AMBER CASSIDY

First Loss

First published by AC Books 2026

First edition

ISBN: 979-8-9890036-9-3

This book was professionally typeset on Reedsy.
Find out more at reedsy.com

Preface

This is a dual-timeline, second-chance romance with a lot of angst and unresolved tension... They both have different versions of their story, and they have to come to terms with their past before they can move forward into their future. But as always, you'll get a happily ever after!

Enjoy!

There is an overlap in the timeline of this book and the last book, First Chance.

TW: There are tough topics discussed, such as Suicidal Ideation and Attempted Suicide—content warning: Violence, Assault, Suicide, Attempted Sexual Assault.

Acknowledgments

I am grateful to have real-life inspiration for writing the friendships in this story. I hope everyone can find the girls who will keep them laughing.

To my best friend, who was the first to read my very rough first draft of the first book of the Chance Encounters Series and has supported me endlessly… Thank you, and I love you forever!

This one is for Robyn!

Chapter One

Liv

Hot breath moistens the skin around my ear, forcing my neck to bow in escape. He doesn't notice as his hips gyrate between my legs, rocking me monotonously atop the arm of the sofa. Without the slightest bit of pressure to my clit, I hardly feel *anything*.

Is this what he came for?

"Come on, let's go to bed," I whisper, pouting sultrily against his shoulder to avoid his ragged breathing. It's becoming difficult to pretend it's not repelling.

"I'm close…" He puffs, jerking his hips stiffly as if he's in pain.

"But–" I don't have a chance to continue my rebuttal before his pinnacled grunt rumbles against my shoulder. We never even made it past the living room.

"Sorry, sweet thing. I'm in a rush."

A rush. He hasn't seen me in over a month.

"Well, maybe next time we can remove all of our clothes before we start," I remark dully, not quite concealing my boiling animosity.

He smirks as he pulls the soiled condom off and drops it on

the coffee table. "I have a hard time getting any work done when all I can think about are the sexy pictures my fiancé sends me. Seeing you naked only makes me cum sooner," he chuckles in amusement, turning away before he notices my lack of enthusiasm.

I used to send him sexy selfies all the time, almost every day, but he hasn't seemed to care that I've stopped sending new ones altogether.

"Then you should focus on making me cum before you take your dick out," I snip, failing to hide the frustration in my voice.

"Don't be crass. You know that I only had enough time for a quick stop. You're the one who chose to move away, not me."

He's right. I made the choice to uproot my life.

I wasn't ready to settle into his penthouse condo. Not when other parts of my life weren't there and parts left unsatisfied. It was too permanent to move into a tower I would never escape from.

Instead, I wrapped up all my clients and found a cottage outside of New Hope, a small Hallmark town in Rollins County in the heart of the Blue Ridge Mountains.

I promised a small reprieve wouldn't affect our engagement. Once we're married, I'll move home, and I'll finally settle down.

Except that our relationship has strained. The distance has grown more than physical. Daily phone calls turned into one every couple of days. Weekly visits turned into monthly, and now we're nearing a wedding date that looks like a vast black hole.

"I know, it's my fault," I mumble, blinking up at the ceiling, waiting for the tears to build up behind my eyes.

"Listen, this is only a phase," Elliot whispers against my shoulder. "Things will get back to normal when you come home. I won't be so busy with work, we'll share a bed again."

Elliot's a Chief Financial Officer for a Fortune 500 company; he's always busy, but that's never mattered because my job keeps me busier. I was a corporate attorney who juggled multiple caseloads, and now I'm balancing an entire county on my shoulders. Yet, somehow, I still have the desire for a hearty sex life when he is content with quickies.

"Come here, sweet thing." He pulls me in, wrapping me in arms that used to be comforting. Now, they feel strange. Forced. "I love you, Liv."

"I love you, too." I do. I mean, I think I do. Everything in my gut churns, and the words feel sour coming out.

This isn't me. I don't question my gut. I've built my entire career around it. My brain carries me, but my gut puts the nail in the coffin for all my cases.

We've been together going on three years… He's right. This is a phase. Everything will be fine.

"How about next time I come to you? I can spend the weekend with you, and we can go over some final wedding details," I suggest, wrapping my arms around his neck. He smiles warmly at me before brushing my thick chestnut hair away from my forehead.

His eyes stay focused there as he speaks. "I was going to surprise you, but the condo is being renovated. I've been trying to keep it under wraps until you can see the finished product."

I attempt to hide my disappointment. I thought he'd be thrilled to spend an entire weekend with me because he always complains that we don't make the time.

"Oh. Well, you could come here."

"I'll check out my calendar and let you know." His lips land on my cheek and disappear even quicker. I feel nothing.

"Right. Drive safe," I mutter as he slips his shoes on by the door. He glances back at me, and I stop spinning the giant engagement ring on my finger.

"You'll get whiplash after you leave this place and move back home. Like you've stepped through time." He winks, leaving out the front door without hesitation.

He likes to remark on the state of my cottage. It's outdated and homely. The outside's yellow facade is faded nearly white and is covered in vines.

I love it.

It reminds me of nature, the earth. As a little girl, I played in fairy gardens and spent my mornings making mud pies and witches' potions, always with smudges of dirt on my cheeks and in my hair.

This cottage, nestled back in the woods, surrounded by the smoke of the mountains, feels like home.

Tossing my hair over my head and back up again, I rake my fingers through my blowout and fluff it until it looks perfect. I stare into the mirror, avoiding my sad eyes in the reflection.

My makeup still looks great. I never shed any of the tears I thought would fall, or God forbid, broke a sweat during that sad coupling.

It doesn't matter. I have somewhere to be, and my personal life does not belong at the forefront of my thoughts. Not with the trial looming over my head.

When I moved to Rollins County, there weren't a lot of prospects related to being a high-powered attorney, but I always wanted to help people, and the public sector is exactly where it's needed most.

I picked up a few civil cases just to put my name in the ring at the local courthouse, and then a family court case led me to Sheriff Malec.

His now-wife, Natalie, needed custody of her little brother, which got me a personal introduction to the sitting judge.

When Judge Reisner retired, and the only prosecutor in the county took his position, I was lying in wait. I was appointed Interim County Prosecutor under the stipulation that I would step down when a permanent candidate ran for the position.

It's been six months, and there hasn't been a single whisper in the wind that anyone is coming to fill the role. Now, I'm heading the biggest case Rollins County has ever seen, and I'm prosecuting two members of one of the oldest families in the area.

Randall Porter and his brother, Jeremiah Porter, are looking at a long list of conspiracy, fraud, assault, and kidnapping. And if I can help it, attempted murder.

Sheriff Malec warned me it could get sketchy, but high stakes don't scare me. Not much frazzles you when you've already lost everything in your life once.

* * *

My palm jabs the windshield wiper button again on this perfectly sunny day, leaving me huffing in frustration when the single daisy, stuck by its stem, doesn't dislodge itself from under my windshield.

I was in a rush to get out the door and to my meeting on time, so I didn't notice it. I know Elliot didn't leave it. He's not a daisy guy. Red roses, only.

Doesn't matter, I'm about to pull into Second Chance Sanctuary, and I need to make sure that Lochlan Dane and Jo Montgomery are on board for how intense this trial will be.

Lochlan runs the black bear rescue that was targeted by Randall Porter. Jo was attacked by Jeremiah Porter because of it.

We have months to prepare, but I'll leave no stone unturned before we ever enter the courtroom.

The weird flowers left on my car are probably just a small-town thing. People notice a newcomer right away. They stare when I stop into the grocery store. The locals know who I am, and I get the occasional request for free representation. I don't mind the occasional pro bono, but my expensive pantsuits aren't going to pay for themselves.

However, the random gifts in my mailbox and on my doorstep are becoming annoying. I thought rural communities were more respectful of private property, but it seems like Southern curiosity is overshadowing.

Last week, I came home to a box of chocolate-covered strawberries on my welcome mat. No note or return address. They went straight into the trash can, and so did my welcome mat. No need to encourage anyone.

The rational part of my brain knows that it's weird, but I have too much going on, and I refuse to put more thought into it.

My Jaguar careens roughly through the entrance of Second Chance Sanctuary, clearly with terrain meant for trucks, and I park next to Sheriff Malec's SUV. Jo is his half-sister, but he insisted on making introductions because of the owner of the property.

Now that I'm seeing Lochlan Dane for the first time, I'm glad for the extra presence. His glower seems permanent on his face, but I feel it assessing me as I meet them on the porch to introduce myself.

"It's nice to meet you, Liv." Jo is bright and kind as she shakes my hand, but he only stares, his eyes shadowed by his furrowed brow.

"Is Liv short for something?" He asks suddenly, gruffly. The unease rolls over me, but not because I'm afraid… It seems as if he is seeing something that I'm not.

"Just Liv," I answer kindly, but bluntly. Everyone calls me Liv, I insist.

I dive into my plan for prosecuting the Porter brothers, ignoring his stare, taking comfort in my craft. I know the law, it's my strength.

I focus on Jo, handing her my business card before navigating carefully to my car. Attempting not to break an ankle barely outweighs keeping the dry dirt off my dark navy pants.

"I'm leaving town in a couple of days. Will that be an issue?" Jo asks, and I offer her a knowing smile.

"Jackson filled me in. It shouldn't be an issue as long as you're here for the trial." He also mentioned her and Lochlan's odd relationship.

As intimidating as he is, his body gravitates towards her, shielding her from my ominous words about what's to come with the Porters, and fixating on her when she speaks.

They continue their conversation as I make my leave, and I can tell tensions are high. Jo's a few years younger than I am, but I know a smart woman when I see one.

If she wants it badly enough, she'll get everything she wants in life. If a man isn't cut out to be a part of it, he can get lost.

"Hey, Loch!"

The toe of my stiletto catches the dirt as I reach for my car door, releasing a plume of dust, and my body lurches.

"Olive?" *That voice.*

Time transcends, and suddenly, I'm not Liv Greenwood, attorney-at-law and Interim Prosecutor. I'm Olive, the shy junior on the first day at my new school.

My eyes lock with Jo's concerned ones across the roof of my car. "I've got to go." *I can't do this.* "It was nice to meet you. Call me if you need anything."

Get out of here. Leave. Leave. My brain screams as my limbs struggle to respond.

"Liv!"

I barely hear my name over the rumble of my engine, but I don't stop. My foot hits the gas before I've shifted into drive, forcing my tires to do the fleeing for me.

I hear the guttural, "FUCK!" But I don't look back, not this time, even as the familiar tremors wrack my body.

Chapter Two

Hayes

I rip the throttle wide open, and my back tire fishtails as my bike rockets out of the garage. I don't contemplate what I'm doing because none of the consequences are as bad as watching Olive get away.

I hit the main road heading down the mountain at lightning speed, but she got a head start. I only catch glimpses of her gunmetal bumper around each curve until the final stretch. She has to slow down to turn towards town.

Her brake lights merely flash before she accelerates across the two-lane highway.

I'm not letting her get away. I've waited too long for this.

I blow through the stop sign without looking, putting me on her bumper. Her eyes meet mine in the rearview mirror, and the wind drowning my eardrums fades away.

Olive. My Olive.

The whites of her eyes expand, tearing away from mine as her car hits the rough shoulder, and she's forced to over-correct to get control.

We're going too fast.

My tires squeal on the pavement as I slam on my brakes,

widening the gap as she swerves onto the patch of dirt and gravel next to the road.

I'm barely off my bike before she's slamming her door and stomping towards me in her navy blazer and slim-fitted dress pants. If she's having any issue in the gravel with her death-trap heels, she doesn't show it.

"What do you want?" She yells, stopping me in my tracks.

What do I want?

"You look good, Liv." She's beautiful. She always was, but this far exceeds the girl she used to be. She's grown up, and everything about her is enhanced.

Her shoulders are tall with confidence she didn't have as a kid. Her curves are accentuated by trim arms and legs, and where her jacket buttons at the waist, cinching her hourglass figure.

Her face has matured and slimmed, where it used to be round with adolescence, highlighting her full lips and angular cheekbones. Her bright hazel eyes are the same, but sharp and *pissed off*.

"Fuck you, Jensen." She turns on her heel and starts to walk away. Grief washes over me…

"Liv, wait!" I beg.

I don't know why, but she stops, standing with her back to me. Her shoulders rise and fall with her flustered breaths.

"Let me-" I start, but she cuts me off by whipping back around to face me. If looks could kill…

"No! You don't get my attention or my time now. You had your chance a decade ago." Her sharp, manicured nail juts out, inches from my face. "I don't know how you knew I was here, but stop leaving me fucking gifts."

"What?"

"I don't care if it's a peace offering. I'm not interested."

"I don't know what you're talking about. I only found out you were here five minutes ago."

The fierceness of her face falters almost indiscernibly, but I watch as the warm skin of her cheeks pales.

She stumbles back a step, avoiding my eyes.

"Is something going on?"

The shake of her head is barely there as she scrambles back to her car.

"Liv!" I grab for her door as she slams it shut, but she locks it as I yank on the handle. "Is somebody bothering you, Olive?" I plead, but she ignores me.

The engine roars to life as she hits the gas and nearly runs over the toes of my boots, leaving me in a cloud of dust as she speeds away.

* * *

Four years ago...

"Is this your girlfriend?" The tattoo artist asks as the needle stabs my skin.

"No," I respond bluntly.

"Sister?"

"No."

He glances up at me briefly, blinking away when he connects with my deadpan glare. I hate questions. I don't like explaining myself to strangers; that's why I do most of my tattoos myself. This spot was too tricky, and I couldn't risk messing it up.

He continues working in silence until the ink's done, snapping his latex gloves off and pointing to the mirror on the wall. "Let me know what you think."

The man in the reflection is someone I've spent years trying to understand. Each tattoo up and down my arms and across my chest represents what I've been through, and who I am.

At some point, it felt like putting a permanent reminder on my skin would help ease the torture in my head.

Right above my diaphragm in the hollow pit between my ribs is my greatest punishment.

OLIVE

* * *

I always wondered where she was and how she was doing. I would lie awake at night, thinking of all the ways I could find her and where I'd need to go to look. And what I would possibly say once I saw her again.

I always wondered if she moved across the country or out of the country altogether... She was destined for great things, and that meant the possibilities of where she went in life were endless.

Now, I know she's a hotshot lawyer. Her success doesn't surprise me, but her career choice does.

And, I find out she is right around the corner...

But she wants nothing to do with me.

Like I'm the nightmare of her past.

Because I am.

I stroll into the local bar in the town she drove off towards yesterday, and sit down at a stool, eyeing two old men and the bartender. It's only about 5 o'clock, so these are the regulars.

If she's working with Sheriff Malec and prosecuting the man who attacked Second Chance Sanctuary, I know she's staying close by.

I want to know where.

I want to know everything.

"What can I get for you, sugar?"

I smile at the woman with teased hair from a different decade, and her demeanor doesn't shift. She's a veteran, my charm won't phase her. "Shot of Jack, please."

She sets the glass down in front of me and refills the next guy's glass.

"Do you know of any good lawyers around here?" I ask casually, fiddling with the full glass in front of me.

"Why? Are you trouble?" The bartender asks sternly. Her name tag says 'Daya'.

"No," I chuckle, downing the amber liquid.

Not anymore.

Chapter Three

Liv

"I need every document, every police report, and every complaint against these brothers since they became adults. I don't care if it seems insignificant; that's for me to decide," I harp at the intern assisting me. She came from the local community college, and I inherited her when I took the job.

Normally, law offices have paralegals and office clerks, people who know how to build a case. Rollins County does not have the manpower. Other than my intern, I share a secretary with the entire floor.

Dotty is seasoned and knows what she's doing, but she's assisting everyone in the court system with all of their paperwork. She's overworked.

My intern is just clueless.

"Anything that I need to know about that weird exit the other day?" Sheriff Malec's voice comes from behind me. We share the building with his office, but he's in a different wing. So this visit is intentional.

"Miley, give us the room, please," I dismiss the intern, and Jackson shuts the door behind her as she leaves.

"There is nothing to tell." I don't bother looking at him as I lie, and he doesn't humor me with a response. I can feel his stare rolling over me.

"Hayes is someone that I used to know," I admit with a sigh, shuffling papers around on my desk until I find the courage to look up.

"Right. People don't usually run away from people that they know."

"Used to know," I correct him.

"I've encountered him plenty at the sanctuary, but I admit that I don't know him very well. I know he has a past, but is there anything that I need to know, Liv? Are you afraid of him?"

Afraid of Hayes?

"Absolutely not."

Fearing him would never cross my mind. He was my safe space. *Used to be.*

That thought rocks me slightly.

Jackson doesn't speak, using his annoying law enforcement tactic of making me stew in my thoughts until I blab. Unfortunately, it's working.

"We had a falling out a long time ago. There isn't any familiarity between us anymore. If anything, it's contempt. He's a stranger now."

"You definitely didn't look like strangers." He opens the door, apparently having got what he came for.

"There's bad blood, Jackson. I can't stand the thought of being near him," I huff in defense.

"Yeah. My wife used to feel that way about me, too." He smirks, strolling out of my office.

"It's not like that!" I shout after him. "There's too much

history," I mumble when he's too far away to hear me.

I shut the door, and a glaring reminder waves in front of my face. My 8-carat engagement ring.

A 6-carat square-cut diamond with single-carat accent diamonds on either side. It's brilliant. And, a little excessive.

Elliot insisted on the biggest and flashiest ring he could find. I talked him down from ten carats.

I wasn't born with money like he was. Wealth isn't something that comes naturally to me. I've made an incredible living with my law career, but I don't marvel in the excess of it all.

It's a beautiful ring, though, and I'm grateful. Elliot has been a wonderful fiancé despite all the confusion in my head recently. He was ultimately supportive when I decided to relocate to Rollins County temporarily. He's handled the wedding planning while I'm away.

He's a good man.

We met when I was fresh out of law school, working in my first law office. Our firm was representing his company. Even though he didn't come near me while we were working together professionally, I always felt his eyes on me. Once the case was resolved, he asked me to dinner, and we were hardly ever apart after that.

Aside from now.

My phone rings from my desk, the special ringtone that only belongs to one person.

"Did you miss me already?" I ask as I answer.

"Of course, I haven't spoken to you since lunch," Thea responds humorously.

"I'm done for the day, I just need to run home and change before I head to your house."

"Well, wear something hot because my mom offered to babysit. We're going out!"

"Dancing?" I ask excitedly. That was our favorite thing to do in college when we were roommates and inseparable, before life got in the way.

"Dancing!" She sings-songs before saying our quick good-byes.

We missed out on so many nights out because of what she went through after undergrad, and then moving separate ways for our jobs.

Now, we get to dance together whenever we have a free night, as long as our shadow tags along. Her husband, Jesse, makes her feel safe enough in every room that she doesn't have to hide.

And, I love him for being that for her.

I'm so excited for the distraction that a night out with my best friend can bring me, I don't notice the gift on my windshield until I drop my briefcase in the passenger seat of my car.

It's another daisy. This time, the white petals are tipped in red dye. Unease washes over me.

I glance in my mirrors, scanning the parking lot, but other than a handful of employees leaving the county building, there doesn't seem to be anything out of place.

I keep my head on a swivel, jumping out and tossing the flower onto the pavement before anyone notices my strange behavior.

No one is watching me. It's all in my head.

* * *

The neon strobe lights and the fog machine might be a bit overkill for a bar, but Casa Amigos is the only place within fifty miles that plays upbeat music and doesn't smell like cigarettes and mildew.

"... So everybody put your hands in the air now."

Thea and I launch our hands out towards the ceiling, jumping and screaming along to the song. We're lost in our own little bubble, letting the beat and alcohol transfix us.

She didn't drink in public for the longest time, but now we get to indulge in tequila shots and margaritas because of the man sitting at the table right on the edge of the dance floor.

Jesse watches Thea closely at all times, always with a disgustingly sweet smile on his face, ready to jump in to ward off stray attention.

Except this time, when I glance over at him, he's not watching us. His head is crooked slightly, his eyes trained across the room in a dark corner.

I twirl around Thea, shimmying against her backside until he glances in my direction and catches my eye.

"Everything okay?" I mouth. It's too loud in here to hear someone from across the dance floor.

He smiles easily and nods, but I notice the tension in his posture. I've won cases by reading body language alone.

"Bathroom," he mouths back before weaving through the crowded bar.

"What's wrong?" Thea asks, and I realize I've stopped dancing.

"I don't know."

She loops her arm through mine, pulling me towards the table Jesse just left, and cranes her neck looking for him once she sees that he's gone.

"He said he was going to the bathroom."

"That's weird," she remarks. We both know that man would not let Thea out of his sight in a public place, not even if nature calls. "Oh, he's over there. He's talking to someone."

I follow her line of sight over the heads of the crowd, and my knees buckle. I see blonde hair that's not so blonde anymore and not nearly as long as it used to be, and the eyes that I used to dream about.

But that familiar form across the room is also taller and stronger than the boy he used to be, and he sits like a predator in the corner, concealing how dangerous his presence is.

If my forearms weren't resting on the table top, I would crumble.

"Thea..."

Chapter Four

Hayes

God, she's beautiful. And, magnetic. Even if I didn't know who she was, it would be hard for me to look anywhere else.

She throws her head back and laughs as she bounces around to the beat, and I feel the muscles twitching in my cheeks. I could watch her every minute of every day, and it would never be enough.

I don't know how I survived this many years without seeing her.

I saw her every day in my thoughts, but it doesn't come close to reality.

Since seeing her for the first time, I haven't been able to stop looking for her. A few innocent questions to the locals gave me all the information I needed. The building she worked in, and where she lived.

I tried not to show my frustration with how easy it was to obtain those details. Especially after I watched her discard a flower from her windshield wiper as if it were a snake earlier. I could see her eyes were as big as saucers from where I sat on the other side of the parking lot.

Having a secret admirer is one thing, but if the attention is frightening her, I won't allow it.

If anyone gets to stalk her, it's me.

"Is there a reason you're watching my wife?" A man's voice comes from beside me suddenly. It's low and controlled, not someone excited and looking for a drunken brawl.

"Who is your wife?" I ask after finishing the last of my drink, slowly turning toward the man. I recognize him.

I've seen him at the sanctuary.

He doesn't respond, looking at me with the same level of recognition.

"I'm not looking at the blonde, if that's what you're worried about."

"I don't like you looking at either of them. What do you want?" He asks, just as seriously as before. He doesn't know me well enough to know my intentions.

I like this guy. I can appreciate him looking out for the woman I care about, even if she hates my guts.

"Liv is an old friend. That's all."

"If she were a friend, you'd go over there and say hello."

I smirk at his accurate assessment. "Yeah, I guess you're right."

"Jesse, we're leaving," the woman with long blonde hair says from behind him, cutting a glare my way.

He wraps his arm around her shoulders and kisses her head. "Alright. Where's–"

He doesn't finish his thought before she cuts him off. "She went outside for some air." I stand up from my seat, and she glares at me again. Clearly, she's already formed an opinion of me.

"Hayes," I introduce myself, reaching my hand out to shake

hers, but her body flinches away. Apparently, she's heard really terrible things.

Jesse pulls her in tighter, reaching his hand out instead.

"I'm taking them home. We don't need an escort." His hand squeezes mine briefly, and I see the warning. He won't let me near Liv unless she allows it. And that's not going to happen.

"Drive safe," I offer, taking my seat again.

As soon as they leave the bar, I make my exit. I watch from the shadows as they all leave in one car, avoiding Liv's tense looks over her shoulder.

I don't bother following them. I know where they're going, and where she'll end up.

It takes about an hour and a half until she's parking in front of her little yellow cottage in the woods. It's like something out of a storybook with absolutely no safety measures, no flood lights, and hardly visible from the road.

She's a sitting duck out here, and she doesn't see me leaning against my bike at the darkest edge of her driveway.

"So, you told your friend about me?" I ask suddenly, and she drops her keys from her purse. They hit the ground with a clatter, but she doesn't turn around.

"Leave me alone."

"Why should I do that?"

"Because I don't want to be near you."

I ignore the sting of those words and saunter towards her slowly. "Seems like I should be the least of your concerns."

"Why is that?" She spits, spinning to face me finally.

Her fierceness leaves me spellbound for a moment. She's a force to be reckoned with, and I'm so damn proud of her.

"You have a stalker, Liv."

"I know. He's standing in my driveway."

I laugh, and she blinks at me in quick succession as if she forgot the sound. "You know it isn't me."

"I don't know that."

"Yes, you do."

She averts her gaze because she doesn't want to admit that I'm right. No matter what has happened between us, she knows I'd never act maliciously towards her. I'd never want her to be afraid.

"It doesn't matter. You need to leave me alone."

"Why? If some freak is harassing you, it needs to stop."

"It's not about that." She keeps her hands tucked under her arms as if keeping her left hand out of sight will change the facts.

"Ah, because you're engaged."

She jolts like she was electrocuted. "How do you know that I'm engaged?"

"Even a blind man could see that rock."

She rolls her eyes. "My fiancé is a generous man."

"I'm sure he is." I don't hide the sarcasm from my voice, and she notices.

"What does that mean?"

"Just doesn't seem like your style."

"You don't know anything about me."

I used to. "Does he love you?"

"Of course, he does."

"Then why isn't he here?" I don't mean to raise my voice, but this situation is ridiculous.

The second there was a hint of danger, the man she is supposed to marry should have dropped everything to be here to keep her safe.

Like I would.

Like I am.

"It's not–" She tries to flee, snatching her keys up to go inside.

"Why, Liv?" I don't back off, following her to her door.

"Stop!"

"Why?" I push, holding the door shut above her head so she can't open it, twisting my head away to ignore how damn alluring she smells.

"He doesn't know!" She shouts.

"What?" I breathe, accidentally inhaling the intoxicating scent on her skin, enriched from dancing so hard. Her natural musk is better than any perfume, and it makes my blood pump painfully through my veins.

God, she smells good.

"I haven't told him," she whispers, twisting that damn boulder around her finger. The brilliance of it has been seared into my brain since the day I saw her at the sanctuary.

"Why?"

"Because it isn't anything. It's not a big deal." She shrugs, trying to convince herself, because she definitely isn't convincing me.

"But you're afraid," I object softly, breathing against her hair.

"No, I'm not."

"Yes, you are. I can see it on your face. I know you."

"No!" She barks, spinning to face me. Her anger shoves me back until the span of the porch is between us. "You don't know me. Not anymore."

"You're right, I'm sorry."

"You're sorry?" She laughs. "Too late for sorry, Jensen. Get the fuck off my porch and leave me alone."

Chapter Five

Liv

F*ourteen years ago...*

All the other kids are crowded around the stop sign waiting for the school bus, while I stare down the street into the early morning fog. It's my first day at my new school, and I don't know anyone.

I'm too sheepish to walk up to any of them to introduce myself, so I keep my distance, balancing on the curb and rubbing my hands up and down my arms to ward off the bite of autumn in the air.

"Most people wear a sweater instead of mimicking a cricket," a boy's voice comes from beside me. My spine stiffens, and I barely glance over my shoulder, checking to see if he's speaking to me.

He's tall with jaw-length blonde hair pushed back behind his ears like the skateboarders you see in the movies. He's not carrying a backpack despite being at the school bus stop.

"I don't have any sweaters," I utter, confused as to why he is talking to me.

"I know it's a shitty trailer park, but I'm sure you're not that poor," he scoffs, pulling out a cigarette to light. I must scrunch my nose because he chuckles and puts it back in his pocket, unbothered.

"The last place I lived was warm year-round, and my mom only believes in sustainable goods. She made us get rid of most of our frivolous attire."

"Frivolous? Are you 75?"

"I just turned sixteen."

"Sophomore?"

"Junior. I placed high on my test scores."

He rolls his eyes, and I don't know why. I'm telling the truth.

"Senior," he replies, and I look him up and down subtly because he looks much older than me, but he catches on. "I got held back."

"Oh."

"Don't worry, smarty pants, I got expelled last year for fighting. Not because my grades suck." He winks as if that lessens my concerns about him.

"I'm sorry?" I utter awkwardly. I'm not sure what else I'm supposed to say.

"I'm not. I beat the shit out of a bully, and he deserved it. My dad trashed my bike as punishment, though, so that sucked."

He notices my confusion.

"My dirt bike." He enlightens me. "Which is why I'm stuck riding the bus like a loser." He glances at me. "No offense."

I shrug because I don't even have my temps. The bus is my only option.

"Your mom won't let you have a coat because it's frivolous?" He continues torturing me with conversation, and my heart is already beating out of my chest with nerves.

I'm starting three months late into the school year, and now a cute boy is looking at me. Cute boys never look at me.

"I have a wool poncho that she handmade, but it's too hot for most situations, and she won't buy me real deodorant. I'm afraid that I'll stink." Heat rushes to my cheeks with embarrassment.

"Yikes," he says, raising his eyebrows.

"I don't know why I told you that." I squeeze my eyes shut, wishing I could hide. "It's also really ugly," I add, and an amused smile grows on his face before he laughs, making me smile bashfully.

"So, don't come near you on the days you're wearing your winter poncho. Got it." He smirks, backpedaling slowly.

I think it's part of his joke, but he continues backing away even as the bus comes rolling down the road.

"Where are you going?"

He shrugs. "Not feeling the bus today."

I'm staring at his retreating form as the air brakes squeal, and all the other kids shuffle through the bus doors. It would have been nice to have one friendly face beside me as I arrived at the school, but I try not to think about it.

I'll keep my head down and find my classes as fast as I can. If I don't draw attention to myself, then the other kids won't realize that I'm a fish out of water.

I went to public school until fifth grade, when my mom pulled me out to start homeschooling. She started a wellness journey, and it overhauled our lives. We bounced around from place to place while she sold her handmade goods and taught yoga classes. We cut out all toxic household products, and then she met my stepdad at a free spirit retreat.

Now, we live in his trailer, and I don't have access to the

internet. It's too radioactive, as they say. My options were to sit somewhere all day that provides free internet or to go back to public school.

I chose the latter. I wouldn't mind more structure when my home life is the definition of flippant. I love my mom, but we're polar opposites. She flows with the wind, and I'm rigid, responsible.

One of us has to be.

Too quickly, the bus screeches to a stop in front of the school, and I suck in a chest full of air. This is it.

My new school.

The large brick building is harsh and overbearing. Not for the first time, I'm regretting my choice to return to traditional school.

All the other students rush around me, heading through the main doors in a controlled flurry because they all know where they're going. I am lost, and I haven't even gone up the concrete steps.

"Hey, hippie girl," the familiar voice calls from behind me. The relief that washes over me makes me blush, but as I turn to look, so does embarrassment. The boy from earlier is jumping out of some girl's car and jogging towards me. She's older, probably a senior, but only shoots me a suspicious look before turning her car towards student parking.

"My name is Olive," I tell him when he gets closer.

"Olive?" he looks at me questioningly.

I nod my head stiffly.

"Damn, even the name is hippie."

The warmth in my cheeks deepens as he hands me a folded gray hoodie. "What's this?"

"For the non-poncho days." He winks, jogging up the steps

towards the entrance. "See you around, Liv."

Liv. My cheeks burn at the nickname. No one has ever given me a nickname.

I unfold the sweatshirt, looking at the faded logo across the worn cotton. It's for a karate studio somewhere in town. The name 'HAYES' is ironed on the back, though the glue is more legible than what is left of the vinyl letters.

And, in the front pocket is a stick of men's deodorant. Nothing natural about it.

I tuck it in my backpack, smiling to myself. At least I don't have to worry about smelling bad at my new school.

* * *

Present...

The final wooden block settles at the top of the tower, completing the castle, and I sit back to admire my work. I'm babysitting baby Kate tonight, and even though she's already tucked sweetly in her crib upstairs, I want her to have something fun to see first thing in the morning.

She's only a year old, but I think she'll appreciate Aunt Liv's craftsmanship.

I never knew how much I could love another human. The second I laid eyes on her, I was in love. No one can convince me that she isn't somehow part of my DNA.

I spent Thea's entire pregnancy mourning because I thought I wouldn't get the traditional aunt experience. We lived on opposite sides of the state, but one look at my best friend holding her sweet baby girl after she was born, and I knew I couldn't miss it.

I couldn't settle down with Elliot without having a chance to be a part of Thea's journey into motherhood. And even though he thought it was a childish decision to make, I think he's under the impression that this phase will help me get over my friendship from college.

But he doesn't understand our relationship; he's never really tried. She's the sister that I never got. She knows me better than anyone, including him, the man I'm supposed to marry.

Having her as my person is something that I'll never take for granted. And, being here for her while she navigates this phase of life was nonnegotiable, so he kept his judgments to himself when I made it clear I wasn't asking his permission.

I was born to teen parents who gave me up for adoption, and my new mom was a single woman in her fifties. I had no family, no siblings or cousins.

Thea is my family. Now, my cottage is ten minutes from her house, and I can be her village. I get to babysit the sweetest baby ever, so mom and dad get a break.

I get baby snuggles and all the giggles.

She's the best. She's–

A wooden board creaks behind me, and my spine stiffens against the back of the couch. Thea and Jesse won't be home for at least another hour or two.

I don't look towards the sound because I can't tell where it came from, but I train my ears to listen closely to my surroundings. It's an old house; it could've been the wind.

But when another faint creak sounds to my left, sweat gathers at the neck of my sweater. It sounds like it came from outside. My hand slides over the velvet couch cushion to grip my phone. Should I call the police?

What if it's nothing?

It's been nearly two weeks since the last flower was left on my car. This has nothing to do with that...

But, even as I think it, my brain is contradicting itself. I don't want to look like the girl who cried wolf. I have a professional reputation to uphold in this county.

I should call Jackson. He's the Sheriff, but he's my friend; he wouldn't judge me. If I call Elliot, I'll have to explain why I'm so paranoid, and I have no desire to open that can of worms.

No, I'm a grown woman, I can handle this. It's probably a stray cat.

I tiptoe towards the door and flip on the porch light, but nothing happens. The dim yellow light normally shines through the small windows at the top, but they're still cast in darkness. *The porch light is out.*

It's nothing. The light bulb probably needs to be changed.

It's nothing.

Another slow creak makes me jump. Was that right outside the door?

My fingernails clack against the screen before taking on a life of their own as I back into the living room.

"Hello?" The sing-song voice answers on the other end of the line.

"Hi, Jo. I hope this isn't a bad time, but I was wondering if you had Hayes's phone number?" My skin tingles after saying his name out loud.

"Yeah, of course. Is everything okay?" She must hear the nerves in my voice. This is stupid.

"Everything is fine. I'm sorry, I shouldn't have bothered you so late. Have a good night!"

"Wait–"

I don't give her a chance to speak, ending the call before I can change my mind. What was I thinking?

Reaching out to Hayes would be opening a door that has been firmly shut for a long time.

My nails tap against my black phone screen as it starts to buzz, vibrating with an incoming call. It's not a number I have saved.

My gut tells me that it's Hayes.

My guilt forces me to ignore the call.

I shouldn't talk to him.

But what if someone is outside? Kate's upstairs.

That thought makes my stomach roll.

The same number pops up again, as my phone vibrates in my hand.

"Hello?" I answer under my breath.

"Liv?"

I ignore the relief that washes over me when I hear his voice, still too nervous to analyze that feeling.

"I shouldn't have reached out."

"But you did."

I can only answer with silence.

"Are you okay?"

"It's nothing."

"What's wrong?"

More silence from me.

"Olive." His stern tone makes me squeeze my eyes shut. It's been a long time, but I know that tone… It isn't anger. It's unyielding protectiveness.

It's exactly why it was too easy to reach out to him.

"I'm babysitting at Thea's, and I got spooked. I shouldn't

have called."

"Are the doors locked?" The rumble of an engine nearly drowns out his voice, but I ignore the implication of that. He isn't getting on his bike for me; he doesn't even know where Thea lives.

"Of course, they are."

"Go hide in a safe spot."

"I'm not hiding. Plus, the baby is asleep upstairs."

"Go upstairs."

"Hayes, this is ridiculous. I was too embarrassed to call Malec, and now you're freaking me out."

"You called me for a reason, Liv."

"It was a mistake." I shrug as if he can see me, pacing back and forth behind the couch.

"Nothing between us is ever a mistake."

I can't respond, and my silence is heavy between us as his engine revs in the background.

I know I should hang up, but a part of me wants to keep him on the line until Thea and Jesse get home.

Even after all this time and everything we've been through, I can't cut off the only connection I have to him. I've never been able to.

But I'm also not the girl I used to be.

"Listen, I shouldn't have called. I'm fine. The porch light probably needs a new bulb, and–" I'm already staring at the door as the brass doorknob twists ever so slowly.

"New bulb? What are you–" I gasp, cutting him off, not hearing the rest as my phone clatters to the floor.

Chapter Six

Hayes

F*ourteen years ago...*

"Just leave her alone! Go to bed, you're drunk!" I slam the storm door, roaring in frustration as I stomp down our rickety wooden porch.

Another night, another disgusting display by my father. He's a loser.

The first beer gets cracked open when his eyelids do, and he doesn't stop until he's belligerent. Somehow, he still manages to go to work and pay the bills on this shitty trailer so he can hold that over my mom's head. And mine, not that I asked to be put on this earth.

He's belittled my mom for so long that she hardly ever speaks, and when she does, she merely whispers. I can't stand to be around them.

I hate my dad, but I love my mom. I hate watching her stay around a man who treats her that way.

If I could get out of this hellhole, I'd get her out of this damn trailer park.

I won't have to stare at this sad neighborhood playground covered in spray paint. I'll buy her a house where the grass is always green, and she never has to tiptoe around. My father can rot by himself in his recliner.

"Fucking, loser!" I yell into the sky, kicking the rusted swing.

The hinges squeak painfully until I grab the chains, halting them. Something shuffles across the playground, and I see her retreating form on the other side of the slide.

"Liv?"

"I'm sorry, I don't want to intrude."

"No, you don't have to go. I'm just pissed at my dad."

She stops walking and turns towards me. She has her backpack on and has a laptop folded up against her chest.

"What are you doing out here?"

"I was trying to get some homework done. If I sit out here, sometimes I can connect to someone's internet."

"You don't have the internet?"

"My mom doesn't think it's safe."

That makes me chuckle. All the bullshit in my head lifts away, and I let myself laugh.

"What classes are you taking?" I sit on the landing below the slide, letting her choose to come closer. And, she does, rattling on about the college-accredited courses she's taking and the classes she needs to graduate with honors next year.

It's refreshing being around someone whose biggest problem is seeing how much they can succeed. She is going to make something of herself. I don't know her very well, but I can tell she's one of those types. She's meant for great things.

Peace flickers inside of me.

Maybe the world isn't as fucked up as I think it is, and I don't have to go down with the rest of them.

* * *

Present...

The second Jo told me that Liv was trying to get in touch with me, I knew something was wrong. I dropped what I was doing and jumped on my bike.

I know where Thea's house is. I memorized the route after realizing how often Liv spends her time here.

Since the day I saw Liv at the sanctuary, I've been keeping tabs on her. She accused me of being her stalker, but I'm only trying to keep her safe.

I accelerate down the street until there's an opening in the curb, driving up onto the sidewalk and into the front lawn. It's dark...

Too dark.

The street lights illuminate the front porch of the old Victorian house just enough that I can see there isn't anyone out front, but all of the windows are blacked out. It's completely dark inside, and my head's on a swivel as I climb the porch steps.

I try the front door, but the handle only twists because the deadbolt is locked above it. I glance up at the porch light.

Jesse doesn't seem like the type of homeowner who would let something like that go. It looks intact above my head, but I reach up anyway to tinker with it. One slight twist and it floods the entrance with light.

My palm halts before it connects with the door. I don't want to startle her. "Liv! It's me!" I shout instead.

I step back, contemplating how I'm going to get in if she

doesn't answer, because I'll break the door down if I have to, but luckily, it swings open.

"Hayes," she pants my name like she's out of breath. Her eyes are wild, staring at me as if she's hardly holding herself together.

"Are you okay?" I keep my tone low as she glances left to right, as if she's waiting for something to jump out at us.

"No," her voice cracks. She's terrified.

Seeing her like this bothers me to my core, and it takes every ounce of willpower not to erase the distance between us, so I can wrap her in my arms.

That's what she needs, and what I've always been good at. But I'm nearly a stranger to her now.

"Do you want me to come in?"

She nods, stepping back to let me through the door, and that's when I see the gun in her hand.

"Liv," I utter her name, staring at the firearm.

"Oh. It's Jesse's gun, I got it out of the safe upstairs." She hands it to me like it's burning her skin, and I stick it in the back of my waistband.

"You know the code to their safe?" I ask as I turn the lights in the living room back on.

"Of course, I do."

"Sit down, and try to relax. I need to put it back." She stares at the door that I've already relocked and then back to me like she's afraid someone will barge in at any moment. "You're safe, now, but I need to put the gun away. I'm a felon."

That word shifts her demeanor entirely, like she finally remembers who I am. I try not to let it gut me.

When I come back downstairs, she's pacing back and forth in front of the green couch.

"The light bulb on the porch was tampered with. Someone was fucking with you," I tell her as I sit down in the chair beside the coffee table.

"Someone was out there, and all I could think about was the baby." Her body sinks to the couch cushions, finally, and she covers her face with her hands.

"What's her name?" I ask, trying to distract her from the real issue at hand because I can see the panic building.

"Catherine Olivia Callahan. But we call her baby Kate." She smiles to herself, as if saying the name brings her that much joy. "Thea wanted her middle name to be Olive, but I insisted that she give her the normalcy I always wanted and use Olivia instead."

"I like your name."

She rolls her eyes. "You're the one who started calling me Liv."

"Because I wanted your full name all to myself."

"Stop, Hayes."

My rebuttal dies as someone raps on the front door, and her face drains of color.

"It's only Malec."

"What? You called him!"

"I called him after your call disconnected. I didn't know what was happening."

"I wasn't ready to tell anyone, and you went behind my back?"

"It's not just anyone, it's the Sheriff."

"Why? You hate the police!"

"It's you, Liv. You! I have to keep you safe." I rake my hands over my scalp, trying to rein myself in. "Do you think I can sit back and let anyone hurt you?"

"Right. Only you're allowed to do that," she snaps after I turn my back to open the door, making my shoulders tense. *I deserve that.*

I stay silent as Liv reluctantly tells Malec what happened. I melt into the wall as the conversation ticks every nerve ending in me until I'm ready to blow.

"How long have you noticed the gifts?" Jackson asks, writing on a notepad.

"It started a couple of weeks after I moved here. I thought it was the locals being friendly at first, until the flowers on my car. They've shown up whether I was at home, work, or the store. Chocolate-covered strawberries have been left on my porch. Bottles of wine."

"Any notes?"

"No," she states bluntly.

"Is this the first time someone has tried to approach you?"

"I guess. I encounter the public all the time in the courthouse and in town. I've never noticed anything odd."

"This shows an escalation. Until we know the intentions of this person, you need to be cautious. We need to save anything left for you. If you notice anyone following you or anything out of place-" She glances at me briefly but looks away just as quickly. "Let me know right away."

"I will."

"Liv! Oh my God! What is happening?" Thea scurries through the door and drops to her knees in front of where Liv is on the couch. Her palm goes to Liv's forehead as if she's checking for a fever. It strikes me as odd, but this is a new mother, maybe it's instinct.

"Someone tried to break in," she utters to her friend, revealing herself fully for the first time since I've been here.

Her chin trembles, letting herself break.

Jesse is sprinting up the stairs before anyone can stop him, only returning a minute later with a ghostly expression on his face.

"She's fine," Thea murmurs to him when he's close. "Liv kept her safe."

He kneels next to her, and their foreheads meet, exchanging a brief but deeply intimate moment in a room full of people, so they don't fall apart.

"Are you okay?" He turns his attention to Liv, squeezing her shoulders and examining her with concern.

"I'm fine," her voice cracks, and Jesse pulls her in for a hug, but not before looping his wife in. Warmth blooms in my chest.

These people love her.

"I don't think you should be alone tonight, Liv," Jackson says from the doorway. "This wasn't random. Whoever did this had to seek you out; they unscrewed the light bulb so you wouldn't be able to see them, and the only thing that kept them out was the dead bolt. They might get bolder next time, especially if they're angry they missed out this time."

"You told me you'd keep me in the loop about creepy flower guy," Thea scolds her as if she suspected this guy would be an issue.

"I have been. This is the first time anything like this has happened. I swear."

Unlike some of her earlier responses, I can tell she's telling the truth. She might be withholding the truth from Jackson, but she won't lie to her friend.

"How do you know it's a guy?" Jackson asks.

"The handwriting was definitely from a man," Thea admits,

and Liv squeezes her eyes shut.

"You said there were no notes," I call her out, and everyone's attention falls to me suddenly as if they just remembered I was here.

"There was one note," she admits. "It said... *Choose me.*"

Whatever warmth there was in my soul earlier ignites into a fiery rage.

Chapter Seven

Liv

"Stay here tonight," Thea insists.

"No, I am not screwing up my life because of some weirdo. I'm going to sleep in my own bed and continue like I would normally."

"I can call one of my deputies in and have them sit in front of your house. At least for tonight," Jackson offers. This is a small county, and I know they don't have people like that to spare. Besides, I don't want to draw any more attention to this. I don't know his deputies, and they might spread my business through the gossip mill.

"No. I'll be fine."

"You're going home to pretend as if nothing happened?" Thea asks, and I can tell by her tone that she's annoyed with me. "This is serious, Liv. And, scary."

"I know..." I exhale slowly.

"I'll take her home, I'll stay," Hayes says from his spot on the wall.

I've done my best to ignore his brooding presence until now because I know it's more than that. He's fuming with his need to protect me.

It's always been that way.

When we were young, it was loud, and he'd throw caution to the wind if someone even looked at me the wrong way. But this is different.

The danger that lurks in his blood is controlled now. Years of reaping the consequences of his actions have turned him into a disciplined beast.

The lean, muscle-laden body I remember is sturdier and more threatening. His arms are thicker, and no doubt holding all of the secrets of the past decade.

"No," I dismiss him.

Thea squeezes my hand, forcing me to look at her. She knew that I would say no to him, because that is what I should say. That's the right course of action.

But she is the only person in the world who knows all about Jensen Hayes.

"He can sleep on your couch for one night. It'll make me feel better," she insists...

Because she knows my heart is screaming yes.

* * *

"You can go, really. You don't need to stay," I tell him for the third time since stepping through my front door.

He ignores me for the third time. "I like the cottage. Did you decorate?"

"Uh, no. Most of it is the owner's stuff."

"The dream catchers?"

"Well, yeah. Those are mine."

He smirks and continues strolling through my living room. Stepping back into my life and invading my space as if he hasn't been a ghost all this time.

"Why are you doing this?"

"To keep you safe."

"And, how do you plan to do that?" I huff, kicking off my shoes haphazardly and settling onto the couch as if he isn't watching my every move.

"I'll protect you. Call it personal security."

"Absolutely not."

"Why? Afraid to be around me?"

Yes. "I don't need a bodyguard."

"You do. You're working the biggest case in the county. Everyone is talking about it. Everyone is talking about you. You should have heard how easy it was to find out where you live. Where you work. Where you like to eat for lunch."

Damn, locals. "So, what? What are you going to do?"

"I'll be your eyes, so you only have to worry about your job." He watches with rapt attention as my thumb knuckles dig against my temples.

I drop my hands. "That's ridiculous."

"Tell me who would walk in front of a train for you?"

"What? Why would–"

"Who would take a damn bullet to the chest for you?"

"Stop," I breathe, as my heart beat whooshes in my ears.

"Who will protect you at every hour of the day?"

I shake my head, refusing to answer.

"Tell me who else would give their last breath for you, and I'll leave you the fuck alone."

My spine tingles because I know there isn't anyone who would do those things. Elliot isn't the savior type. Thea loves me eternally, but she has a baby now, a husband.

There is only one answer, and it kills me inside.

"Why? I'm not your problem, and I don't even know if this guy is dangerous." I avoid his gaze, launching up from the couch to rifle through the linen closet. "It's not like you bothered to check in over the last ten years."

"Eleven years. Three months. Six days."

My lips part, and I can't force them back together. "What the fuck is wrong with you?"

"A lot, probably."

"Whatever." I throw a spare pillow and blanket across the back of the couch, ignoring them as they bounce and fall onto the ground. "I'm going to bed."

"Have you told your fiancé yet? I didn't see your lips moving as I was following you home."

Yeah, I was too busy watching him behind me on his Indian Motorcycle. "I just got laid out and filleted in front of everyone in Thea's living room because someone won't leave me alone. Can I have a minute to process all of this?"

"A man should know if his woman is in trouble."

"He's busy, I'd rather get it straightened out before I worry him."

"Bullshit."

"Excuse me?"

"That's bullshit, and you know it."

"You don't have the right to an opinion."

"Yeah, and what does Thea think? Does she think your fiancé should be here?"

"Don't," I warn him. "You don't get to pretend to be on a little team with her. You aren't even close to her level."

"Well, someone needs the unconditional truth from you,

not the sugar-coated shit you were trying to pawn off on Malec."

"She knows everything about me. She knows *everything*." I glare at him pointedly so he knows what I mean.

"You told her all about us, huh?"

"Of course, I did. She's my best friend."

"I used to be your best friend."

"Until you left me!" I scream, smacking my palms against my bedroom door. "You were gone, and Thea picked up the pieces! She took me in and loved me like you never could. She stayed! Through everything!"

He doesn't move as I crush him with my words.

"Every milestone. Every heartbreak, every terrible fucking thing that happened to either of us. She couldn't push me away, and I wouldn't let her! Because that is what best friends do. You left!" I jab my finger into his chest, and he takes it, staring at the contact.

"You don't get to come back into my life and pretend that you care about me. You aren't allowed to! Not after you threw me away like garbage!"

"That's not fair," he thunders, knocking me back a step. It's calm but stern, and it only fuels me. I love a fight.

It took me years to grow a spine, and then I built my career on it.

"What part? Did you reach out all these years, and I missed it? Did you need my address?" I pick up a stack of junk mail and launch it across the room. A rare flourish that I don't usually partake in during court.

"I never wanted things to happen the way that they did. I never stopped thinking about you."

"Wow, means a whole lot now." I roll my eyes, and he grinds

his teeth together.

"I lost everything," he grits out.

"I lost you!" I grasp my door frame to keep from slamming it and take a deep breath. "*You* abandoned *me.* That was *your* choice."

I don't look as I shut him away. Shutting him out like he did to me. Eleven years, three months, and six days ago.

* * *

Glinting sunlight streams through the bottom crack of my blinds, shining directly on my face as it does every morning.

Despite averaging five hours of sleep a night, waking up to the natural light helps rouse me without setting off my nervous system like a normal alarm would.

Today, I feel hungover, and I didn't have any alcohol last night.

I take my time twisting my hair into a claw clip and washing my face, and I only leave the safety of my bedroom after I've tightened my robe around my waist for the fifth time.

My living room is silent and empty. The blanket and pillow are stacked neatly on the end of the couch. My shoes are placed upright beside the door, and the junk mail I threw across the room is back with the other envelopes on my counter.

He isn't here.

The deep pit of grief in my stomach simmers with anger. Of course, he left.

It isn't until I walk into the kitchen to see my teapot

percolating on the stove that I take pause, and the anger turns solemn. He started my tea?

Maybe I'm being unreasonable, but I can't let myself forget, even though it'd be so much easier that way. All the years of sadness can't be erased.

I sigh, ignoring the tea, and reaching for the back door instead, but it's already unlocked. I swing it open, staring at the closed screen door in front of me. That means...

"Good morning," the low timber of voice glides over my shoulders as I step outside. He's sitting at my little metal outdoor bistro set that came with the cottage. Its aged flower design matches perfectly with the cottage aesthetic and the cobblestone back patio.

"I thought you left."

He sips out of his own mug, ignoring my statement. "I was surprised to find tea in your cabinets."

"I could never stand the taste of coffee. Started tea in college."

"Much to your reluctance," he guesses.

"My mom was off her rocker with her beliefs, but I've come to understand some of her choices as an adult," I admit.

He looks at me thoughtfully, urging me to continue.

"Nature is important for the soul. I like being barefoot when I can. I do yoga every day, and I hate food dyes." I shrug. "But I believe in modern medicine, and don't want to think about all the chemicals in my nail polish or shampoo."

"And, do the dream catchers still keep the nightmares away?"

"Sometimes."

Chapter Eight

Hayes

13 years ago...

I tap gently on the window pane with the light green dream catcher hanging in it, and it's only a moment before there is indiscernible movement at the corner of the curtain.

Seconds go by, and I think she's ignoring me until the curtain is shoved aside completely. Olive is looking at me with the most confused expression on her face as she cracks the window open.

"What are you doing?"

"I haven't seen you in a few days. I wanted to say hi."

"You haven't seen me because you got in trouble for fighting. Again," she scolds.

We've been friends for a few months now, and she's set me on a better trajectory, but I still have lapses from time to time.

"Bobby was showing off his cousin's girlfriend's nudes. Even the principal couldn't blame me for clocking him."

She rolls her eyes and leans her elbows against the window frame. I'm standing on an old milk carton, putting our heads nearly in the same place.

"You have to graduate in two months. No more trouble."

"Trouble finds me, Liv. You know that." I smirk and watch pinkness creep into her cheeks.

I'm not a stranger to girls' attention, but I'm older than her. I shouldn't enjoy seeing her blush like that, and I shouldn't hope that she likes seeing me as much as I like seeing her.

Liv isn't like that, though. If she has a crush on me, she's never said. She doesn't try to flirt with me, and she's never trying to get anything from me.

I don't want anything from her besides friendship.

She's beautiful, of course, but I know what a girl like Liv is destined for, and it is a whole lot better than anything that I could give her. Friendship is all I'll let myself hope for.

"What will you do once you graduate?"

"I have a job lined up at Brody's auto shop. He's going to let me apprentice with him until I can get all my certifications."

"Have you always wanted to be a mechanic?"

I laugh. "No, but it'll pay well enough. I want to save up enough money to hire a trainer."

"Trainer for what?"

"MMA. Mixed Martial Arts."

"You want to be a professional fighter?"

"That's where the real money is. I can make it big, I know it."

"I believe in you." She smiles, resting her head against the edge of the window.

"I'm sorry, it's late. I should let you get some sleep."

"It's okay. I'd rather talk to you." Her lips tip in a smile, but she hides it quickly, shyly.

"You're something special, Liv. I can't wait to see the great things you do someday."

"Like what?" She laughs. "I don't have a clue what I want

to do."

"Surgeon?"

She grimaces. "Not a fan of blood."

"Teacher?"

"Kids scare me."

"Kids scare you because you are still a kid."

"Okay, I'm not that much younger than you," she argues.

Young enough. "A couple of years out of high school and you'll realize how young you are now."

She rolls her eyes, making me chuckle. "How mature of you," she teases.

"That's why I watch out for you. I have to make sure no one takes advantage of you."

"Please. Boys don't even look in my direction."

"They will. And when they do, remember that you're the prize and they don't deserve you."

"None of them?" She scoffs.

"Not a single one," I insist seriously, sobering her.

"And if I want someone?"

"Just don't let anyone stop you from achieving your dreams. I watched it happen to my mom, and she'll never get those years back."

She could be living a much better life if she hadn't settled for my father. I'd gladly snuff out my existence if it meant she got a redo.

"You're a good guy, Jensen. No matter what anyone says."

"Oh, and what do they say?"

"I've had two teachers warn me about you. A couple of classmates have whispered their concerns after seeing you walk me to class. They say you're bad news."

"That's true. But never something you have to worry about,

dove." I smooth my thumb against her chin, memorizing the way she dips her head bashfully.

The purest thing I'll ever touch.

* * *

Present...

"Have you made your decision?" I study her closely as she avoids my gaze.

"About what?"

"Are you going to let me protect you?"

"Oh, I have a choice?" She asks sarcastically.

"You always have a choice, Liv. I'd never force anything on you." *But I'd watch from a distance no matter what.*

"Hmm," she sighs, stepping over to a metal tub I'd been pondering earlier. She peels back the cover, and I realize it's full of water and not a garden bed as I'd suspected.

"If you're still afraid to be near me, you can just say that."

"I'm not afraid of you, Hayes. Never have been."

"I know. You're a poor judge of character."

She throws her head back, letting out a full belly laugh, and I'm mesmerized. Her eyes crinkle, and her smile leaves little dimples at the corners of her lips.

Her teeth are nearly perfect, aside from her incisor on the left side that's always had a slight angle to it.

I always thought the uniqueness of it made her prettier, something that made it even harder to look away when she smiled. She has a beauty that can't be duplicated. I'm glad she never got it fixed.

My eyes trace a line down her neck until it disappears under her robe.

"I might have been a poor judge of character back then, Jensen, but now I'm a grown woman and eat men like you for breakfast." She drops her robe suddenly, stepping into the tub of water in the tiniest bikini I've ever seen.

I don't blink as she sinks to her neck, gripping the sides as she battles the icy water. Her head tips back, and for a moment, she looks relaxed.

Maybe it isn't as cold as it looks.

"You can play bodyguard, Hayes. If that eases your burdens. For repentance, whatever." The tremor in her voice is a good indicator that it really is that cold, but the goose bumps across her skin draw me in anyway.

Her eyelids pop open when she senses my approach.

"But nothing changes between us," she rasps as I dip my hand into the water near her thigh, letting it bite my skin as it does hers.

"As long as there's an 'us', that's all I care about." I should move back, give her more space, because I can see the cold taking effect as her entire body trembles.

But I don't move.

She pushes to her feet, sucking in a chestful of air as the temperature change shocks her body. Only then do I move, stepping away so she can grab her robe, but my gaze never leaves her.

She's all woman, now, and I don't feel guilty for admiring her like I did when we were teenagers.

And, I think it pisses her off.

"Be here tomorrow morning at 7:30 sharp. Wear something professional," she suggests, condescendingly.

"Yes, boss."

She cuts me a glare as she walks inside. "*Don't* call me that." The door slams behind her, and a smile stretches across my face.

Chapter Nine

Liv

There was no waking with the sun this morning. Instead, I've been up since 4 a.m. because I was sick of tossing and turning.

Spending an entire day with Hayes, on purpose, feels like a mistake even though I know the reasoning is sensical.

Someone is stalking me, that's why he is doing this. That's all.

But I still can't erase the way he looked at me yesterday morning when I did my cold plunge. The way his eyes burned a path across my skin.

It was a heat that I haven't felt in a long time.

I shove my folder of paperwork and my laptop into my briefcase as hard as I can, pushing my thoughts away.

It's 7:28, he should be here, and I wish the anticipation of that was simply about being on time to work, but I meant what I said. I'm not waiting on him.

I slip on the same heels from the other night that he placed by the door for me and step into the cool morning air.

"Good morning," he startles me, and I nearly drop my briefcase. He's wearing a black suit with a black dress shirt.

No tie.

He's always been handsome, but this is something else entirely. His aura is overwhelming, his charm is palpable.

He's no pretty boy; he's a killer in a suit.

"I didn't know you were here." I clear my throat, stepping past him.

"I was going to knock at 7:29. You're ahead of schedule."

That makes me roll my eyes. "Let's go–" I stop at the edge of the porch. Parked next to my silver Jaguar is a black SUV.

"Whose car is that?" It's nice, with tented windows and shiny wheels.

"Mine." He opens the passenger door for me, but I don't move.

"Where did you get this?"

He looks at me in confusion.

"You didn't steal it, did you?"

"Jesus Christ. Get in the car, Liv."

I climb in, needing the grab handle to hoist myself up into the lifted vehicle because of my pencil skirt. The interior is just as luxurious, and it smells brand new.

"How did you afford this?"

"Did you assume that I've been unemployed all this time?"

"Well, no, I guess not, but I didn't think the sanctuary paid that well."

"So do you think I stole it? Or that I came about the funds illegally?" He asks in exasperation.

"I'm sorry, I guess I don't know what to think. I don't know anything about who you are, now."

He sighs, throwing me slack like he always does. "When you're first hired at the sanctuary, the pay does suck. But that's because you get free housing and food. The little bit of money you save can get you started, and for most guys, that's enough. That's all they need, so they move on. I stuck around, and the pay got better as my responsibilities increased, but I didn't rely on it.

"I learned different trades, skills, and taught myself how to invest. I don't have lawyer money," he glances at me, "but I'm doing okay for myself."

"I'm glad," I whisper, only because I can't get my throat to work. All I ever wanted was for him to be happy.

He jerks his head as if nodding is even too much to express his response. Silence falls over us, and I can't stop my mind from wandering.

He was in prison for six years.

He's been out for five...

"Were you ever going to reach out to me?"

"What?" He asks, lost in his thoughts also.

"If we didn't run into each other at the sanctuary... Would you have ever tried to find me?"

Each rotation of the tires against the pavement grates my eardrums as the deafening pause grows longer. Louder.

Each breath that fills my lungs becomes painful until I can't stand it.

"So, that's a no," I laugh humorlessly.

"It's not a no," he argues.

"Then what is it?!" I don't know why I let my temper flare or why I keep beating the same dead horse. We were not meant to cross paths again, and it's becoming clear.

"I don't know, Liv." His hand grips the top of the steering wheel until his knuckles turn white. "I don't know," he utters softly this time, tortured by the words.

"I'll talk to Jackson today to see if he can spare any deputies.

I wouldn't want to put you through more torture." I throw the door open as soon as he's parked outside the county building and slam it shut behind me.

Part of me expects him to stay behind, but the bigger part of me isn't surprised when I feel him trailing behind me.

I don't have to look to know he's there. I can sense him.

I always could.

* * *

13 years ago...

"If you keep walking ten feet behind me, everyone will think you're following me," I yell into the air as I walk home from the bus.

"I'm not following you," Hayes responds, jogging to close the gap. "You left school without me."

"No, you missed the bus. That's not the same thing. Besides, you were too busy talking to *Valerie*."

His charming smile spreads across his face, and I have to look away. It's like the sun, except if you stare it'll scramble your good senses.

"She wants me to take her to prom."

"Her and every other girl in school," I mumble.

"Jealous?" He wiggles his eyebrows, and I scoff.

"No, I'm not allowed to go to prom until I'm a senior." *Not that anyone asked me to go anyway.*

"Don't worry, it isn't as cool as everyone makes it seem."

"You've never even been to a school dance."

"That's not true. I snuck into homecoming once." He winks

and jumps onto the dilapidated playground that has turned into our hangout spot, lounging at the top of the slide as if it's his personal hammock.

"How do you do that? Break the rules. Don't they mean something to you?"

"Most rules don't mean much to me at all."

"Why not?"

"Because they don't matter. At the end of the day, only certain things change the course of your life. Abiding by certain things matters… Keeping people safe, doing what's right even if it feels wrong. I don't know, morals mean more than rules."

"You get in fights all the time. How is that keeping people safe?"

"I don't hit anyone who doesn't deserve it, Liv."

"Did they teach you that in karate?" I tease. I asked him about the sweatshirt he gave me the first day we met, and he told me that he earned a black belt by the time he was fifteen.

He stopped going shortly after that, but refused to tell me why.

"Something like that." He looks up at the clouds as raindrops scatter down around us.

"I guess I'll see you tomorrow." Before I can throw my backpack over my shoulder, he slides down the slide and grabs it from me.

"Come to my house for dinner."

"Oh. Are you sure?" He's never invited me to his house. But to be fair, I've never invited him to mine either.

"My dad has a late shift at work. My mom always makes my favorite." He backpeddles towards his trailer, holding my backpack hostage, forcing me to follow, but truthfully, he pulls me easily like a magnet.

"Mom," he announces as he enters the door. "Liv is coming for dinner."

"Hi, Mrs. Hayes." I've come across her a time or two when she's called Hayes in for dinner after we'd been sitting on the playground all afternoon.

She's always been kind, but I've also noticed the deep sadness that weighs down her shoulders. Today, she smiles, and a small part of it touches her eyes, and I watch as Hayes mirrors it.

He loves his mom. It makes him softer, and it's the sweetest thing ever.

We end up doing our homework in the kitchen while his mom cooks, which is mostly me doing my homework while Hayes talks to us. He's incredibly intelligent, but no one gets to see it.

He does well on tests when he bothers to show up for class, but in the grand scheme of things, it's not enough. He'll graduate next month by the skin of his teeth.

"Dinner is ready." Mrs. Hayes serves us beef enchiladas, and they're plated with love, garnished prettily on ceramic white plates that have finely painted blue flowers around the edge. They're not fine china, but they are definitely special, and I start to ask about them when the front door blows open, hitting the wall with a bang.

Hayes jumps from his seat as his dad walks through carrying a 12-pack of beer.

"What the hell is that smell?"

"Dinner," Mrs. Hayes says hurriedly, grabbing the case from him and taking it to the fridge.

"Smells like shit," he grumbles, kicking off his boots. He's still wearing his police uniform. He's a veteran at the local department, although you'd never be able to tell from his demeanor.

"I thought you were working late," Hayes says through gritted teeth.

"A mailbox ran out in front of me and wrecked the front of my cruiser. They let me leave to heal up before my shift tomorrow," he chuckles, gruffly.

"Wonder why," Hayes scoffs, sneering at the beer his mom hands him.

"You got something you want to say in front of your girlfriend, boy?"

"No."

"What was that?"

"No. Sir," he grinds out.

He hates that word. He doesn't like it when teachers push the respect rule, either, but I thought he just couldn't stand authority.

I'm still gripping my fork in my hand, and I haven't been able to move. I'm not used to being around angry men. My stepdad is a stoner. He hardly strings sentences together, and I never have to worry about him yelling at my mom or me.

"I'm sorry, Liv. You'd better go." Hayes peels the fork from my hand, noticing my rigid posture.

"You embarrassed of me, boy? Nah, you just don't want your girlfriend around a real man." He barks a laugh, and I feel Jensen go from a simmer to a boil.

"Of course, I'm fucking embarrassed," he yells, throwing the fork that he took from me across the room so hard it dents the wall before clattering to the carpet.

"What did you say?" His father launches up from his

recliner and yanks Hayes's head back, gripping his hair in his meaty palm.

Mrs. Hayes must've expected it because she's lifting me from my chair and out of the way before I get shoved in the commotion.

"Liv, go," Jensen grumbles under his breath, staring into his father's bloodshot eyes.

I can't make my feet move. His mom's hands under my arms try to shove me towards the door, but she's a small woman, and I'm a foot taller than she is.

I can't stop looking at my only friend's face. The anger and disgust he has aimed directly at the man in front of him.

And the strength he has to be able to put up with it.

"Liv! GO!" He yells, spurring me out the door.

His mom slams it shut behind me, leaving me slumped against the porch railing to listen to the fight ensue.

"You're a worthless, no good, son of a bitch," his dad yells. The next thing I hear is a loud crash as dishes shatter.

I start running, and I don't stop until I'm safely home and behind my bedroom door, letting the anguish rip through me.

Chapter Ten

Hayes

13 years ago...

Tap... Tap... Tap... The curtain draws back achingly slow. "Hi, dove."

She opens the window just as slow, avoiding any noise that'll alert her mother to my presence outside her bedroom. "Are you okay?" She asks with the biggest eyes I've ever seen, but it's the shakiness of her voice that guts me.

"I'm fine. My dad is always like that when he drinks. I'm used to it. I wanted to apologize."

"Apologize?" She whisper-screams, and I shush her, but she doesn't relent. "You shouldn't have to live like that!"

"Your mom is going to hear you."

"I don't care! She's probably already blazed out of her mind," her voice cracks on her last word. "I've been worried sick about you."

"Look, I'm fine." I hold my hands out, grabbing hers on the window frame and squeezing her delicate fingers. "I'm out of here soon, don't worry."

She blinks at me, and her entire face breaks as tears stream down her cheeks.

"Hey, stop, don't cry," I beg as she covers her face with her hands and flops back on her bed.

"I can't stop thinking about how mean he was to you," she cries into her comforter, and I can't handle the way it makes my heart ache.

Gripping the top edge of the trailer, I pull up until my feet clear her window, easily lofting my body through the opening.

I drag her into my arms like it's the most natural thing in the world, and hold her until the heaving sobs turn to soft whimpers.

I've never touched her like this. We've barely done anything more than side-hug, but that was always out of friendliness. This goes a lot deeper than that.

It's not romantic. This is intimacy beyond that.

I've never experienced this before, and I don't think I can ever let her go.

"He's a terrible father. A shitty cop. And, a miserable human being, but he doesn't deserve your tears."

"I'm not crying for him, I'm crying for you." Her sad eyes find mine, and I can't look away.

Her beautiful hazel-blue eyes that shine with gold flecks during the day, and apparently deepen when she's crying. The dark ring around her iris is thick and angry.

"Don't cry for me, Olive. I can't stand to see you cry." The pad of my thumb traces her cheekbone, and her eyelids flutter when I reach her temple.

She's the most gorgeous thing I've ever seen, but I've put her so high on a pedestal that it's hard to fathom that she's real.

"You're my best friend, Jensen. I think I'd die if something happened to you."

"Don't say that. Don't ever say that. Your life is more important than mine. You have so much to offer the world, and it needs you because of it."

"The world needs you, too."

"Some of us are expendable, and I'm one of those people. That's just life." I offer a faint smile, feeling the canyon that will divide our paths.

"Don't say that." She smacks my chest, and I chuckle.

"At least I know the one good thing that I've ever done in my life is tricking you into being my best friend."

I watch the dimples form at the corners of her lips and have to fight the urge to kiss them.

Olive is too good for you.

"I love you, Jensen," she murmurs against my chest, and I pull her in tighter.

"I love you, too, Olive."

* * *

Present...

"I can help you with something," I offer for the fourth time today. She's drowning in stacks of legal documents, and the intern keeps bringing more.

"What exactly do you think you're qualified to help me with?" *Ouch.*

"I don't think it takes a genius to sort through paperwork."

She sighs, rubbing her temples. "I'm sorry, I don't mean to be a bitch. This case is complex, and I'm used to having a team of litigators and paralegals."

"How can I help?"

"I don't know. I need to know everything about Randall and Jeremiah Porter, so there is a definite timeline of their crimes and escalation. Unless you can inject that knowledge into my brain, I don't think you can help me."

"Well, what do you have so far?"

She slaps a stack of papers on the edge of her desk, and the top sheet slips onto the floor. When I pick it up, there's one single highlighted line among an ocean of words.

"This part is all you need?"

"That's the main point. I can tie it all together later. Hey, where are you going?" She shouts after me as I leave her office.

When I return, I'm dragging in a giant whiteboard on wheels that barely works.

"What are you–" She stops. "Where did you get that?"

"Don't worry about it."

"Hayes, I don't own the building, you can't just take stuff..." She continues berating me, but I ignore her, carrying on with my self-assigned task.

I draw two horizontal lines across the board and add one hash mark at the very beginning, jotting down the year and the incident.

"I'll pinpoint the details. It'll be all laid out, and you won't have so many papers to dig through."

Her mouth opens and shuts as if she's going to argue for argument's sake, but then she hands me the rest of the stack silently, giving me the green light.

"Thank you," she utters softly after I get to work.

"It's what I'm here for, Liv."

"You're here to keep an eye out for my stalker, not to be my assistant."

"I'm here to be anything you need."

She doesn't respond, and when I turn to look at her, she's staring straight through me.

"We're not friends. This is a working relationship. That's all it will ever be." Her eyes dart to mine to punctuate her statement.

"I don't expect anything from you."

She nods, and we continue on our islands, separated by a sea of unsaid thoughts and turmoil.

It isn't until the end of her workday that I dare to bridge the gap and speak to her unprovoked.

"I need to go check the parking lot. I want to see if anyone is out there lurking. Stay in here until I come back, and we can walk out together."

"Doesn't that seem a bit unnecessary?"

"No."

"Hayes..."

"Liv, let me do what I'm here to do."

"Fine." She tips her head back down to her laptop, and I shut her into her office before I go down to the employee lot.

Nothing seems amiss as I check my SUV. We parked in her assigned parking spot, but threw off the routine by not driving her car. No flowers today.

I don't like how many places there are to hide out here, and I don't like how easy it is to get into the building. I have a visitor's key card, but I bypassed each of the scanners because other employees were exiting for the day. I slipped back in easily.

The floor for the prosecutor's office is empty when I exit

the stairwell, but it doesn't concern me until I notice Liv's door is wide open...

I shut it. I know I did.

"Liv," I announce, but she doesn't respond. I confirm she isn't in her office and whip back around toward the common area. "Liv!"

My feet thunder down the silent hallway as I scan each office and room for a sign of her. "Liv!" I yell again, ignoring the tightness in my chest.

I nearly miss the water running when I pass the bathrooms. Decorum out the window, I shove into the women's restroom and don't take a breath until I set eyes on her.

Her startled expression finds mine in the mirror as she washes her hands. "What are you doing?"

"I told you to wait in your office."

"I am in the office."

"No, not *the* office. *Your* office."

"You're ridiculous."

"Dammit, Liv. I'm trying to keep you safe."

"I'm not living in fear!" She snaps back, aggressively chucking her paper towels in the trash can. If only she were as passionate about her safety as she was about hating me.

"You wouldn't have to live in fear if you'd only listen to me and let me take care of you."

"Yeah, sorry if I have trust issues. I've been burned in the past," she flings at me as she breezes by me out to the hallway.

I sigh because I know I deserve it, but I still wish she'd give me even an ounce of the benefit of the doubt. I'm not the boy she knew a decade ago.

And, I'll prove it.

Chapter Eleven

Liv

I'm going to explode out of my skin. Being in such proximity to Hayes all day has fried my nerves, and I am close to jumping out of the car before he's even made it up my street.

He didn't catch me going to the bathroom earlier. The moment he walked out of my office to go check the parking lot, I sprinted to the sink to splash cold water on my face.

I felt like I was suffocating.

I don't know how I'm supposed to pretend that being near him isn't painful when he acts like there isn't anything strange about this.

"Your phone is ringing," he utters, pulling up my driveway.

I have it on silent, resting on the center console, but Elliot's name is displayed on the screen. Dread twists my stomach.

"I'll call him back late–"

"Someone's here," he interrupts, and my head snaps forward.

I'm going to be sick. "That's Elliot's car."

"Were you expecting him?" He asks dully.

"No, it must be a surprise."

"How thoughtful." His voice is nowhere close to sincere. He starts to get out of the SUV at the same time I do, but I try to stop him.

"Please, don't."

"Why?" He gets out anyway.

"Liv?" Elliot gets out of his car, and we're suddenly standing in an awkward triangle in my driveway.

"Elliot, this is Jensen."

"Hayes," he introduces himself, offering his hand to shake. The moment their palms touch, electricity zaps me. My old life and my new life were never meant to merge.

"Friend from work?" Elliot asks me. There's no recognition because I've never told him about Jensen.

There's also no accusation in his tone about me being with another man because he would never suspect I'd be cheating on him. He's not the jealous type.

Hayes looks at me, waiting for my response, and both their gazes on me is suddenly too much. "I'm sorry, I need to go take my shoes off, they're killing my feet."

"Hayes, I'll see you tomorrow." I glance at him as I walk past, and he holds my focus until I'm forced to look away.

"Yes, boss."

As soon as I'm in the front door, I slip my shoes off and fall backward onto the couch, propping my legs over the arm while I rub my head.

"Something wrong with your car?" Elliot asks from the kitchen, making himself at home and pouring himself a glass of scotch. It's not my preference, but I always keep a bottle in stock for him.

"No." I sigh, preparing myself for more truths to be forced out of me. "Someone has been leaving me creepy gifts. Hayes offered to shuttle me to and from work until we find out who it is."

"Anything good?" He scoffs into his glass.

"What?"

"Are the gifts any good?" He laughs to himself, and I roll my head back to look at the ceiling.

I never expected him to be alpha-asshole protective about it, but he doesn't seem to be concerned at all. Not like Hayes was.

"I have a stalker, Elliot," I state plainly.

"Of course, you do, Livvy." I hate when he calls me that. "You're a beautiful woman."

"This isn't funny."

He raises his hands in surrender. "I'm sorry, that was distasteful. I just assume you already have everything under control. No need to worry."

No need to worry.

"God forbid my fiancé worry about me," I snap, swinging my feet to the floor.

"You know that isn't what I meant." He stands in front of me, tipping my chin up with his finger. "I do worry about you, but I also know you can take care of yourself. You've made that abundantly clear to me during our relationship."

I guess he's right, though it seems out of context in this situation.

Regardless, I've already hit my limit of mental gymnastics for today, and I don't have the energy to rein in my emotions.

"How long do you plan on staying this time?" I ask coldly.

"I thought we'd have a quick dinner." He smiles and wags his eyebrows suggestively. "But, I need to head back tonight."

A quick dinner. A short visit. It's always the same.

"I already have dinner plans with Thea."

"Ah, I see. I should have called first." He finishes his scotch and leans down to kiss me, but I give him my cheek.

He pecks it and straightens as if nothing is amiss. "I'll make arrangements for my next visit. See you soon, sweetie."

He leaves without a word from me.

I don't actually have plans with Thea. I shouldn't have lied. But my thoughts are so jumbled in my head, I can't pretend to be the perfect fiancée tonight.

I need my best friend.

All I do is change out of my work clothes before I walk out the door to go to the one place that I always feel like I belong.

I walk straight through Thea's front door without knocking, and she smiles when she sees me. She's sitting at her kitchen table next to baby Kate and twists the high chair until my best girl sees me, too.

A smile puffs her chubby cheeks, and it's exactly what I needed to reset my state of mind and remind myself of who I am.

I'm not frail. I'm not incapable of handling hard things.

Tomorrow will be a better day. The awkwardness of being around Hayes will dissipate, and I'll make a point to call Elliot to apologize for my behavior lately.

We're getting married soon, and we need to be solid. *I* need to be stable. No more detours in my plan. I'll finish my work in Rollins County and go back to the city. I'll forget about having a stalker. I won't have to see Hayes. *And I'll only see Thea and Kate one weekend a month, if that.*

The cracks in my perfectly drawn-out life are starting to loosen the ground beneath my feet. The things I thought I wanted are starting to look like flaws… A high-powered career and an affluent lifestyle.

They don't mean anything if they aren't in the place I want to be.

By the time I get home, the front of the cottage is darkened by night, and I'm immediately wary of my surroundings.

I never used to be afraid of the dark. Now, every shadow is shaped like a man. Every noise sends my pulse racing.

All because some creep out there feels entitled to corrupt my autonomy.

"No one is here. No one is watching me," I grumble to myself as I back into my normal parking spot.

My eyes are still scanning every dark corner when my headlights illuminate the large oak tree in front of the cottage. I slam my hand on my steering wheel in fiery annoyance, forcing it to overpower the disgust.

"What the fuck!"

Hanging from the tree is a mutilated animal, sliced and mangled. Drenched in blood, it's hard to tell if it's a cat or a fox, or some other small animal. But the paper nailed to its stomach, or where the stomach should be, is painfully legible.

SLUT

* * *

My tires crunch across the gravel until they come to a stop in the center of the dirt lot.

There's the farmhouse to my right, but it's dark. The big barn to my left has the door propped open, and I can hear voices from within.

This is a bad idea.

I don't know what I'm doing, but this is where I ended up when nothing else felt right.

I blink to adjust to the lights inside as I step through the door, and the noise of multiple conversations dies completely by the time both of my feet come to a stop.

At least six men are staring at me, but no one moves until an older man by the pool table leans his stick against the side and steps towards me.

"Can I help you, ma'am?" His scratchy drawl comforts me, but it doesn't erase the anxiety coursing through my veins. I haven't stopped shaking since I peeled out of my driveway.

"I'm looking for Jensen, err, Hayes, I mean."

"He's probably in the garage, but let me call him first to chec–"

"Liv?"

The adrenaline keeping me afloat deflates hearing his voice, and my knees nearly buckle, but my self-preservation keeps me upright.

"Thank you," I utter to the older man before turning towards the door.

Jensen is standing in the doorway, looking at me as if he's checking for injuries. His serious gaze scans me from head to toe, and I tremble under his assessment.

All the fear that I've tamped down catches up to me now that I'm in his presence. The disgust of seeing a mutilated animal left purposefully for me washes over me.

"Get me out of here, please," I beg under my breath as black shadows lick at the edges of my vision.

He hardly blinks at my request, offering his hand to me, but my focus only narrows, and as hard as I try, it's out of reach.

My neck muscles go lax, and my body sways, but I only fall against a hard wall of muscle. "Olive, what the hell is going on?"

"Nothing," I breathe, sucking in his distinctive scent. It's exactly as I remember, but somehow better.

"Olive," he growls, steadying me on my feet. Some alertness snaps back into my brain.

"I just need to sit down," I whisper, remembering there are people behind me witnessing this.

"Not in here," he grumbles. "Can you walk, or do you want me to carry you?"

"I can walk," I admit regretfully, but he doesn't let me go.

He wraps his arm firmly around my waist before leading me back outside, and doesn't let it slip until I'm placed solidly in a fold-out camping chair in a big garage.

The warmth of his skin leaves me too quickly, and a chill zips down my spine.

"What do you need?" He asks, worriedly, examining my face just as closely as before.

"I'm fine," I breathe in relief now that my head's stopped swimming.

"You are not fine," he grits again.

"This has been happening lately. I just need to rest."

"What the fuck do you mean? You've been having dizzy spells? Passing out?"

"I've been passing out."

He swipes his palms across his face harshly. "Why?"

"I don't know."

His jaw tenses, making the muscle in his cheek twitch.

"Are you lying to me? Because I swear to God I'll call Thea

right now and get the truth out of her."

I know I'm doing better because I roll my eyes at him, and it doesn't give me vertigo. "My doctor thinks it might be stress-induced, but that's just a non-answer because they can't figure out what's causing it. And, before you ask, Thea knows all of this already."

"Oh, I'm sure she does. I can see the secrets transmitting back and forth between the two of you every time you're near each other."

"They're not secrets. You just don't have the privilege of knowing everything about me anymore."

Chapter Twelve

Hayes

You just don't have the privilege of knowing everything about me anymore.

As if I don't already fucking know.

"I get it, Liv. I fucked everything up. I'm a horrible person, and you hate my guts. I fucking get it. But, please, stop hiding things from me. I am begging you." I fall to my knees in front of her so she's forced to look me in the eyes. "I cannot do everything in my power to help you if I don't know what the fuck is going on."

Her mouth twists down, and I think for a moment that I've upset her. I'd rather her be pissed at me than upset.

"My stalker left me another gift," she admits, and her bottom lip trembles.

"What was it?" I ask softly, gravitating towards her as she leans closer to me.

"A horrifying, sad, dead animal and another note."

"What did it say?" I grit out.

She squeezes her eyes shut, shaking her head. "It said 'slut' but it was written in blood."

I'm going to kill him. Whoever this fucker is, he's going to die. "It's alright, I'll take care of it."

"I called Malec on my way here. I don't know why I came."

"Because you wanted to feel safe." She looks at me like she wants to argue, but she doesn't. "I'll keep you safe."

She relents, nodding her head and resting it against my shoulder. I don't move, I hardly breathe as she takes the comfort she's willing to tolerate.

We both know it isn't enough, but her pride won't allow more.

"Can I stay for a little while? Jackson said he'd get it cleaned up, but I don't want to go home until it's gone."

"Of course, you can."

She shifts back in her seat, breaking our contact and erecting the wall back in place. "You can go back to doing whatever you were doing. I'll stay out of your way."

I wasn't doing anything overly important before she came, but if she wants normalcy, I'll oblige.

* * *

12 years ago...

"Liv, I think you earned employee of the month."

"Shut up," she scoffs, hopping up on the only clear workbench in the shop. She comes every day after school to hang out with me. She does her homework while I work on cars.

Some days we work diligently in silence, and some days the conversation never ends.

She's a couple of months into her senior year, and I've almost completed all the certifications I need to be a full-time mechanic here instead of an apprentice.

"How was your birthday dinner?"

"It was fine. My cake was terrible. Organic and all-natural sugar." She makes a sour face, and I chuckle from my spot under the hood of a 1975 Ford Pickup.

"Just think, one more year until you're legally an adult and don't have to put up with the hippie mom recipes."

"Yeah, I'll be far away at college hopefully."

If I didn't know better, I'd think a wire stabbed me in the chest, but I know it's just the thought of her leaving. She hasn't picked a college yet, but I know she's one foot out of the state already.

"Have you decided what you'll major in?"

She sighs like she always does when this topic is broached. "I'm doing really well in AP Calc. Maybe I'll do something with mathematics."

"Do you enjoy it?"

"Well, no."

"Pass."

"Not everyone gets to do things they love for a living."

"Not everyone, but you should."

"Hmm. Business?"

"Do you want to be someone's boss?"

"Maybe. I like bossing you around."

"HA! That's only because I let you. Not everyone will be as nice as me." I give her a cheeky grin, and she throws her head back and laughs. I love it when she does that.

"I don't know. I'd like to help people but…" She shrugs.

"You have time, don't worry about it."

"I could go into Social Work."

"Why would you do that? The pay would be terrible."

"I don't know, I always had a nice social worker."

It's one of those things that she brought up once, and we don't talk about. She was a newborn still when hippie-mom adopted her, although she swears she was less weird when she was a kid.

"So you want to be one?"

She shrugs. "I could help other families."

"You don't think that would mess with your head?"

"I guess it might. I'd probably have a hard time not checking all my sealed records."

"You wouldn't do that. You're too goody goody."

She flips me off, and I bark a laugh. "Calm down, dove, I wouldn't want to be on your bad side."

"That's right, and don't you forget it." She smiles, and it pulls me from the truck.

"Any plans this weekend?"

"I have a study group on Saturday morning, but other than that, no."

"A study group… On the weekend?"

"I'm not doing great in AP Chemistry."

"Oh, I'm sorry. You have a B+ instead of an A?"

"No, I have an A, but it's not about that." She crosses her arms. "I need to score well on the AP exam."

I raise my hands in surrender. "You're right, sorry."

"Besides, I have nothing better to do. Not like any boys have asked me on a date."

I try not to flinch externally. "Have your eye on someone?"

"No, not particularly. But I'm starting to feel like a pariah since you aren't there every day to talk to me between classes. I see the other girls talking to their boyfriends, and it would be nice if anyone noticed me at all."

"They know you're my girl, Liv. That's why they don't bother." I wink at her, and she huffs.

"Don't say that. People will get the wrong idea."

"What? You don't want people to think you're mine?" I ask casually, though my chest has an anvil on it.

"Not when you go around giving every other girl you see a hickey from Hayes."

"Oh my God. Not this again. It's been a couple of girls. The nickname is unnecessary."

"Still." She shrugs.

"Sounds like you want a hickey from Hayes," I taunt, slinking over to her.

"Shut up," she laughs, pushing my face away when I teasingly lunge for her neck.

I laugh with her even though my mouth waters thinking about sinking into her soft skin. She's a senior now, but she's only 17...

She's too young, and I'm just the knucklehead who will screw with her head.

"Love you, Liv," I tell her unceremoniously because we say it to each other all the time. "Sorry, boys are idiots."

She rolls her eyes. "Yeah, love you, too."

Even though I mean it more than each time before, I'll never cross that line, because there will be no going back.

And, I won't derail her life.

Not even when I would move mountains to have her in mine.

Chapter Thirteen

Liv

My mother always spoke of nirvana when I was growing up. An unattainable goal perceived as otherworldly, complete peace.

I thought she was crazy then, but once I became an adult, seeking nirvana didn't seem so bizarre. Life has a way of beating you down. Why not strive for utter happiness?

Wrapped in a nest of blankets in the center of my bed is as close to this feeling as I've found so far. Those first few minutes after waking up from a deep and restful sleep without any aches from tossing or turning, and before you realize your bladder is full.

Lulling in and out of consciousness, remembering those scattered bits of your dream…

A sigh escapes my chest as I stretch, and then my body goes taut once my foot hits a wall.

I have a queen-size bed, and I sleep in the middle of the room…

It's still dark, and I peek over the blanket in front of my face, but it is obvious that this is not my room. I'm not in my bed.

My body lurches into a seated position as my eyes scan the room. Except it's hardly a room. It looks like a loft. I can see the railing that oversees another space below.

My vision finally adjusts to the dim light, and I notice the body sleeping beside me. Thankfully, on the floor.

Hayes is on a thin blanket with a single pillow that looks like it's from a couch, not a bed.

I'm in Jensen's bed. I grip the blankets under my chin, inhaling his scent on them before I can stop myself.

I need to find my phone. My keys. I need to get out of here, but I can't move. I can't stop staring at him asleep on the floor.

He's wearing a t-shirt, and his arms are folded loosely over his stomach. I can faintly see the tattoos that are scattered across his skin.

While he was working on his motorcycle, I examined each one, looking as closely as I could from the safety of my camp chair.

Most of them are palm-sized and black and white. They're similar styles but aren't meshed together like a sleeve would be.

There's a code of numbers below his wrist on the top of his hand that I haven't been able to crack.

Claw marks down the inside of his forearm.

A snake.

A dagger.

A compass.

There's a tattoo that peeks out from the collar of his shirt, but I can't tell what it is, and I can only imagine what else he's hiding.

He didn't have any tattoos when we were teens. He never

had the money.

A gentle smile tilts my lips. We were so young and naive about the world back then, always dreaming of making it big and getting out of the trailer park.

The corners of my lips fall. We got out of the trailer park, but at what cost?

"I have an alarm set. Go back to sleep," he mumbles sleepily from his makeshift cot.

"How did I get in here?"

"I carried you."

Jitters erupt in my stomach, and I can't tamp them down.

"You fell asleep, and I didn't want to wake you, but I also didn't want you to wake up with a broken neck from sleeping in that chair."

"Where are we exactly?"

"My room in the bunkhouse. All the other guys sleep on the other side of the loft."

"Why do you still live here?"

He sits up, wiping the sleep from his face. "I haven't had a reason to leave."

"Oh."

"Lochlan is to me what Thea is to you, Liv. He's the reason I'm here. I owe him a lot."

I know he's the one who started Second Chance Sanctuary, but I don't think that's what we're talking about.

"He's your best friend." I don't know why the words taste bitter on my tongue.

"He was my cellmate when I got to prison. He showed me the ropes and had my back from day one. I wasn't in a good space, mentally. He saved me, gave me something to look forward to when I got out."

"What happened to being a professional fighter?" I saw his punching bag in the garage earlier, but I was too afraid to ask him.

He sighs. "It was a silly dream, and I had to grow up. Lochlan and I spar sometimes."

"For fun?"

"Kind of." He doesn't elaborate.

"I'm sorry you didn't get to live your dream," I whisper in the darkness.

"We aren't all meant to get what we want."

After all he's been through, and everything we went through… I still want him to get everything he wants in life. I hope he does.

"Does Lochlan… Know about me? About us as kids?"

"He does."

Embarrassment fills me. "He knew who I was when I came here that day to introduce myself to him."

"Technically, no. This is the girl he knew of…" He opens the top drawer of the nightstand behind him and grabs a photo, handing it to me.

The corners are worn, and the picture itself is faded, but there is no mistaking it. It's us, 12 years ago. A selfie that I took with my digital camera. I gifted him the photo before…

Before everything happened.

"Why do you have this?"

"I've never been without it."

"I don't understand."

"I only had a handful of possessions when they locked me up, and even less when I got out, but I always had the photograph."

"Why?" I ask angrily.

"You know why."

"No, I don't."

"Can we finish this conversation in the morning?" He glances around like he's afraid we'll disturb the others.

"No, let's not finish it at all. You have your truth, and I have mine. Let's keep it that way." I don't bother attempting to storm out.

I yank the blankets up to my neck and roll over, facing away from him.

It isn't until I realize that I'm still grasping the photo against my chest that tears begin to well in my eyes.

I've had to miss him for eleven years. Burn with betrayal for eleven years. Fight sickness every time I think of a memory.

The bed dips behind me, and my body rolls as he pulls my nest of blankets into his arms. There are inches of padding between us, but I feel a million miles away.

"It was never supposed to be like this," I cry, letting myself mourn out loud for the first time in a long time.

"I know," he whispers.

"You ruined everything," I cry harder.

"I know," his voice breaks, tightening his hold on me.

"I'm getting married."

His body goes rigid, but he doesn't respond.

"I'm moving back to the city once this case is over," I add. I don't know why I'm telling him all of this.

Maybe because I feel guilty. Or because I'm wrapped in his arms when I shouldn't be.

Or because I want him to tell me not to.

"Okay," he says instead, pushing a fresh wave of tears down my face.

He doesn't care.

I know better.
Jensen Hayes is only ever going to break my heart.

Chapter Fourteen

Hayes

Every morning, I pick her up at 7:30 sharp and drive in relative silence to her office. We exchange logistics as the hours pass, and as soon as we're back in my SUV, the silence continues.

She won't look at me a second longer than she has to. She won't talk about the night she stayed in my bed at the sanctuary.

She doesn't want to talk about her stalker either.

I stay in her driveway all evening, always watching, waiting for anything to go wrong.

If she cares, she hasn't said anything. But I suspect it would only end in an argument regardless.

That's the only thing we can accomplish when we do speak. I'd hate to face her in the courtroom. She has a way of lunging for your throat when she wants to get her point across.

It thrills the hell out of me.

If I knew my presence wasn't upsetting her, I'd make her mad at me on purpose just to hear her voice. More so to experience her fire.

She did it. She grew up to be a powerhouse and achieved

her dreams. She has a successful career, and people who love her. I couldn't be prouder.

I only wish there was a small corner for me. Not that I deserve it.

I hear an engine slowing before I see the vehicle, and I watch it closely as it pulls into her driveway. My shoulders ease when I see who it is.

Thea and Jesse get out of their car and exchange a quick word with one another before they split. He goes to the backseat to get the baby, and she walks over to my SUV.

"Hi." She waves because she probably can't see through my window tint. I lower my window, and she smiles warmly, but hesitantly. "We're here for dinner. Jesse can keep an eye on her for a while if you want a break," she offers. "Liv said you've been here late every night."

Ah, so she has noticed.

"I don't mind. I don't have anywhere else to be." That's not true. I have a shit ton of responsibilities I'm slacking on at the sanctuary.

"You should come in and eat with us."

"She wouldn't want that." I smile stiffly at her, and she tilts her head, observing me thoughtfully.

"Come inside, please. I'd like to get to know you better."

"Why?"

"Because she means a lot to you, and that matters to me." She turns away from me, joining her husband and baby on the porch where they're waiting, and that's when I see Liv watching from the doorway.

I don't follow. I don't know that I should. Not until they disappear inside and Liv gives me a subtle nod.

She doesn't wait to see if I take the bait, but of course, I take it because I'll take any inch she gives me.

I walk into a house of radiant joy. Jesse and Kate are rolling around on the floor. Thea starts collecting dishes as Liv prepares dinner. They're dancing around each other in the kitchen, speaking to each other, and having two conversations at once.

It takes me thirty seconds to figure out that they're talking about a disaster meal from college and simultaneously whether or not they should call Natalie to ask her a question about what Liv is cooking right now.

"But if I put it back in the oven, it will get over-cooked."

"If you don't put cheese on it, then it defeats the whole purpose of the meal." Thea crosses her arms like she means business. "Hayes," she turns to me suddenly, expecting me to forge an opinion about the casserole dish Liv is holding.

"Cheese," I say after glancing at the somewhat colorless chicken and rice. "If you put it under the broiler for a few minutes, it won't ruin anything," I add.

"Fine! You both better eat it, then," she relents.

"Liv hates to cook," Thea divulges. "She only offered because she's afraid to leave her house after dark now to come to my house."

"Hey!" Liv rebuts her friend's honesty.

"You could have told me. I can take you to Thea's anytime you want."

"I wouldn't ask you to do anymore than you already are, Hayes."

More like she doesn't want to ask me.

"I'm here to do whatever you need," I promise.

"See, there you go." Thea shrugs, and I realize this is one of those conversations they've already had that I'm only now becoming privy to.

"Just because you know he used to be my friend doesn't mean you guys can gang up on me." Liv narrows her eyes at her, the throat lunge comes next…

But Thea's face beams, completely undeterred. "You're only mad because it's working and you hate to lose."

"Of course, I hate to lose. Who likes losing?" Liv glances at me, but her attention falls to my mouth quickly. I hadn't realized that I was smiling while watching the exchange. "What?"

"Nothing." *I missed this.*

Her.

Almost as if she could read my thoughts, she busies herself in the kitchen again, actively avoiding any opportunity to look in my direction.

"So, Hayes, Jesse told me that you helped them find Dec last year when he was lost at the sanctuary."

Dec is Natalie's brother and Sheriff Malec's new little brother-in-law.

"We all did. As soon as we found out he was in with the bears, none of us hesitated."

Thea sits down on the bar stool at the kitchen counter and pats the counter top opposite her, and I feel like I'm taking my seat for an interview.

"After I saw how you guys operated, Lochlan did me a solid by hiring Curtis on," Jesse says. "He swears he's still glad Lochlan gave him the job, even after everything that happened."

Curtis was badly injured by Jeremiah Porter when he terrorized the sanctuary.

"How's he doing? I haven't made it to the hospital in a

while." I sigh. "If I were a couple of minutes faster, I would have been there, and he wouldn't have been alone. Hell, it should have been me."

"Still a long road to recovery, but he'll get through it. He always has good things to say about you guys. He respects you a lot, Hayes." Jesse pats me on the shoulder, and I nod my head in appreciation.

"He's one of my key witnesses," Liv says from her corner of the kitchen. "If he's well enough to testify."

"He's hard-headed. He'll be ready," Jesse assures her.

I feel tugging on my pants and look down at the head full of blonde curls. "Hi," I say softly, hoping not to startle her. I don't know if she meant to grab me or if she thinks my leg belongs to her dad.

Her big green eyes stare at me as she bounces in place, gripping my leg. I put my hands out, and she reaches for me instantly, accepting it as I pull her onto my lap.

"I think she was feeling left out," Thea coos at her daughter. "She just started trying to walk, but luckily, she isn't much of a climber yet."

Her little palms beat on the counter, and she squeals. "I think that means she's hungry," Jesse says suggestively since Liv is the dinner host.

"Oh, right." She pulls her eyes off of baby Kate and me. "Let's eat!"

* * *

12 years ago...

"You know what I think?" Liv states suddenly, curling her knees up in the center of her bed.

"What?" I throw my crumpled paper ball again, trying to get as close to hitting the ceiling without actually touching it.

"I think the boys at school are too immature for me. I need someone older."

The paper ball comes down and smacks me in the face. My hand is still open.

"Excuse me?"

"I've always been wise for my age, that's what everyone says. An old soul. Why not date someone older?"

"Because you're 17."

"So?"

"Liv, be serious. You have no reason to worry about dating when you're about to leave for college in a few months."

"I don't need to date for marriage. I can have a fling."

"I'm going to be sick."

"Just because you see me as a sister doesn't mean I don't have needs."

"A sister? You think I see you as a sister?"

"Well, yeah." She doesn't have time to scream as I grab her ankle, yanking her down the bed towards me.

"I wouldn't have wet dreams about my sister, Olive."

Her mouth gasps for breath. "What?"

"You're my best friend, and I respect that, and I respect you. But don't get it twisted. I think you're gorgeous and sexy as hell. That's why no man deserves you."

Her mouth opens and shuts as she stares at me with wide eyes.

"So you'd rather me die alone and miserable because I'm too good for anyone?" She twists her body, trying to put distance between us, but I anchor my arm around her waist until she can't budge.

"No, I want you to live your life. Make bad choices, get drunk in college, and I want you to find yourself without giving anything up for some guy."

She finally stops fighting to get away from me. "I'm not your mom, Hayes. I won't end up with someone like your dad."

"I know." I sigh into her shoulder. "I know."

"If you think I'm so... Hot," she mumbles as if she had a hard time saying the word. "Why haven't you ever told me?"

"You deserve better than me, dove."

"Shouldn't that be my choice?"

"Of course, it is."

"Then kiss me," she breathes, searching my eyes.

God, I want to. "If I kiss you, then one will never be enough." My thumb traces her cheekbone as she swallows thickly.

"Okay," she whispers, letting her eyes flutter closed.

"I'd ruin your life."

"What?"

"I'll consume your every thought," I utter against her neck. "I'll demand all of your time." She gasps as my teeth scrape her tender skin.

"But worst of all, I'll never let you out of my sight. All of your dreams would take a back seat because I'd make you fall madly in love with me."

Her eyes blink, grasping for rational thought when my lips trace her jaw line. "I'd make you drown in this feeling that I've been struck by since the moment I laid eyes on you."

"Jensen," she utters my first name. The one that few people have the privilege of using.

"If you still want me to kiss you in, let's say, ten years, I will. But only after you've accomplished all of your dreams and are ready to settle for a loser like me."

"Ten years?" She gasps.

All part of her perfectly curated life's plan.

Go away for undergrad.

Complete some sort of graduate program.

Be done with school by 25.

Engaged by 28.

Married by 30.

Kids by 33.

A silly conversation we had one evening swinging at the rusty playground that I haven't forgotten for a second. The bullet points are fundamentally a part of me now.

"Yeah, dove. I'll be waiting at the altar when you're 30."

Chapter Fifteen

Liv

"It's outside of your contracted hours to be here so early," I speak into thin air when I step onto my back porch at six am.

The tingle on the back of my neck recognizes the aura emanating from my patio furniture.

"Seeing that you're not paying me, I'd consider a contract pretty irrelevant. Besides, I'm not here early if I never left."

"Did you sleep back here?" It must've gotten down to 40 degrees last night.

"No, I slept in my car. Just came back here to take a leak in the woods."

I roll my eyes. "Nice," I chuff sarcastically.

"Well, go inside and make yourself decent for work. We're still leaving on time."

"Yes, boss," he smirks, rising from his seat slowly. Except he stops before he gets to the back door, watching me with his hands in his pockets.

"What?"

He shrugs, but has a glint in his eye.

"Are you waiting for me to disrobe?"

"Can you blame me?" He smiles, and I hear the challenge in his tone.

Never one to back down easily, I don't blink as I let my robe fall, revealing one of the little cheap bikinis I keep on rotation for my cold plunge.

His jaw unhinges, and he doesn't move until I'm submerged to my shoulders in the ice water.

"What?" I breathe through the cold.

"You have your nipples pierced?"

He has seen me in a bikini before, but this one doesn't have the padding in the top like the last one. "One of many reckless decisions made in college."

He still doesn't move, and his eyes look almost completely out of focus.

"Are you okay?"

"Yeah," he clears his throat. "Just a lifetime worth of fantasies in my head I need to rewrite."

I almost laugh, but my breath gets caught in my throat. He looks distraught as he turns to go inside. He's completely serious...

Excitement tingles in my core, and I force my head underwater, punishing myself for where my thoughts were going.

I have a fiancé.

I'm getting married.

I'm gasping for breath by the time my head resurfaces. I need him to fuck me ruthlessly to erase Hayes from my mind altogether.

That's all it is.

I'm lonely living away from Elliot.

That's all.

I'll visit him this weekend, get thoroughly fucked, and get

myself back into the excitement of walking down the aisle.

When I pass through the living room, Hayes is sitting on the couch, pulling his shoes back on. He hasn't put his dress shirt on yet, and the tattoo on his tricep bulges from the edge of his t-shirt.

Each tattoo down his arm draws my focus until I'm once again staring at the code atop his hand.

50.1.5

Are they coordinates? It can't be a date.

"Everything okay?" He glances over his shoulder, noticing my attention.

"What are those numbers for?"

He rubs his wrist. "Just something important to me."

"Hmm, cryptic," I harrumph. "You know I have nipple piercings, but I don't get to know about your tattoos."

"To be fair, you only asked about one. Ask me about another."

"I don't want to know about the others." That's not true, but for the sake of argument, I'm standing strong.

"And I don't want to think about all the guys who have gotten to see your tits."

"Sucks, huh?" The venom that lies dormant in my soul, that's usually reserved for big cases, can't seem to stay tamped down near Hayes. "And whose fault is that?"

I don't wait for him to respond because nothing he says will ever be good enough. It'll never erase the past. Or rewrite it.

I don't emerge from my room until I'm sculpted to perfection. Suit, blowout, makeup. Because I'm Liv Greenwood. Not, little Olive, consumed by boy problems or distracted by Jensen Hayes.

As he does every morning, he's waiting by the door, holding

it open for me as I breeze past him, and somehow making it to the car door before I can, opening it before I'm able to reach for the handle.

It's overwhelmingly annoying and downright chivalrous.

We don't speak on the commute or the walk up to my office.

It isn't until his arm beams out in front of my chest that I realize how unbothered I've been about checking my surroundings. I was in lala land thinking about my case, disregarding that I have a stalker on the loose.

"Your office door is open."

"Maybe the cleaning staff is in there."

He glances at me, unconvinced. "Stay right here," he demands, and I roll my eyes. "Please," he adds softly.

He slinks through the door, disappearing for a few seconds before he pops back into view, rubbing his hand over his chin.

"What?" It's bad news, I can tell.

"You were ransacked."

"No!" I run past him and nearly fall to my knees. Every paper from every file is strewn across the room.

My blinds are broken, the trinkets on my desk are in a heap in the corner, and the whiteboard outlining the Porter Brothers' criminal timeline is erased. In its place are five words in black marker.

I thought you were different.

"What does that mean?" I screech, too pissed off to keep my composure.

"I don't know, but we'll fix this. We'll get it back in order."

"I needed to have everything ready to move forward with the pre-trial."

"We'll start over."

"No, it'll take too long."

"Liv," he starts, but I stumble back into the hallway.

"No." I try to catch my breath, but it becomes too hard to inhale. "They're counting on me. Everyone in this damn county is counting on me to get these guys."

"We'll figure it out. Just sit down," he begs, but I swat him away.

"Fuck! Not now," I cry as the world starts spinning. I hear Hayes, but I can't focus long enough to speak as I slump unseeing against the wall.

"She's blacking out. What do I do? How do I help her? No, I don't. Does she keep some on her? Thank you, Thea. I'll let you know.

"Come on, dove."

My body is hoisted into the air, and my head falls back until flashes of the ugly ceiling tiles pass over me.

Cold water touches my temple, and I follow the sensation as it trickles down my neck. More water, until it's soaking the collar of my shirt.

"Right here, Liv. Look at me." His voice coaxes me, but I'm still in a dreamlike state.

Something spicy hits my tongue, and my cheeks pucker instinctively against the cinnamon.

"That's it, feel it." His breath caresses my skin, and I blink against it. "Look at me, pretty girl. Come back to me."

I squeeze my eyes shut, fighting against something completely different now.

"Don't shake your head at me," he scolds, but I hadn't realized I was.

His fingers swipe at the wetness on my skin, but it isn't until his thumb caresses the pulse in my neck that I open my eyes to the bright bathroom lights.

"There she is," he smiles, but it takes another moment for the concern to turn to relief.

"Why the fuck does this keep happening to me?" My head falls back against the mirror with a thump.

"Hey, you okay?" Jackson's voice comes from the doorway. "Someone down the hall said something was going on..." His voice trails off as he sees our predicament.

I'm atop the counter between the sinks, and Jensen's body is shoved between my thighs. We're both wet and flustered.

I think this is worse than passing out.

"I'm fine." I shove him back, hopping down from the counter too fast, and my knees buckle before I can control it.

He catches me without a word, even though he has every reason to let me fall on my ass. "She's not fine," he grumbles. "Tell him, or I will."

"Fine," I grit through my teeth. "But can we please get out of the bathroom?"

Jackson follows us to my office, taking his time to catalog the damage, snap photos, and look for any evidence. As he's leaving, I think I'm in the clear, but he stops in the doorway to lean against it.

"So, what's going on with you?"

I glance at Hayes, and he's staring at me seriously, making me roll my eyes.

"Since moving here, I have been having fainting spells. It used to be less frequent, but now it seems like it's happening every few days."

"It happens every time this punk messes with you," Hayes adds, and I cut him a glare.

"Doctors think it is stress-induced," I clarify.

"Liv, if this case is going to affect your health, we can pull you from it. Judge Fulton can call in some favors, get someone else to prosecute."

"No! This is my case."

He holds his hands up. "Fine. You're my colleague, and you're also my friend, but if this gets out of hand, I'll go over your head."

"It won't. I have it handled."

He nods and leaves the room and the mess to us.

"Do you have it handled?" Jensen looks at me as if he's still expecting me to keel over any second.

"We handled it a moment ago, didn't we?"

He scoffs. "Liv, you scared the shit out of me. That was not ideal."

"Now you know for the future."

"Right, I know that cold water and cinnamon candy help to wake you up. But what if it's worse?"

"Lying down with my feet up also helps."

"Dammit, Liv! This is serious."

"I know! But no one gets to take this case from me. I need it."

"Why?"

I turn my back and ignore his question because I am too prideful to admit the truth.

I need this case to prove that I didn't make a mistake by coming here. I need to prove that I can handle this career without the cushion of a bougie law firm.

I need to prove that I am accomplishing all my dreams before I walk down the aisle and lose myself.

Because the truth is, I've already started to.

Chapter Sixteen

Hayes

"What exactly is your plan?" Lochlan asks as we sit around the fire pit.

Liv is spending the night at Thea's, a seemingly normal endeavor, and I needed the opportunity to catch up with my real boss. Lochlan's been chill about my comings and goings, but I think it's because he knows what having Liv back in my life means to me.

"I don't really have a plan. Being around her is more than I ever thought I'd have again."

"Yeah, but I know you, Hayes. You've pined after this woman long enough. Being near her won't be enough."

"It has to be. That's all she'll give me."

"You know she's supposed to get married?"

"I know."

"And, as a sane person, you have to let that happen."

I chug my drink instead of responding.

"Hayes," he warns.

"I know. Damn, Lochlan. Just kick me when I'm down."

"Believe it or not, I'm trying to protect you."

I do believe him because if anyone knows anything about

me, Lochlan knows that I am not a sane person.

He's protected me since the day we became cellmates, including saving me from myself.

"The last thing I want to do is cause her more grief in her life. I want her to be happy. If marrying that jerk off will do that, then..." I shrug in indifference, letting my sentence die.

Lochlan only stares into the flames, ignoring my attempt at being an honorable man.

"What's Jo up to tonight?" They've been inside each other's skin since they made things official. I'm surprised she isn't curled up on his lap right now.

He finishes his drink instead of responding.

"Loch?"

A deep grumble escapes his chest. "She was invited to a girl... Thing."

"A girl thing?"

"Yes."

"Lochlan." My brute friend does not do coy well.

"She was invited to a bachelorette party."

"A bachelore–" My thoughts finally catch up to my mouth. "Oh. Liv's?"

He pauses before taking a drink from his new bottle of beer. "Yeah."

My skin starts to itch as a thousand-pound boulder weighs on my chest. "What exactly were they doing? Or, where were they going?" I ask as pain grips my throat.

"Nope, not telling you a damn thing."

"Fuck you, Loch!" I yell, uncharacteristically, and yank at my hair.

He stands from his chair. "Alright, let's go."

"No, I'm fine. I'm cool."

"Get your ass to the garage, or I'll drag you there myself."

Thirty minutes later, I'm drenched in sweat as Lochlan and I spar, taking turns with the punching bag that I've worn into a heap of faded leather and frayed seams.

It's my place to work out the aggression that I let control my life for too long, the outbursts that always got me in trouble. Whenever I need to blow off steam, I end up in this corner of the garage, punishing my fists.

Another thirty minutes go by until I'm bent over and braced on my knees, catching my breath.

"Feel better?" Lochlan asks through his own exhaustion.

"Yeah, thanks, man."

He studies me for a minute but nods, leaving me to my thoughts as sweat drips down my face.

* * *

12 years ago...

"Stop following me, Jensen. You're not invited."

"You never told me what you were doing."

"It's none of your business."

"I'm your best friend, of course, it's my business."

"Fine, best friend. I'm going on a date."

"With who?"

"A boy from school."

"Yeah, who?"

"I'm not telling you."

"Why?"

"Because you'll try to scare him off."

"Why would I ever–" I start to lie, but she cuts me off.

"I *know* that's what you've been doing. Scotty let it slip when he was canceling our study date last week."

"He's lying."

"No! You're lying, and I'm sick of it. You don't get to sabotage me!"

"I'm not trying to sabotage you, Liv. I'm trying to look out for you."

"Well, stop. I might have daddy issues, but I didn't ask for a father figure. I can make my own choices."

"I'm sorry," I utter, but she's already storming away from me.

She's not even off to college yet, but I'm already losing her.

"Liv, wait!" I close the distance between us, but she doesn't turn around. I have to cut her off to force her to look at me. "You're right, okay? I'll stop interfering."

"Really?"

"Yes."

"You're going to stand back while I talk to boys?"

"Yes."

"You're going to be cool if I get a boyfriend?"

"Yes."

"And, what made you see the light suddenly?"

"You're my best friend, and I don't want to lose you. You're too important to me."

"You're important to me, too." She wraps her arms around my waist, and I squeeze her to my chest.

Too soon, she's pulling away, and I know I'm fucked. Seeing her with anyone else is going to kill me.

She's mine. That's the way it's supposed to be.

"Meet you at the swing set later?" She asks as she skips

away.

"I'll be there." *I'll always be there.*

* * *

Present...

"I knew you couldn't leave well enough alone," Lochlan calls to my back. He must've been waiting around the corner to catch me sneaking out.

"I'm not going to see her."

"Liar."

"What if she needs me?"

"Why the hell would she need you?"

"She could be drunk. Her stalker could be waiting for his opportunity."

"Are you sure you aren't the stalker?"

"Fuck off, Loch." He chuckles to himself. "What if it was Jo?"

"Don't bring her into this."

Ever since he met Jo, he was a grizzly about her. He protected her before he was ever ready to admit how in love he was. Now they're playing house, and I'm still the lone loser pining after the one that got away.

"If Jo had a stalker, you wouldn't leave her alone for a second."

He sighs. "I know, but this is different. Liv isn't yours to protect."

"She'll always be mine to protect."

He nods in understanding because he knows. Men like us

don't let anything hurt the people we love.

"Jo already texted me. She said they're all hanging out at Thea's, drinking margaritas. She's fine."

"Great, then she won't even know I'm there." I ignore any of his objections as I get on my bike, twisting the throttle before the engine has a chance to warm up, pretending I can't hear him.

I'll pay for that later, but I don't care.

I'm an addict who needs his fix.

Chapter Seventeen

Liv

"Alright, last game of the night," Thea announces, setting a bottle of tequila and a stack of cards on the coffee table that's already covered in obscenely shaped confetti.

"If I take any more shots, I might puke," Callie, Thea's sister-in-law, giggles.

"Me too," Jo adds. She and Callie only met this evening, but have become fast friends.

"Natalie and I have been drinking more than all of you," I say, hiccuping as I adjust my BRIDE crown. "Thea should be the most drunk since this is her house."

"I'm still building my tolerance back up," she giggles. She hardly drank for six years, but she isn't holding back for my bachelorette celebration.

"What's the game?" Natalie asks, divvying out the shot glasses. She's fun to hang out with. She's a lot looser than Jackson is, but even though they're such opposites, they seem to work.

"Truth or drink," Thea shuffles the cards as Callie and Jo moan simultaneously.

"I'm going to need a week to recover," Callie feigns distress with her pink feathered boa, and we all laugh.

"That's why I saved this game for last! Everyone has to spill their guts," Thea threatens humorously. "Okay, the bride-to-be goes first!"

"**Where is the most dangerous place you've had sex?**" I set the card down, starting the discard pile. "Umm, probably the roof of our dorm building. The door to the stairs locked, and we were stranded for hours until someone could sneak up there and set us free."

"I remember that! They put a chain on the door after that," Thea cackles with laughter, and I mirror it, losing my breath because I'm laughing so hard.

"My turn," Callie says. "**Does your most recent partner/significant other arouse you without touching you?**" She ponders her response as she discards. "Sorry, Thea, but hell yeah!" She raises her margarita, and we all clink glasses even though we're beyond wasted already.

Elliot doesn't even arouse me when he does touch me. I down my drink.

"Ugh, gross. That's my brother." Thea shivers in disgust and picks up the next card.

"**When's the last time you had sex? The person who has been without the longest has to drink.**" She thinks for a second. "Jesse and I did it in the shower yesterday morning before Kate woke up."

"I gave Jackson a bj in his cruiser last night, does that count?" Natalie admits, tossing her pink boa around her neck proudly.

"Ew, I did not want to know that," Jo says as she giggles because Jackson is her half-brother. "Lochlan and I have been taking a few days off. I was pretty sore after we got home from our weekend trip." Her cheeks flame, and we all end up doubled over in laughter.

"Nathan fucked me twice before I came over earlier," Callie adds, and we all lose it further until tears are streaming down our faces in laughter, and Thea has to run to the bathroom before she pees herself.

"Well, I lose. Long-distance relationship," I shrug, pouring myself a shot of tequila. The smell hits me, and my entire body cringes. The shot burns all the way down my throat into my belly.

Thea locks eyes with me as she sits back in her seat, and I ignore the sympathy. She knows that it's more than the distance between Elliot and me.

I didn't even want a bachelorette party, but she insisted that we stick with some normalcy as the wedding approaches. Everything is so hectic in my life, as my best friend and maid of honor, she's doing her best not to see me spiral.

"My turn," Jo says. "**Anal?**" She throws the card like it's on fire, and the hyena laughter ensues again.

"Stop, I'm going to pee again," Thea wheezes.

"The trick is really good lube." Natalie winks at Jo, and her eyes go wide, pinging to mine.

"Don't look at me. I've never done it. Willing," I amend, "but have never tried."

"Oh my God!" Jo covers her face with her hands until our giggling fit subsides.

"**Have you ever thought of another person while having sex?**" Natalie lays her card down and shrugs. "Definitely in the past, but not with Jackson. Boo, that was an easy one."

I don't know why my eyes find Thea's right away, but the sadness I see on her face isn't anything but a direct reflection of my inner thoughts.

I've definitely thought of someone else while having sex. One person specifically.

"I'm sorry, guys, the tequila is getting to my head. I need some air."

"Are you sure that's a good idea?" Thea asks, standing up when I do.

"I'll be right on the porch, I'll be fine." I walk to the door, and her concern follows me. "I'll keep it cracked."

My skin is warm from the alcohol, and the breeze feels cool as it sweeps over me. Giggles filter out here to the porch from inside, and it makes me smile.

Being around this group of women is healing, but it's a reminder of what I'll be missing once I leave.

Once I got to college, I never had problems making friends, but once I went to law school, socializing wasn't my main focus. By the time I landed my first job, I was back to calling Thea my one and only.

Even through the distance, we never faltered. So why doesn't it feel the same with Elliot?

We're living two different lives, and neither of us seems to mind that much. It's odd for us to talk on the phone more than once a day, but even during that one call, it never seems like we have much to say.

"Is this what my life is?" I utter towards my feet, letting the gravity of my situation crush me. *I'm supposed to be happy.*

I'm supposed to be counting down the minutes until I can say 'I do'.

I shouldn't be dreading the day I need to leave my little cottage to move back to a condo in the city.

I shouldn't be begging to work on a case that will keep me

from my fiancé longer.

It's not supposed to be like this.

"Nice feathers," *his voice calls to me.*

I know who it is without bothering to look up, but when I do, he's hardly visible in the darkness. He's leaning against his bike on the curb.

"I didn't hear you pull up," I say, pulling the pink boa from around my neck and dropping it on the bench by the door.

"Not surprised. I'm pretty sure you guys broke the sound barrier with your hysterics in there." *So, he's been here a while.*

He strolls a few steps closer, and the light finally touches his face.

"We're all a little drunk," I admit, and he chuckles, shaking his head in amusement.

His smile radiates through me, wrapping me in a security blanket that I know I should toss aside. Instead, I let the warmth take hold and comfort me in ways I've been desperate for.

The fear and anxiety that I'm constantly shoving down, that always finds a way to resurface, mystifies when Hayes walks towards me.

When he looks at me.

Because he has me.

The deep guilt for thinking that way claws back to the surface, strangling me.

"What's wrong, Liv?" He knows. He always knows.

"Um, I'm just feeling a little…" I motion wildly around my head, not explaining further.

"I'm sorry, I can leave."

"No," I say too fast. "I'm not ready to go back inside yet. I don't want to ruin their fun with my sour mood."

"Do you want me to take you home?"

The answer should be no.

"Liv? Is everything okay?" Thea asks, staring back and forth between Hayes and me from the doorway.

"Yeah, everything's fine. I–" *What am I doing?* "I'm not feeling very well. Hayes is going to take me home."

"Liv," she warns, her eyes filled with concern.

I take my crown off, setting it next to the boa on the bench. "It's fine."

She doesn't look convinced, but she knows better than to argue with me. Once I set my mind on something, it's hard to dissuade me. "Text me when you get home safe. And, call me *first* thing in the morning." She hooks her pinky finger around mine before I step away. "Promise?"

"Promise," I assure her. Kissing our joined pinkies, a habit we haven't kicked since college.

"You better have a helmet on that thing, and she needs water, Hayes," she shouts down her porch to him.

He nods seriously. "I'll take care of her."

"I'm sure you will," she mutters, looking at me slyly as I back away.

"Do you have a jacket?" He asks when I meet him on the sidewalk.

"No."

He shrugs his off, holding it so I can slide my arms through. "Here."

I barely have time to register how warm it is from his body, or how his smell is infused in the fabric when he's handing me a small bucket helmet.

"Is this what all your bitches wear?" The words come out before I have a chance to filter them, but he laughs easily.

"No bitches have been on this bike. This helmet has never been worn." He pulls it taut on my head and buckles it under my chin.

"What about your helmet?"

"I don't usually wear one."

"That's stupid. You could die."

He smiles at my crassness. "Death doesn't scare me."

"Well, it scares me."

"Do you want me to start wearing a helmet, Liv?"

"Yes."

"Okay," he agrees. Just like that.

"Tomorrow," I push, because I expected more of a fight.

"I'll get one tomorrow." He straddles his bike, kicking the kickstand back with his heel. "Have you ever ridden on a bike?"

"No."

He doesn't say it, but I see the relief on his face from my response. "Plant your foot here," he points to a metal bar behind his knee. "Grab my shoulders and throw your other leg over.

I do as I'm told, too conscious of how his shoulders feel through the thin fabric of his t-shirt.

"The pipes get hot. Don't rest your legs against them." He starts his engine, revving it twice. "Wrap your arms around my waist."

I hesitate, and he twists his head slightly. "Not a request, dove."

That stupid nickname makes my heart misfire, and it only worsens when my forearms circle his torso, flattening my front to his back.

He twists his head again, and it's closer now that my face is pressed against his shoulder blade. “Scared?” He asks huskily, barely audible over the sound of the engine.

I swallow thickly. “No.”

A smile spreads across his face, and it scares me a lot more than anything this bike could do. A smile like that from Jensen Hayes is deadly.

Chapter Eighteen

Hayes

12 years ago...

"Liv!" I shout across the parking lot when I see the familiar brown ponytail bouncing up the steps towards the school.

She whips around at the sound of my voice, searching through the other students to find me. She's always had a way of sensing me.

"What are you doing here?" She looks stricken, glancing around as she jogs up to the no-parking zone where I'm leaning against my dirt bike.

"I haven't seen you in almost two weeks. I was starting to forget what you look like," I smile easily at her, but my cheeks grow heavy when she doesn't return my enthusiasm.

"I've been busy."

"Too busy for me?"

She huffs a curt breath. "Believe it or not, Hayes, I have a life outside of you."

"Ouch." I rub my chest, and she squeezes her eyes shut in regret.

"I'm sorry. I've just been stressed with school stuff and getting all of my college applications submitted by the deadline. I've been here more than I've been home."

"You could've called me. I'd come sit with you, or help you fill out forms."

"I know, thank you, but I have a friend helping me. They're in the same boat, getting college apps in."

They. So it's a guy friend. A guy who is smart like she is. Going to college like she will.

"My mom's been asking about you. My dad will be out of town next week, and she wanted to have you over for dinner."

"Oh, I don't know. I've been swamped with this stuff." She waves distractedly at the high school building.

"Right, I get it. I'll let her know, we can wait a while."

"Okay, thank her for the offer for me." She finally smiles at me, but it's softer than normal, and doesn't feel as familiar. "I'm glad you'll have a week off from dealing with your dad, though."

For a moment, we stare at each other because minimizing my terrible relationship with my father to that singular sentence feels... Wrong. "Yeah, me too."

She takes a step back and nods, starting to turn away from me.

"You know I'm always here for you, Liv. For anything, no matter what."

Another soft smile stretches her cheeks. "I know."

She walks back towards the entrance to the school, and I watch her as the air she normally breathes into me is sucked away until I'm nearly suffocating.

* * *

CHAPTER EIGHTEEN

Present...

Death has been on my mind my entire life. Even as a small child, I recall begging God to take away my suffering. I couldn't handle any more pain.

One particular instance, after my father beat me with his belt and locked me in the hall closet, I vividly remember imagining all the ways I would kill myself.

All the ways that a seven-year-old boy could conceptualize.

Jumping off the roof of our trailer seemed like a good option at the time, though in reality, I would have been lucky to escape with a broken bone or two from that unexceptional height.

Running away always felt like an option, but even as a kid, I couldn't fathom leaving my mom. I lived with a monster, but I needed my mommy.

One early morning after a brutal beating from my old man, I walked right across the closest two-lane highway near the trailer park, praying a car would take me out.

I was eight.

People knew. My teachers, my friends. But no one did anything.

Why would they? I was a troublemaker, and he was one of the boys in blue.

I'd get in fights at school, unleashing my raging emotions on bullies who reminded me of my dad.

I'd end up in the principal's office, but no one cared why I did it. They didn't ask me why a fifth grader knew how to throw a right hook so well.

My father would sign me out, promising to work with me at home, and then beat me until I was purple.

Eventually, as puberty approached, and I got bigger, my

dad couldn't lay his hands on me without feeling the exertion. I wouldn't flinch at his fists. In fact, I could take quite a few punches without ever losing my balance.

That pissed him off, and it made him drink more, take it out on my mom more.

But that wasn't acceptable, so I played along. I would let him think that he hurt me. I'd pull away and try to dodge his evil, but I always let him get his final blow.

Once the fighting got so bad that the school complained to the local police department, and my dad's job was on the line, he put me in karate. Not to help me, but to justify to his coworkers that he was a good father.

Luckily, it did help. Through the initial apprehension, I found a safe place for the first time in my life. I was surrounded by kids who were like me, channeling their emotions and budding hormones into a physical escape.

My sensei was the first positive adult role model that I ever had. He listened without judging, taught me without critique, and shaped the man that I would eventually become.

I finally stopped fighting and started flourishing in school. I even went my entire Freshman year of high school without getting into any disciplinary trouble.

I was still seen as a troubled teen, but I didn't care. I found purpose in martial arts, and I was fulfilled for the first time in my life.

It made my dad angrier. He'd hit me harder and spew vile remarks at me because he knew he couldn't affect me physically. So he attacked me mentally.

I was still left with the bruises.

My sensei was the first person to see the truth behind the marks.

He went to the police behind my back to report his concerns, but it only made everything worse. My father's harassment spread to the karate dojo.

He left parking tickets, placed speed traps, and even went as far as accusing my sensei of being a pervert.

Unfortunately, since he had offered me refuge, it didn't look good from the outside, and the burden of public opinion ultimately meant he couldn't keep the business afloat.

He shut the studio down, but he never blamed me.

He wrote me a letter, begging me to find a path that would lead me towards good. To only fight when it means I'm standing up for what is right.

And, at the end of it, he asked that I forgive him.

The day after I received the letter, I found out he hanged himself in his office.

The false accusations and the bankruptcy brought him too much shame, and he couldn't live with it.

I blamed my father for all of it, but no one believed me.

I carried the burden of his death and lost myself.

Any wrong move by anyone, and I was taking it out on them with my fists, again.

Getting expelled and being forced to restart my senior year was nearly my final straw. I couldn't handle it.

I planned to leave a note for the administrators, like the one my sensei left me.

Except I wanted them to know exactly how their lack of action killed one of their students. I wanted them to know I blamed them.

Then I saw the new girl standing at the bus stop, shivering in the early light of dawn, and I forgot briefly why I was so angry.

I worried about her being cold, and she made me laugh.

Looking at her, I knew there wasn't evil in every single person because she was good. She was a beacon of light when all the paths in my future were utterly dark.

So I went home, crumpling my final 'fuck you' up and set it on fire in the sink. I watched it burn until it turned to ash, and washed it down the drain.

Then I went to my room and dug my box of reminders out from under my bed. My martial arts trophies. My black belt. And, my Noble Paths Karate sweatshirt.

I never intended to wear it again. It was two sizes too small, and the words were mostly gone, but I knew when I held it up that it no longer belonged to me. I didn't need it as a reminder of all the lessons I learned.

I needed it to guide me towards the future I wanted.

Olive was everything to me. She was the only person who wept for me when she saw the monster that I lived with.

She was the only one who cared.

Then I lost her, and the desire to end it all never felt heavier.

I nearly never saw outside of those prison walls again.

I had to remind myself every day that I needed to live.

Now, I have a particular desire to drive off a bridge. Not because I want to die, but because life can't get any better than this.

I finally have Liv back. Not completely, not enough, but I have her back in my life. She has her arms wrapped around my waist, and I can feel the warmth of her cheek against my back.

This could be the best I'll ever have.

But I'll keep living for her.

It's the only reason I've ever had.

Chapter Nineteen

Liv

The power of the engine vibrates my skin, penetrating through muscle into my bones. The sharp wind swipes at my face and tousles the ends of my hair against my back.

The most unnerving part of it all is being attached to the one man I thought I'd never be close to again.

He feels completely different, but having my arms around him still feels like home. The depth of my grief has been buried so long that it feels like a cork has popped, and ribbons of emotional turmoil are bursting out of me.

It's impossible to stomp those feelings back down when he's right in front of me and refuses to go away.

It isn't fair.

I have a life. I was doing everything right. I got the degree, the career, and a fiancé.

But it isn't enough. Not when the one person whom I would have chosen over all of it stumbles back into my life and refuses to leave.

He shows up, and this sick part of my brain can't leave him alone. The compass over my broken soul always points to him.

His hand covers where mine overlap over his stomach, holding me steady as he pulls over the curb into my driveway and up to my little yellow cottage. Before he lets go, he squeezes, and that small gesture twists my already mangled mind.

Why is he doing this to me?

I stand up, struggling to get off the back of the bike before he tells me it's safe to, desperate to escape the situation I've put myself in.

I'm unbuckling my helmet at my front door by the time he turns his bike off and catches up to me. "I forgot my keys," I utter towards the door instead of facing him. The alcohol is making my head spin.

"Do you keep a spare?"

I shake my head, letting it thud against the wood.

"Alright, just give me a second." He disappears off my porch, and I don't bother checking to see what he's doing. I'd rather drown in self-pity.

The door whooshes open after a minute or two, and my head drops before I catch it and look up into his grinning face. "Madam," he gestures sarcastically. "The lock for your kitchen window probably should have been replaced a decade ago."

I hardly hear him, though, because my eyes zero in on the tattoo under the collar of his shirt. One of the tattoos that I've never been able to see very clearly, but tonight his t-shirt is looser, and the collar doesn't fit snugly at the base of his neck.

"Are those... Olive branches?"

He glances down at his ink as if he doesn't know it's there, or is considering whether he can get away with lying. But I can see it clearly enough, and my question was rhetorical.

Along each collar bone is an olive branch, curved slightly to follow the path of his clavicle. He doesn't insult me by trying to dismiss it, but he also doesn't respond at all.

"Did you get those because of me?"

"Liv…" He starts, but I cut him off.

"Yes, or no."

"Yes."

I shove past him into the living room, raking my hands through my windblown and tangled hair.

"What do you want from me, Hayes?"

"I told you I'm here to keep you safe."

"Why?"

"What do you mean?"

"After all this time, after all we went through, what do you want from me?"

"I don't want anything from you. I just want to be part of your life."

"Why?" I cry, flinging my hands towards him.

"Because you're my girl."

"I'm not," the words come out barely above a whisper, caught in my throat.

"Yes, you are. You always have been."

"I'm not!" I yell, throwing the couch pillow at him. He snatches it out of the air easily. "I'm engaged!"

"I know!" He yells back, squeezing the discarded pillow in his hands.

"Then what do you want from me?" I beg him to answer as I break further.

"Anything you'll give me."

"Anything?" I ask condescendingly.

"You need a bodyguard? I'm here. You need a guy to fix your car? Done. I can build you a house, I can give you a tattoo. I know how to sew. I can play guitar. I don't do a lot of cooking, but I'd learn if you never wanted to cook another meal."

"Why?" I shrug in exasperation. "Why do you want to do any of that for me?"

"I taught myself how to do everything so I could be something to you someday. Even if it's only a glimmer of what you need."

"But why!" I beg this time, losing control of myself.

"Because I messed up! Is that what you want to hear? Will that make you feel better?"

I shake my head, not bothering to humor him with a response.

"I fucked up and lost the most important person in my life, and now I'm begging her to give me a crumb of forgiveness. I will be anything you need as long as you don't shut me out.

"You need a ride home because you're drunk or because you're scared? I'll break every traffic law to get to you. You need someone to fill your gas tank? I'll make sure you never go below a quarter tank."

"That's ridiculous," I mutter to myself, and he just shrugs. "That's ridiculous," I say with more gusto, regaining control of my emotions.

The frustration feels better than the sorrow, and I focus on that as I pace back and forth in front of him, suddenly coming to a grinding halt.

"My feet hurt." I spin facing him fully, and he sees the challenge on my face immediately.

He takes a step back, falling onto the couch, and patting his thigh.

I grit my teeth together because I'm not actually bold enough to let him touch my feet.

I keep pacing. Burning hotter with each lap back and forth. "What if I want you to be my little bitch boy, fetching me coffee and scrubbing my floors?"

"It'd be my pleasure." His face is calm, not offended or put off by my suggestion. He's not bluffing, and it only angers me further, but I'm not entirely sure why.

If you had asked me years ago, I would never have believed that he and I would be relatively strangers. But to equate our relationship to something as meaningless as a formal relationship, servitude even, it feels like a slap in the face.

My knee digs into the cushion right in front of his crotch, making him flinch slightly. But his eyes only darken when my hand grips the underside of his jaw, holding his face taut.

"And, what if I spit in your face and tell you to fuck off?" I threaten, leaning closer to him than I should. My entire body hovers over his, and even without touching, the static between us clings to my skin.

His face is stone, but his eyes tell a different story, wild to the brim with the Jensen that I know.

His head tips back a fraction, hooding those wild eyes ever so slightly, then his mouth opens…

Not a single word comes out as he stares at me…

Willing me to spit in his mouth.

I stare at him, fighting against myself not to take the challenge, not because I want to win so desperately, but because to my core… I want to know what it's like.

I want to know how he'd react.

And that's dangerous.

Heat curls in my belly, and I gasp, shoving his face to the side, roughly. I launch myself backwards to put distance between us.

I never should have let myself get that close.

"Be gone before I get up in the morning," I dismiss him, slamming my bedroom door.

* * *

12 years ago...

"Do you want me to wait until you're finished so I can give you a ride home?" Noah asks me as he logs out of his computer. He's been staying after school most days, like me, to work on college prep.

We sit in near silence most days, focusing on our computers, and sometimes he will share his snack with me, but this is the first time he's ever offered me a ride.

"No, you go ahead. I'll catch the city bus, it runs in an hour."

"You sure?" He asks kindly.

He smiles at me, but I don't think he's flirting with me. I'm not used to anyone paying me any attention, so sometimes I'm not sure.

It doesn't matter, though. Boys at school have never given me butterflies like Jensen does.

"Yeah, I'll be fine." I smile at him as he throws his backpack over his shoulder and says goodbye to Mr. Arkett at the front of the computer lab.

Once Noah leaves, Mr. Arkett leans back in his chair to look at me. He's my chemistry teacher, but he picks up the extra shift in the evenings to monitor the computer lab for students like me who don't have internet access at home.

"Always the last one standing, Livvy."

"I know," I giggle. "I can leave now if you're ready to head out."

"No, I don't have anything to get home to." He stands up from his desk and stretches his arms above his head. It pulls his school polo up just a bit, exposing his flat stomach.

Mr. Arkett is only 26. He's a graduate of our high school and started teaching here right out of college. He teaches my chemistry study group, too, so I see him more often than my other teachers. And most Saturdays.

He's really quite handsome. His dark hair is always tousled and kind of messy. There are a few girls in school who signed up for Chemistry just because he teaches. I didn't, I needed the extra science credit to graduate with honors, but I don't blame them.

"Well, I'm just going to submit this scholarship application, and I'll be done."

He sits down at the seat next to me, where Noah was sitting, and spins the chair to face me. "Take your time."

It's hard to focus when I know he's sitting so close. His knees are only a foot away from the side of my chair as he swivels back and forth on his wheels.

"You're a smart girl, I think you'll do great things in college."

"Oh, thank you." I feel the blush creep up my neck at his compliment, but it only worsens as his attention stays on me.

"You're pretty, too. The boys will love you."

I'm not shocked at his words because he's complimented me before, but I'm still unprepared with a response.

No one ever says things like that to me, aside from Hayes,

but he's different. He made it firmly known that I was his best friend, and he's not willing to be more than that. The disappointment of that stings badly, and I've decided to stop hoping he'll change his mind.

I clear my throat. "I'm done." I shut my computer down without facing my cute teacher, begging my red cheeks to calm down before I have to look at him.

"I can take you home."

"I was going to catch the bus."

"Nah, it's late, and there are too many creeps out there. I'll drop you off."

"Okay, thank you, Mr. Arkett." Nerves tingle across the back of my neck as I smile shyly at him, and they only intensify when he smiles back.

"Call me, Landon, after school hours. Remember?"

Chapter Twenty

Hayes

R*ight. Right. Left under cut, right jab. Left hook.* Each punch drives through the punching bag until the exertion radiates through my muscles, from my arms to my shoulders, back, and stomach.

I put the weight of my body into every jab, begging for exhaustion so it will distract me from my thoughts.

She's back to treating me like a ghost, but I can't pretend we're strangers. I can't erase everything that's happened between us. I can't forget the way her arms felt wrapped around my waist.

I can't stop thinking about the way she smells. The twinkle in her eye when she smiles. The lithe body in those damn bikinis.

Beautiful, beautiful, Olive.

And the diamond ring on her finger. Because she'll never be mine in the way that I want her to be.

She went to visit her fiancé this weekend, and all I can imagine is his hands on her. His mouth touching all the places that I've dreamed about.

The bastard won't ever understand how lucky he is to be

chosen. He will never cherish her the way she deserves. She's Olive-fucking-Greenwood.

My fists slam into the bag again, pummeling the leather until I'm gasping for breath, letting strangled grunts of frustration tumble out of my throat.

It's not enough.

My leg whips out, and my shin connects, once, twice. Jab, Jab. Left kick.

He's probably peeling her clothes off now.

Right, right, left. Right kick.

Dragging his lips across her delicate collarbone.

"AHH!" Roundhouse right kick.

I collapse to my knees, staring up at the rafters of the garage. She's going to leave. Once she's married and done with the Porter case, she'll move back home to her condo with her *husband.*

I finally got her back, and I'm supposed to say goodbye?

I should. I should let her move on and live her life the way I always wanted her to. It's not her fault that I never actually wanted to let her go.

My phone starts ringing atop my workbench, and the vibration has it nearly falling off the table top by the time I reach it. *Olive.*

Doesn't matter where she goes. Whenever she needs me, I'll be there.

"Hello?"

"Hi," her voice cracks. It's nearly 10 pm, and she should be with *Elliot.* Such a stupid name.

For a stupid fucking man.

"What's wrong?"

She doesn't respond, but I hear rustling and sniffling like

she's trying to pull it together. I don't give a shit about that. "Olive?" I need to know what is wrong.

"I messed up."

"What happened?" *Maybe she accidentally killed him, and now she needs help hiding the body.* No. That's ridiculous. Don't get your hopes up.

"I came here to surprise Elliot, but he wasn't even home. He's on a business trip." I hear her roll her eyes. "I got mad because I didn't even know about it, and I turned around to drive home, but I ran out of gas."

"Are you stranded on the side of the road, or could you pull in somewhere?"

"I pulled into some hotel on the side of the freeway, but I haven't gotten out of my car. I'm pretty sure I see lot-lizards," she whispers as if someone could hear her.

A small smile tugs at my lips, imagining her panicked eyes. "I'll be right there."

"No, you don't have to come. I'll call AAA."

"You called me, Liv."

"I know."

"You can always call me."

She doesn't respond.

"Drop a pin, I'll leave right now."

"Can you drive your SUV?"

"Sure." My bike would be faster. "Why?"

"I was hoping you'd stay on the phone with me until you get here."

"Yeah, dove. I can do that."

Unfortunately, all that is left unsaid between us makes small talk difficult. I can hear her hesitation as the silence on the line grows. She needs something to take her mind off the situation she's in currently.

"Talk me through the Porter case since we have pre-trial next week."

I can't see her, but I imagine her smile. "Okay, well, I'll start by showcasing my evidence regarding Randall Porter's conspiracy to obtain Second Chance Sanctuary by illegal means to build his private properties. I have multiple witnesses, including contractors and city ordinance officials who he discussed building plans with.

"I have multiple letters from Lochlan Dane refusing to sell his property. I also have all of the communication and letters of harassment that Mr. Porter sent him under the guise of legitimate mayoral duties.

"But most damning will be the text message communication between Randall and his brother Jeremiah. So, I'll express to the judge that Randall used his brother to do his dirty work. I'll be able to provide a lengthy criminal record for Jeremiah Porter.

"I'll also show the judge that I have financial statements proving that Jeremiah was in financial distress and likely more easily swayed to do Randall's bidding."

"That's a strong case, Liv."

"I know," she states proudly. "This is only pre-trial, so all of that might not be necessary, but I want to make sure that the judge knows I'm going to nail these suckers. Hopefully, their defense attorney underestimates me because I want to get them on every last charge."

"You want them to underestimate you?"

"Absolutely. That way, I can wipe the floor with their lame arguments."

"You're an incredible lawyer, Liv. They'll never see you

coming."

"I know!" She sing-songs. "I love seeing the opposing attorney's face when they realize they're totally fucked."

"Easy killer," I laugh with her until the silence returns. "I'm really proud of you, you know that?"

The sounds of the road are all I hear for a few minutes, and I think she won't respond until she finally sighs. "I went to law school because of you."

"What? Why?"

"After seeing what happened to you... I never wanted to feel that helpless again. Seeing all of the people in the courtroom who held all the power shifted something in my brain. People need advocates during vulnerable times in their lives. I always wanted to help people, and I realized that I could use my knowledge to my advantage."

There's a lot we haven't talked about with our past, especially the day I got sentenced to prison, but I still remember it like it was yesterday. It was the last time I saw her.

"I'm sorry," I choke out. "I'm sorry for how everything went down. I–"

"Don't, Hayes. I'm not ready. I certainly don't want to discuss this over the phone."

"I know. Just tell me that you believe that I'm sorry. I need you to know that how I left things with you is the biggest regret of my life."

"I believe you."

It doesn't change things, but at least she believes me. That's one bit of closure that I've needed for a long time.

"I'm almost to the hotel," I update her, trying not to trap her in another serious conversation.

"I thought about you every day," she admits, surprising me.

"I went to college and cried myself to sleep every night. Thea was my roommate. That's why she knows about you. She held me when the sobbing became uncontrollable."

"Liv..."

"I'm in the back part of the lot. See you when you get here." She hangs up, and I'm left staring at the black screen.

I'll never be able to fix all that I've broken.

* * *

11.5 years ago...

Tap. Tap. Tap. I wait as I listen to the rustling of movement behind the window, and her to slowly open it.

"It's so late, Hayes."

"I know, I'm sorry. I've just missed you, Liv. Haven't seen you in forever."

"I've been busy–"

"Busy, I know. I'm starting to feel like you're avoiding me."

She smiles softly and chuckles. "That'd be silly. I'd never be able to hide from you."

"That's right. I'd track you down." I smile. "Can I come in?"

Her eyes grow a little wide with panic. "No, I don't think that's a good idea."

"Why not? I've spent the night before. I'll be gone before your mom wakes up." We've slept in the same bed on numerous occasions, and I've always been a perfect gentleman. I don't know why it would be a concern now. Unless...

"Do you have a boyfriend, Liv?"

"What? No."

"Then why can't I come in?"

"You've made it clear you only want to be my friend."

"You're my *best* friend. I just wanted to hang out with you, I wasn't going to jump your bones."

"Right, because why would you do that?"

"What is going on?"

"Nothing, Hayes. I'm just setting boundaries."

"Liv, we've talked about this."

"No, you've talked. You put up the wall between us because you think I'm not old enough to make my own choices."

"That's not–"

"My friend thinks that I'm very mature for my age and that I'm way too smart to date high school boys. But you still think I'm a kid."

"I don't think you're a kid. And, what fucking friend is telling you that you're mature for your age?"

"Why? Are they wrong?"

"I mean, no, but it just seems odd..."

"Bye, Hayes." She closes the window in my face, and I'm left staring at my befuddled expression.

Chapter Twenty-One

Liv

His headlights sweep across my front windshield, and I brace myself to see him again. It should be easier, but it's not.

The pit in my stomach is still begging for the void that he left to be filled.

"I brought a gas can, I'll dump it in and then follow you to a gas station," he says through my window as if nothing is amiss.

I climb out of my car for the first time because I haven't felt safe enough to until now. "Thank you for coming to help me."

"Anytime," he responds, like he has nowhere better to be than right here. Saving me even when I've been pretty terrible to him lately.

He focuses on my car until the cap is screwed back on the empty gas can, and my gas tank lid is closed, but when his eyes finally meet mine, a breath escapes me.

He's always been beautiful to me. When we were young, I was always too afraid to say it. He took my breath away. He still does, but now there is pain I see in his eyes every time he looks at me.

He's been utterly broken.

Just like me.

I'm reaching for him before I have a chance to stop myself, wrapping my arms around his neck like I did so many times a lifetime ago. "Thank you for coming," I utter more wholeheartedly as I hug him.

He's only stunned for a moment, but I hear the empty gas can thud as it hits the ground, and both of his arms coil around my waist, pulling me in tighter like he always used to.

Holding me like only he could.

A hug that entangles two people, plastering their souls together into one place and time. Hurricane-force winds couldn't tear us apart.

I missed this.

I've missed him and the closeness we shared. Two atoms fused into one.

I could stay like this forever, with the heat of his palms encasing my ribs.

I want–

"Care if we watch?" A man's voice croons from the other side of my car, and someone else snorts a laugh.

Jensen's comforting body turns to stone in an instant before he spins me behind him. He did it so quickly that I would have stumbled if not for his arm keeping me plastered to his back.

I'm tucked between him and his SUV as he stares down the unperturbed guests. One of them is leaning against my passenger window, the other is standing a few feet off to his side.

"We've got nothing for you," he says easily, but his voice is deep with warning.

"We've been waiting for the pretty thing to get out of her fancy car and come pay her lot fee." He chuckles to himself, spitting a toothpick out of his mouth onto the roof of my car.

"We were just leaving," Jensen responds with a lot more patience than he had when we were teens. If I weren't scared shitless right now, I'd commend him for his progress.

"Not til you pay."

"Liv, get in my car." His tone is low and controlled, blanketing me in security, but I can't make my feet move. "Now," he commands.

The guy leaning on my car huffs a laugh and leans back onto his feet, readying himself, but he only watches as I shadow Hayes and slink along the SUV.

As I climb inside the passenger seat, he taps the side coolly, signaling me to lock the doors, and I do immediately. Even though my window is up, I can hear them clearly.

"Take off," Hayes warns again, but the calmness in his tone sends a chill down my spine.

"Hundred bucks," the smaller guy lingering in the shadows pipes in with their apparent price.

Hayes laughs, and I do a double-take. He's so nonchalant, but that's not the Hayes that I know. "No cash, sorry." He shrugs.

"We'll see about that," the main guy threatens, popping open a switchblade in his hand.

I want to call 911, but my phone is in my car, and I don't know where Jensen's phone is. He didn't even flinch at seeing the knife.

He strolls out from between our cars into the open lot and just waits, summoning the guy forward with his uncaring.

It isn't until the guy is within feet of him, slashing his knife in the air, that Hayes even uncrosses his arms.

He lunges, jabbing his blade towards his chest, but he's too slow. Hayes's hand shoots out, pinning the guy's wrist in the air and snatching the knife away from him easily. "Get the fuck out of here," he growls in his face, throwing his arm with enough force to knock the guy back a few steps.

"AHHH!" The guy lowers his head and barrels towards him like he might try to take him down, but Hayes is quicker, stepping to the side at the last second, forcing the guy to tumble onto the pavement.

Luckily, the sidekick is still hiding in the bushes as the big guy stands up sluggishly. Hayes looks at me through the windshield and blows an exaggerated breath out, shrugging at me with a premeditated apology.

Big guy takes one step towards him, and Jensen's fist strikes the guy in the jaw, knocking him out cold.

I don't have a chance to breathe before he turns on a dime, whipping the pocket knife out of his hand.

It lodges into the tree next to the sidekick.

A muffled noise of shock escapes my throat, and I clap my hands over my mouth. I watch with bug-eyes as Hayes drags the guy into the grass and pats his unconscious cheek, never taking his eyes off the other guy, who was never brave enough to join his partner.

He wipes his hands as he strolls casually to where I'm staring out the window. "All good now. Are you okay?"

I nod, but I'm not sure I've blinked.

"Drive my car to the gas station, I'll drive yours."

All I can do is nod again before shuffling over the middle console to the driver's seat. I drive the two miles to the closest gas station in shock as my car's headlights follow closely behind me.

Jensen is deadly. He always has been, but now he's calculated. It should scare me, but the emotions I'm feeling don't feel like fear.

It's the warmth that blooms whenever I'm near him. The comfort that a man as violent as he is would do that to protect me without even breaking a sweat.

Because he cares.

He's always cared.

* * *

11.5 years ago...

I know I should be disappointed that I didn't go to my senior prom, but I keep reminding myself that high school is only a small part of all that I'll accomplish in life. In ten years, it won't matter that I didn't have a date to prom.

I probably won't even remember this night.

Even though I didn't attend the dance, I decided to come to the school for the bonfire they hold afterward. The upperclassmen are invited, and the teachers are handing out hot chocolate and pizza or coordinating corn hole tournaments.

I'm standing off to the side, resting my arms on this wooden split-rail fence, and watching the flames dance. Keeping to myself as usual.

"They're taking turns blasting each other in the faces with whipped cream pies over there if you want to join." I turn to the voice as it comes towards me.

"Hi, Mr. Arkett. I mean, Landon." He smiles when I use his first name, and it warms my cheeks.

"No interest in a cream pie?" He winks.

"Uh, no." I laugh, awkwardly. "I'm not really cool enough to join in with their games."

"You're cooler than all of them, Livvy. Don't let it bother you." He leans against the fence next to me, and our arms nearly touch. I'm surprised, but we're hidden away in the shadows outside the glow of the bonfire, and most people are focused elsewhere.

"It doesn't bother me," I utter. "I'm used to it."

"Well, you're my favorite, if that counts for anything." He nudges my arm with his elbow and lets it linger there.

"Thank you." The blush creeps down my neck, but the heat feels overbearing, and a little wrong. We haven't done anything wrong, but the good pupil in me knows that we're breaking unspoken rules.

It's just nice to feel like someone likes me. Jensen's rejection has worn me down. He'll never love me like I love him, and I can't stand his pity.

"Are you coming to the study group tomorrow morning?"

"Yeah, I planned to."

"It's at my house, if you didn't know."

"Oh, no, I didn't. Did they double-book the library?"

"Yep. I offered to have it at my house since only a few kids show anyway. Besides, you're the only one that matters."

"That's not true." I tip my head down to hide my smile.

"I really like you, Livvy. You're a good kid." His words confuse me. Calling me a kid makes me think that I'm misreading our interaction, but then I feel his hand skirt down my spine.

I freeze as his palm rubs circles on my lower back. My body is tingling, and I don't know if I want him to keep going or if I want to run away.

When his fingers tickle my bare skin under my shirt, my brain screams for him to stop. But the words don't come out of my mouth. *Stop. Stop. Stop.*

I'm smarter than this. I should be able to save myself, but my body doesn't move.

His finger tips skim the band of my bra, and my teeth clench.

I don't like this. This is wrong.

Why can't I move?

Why can't I speak?

"What the fuck is this?"

His voice. I know exactly who that voice belongs to, and it breaks the spell I'm under.

I whip around. "Hayes, what are you doing here?"

"Me? I came here because I thought you might've been sad about missing prom," he's yelling at me, but his eyes are focused on Mr. Arkett. "Why the fuck are you touching her?"

"She was upset. I was only comforting her." He puts his hands up, trying to convey innocence, and I can only look at him in shock.

I didn't expect him to admit that he was behaving inappropriately, but hearing him sound like such a coward is jarring.

"It's him, isn't it?" Hayes accuses. "He's why you've been so distant with me?"

"No. I mean… I don't know, maybe." I've always prided myself on being a smart girl… But that was the absolute wrong thing to say.

Mr. Arkett starts to back away, fleeing to the safety of the group when Hayes snaps. He lunges at him without warning and tackles him into the fence.

"No!" I scream, hearing the wind knocked out of my teacher, before he takes him to the ground.

That's all it takes to garner attention from other students, and the swarm starts gravitating towards us.

Jensen's punches are wild and erratic, hitting Mr. Arkett in the face over and over again until I realize he's lost it completely. He's crazed...

"Hayes! Stop!" I beg, screaming his name until my throat is raw. "STOP!"

He throws blow after blow, even after Mr. Arkett has long been out of it. It feels like the entire school is watching as teachers shout and run towards us.

My fingers tear at Jensen's shirt, but it's no use. He's fueled with fury, and I'm nothing compared to him.

That's when I see all the blood.

It's everywhere, spraying out of Mr. Arkett's face each time Hayes's fist connects.

Raw flesh splits open, flooding his face in red.

My stomach lurches, and I fall to my knees in the grass.

"Hayes, stop!" I beg again, barely able to get sound out.

Noah rushes over, pulling me further from the violence happening, but I fight him as he does, even though my body is weak and I'm near fainting from seeing the blood.

"He's a fucking psycho. Stay back," Noah warns, forcing me to stay in one spot.

Everything in front of me happens in slow motion.

One of the football coaches rushes Hayes, tackling him off of the lifeless teacher, but he doesn't stop. He keeps fighting to get up like a rabid animal. Flinging his arms and kicking his legs as he yells.

"THAT'S ENOUGH!" A voice demands, and time stops altogether. Hayes's blood-spattered torso goes limp as his father arrives on scene. Accompanying him is half of the police force.

He grabs Hayes by the collar, yanking him up off the ground. "You've embarrassed me for the last fucking time, boy. You're finished."

He tosses his son to the officer on his left and wipes the disdain off his hands. "Throw the book at him. He's no son of mine."

Chapter Twenty-Two

Hayes

"I watched you disarm a lunatic with a knife, you'd think this would be a walk in the park," Liv blurts out, shaking her hands in the elevator as we head to the courtroom.

"I had that under control. This is all you."

"I have it under control."

"Yes, you do." I hand her the briefcase I was holding, and she straightens her spine as the doors open to the ground floor.

The scene in front of me glitches, and I'm suddenly experiencing déjà vu. The standard oak woodwork and shitty carpet...

I haven't been in a courtroom since my day in court 11.5 years ago, but if you've been in one, you've been in them all.

In front of the bench or behind the bench, the suffocation feels the same.

Liv walks confidently to her place and starts readying her paperwork, but I don't have the same ease. My collar feels stiff, and I don't want to sit down just yet.

"Hayes," Liv whispers. "Jensen," she whispers again, forcing me out of my claustrophobia. "You don't have to stay in here if you're uncomfortable."

"I'm fine." I tug at my collar absently, and her eyes clock it. "There's a deputy in here. I'll be okay."

"Your stalker has been suspiciously quiet. I'd rather stay close." *As if that's the only reason.* "Besides, I'd like to watch the Porter brothers sweat."

Their actions directly affected my friends and my home. Jeremiah nearly killed Curtis. I can't wait to see them go down for what they put everyone through.

The judge enters, and I go through the motions on instinct, rising and sitting as if I'm on trial again. It's a hard feeling to shake when it was your nightmare for a decade.

Liv talks through her evidence exactly as she had practiced with me the other day, delivering her spiel confidently. Judge Fulton looks pleased and doesn't ask any clarifying questions, which makes Liv's shoulders relax.

"Alright, Defense, let's hear your side."

"We'll be providing alibis for Randall Porter's whereabouts and proof that all of his business dealings were done by legal means. This counsel requests a separate trial from Mr. Porter's brother, Jeremiah–"

"What?" Jeremiah yells, jumping up from his seat. "You said you'd take care of me?" He lunges at his brother, who barely reacts.

The deputy on duty quickly separates them as the judge pounds his gavel. "Order," he demands. "This is only the pre-trial, Mr. Porter. You have time to obtain your own counsel. If you cannot afford it, counsel will be appointed for you."

He waits until the room settles before continuing. "Miss Greenwood, is this going to be a problem moving forward?"

"No, your honor. The county is ready and willing to

prosecute the defendants separately."

"Great. Let's set trial dates for both and move on with our day. Any time constraints or schedule issues coming up?"

"I'll be out of the office for the next two weeks, but after that, I am available."

Two weeks.

The rest of the conversation in front of me disappears as I contemplate those words. She's going to be gone because she's getting married…

She's getting married this weekend…

She's getting married…

I tug at my collar because I'm having trouble breathing again, but it has nothing to do with the stuffy courtroom.

"Hey, you okay?" Liv asks suddenly.

I blink towards her and realize the room has been dismissed. I'm the only one sitting down. "Sure, what's next?" I croak out.

She looks at me with underlying concern but doesn't push it. We haven't talked directly about her wedding day, but we both know it's happening.

"I need to get my things from my office, but I'm done for the day."

I nod, and we head back upstairs in silence, but I can't shake the noose around my neck.

She's getting married.

And, as if the universe gets off on cruel jokes, there's a big white box with a big white bow sitting outside her office door.

"Miley, did you see who left this?" She asks her intern.

"No, ma'am. I was out getting a coffee, and left for about ten minutes."

"Let me just..." She starts to hand me her briefcase as if that'll make this less awkward.

"It's okay, I'll get it." I bend to grab it, and as soon as my hands are under it, the cardboard saturates my fingers, and I freeze.

"Hayes?" She asks from behind me when I don't move.

"If I ask you to turn around, would you listen?"

"No."

"I didn't think so." I spin to face her and hold the box up, watching her eyes go wide. "It's blood... Isn't it?"

Her hand covers her mouth, and she nods.

"I guess your stalker knows you're getting married Saturday."

* * *

"There are cameras at all the entrances in the building, but it's a public courthouse; we've had over three hundred people in and out today," Malec says, scanning the security footage at the courthouse.

He pulled a chair up and told me to sit next to him so we could go through the footage. I hate to admit it, but he's growing on me despite his profession.

"A big white box isn't normal," I utter, staring at the split-screens.

"No, it's not. And, it should have been pulled aside at security."

"Are you sure it was a deer heart? Not human?" Liv asks, pacing back and forth in front of Malec's desk.

"I'm positive," I reassure her. "My dad always made me gut the deer when he forced me on his hunting trips."

"Didn't like to hunt?" Malec asks me absently.

"Didn't like my dad."

He nods in understanding and leaves it at that.

"He was abusive and horrible. He was a cop," Liv scoffs. "No offense," she says directly to Malec, and I look at her in disbelief. She shrugs, "Sorry, I ramble when I'm stressed."

"No offense taken," Malec says, completely unbothered. "Right here. The office supplier loads his dolly with four boxes of paper, but when he gets into the building, there are five."

"The office supplier is my stalker?"

"Doubt it. He probably was just an easy target. No one pays attention to the paper delivery."

"What happens next?" Liv leans over my shoulder, and I stop paying attention to the screen in front of me.

"We don't have cameras inside the offices. Our guy must've snuck in the public entrance and retrieved his package somewhere."

Her hair falls over her shoulder, brushing against my ear.

"So, we've got nothing?"

"I'll send the fingerprints to the lab. This guy isn't in the system, but I'll at least match them to the other evidence he's left behind to start building a case."

She smells like vanilla and green tea.

"What should I do?" They continue to converse over my shoulder, and I can't untangle myself from her proximity.

"All we can do is wait, but you'll be out of town for a bit, so that'll help. Give this guy time to get antsy and slip up."

Out of town.

Because she's getting married.

I struggle to come up with anything to say the entire drive back to her cottage. I feel her subtle glances in my direction, but I'm afraid that if I look at her directly, I'll blurt something out that I'll regret.

Don't marry him.

Don't do this.

I wouldn't regret it because the thoughts are untrue, I'd regret it because of the position I'd be putting her in. I've put her through enough for one lifetime, and I want her to be happy.

Even if it doesn't include me, killing me inside, that's my burden to bear.

"I won't need a ride for a while," she says once I park.

I squeeze my eyes shut, willing away the nausea I'm experiencing. "About two weeks, right?"

"Yeah."

I nod stiffly as she shuts her door, and I watch her walk across her porch. "Liv, wait!"

She spins to face me, and I'm already across the driveway. "Can we talk?"

"About what?"

"I don't know. This." I motion between us.

"What about this?"

"I finally got you back, Liv. I feel like I'm losing you, again."

"I'm not a toy, Hayes."

"You know that isn't what I mean."

"What do you want me to say?"

That you won't marry him. "Are you happy?"

"What? Of course, I am."

"Have you gotten everything you've wanted in life?"

She hesitates. "Almost."

"Do you think Elliot is your soulmate?"

My question knocks her back a step, and her eyes turn to slits. "We're not children. That's a silly notion, and you're overstepping."

"Liv," I stop her before she slams the door in my face. "I just need to know if it was all worth it."

"If what was worth it?"

"Making you live your life without me."

Her lips part, and a ghost of agony crosses her face before the door slams closed.

* * *

11.5 years ago...

My court-appointed lawyer keeps telling me to keep my head down, act cool, and not to show them I have a temper.

But all I can think about is his hands on her. A grown man touching my Olive.

I laid awake in my jail cell last night thinking about it.

I think about every conversation I've had with Liv the past few months and why she didn't tell me about her teacher.

I wasn't able to protect her from it, not until it was too late.

The correction officers told me that she tried to visit me, but she's a minor and not a relative, so they turned her away.

I couldn't face her anyway.

I was only brave enough to call her once. To tell her to stay away from me.

"Hayes, I'm here." Her voice whispers over my shoulder,

and my eyes squeeze shut.

"You shouldn't be here," I grit through my teeth without turning around. Not here, in this courtroom, with the shame I feel. I can't stomach looking at her.

The girl I'm about to lose.

"Please, Hayes. I'm so sorry. I messed up. This is all my fault."

"Don't. Don't ever say that. This isn't your fault. It's Mr. Arkett's fault, and mine," I argue, barely turning my head.

"Nothing happened. Please, you have to believe me." I hear the tears in her voice, but I still can't look at her. It's too painful.

I failed her.

My lawyer silences whatever else she's about to say with a look, and I fight the urge to punch him.

I'm a fucking mess.

"Go home, Liv," I dismiss over my shoulder as the judge enters. "Go!"

I know she doesn't leave. I would feel the air shift if she did. My self-hatred boils to an all-time high as they talk through my charges in front of the entire room.

My juvie record is sealed because I'm an adult, but they know me here. They're familiar with my reputation, and they know who my father is. The man sitting on the opposite side of the room is ensuring that I get what's coming to me.

It hurts worse that my mother chose to sit beside him.

"This is a heinous crime. I have it on good faith that Mr. Arkett is a beloved member of the community and wouldn't harm a fly, let alone provoke such a violent attack. He won us the conference championship eight years ago. Everyone loves him. Now, he'll be recovering from his injuries for months.

What do you have to say for yourself, son?" The judge asks, acting as if he cares what I have to say.

I don't speak. I don't even stand. My lawyer nudges my shoulder, but I don't move. Fuck him, fuck this place.

"Your honor, I'd like to make a plea deal. My client will plead guilty to aggravated assault and a four-year sentence." My lawyer adjusts his tie, waiting for the judge's response, but I don't get my hopes up

Things never go easy for guys like me.

"This young man has shown no remorse. I recommend updating his charges to attempted homicide and a twenty-year sentence."

My head snaps up, "What?"

The room buzzes with reactions to the judge's harsh recommendation, but my ears only focus on Liv's sobs behind me.

"Prosecutor?" The lawyer on the other side shrugs and nods, clearly as confused by this as the rest of us.

The judge raises his gavel, and I realize the gravity of a single fucking mallet. He's about to end my life.

"NO!" Liv screams, and the room grows louder with chatter. "You can't do this!"

Court deputies come barreling towards her to take her out of the room, and my chair tips as I lunge for them. "Don't touch her!" I yell, shoving my lawyer's hand off.

"Order! Order!" The judge yells.

"No!" She screams as one of the deputies grabs her arm.

"Get off of her!" I yell again as arms wrap around my shoulders, holding me back. Two deputies strong-arm me as I fight with no sense of reason, no logic.

It's Liv, nothing else matters.

"Order!" The judge pounds his gavel.

"He was only protecting me! He was protecting me!"

"Liv, no!" I don't want her to get involved. She doesn't need to be dragged into this and tarnished by the actions of men.

"Son, stop fighting, or I'll throw your girlfriend in jail, too!" He yells, and as soon as I process his threat, I go limp. "Now," he huffs. "I want to hear what she has to say."

My strong, brave Liv pulls her bicep from the deputy's grasp and wraps her arms around herself instead. "Jensen is my best friend. Not my boyfriend. He witnessed Mr. Arkett initiating a relationship with me. That's why he attacked him."

"That is no grounds for the level of violence displayed."

"Liv, don't. That's enough," I beg as tears stream down her cheeks.

"I'm only 17. Mr. Arkett is my chemistry teacher." The room gasps collectively.

"He was behaving inappropriately?" The judge asks.

"Yes, your honor. He liked to drive me home after hours. He would talk to me about boys and college. He complimented my appearance often. The night this event took place, he asked me to attend a study session at his house and hoped we'd be alone. He was touching me out of sight of the other teachers and rubbing circles on my back. He was underneath my shirt, touching my bra when Hayes found us."

I rock back and forth in my chair, gripping my head in my hands as I hear her speak. *He was touching her. He would have done worse.*

"It's my fault, your honor," she cries. "I should have known better."

"No," I mutter. *Don't martyr yourself for me.*

"I was too afraid to tell him to stop. If I had told him no, this wouldn't have happened, but I froze," she cries.

"Young lady, this is not your fault. I have daughters, and I can appreciate your bravery today, but your friend nearly killed a man." He taps his fingers against his podium. "I'll allow the plea deal, but six years instead of four." He bangs the gavel and seals it.

Chapter Twenty-Three

Liv

I wasn't a girl who dreamed of her wedding day. I wanted to be married by 30, but I didn't fixate on the details. I didn't consider which season was best or what florals I'd love to decorate with.

All I really thought about was the man I imagined standing at the altar. The man who promised to be there for me.

When he disappeared from my life, I stopped thinking about a wedding. I hardly thought about the man I'd end up with, only that I needed to be with someone in time to have children by 33 and 35.

That was the goal, and all I had to do was stick to the plan.

Now, I'm 30 and some change, staring at myself in the mirror with bridal lingerie on, and I feel no accomplishment. Only deep-pitted hollowness.

I loop the hanger over my head, letting the satin hang down the front of my body, and the pearl straps lay against my skin. The dress is light and drapes my curves when it's on, leaving my back exposed nearly down to my tailbone.

It's stunning. The pearl work is beautiful.

"That's not your dress," Thea says from my doorway.

She's right, this is a dress you'd wear at an outdoor wedding, so the sun could kiss every inch of skin as you marry the person you love.

It isn't the dress that I'm wearing to marry Elliot.

"I couldn't help it. It was so perfect when I tried it on... I knew it didn't match the wedding aesthetic, though." I shrug. "I forgot it was in my dress bag."

Thea scrunches her eyebrows but doesn't question me. "It is beautiful. Her fingers glide down the silky satin. It looks like you."

Her words nearly force a sob from my throat, but I choke it back as I take the dress off and hang it back in the closet. The correct hanger hangs heavy in my hand as I carry it over to the mirror.

Someone help me.

"Here she is," I announce, pulling the dress from the hanger. It's corseted at the top with long lace sleeves, and the billowing satin skirt starts at my hips and flows out to the ground. Perfect for an indoor wedding at the tail end of winter.

I hate the cold.

"It's beautiful, too," Thea voices, interrupting my thoughts. "Liv, are you sure..."

I don't know exactly what she's about to suggest, but I cut her off anyway. "How much time do we have?" I ask, fluffing the skirt absently.

"Does it matter?" Thea asks sternly. I look at her reflection in the mirror, and she's looking at me with furrowed brows.

We're in a fancy hotel with a small number of guests arriving any time now. My friends are sitting in the living room of this fancy penthouse, and my best friend is looking at me like she's about to tell me I have cancer.

"What do you mean?" I ask breathlessly. *Please, save me.*

She tilts her head in that way that always convinces me that she can read my thoughts. "Do you even love him?"

My mind goes blank. None of the normal responses to that type of question even attempt to roll off my tongue.

"Liv," she utters, seeing the battle warring on my face.

"I'm supposed to get married, Thea. This is ridiculous."

"It's not ridiculous. I hardly recognize you right now, and I'm worried." Thea knows me better than anyone, and I know I can't look her in the eye and lie to her. Not only would she know right away, but I'd be a terrible friend for it.

"Things have been hard, lately," I admit through a frog in my throat, and she nods in agreement.

"You can say that you don't want this."

"I can't."

"Yes, you can." She wraps her hand around my arm delicately, and the first tear rolls down my cheek.

My makeup is already done. I shouldn't cry.

"If you want to marry Elliot and stand by his side for the rest of your life, then I'll support you because I will always be here and I love you, but I think you know this doesn't feel right."

Another tear rolls down the other cheek, leaving a streak in its wake.

"Everyone is expecting me."

"Your mom isn't even here. Doesn't that mean something to you?"

My mom was invited, but she disappeared on one of her retreats, and I haven't heard from her in about two months. It isn't odd for her, but it still stings regardless.

"Elliot is a good man."

"He might be, but that doesn't mean he's the one for you."

The one for me...

"This isn't about Hayes."

A small smile quirks her lips. "I never said it was."

I drop the dress, letting it gather at my feet. "I don't have to do this?"

"You don't have to do this," she confirms, squeezing my arm tenderly.

"But what do I do? What do I say?"

"Don't worry about that." She jogs over to the door in her heels and peeks out. "I need you both, now."

Callie and Natalie rush through the door in their matching bridesmaids' dresses that complement Thea's maid-of-honor dress, expecting to see me in my wedding dress. Both of their faces fall when they see me standing in nothing but my bra, lace thong, and thigh-highs.

"What's wrong?" Callie asks first, scanning my face.

"I can't do this." The words leave my mouth, and the weight of them finally crashes into me. My knees hit the carpet as I fall to the floor. "I can't do this," I cry, feeling multiple sets of arms wrap around me all at once.

"I'll tell Nathan to get the cars."

Their voices converse above my head, but I let go and let them take over as my body and mind fall apart in a pool of satin.

"Jackson and I will stay here and talk to the vendors."

"I'll pack her things." Thea starts scurrying around the room.

"We need to tell the guests," Callie's statement stops Thea in her tracks.

"I'll do it. I've always dreamed of having a chance to do something like this," Natalie volunteers with a glint of mischief in her eyes. It eases some of the guilt burdening me and I exhale roughly, letting it out.

"Elliot," I murmur his name. "I need to talk to Elliot."

"I can tell him," Thea offers. The woman who avoids men like the plague would tell my fiancé the wedding is off. I'm such a coward.

"No, I'll do it." I pull myself to my feet, and someone drapes a robe over my shoulders, helping me shrug it on. "Ask him to come to my room and make yourselves scarce. I can do it."

Sympathetic looks blanket me for a moment before I shake them off. "I swear, I'm fine. Go get him."

Thea nods, and they exit quietly, their support dissipating along with them, and my knees go weak again. I'm slumped on the floor, staring into the mirror that was supposed to reflect a beautiful bride today.

Instead, it shows a train wreck. Someone who wasted years of her life on a relationship that she knew wasn't the right fit.

"You're such an idiot," I mutter to myself. "IDIOT!" I scream, ripping my pearl earrings out and beaming them at the mirror.

Streaks of tears stream down my face, and I stare at them until I see a monster.

A horrible person.

I am a monster.

A sob racks my body, and I double over onto my knees. So stupid…

I wish…

I wish Jensen was here.

Another sob heaves from my lungs.

I'm an evil person for wanting him here after I've been so cold towards him, but I know that a hug like the one from last weekend is the only thing that would make me feel better right now.

It could keep me together when my world is falling apart.

A knock raps at the door, and a startled huff escapes me. I scrub my palms across my cheeks, swiping at my tears, and stand up on shaky legs.

"Come in."

Elliot enters the room wearing a dashing tux. I haven't even seen what he'd be wearing until now. The final wedding details were tossed together by our wedding planner.

"What's going on, Livvy?"

I shudder at the nickname. "I'm sorry, Elliot."

His posture stiffens, and he sighs as he loosens his bow tie. "What is this?"

"What?"

"I gave you a luxurious life. Connections. My name means something. And you're willing to throw it away?"

"I didn't need those things. I made my own money. I've worked hard to get where I am." *I definitely never gave a shit about your name.*

"Where? Some prosecutor in Hicksville? Renting some shack?"

My jaw goes slack at his callousness. "I told you why I wanted to be there."

"Right, for your little friend. She has her own family, you know? She doesn't need you like you think she does. You're pathetic."

"That's enough," Thea's voice demands from across the room. "Liv, we're going home." She stares at Elliot with all of the strength in her sunshine-filled body, reminding me that I can be brave, too.

"For the record, I stomp past him, joining my best friend. I *bought* that shack months ago. That little cottage is more my home than your condo ever was. And, maybe if you learned how to please a woman, she'd actually want to come home to you."

His jaw works back and forth as we get the hell out of that hotel room, but as soon as my feet hit the hallway, I hear him coming back for more.

"You're a joke. You'd better hope that hole in the wall town still wants you because I'll make sure your career is over. No one will hire you," he spits his words, coming to a stop once he reaches the hallway.

I'm standing beside Thea with an army behind us. Natalie is on my left side with Jackson towering behind her.

Callie is beside Thea, holding baby Kate as Nathan and Jesse step forward, putting a wall between Elliot and me.

This might be a shitty day, but at least I'm not alone.

"I'm leaving now. Good luck, Elliot. I really do wish you the best." I turn my back on him, strutting down this hallway as if I don't have a care in the world, as my flimsy robe flutters around my thighs.

I might be losing a fiancé, but relief fills my body as every step takes me further away.

I've experienced loss. This feels like freedom.

"I've been fucking the wedding planner," he yells pathetically down the hallway as I enter the elevators.

A puff of laughter escapes me. "Fuck you."

Chapter Twenty-Four

Liv

"Honestly, I'm fine. Or, I was fine until I sat next to Kate on the way home," I laugh-cry into a tissue, curled up on the couch in my living room.

"You'll be fine, Liv. You have plenty of time to start a family," Callie says. All the girls have stayed by my side since this afternoon, and now it's late into the night as I drink away my sorrows.

"I know. I know. But now I have to start all over..."

"Jesse and I got pregnant before we were technically married. You don't always have to follow the perfect timeline." Thea looks at me pointedly because she knows about my stubborn life plan.

"That's different, you and Jesse are..."

"Soulmates?" She says teasingly, and it brings a wave of sadness over me. I guess I do still believe in soulmates.

"Everyone is going to think badly about me now. A failed engagement," I sigh, shaking my head.

"No, they won't," Natalie says, coming to kneel in front of me. "You are an awesome person. You're an admirable woman, and whether you're married or unmarried is the least interesting thing about you. No one will judge you. They'll see the strength that it took to make the right choice for yourself. Especially when most people could never be that brave."

"Are you sure you're a chef and not a therapist?" I wipe fresh tears from the corner of my eyes before they fall.

"That's just what a life of trauma does for a person. It really shapes you," she laughs, and it steamrolls a giggle fit among all of us.

We're still catching our breath when someone knocks on my door, and everyone's eyes go wide.

"Are you expecting someone?" Thea asks.

"No." I see the worry on her face, and I realize how screwed I am in the head because she's thinking of my stalker, but I'm hoping it's someone else.

"I'll check." Callie grabs something from her purse and tiptoes to the door.

"Does she have a gun?" Natalie whispers.

"My brother has turned her into GI Jane," Thea whispers in exasperation, but her eyes are still wide with worry as she texts on her phone. Most likely to Jesse.

I never had that type of relationship with Elliot. He wasn't the person I'd call in distress. He wasn't my person.

"Oh, it's Jo." Callie flings the door open, tucking her gun behind her back nonchalantly as she smiles. "Hi!"

"I came as soon as I heard."

I felt bad not being able to invite her to the wedding since she's technically a client and that'd be frowned upon. Now I'm just glad I didn't waste another person's time.

"Are you okay?" She sits on the coffee table in front of me, offering a tender smile.

"I'm fine. I feel silly canceling the wedding at the last minute, but I know it was the right choice."

"Don't feel silly. Imagine how difficult it would have been if you'd gone through with it and were actually stuck with the guy."

Her seriousness makes me laugh, and I'm overwhelmingly glad to be surrounded by such good friends. Even with them here, though, my mind keeps wandering to someone else I wish were here.

"I know I hurt him, but he was so horrible earlier. I'll have to go get an STD test now that I know he was cheating."

"I'm sorry, Liv. You didn't deserve to find out that way."

"But at least it wasn't after you signed the marriage certificate." Natalie clinks her glass with my tequila-soda.

"I should have punched the bastard in the face," Thea says with conviction, downing her drink.

"You've never hit anyone in your life," I giggle, and she shrugs.

"Listen, I don't want to make you uncomfortable," Jo starts. "But, I need to know what you want to tell Hayes..."

Hearing his name out loud is like a record scratch. "What?"

"As of right now, Hayes thinks that you're married."

"So?" Thea speaks for me after our eyes lock, and she sees my distress.

"I mean, you know, he was upset?" Jo asks in confusion.

"It was awkward the last time I talked to him... But he didn't tell me not to go through with it. He only asked me if I was happy."

"What did you say?" Callie asks, and everyone leans in, locked onto this conversation.

"I think I said yes, I don't remember. I was feeling pretty

defensive at the time."

"I've been trying to stay out of it because it isn't my business, but he's a mess, Liv. He has been since that first day he saw you at the sanctuary," Jo admits. "He and Lochlan got into a... Physical altercation this morning," she adds delicately.

"About what?" I panic, imagining Hayes hurting someone he holds in such high regard, but Lochlan is a large man... I don't want to know how ugly things could get between them.

She hesitates but relents when she sees my worry. "You need to know that Lochlan loves Hayes, and he sees him as a brother. He'd never do anything to hurt him on purpose."

"What happened, Jo?"

"He was trying to get to you."

My lips part. After all this time and not saying a damn word about it... "He wanted to stop the wedding?"

She nods. "Lochlan knows how important you are to him, but he also knows how serious Hayes was about not interfering in your life. Hayes had already said he'd never put you in the position to choose, and he didn't want to upset you on your special day."

"So, he was going to let me get married?"

"Well..." She wipes her hands nervously on her legs. "I think the plan was to let you get married, but this morning it's like a switch flipped, and he went off the deep end. He was acting crazy."

I stare at her, dumbfounded. We all are. But I know exactly what type of crazy she's referring to. I've seen it with my own eyes.

"He tried to leave, and Lochlan took his keys. He ordered everyone on the property to hide the keys to the work trucks... Hayes destroyed the garage. He destroyed the bunkhouse.

"I mean, they're hot-headed men, and sometimes they take their aggression out on each other, but this is nothing like I've ever seen. Normally, if Lochlan and Hayes get into it, it ends with a couple of bloody towels and beer... This wasn't that."

"Tell me, Jo." I'm sitting on the edge of the couch, staring at her as she hesitates to finish the story.

"Lochlan locked Hayes in a bear cage."

"What?!" A chorus of surprise rings out among all of us.

"He was losing it. He was fighting everyone and hurting himself in the process. I'm pretty sure Lochlan has a black eye and a broken finger... But he knew Hayes would regret putting you through more grief."

"He's in the cages with the bears, right now?"

"No. No!" She clarifies. "He's in a cage on the trailer that they use to transport the bears. Totally safe, though slightly unorthodox."

"I need to go tell him," I jump up, and everyone around me stands at the same time.

"No, you need to stay here and rest. You've been through enough today, Liv. Seeing Hayes is not a good idea," Thea warns. "I know you care about him, but your emotions are raw, and you've been drinking."

I slump back in my seat. "I know, but he's so upset and I never..." I look at my best friend. "I don't want him to feel like I did when I lost him."

She looks at me in understanding because she knows how terrible those first few months were after Hayes went to prison. She met the version of me that was in pieces when he told me goodbye.

"Tell me what you'd like me to say, I'll deliver the message," Jo offers.

"I need a pen and paper."

* * *

11.5 years ago...

—

Dear Jensen,

I miss you. I keep hoping to hear from you, but I know you're probably getting settled in. My college acceptance offers are rolling in, but I think I want to stay here and visit as much as I can. These six years will fly by, I promise.

I read online that you get to make phone calls, so please, call me. I feel like you're mad at me.

Love,

Liv

—

Dear Jensen,

Please, reach out to me. I miss you. I'm worried sick. If you're mad at me about Mr. Arkett then I apologize and will apologize over and over. I knew it was wrong, and I never meant for you to find out that way.

I knew you'd be protective of me. You always have been. I'm sorry for everything.

Your best friend,

Liv

—

Dear Jensen,

I'm falling apart without you. I need you. I'm not going to college. I can't live my life knowing that you're stuck in there because of me. I'll wait for you.

I need you. Please, talk to me.

Yours, always,

Olive

—

Olive,

I don't want to talk to you.

I don't want to see you.

Don't try contacting me again.

By the time you read this, I'll be dead.

—

Chapter Twenty-Five

Hayes

"You feel like eating?" Lochlan asks from outside my temporary prison cell. He was in one long enough. He knows how to make something work on the fly.

"No."

"If I open the gate, are you going to try to leave again?"

"Yes."

He sighs, rubbing his hand over his head. "It's nearly midnight."

"So?" The moon has been out for hours, but the floodlight beside the barn is the only thing providing me with any light.

He holds up a piece of folded paper in his hand. "I want to give you this, but I need to know that your freak show from earlier is over with."

"Why? Afraid I'll hurt you again?" His purple cheek and swollen eye socket stare at me through the cage bars.

He chuckles. "You look worse than I do, pretty boy. Besides, I got you in here once, I'll do it twice if I have to."

"You only managed because you got me in a headlock when I wasn't looking. It was a cheap shot."

"A cheap shot that saved you from doing something stupid."

"Doesn't matter now." *She's a married woman.*

He tips the paper forward between the metal bars, handing it to me.

"What is this?"

"Jo told me I needed to give this to you asap."

I unfold the first crease, but my cracked and bloody hand stills.

—

Dear Jensen,

—

"Is this a joke?" I don't take my eyes off the handwriting that I know by heart.

I don't have to unfold the second half of the paper to know it's from her.

"Read it, I'll be on the porch." He unlocks the padlock on the cage but doesn't open the door, strolling back up to his farmhouse, and leaving me to read the letter in my hand.

I unfold it slowly, exposing the rest of the words.

—

Dear Jensen,
I wasn't happy.
He's not my soulmate.
Still,
Olive Greenwood

—

I read the words again. And again. Convincing myself that I'm comprehending them wrong, and that I'm only seeing what I want to see.

I read it again, but this time I'm on my feet before I can finish, shoving through the cage door and sprinting up to the big house.

"She didn't marry him?" I ask breathlessly, holding the letter in front of me.

Jo's sitting next to Lochlan, looking at me tenderly. "She didn't marry him."

The gravel bites my knees as I fall to them. "Is she okay?"

"She will be," Jo assures me.

My hands scrub at my arms as if I can wipe away the blood and grime caked to my skin. As if I can erase my psychotic break. She needs me, and she shouldn't see me like this. I need to shower.

"Hayes," Lochlan says, grabbing my attention. He waits until I look at him, and he shakes his head. "You can't see her yet."

"What? Why? I need to be there for her."

"She needs time." Jo looks at me sympathetically. "Alone."

"Alone? She still has a stalker out there!"

"She's staying with Thea for a while. Let her come to you when she's ready."

I grab the porch railing, letting my head hang between my shoulders. "And if she's never ready?"

Jo shrugs. "I don't know."

"Just be ready for her when she is," Lochlan adds, trying to give me an ounce of hope.

He knows I won't survive losing her again.

* * *

11 years ago...

I can't ruin her life. She has to go to college and escape the storm cloud that I live under. I love her more than life itself, and I can't rot in here knowing she isn't moving on.

"Cell 247, open," the guard announces, waiting for the automatic buzzer to signal it's unlocked. The heavy metal door creaks as it opens. "Cell 247, close."

It slams shut behind me.

I'm alone. Lochlan must be at visiting hours. I just got done having my stitches removed from our scuffle the first day I was assigned to his cell.

The guard had let it slip that Lochlan was in for a sex crime, and I let all of my rage at my own situation loose on him.

But he fought back, and we both ended up bloody and bruised.

He's the first person who has ever been able to put up a fight against me, and it made me angrier.

"I know you're pissed off, kid. I would be, too, but I didn't rape anyone. I didn't do it."

He spit those words at me while his forearm was pinned to my trachea, but I still didn't believe him.

He backed off anyway, seeing the malice in me.

"Fine. Go ahead. Kill me. I'm tired of fighting."

The defeat in his voice had nothing to do with our current confrontation, and for some reason, I took pause, watching blood drip down his chin. He didn't bother wiping it away.

He already had scars, and I definitely added a few more, but it was his eyes that were the most marred.

He was dead inside, just like me.

He told me his story, and I believed him. He was disgusted to be labeled as a predator.

I told him my story while we were getting stitched up in the infirmary. I told him about Liv and how much I loved her.

I told him about the night of the school bonfire.

And that the only thing I regretted is that I didn't kill the fucker.

Lochlan didn't condemn me for admitting it.

"We make choices in life that we have to live by forever. There are no do-overs. It's better to do what you think is right than to sit by and let innocent people suffer."

It was a relief to hear someone think like me, and I wish I told him that, but it's too late now.

I have to make sure Liv moves on without looking back, and the only way I can do that is to not be here at all.

We're too connected on this plane. She'll always seek me out just like I would if I were on the outside. I will never be able to live without her, but all my existence will ever do is drag her down.

I stare at the empty glass vial in my hand that I swiped from the infirmary cart before I smash it against the side of the bed frame.

It shatters across the floor, but all I need is one piece bigger than the rest.

"I'm so sorry, Liv." Tears prick at the corners of my eyes as I whisper my final goodbye to the gray walls. "Thank you for being my best friend when I had no hope left in my life."

The sharpest corner of the glass shard pricks the skin at the base of my wrist. "I love you, forever, dove."

The shard digs deeper into my wrist until blood wells up around my fingers, and before I give myself another second to think about it, to think about her, I rip the glass up my forearm, flaying my skin several inches.

The blood pours out, covering my arm, splattering down my legs, and I sink to the floor as I watch it pool around me.

"Do great things, baby girl," the words escape me as my consciousness fades.

"Open 247." The door buzzes as it opens, and my head lolls to the side.

"Kid! NO!" Lochlan's voice thunders.

His body collides with mine on the floor, and he reaches for my arm, wrapping his hands around my wound as if he can put it back together.

It's too late. The blood is blanketing the cell and both of our bodies.

"HELP!" He yells. "HELP! You're going to be okay. HELP US!"

His words barely seem real as darkness closes in around me.

"I'll take care of you, kid."

"You're not alone."

"Fight, Hayes!"

But I didn't fight.

I had no reason left to.

Chapter Twenty-Six

Liv

I exhale, pushing the smoke through my lips until a cloud forms above me, and it slowly dissipates. It's so late that my eyes are heavy from exhaustion and all the tears, but I couldn't sleep for the life of me.

Thea's in my bed, Callie's on the couch, and Natalie was curled up like a cat on the chair in the living room when I tiptoed to the back door.

Tomorrow morning, I'll pack a bag and go to Thea's instead of going on my honeymoon, and as much as I love her and her little family, it's a tough pill to swallow.

"You shouldn't be out here alone." *That voice.*

It stops me from pulling the joint from my lips, so I take another drag and blow the smoke out, giving me some time to process.

"I figured the day couldn't get much worse," I say into thin air.

"Is Olive Greenwood breaking the law?" He asks, making his silhouette visible in the dark outskirts of my porch.

"A nasty little habit I picked up in college," I tell him sarcastically as he comes into the light of the back porch.

It's nearly 4 am. "What are you doing here?"

"I was out for a stroll." He steps closer, and I don't muffle the gasp that escapes me.

"You look terrible."

He snorts. "Thanks, I'd say the same to you… But that'd be a lie."

"Shut up." I know I have bags heavier than concrete under my eyes and remnants of wedding makeup smeared across my face.

"I got your letter."

"You were also supposed to get the memo to leave me alone." I pull my knees to my chest, wrapping my free arm around my shins.

"I had to check on you."

"I'm fine."

He glances at the pot on my patio table, totally unconvinced.

"Besides, I heard you were the one losing it today."

"I might've been a little upset."

He would have come for me. "Are you pissed at Lochlan for putting you in a cage?"

"No, he meant well."

"He meant well… Really?"

"Lochlan knows me how Thea knows you."

"He's your best friend. You can just say that you know?"

He rolls his eyes. "He's more like a brother, honestly."

"You regularly get into physical fights with your *brother?"* I air-quote.

"Well, yeah, actually. He's the only person who encourages me to fight because I need to. He gets me on that level. We've been there for each other all these years. Keeping each other in check when we need to, punching each other in the face when we need that." He shrugs.

"Men are idiots."

He chuckles, scrubbing his hand over his chin. "Yeah, I guess we are."

Silence descends as the sounds of the night linger around us.

"I'm glad you didn't get married."

My stomach somersaults, and I take another long drag, letting that statement sink in. "Why?"

"You know why."

"So you can keep toying with me?" I take another deep pull, and I choke on the smoke, coughing until my airway clears.

"Put that out," he demands, stepping closer.

"Do I seem like the type of woman who follows orders?"

"Not yet." He sinks into the seat in front of me, letting his knees brush the tips of my toes.

I hate to admit that something instinctual inside of me almost makes me snuff out the joint, but my mind fights it. Instead, I put my hand out and tip my head, offering it to him.

His eyes don't leave mine as he plucks it out of my fingers and places it between his lips. The smoke fills his mouth, but he lets it out quickly and smoothly before jamming the burning end into the ashtray.

"Not in the mood to get high?"

"I don't do drugs." He relaxes into his chair, clasping his hands over his chest. "I just wanted to taste where your lips had been."

"Jensen, don't," I breathe, overwhelmed with the implication of that.

"Why?"

"I just ended my engagement 12 hours ago."

"I can wait."

"Don't say that."

"Why not?"

"Because I already waited for you!" The words fly out hotter than I intended, and I have to squeeze my eyes shut to regain my composure. "You made me think you died instead of manning up and breaking up with me– I mean…" I scrub my hand over my face. We weren't ever dating or even technically together, but I was in love with him. It felt worse than any breakup.

Including the one I had today.

"I did."

"You did what?"

He pulls his sleeve up, showing me the tattoo on the inside of his forearm. The claw marks. "Give me your hand." I don't respond. "Olive," he insists, holding his out to take mine.

I put my palm gingerly in his, ignoring the way it feels as he tugs me closer, letting my fingertips run along the length of the tattoo. "Feel that?"

"A scar?" He nods, and the gravity of it hits me. "You attempted suicide?" The words barely escape above a whisper.

"Succeeded actually. They said my heart stopped beating for almost four minutes."

Four minutes... He really died.

"You bastard." The anger explodes out of me, and I jet from my seat, bashing my fists against his chest. "How could you?" I demand, pushing so hard that his chair tips back and he barely saves himself from falling with it.

He steadies his feet and grips my fists in his hands at the same time, pulling me into his chest.

"How dare you?" I cry, still trying to beat him. "I didn't know if you were alive or dead for months! I called every week, trying to convince someone, anyone, to give me information. I only knew you were alive because one person slipped, and they confirmed that you were an active prisoner. You never called me. You never told me what you did!"

I cry until my arms fall limp, and he pulls me in until my face is buried in his shirt. "I didn't want you to know." He shakes my shoulders gently, trying to get my attention. "I didn't want you to know," he repeats, softer and filled with pain.

"I was so fucking ashamed of everything I did. You told me you were going to drop out of college, and I lost my mind. I thought you'd be better off if I were gone. I thought you could move on."

I shove away from his embrace. "You thought I'd move on if you *died?*" I screech. "All these years, I thought you hated me because of Mr. Arkett. I thought you were punishing me."

"Don't say his name," he begs.

"I thought you didn't want to see me because I disgusted you. I thought you were mad at me. I knew you'd flip out if you saw what was happening. I knew you'd be angry, but I liked the attention," I seethe.

All of my emotions are at a tipping point today, and I can't hold anything back.

"He told me I was pretty and he *wanted me*. He would have acted on it too, when you never did!"

"STOP!" He begs, grabbing his head in his hands. It's like déjà vu, seeing him react the same way he did in the courtroom when I told my truth to the judge.

"I carried that with me for years! I held all of that guilt

because you wouldn't talk to me! You abandoned me!"

"I went to prison for you!"

"I would have waited!"

"Exactly!" He yells, throwing his hands out. "You would have waited for me, and your life would have been over. You would have put everything on hold, and you wouldn't have any of this." He motions around me.

"Your education, your success, and all of your plans for the future would have been ruined because of me!"

"That was my choice," I mutter.

"What?" He asks in utter disbelief, stepping closer.

"That should have been my choice! But you took it from me."

He shakes his head in disbelief. "You don't know what you're talking about, Olive."

"I would have chosen you," I cry. "I would have, but you didn't choose me."

"Yes, I did! You just can't accept that I did what was right for you."

"Well, I guess we'll never see eye to eye on this then."

"I guess not."

This is when I should go inside. I should slam the door in his face like I have so many times already, but I can't seem to walk away this time.

I hug myself, trying to calm the shakes taking over my body.

"I shouldn't have come. I'm sorry," he whispers. "I just can't stay away when I know you're so close, and I know you're hurting." He sighs. "I guess I only made it worse."

"Why didn't you come for me when you got out of prison?" I repeat the question I asked him months ago.

"I assumed you had moved on. Or, I guess I hoped that you

did. Besides, I had nothing to offer you. I kept telling myself that once I was stable and could do something to make you proud, I'd come for you. I'd finally apologize for everything I did, and I would see that you were happy."

"That's all?"

He closes the distance between us and hesitantly cups my cheeks in his hands. "That's all that matters. All I ever wanted was for you to be happy."

"Do I seem happy now?"

"No, you seem fucking miserable."

I scoff, letting my face lean heavily into his palm. "I've been through worse," I whisper, looking at him sadly.

"Will you ever forgive me?"

"I don't know," I answer honestly, and his face pinches in pain, but he nods.

"I'll give you some space. As long as you're staying with Thea, and Jesse is around to keep an eye on you, I'll back off. But I'll be back to work with you as soon as life returns to normal. Nothing has changed, Liv. I'm going to keep you safe." He lets his hands fall, backing away from me slowly until there is a void between us once again.

Nothing has changed.

Everything has fucking changed. My entire life imploded today, and Jensen is here.

All of the bad days I've had since he went to prison, and I wished he were there to help me through them, and he never was.

But he's here now.

"Jensen," I utter brokenly to his back just before he disappears into the darkness. His feet freeze midstep, and he turns to look at me. His brows are furrowed in concern as his sad eyes find mine.

"Can I have a hug?" My voice cracks on the last word, and a huff of breath escapes him as he closes the gap between us in two steps.

There's no hesitation as he wraps his arms around me. I can't even lift my arms to hug him back as I bury my face in his chest and sobs heave out of me.

His hand threads through my hair, cradling my head to his heart, holding me tight and letting me fall apart in his arms. I don't know if I'm crying because of my wedding or because of everything else...

But I don't stop crying until the skin around my eyes is raw and swollen.

Even after the tears stop, I stay in his embrace, soaking in the feeling after being without it for so long. The hug he gave me the night I ran out of gas wasn't long enough, and I'm starting to realize that none ever will be.

I don't want him to let go. My hands clasp behind his back, melting into him further.

"I am so proud of you, Hayes," I whisper into his chest, cherishing that I get to be this close to him, even in the shadows of darkness. "I hope you can find it in you to be proud of yourself, too."

"Maybe one day," he murmurs above my head.

"Were you really going to try to stop my wedding?"

He tenses, and I hear him swallow thickly. "I don't know what I would have done. I kept telling myself that I needed to look at you one more time. If I walked in and saw your face, I'd know."

"You'd know what?"

"If you needed to be rescued or not."

A laugh escapes me, and I smother it against his chest. He knew I needed to be rescued even when I was too stubborn to admit it.

It felt like it was too late.

"And, then what?'

He palms the back of my neck, tilting my head up towards his. "Then I'd do whatever it took to get you smiling again."

Jensen Hayes has always had a way of putting me under his spell. Even when there was nothing between us but friendship, I was in love with his smile and his charm. I'd dream about the day he looked at me like a man in love…

With nothing to hold back, no friendship to preserve. I wanted his full, undivided infatuation.

But now I'm seeing that look on the night of my canceled wedding to another man, and it's entirely too much to process.

My emotional cup is empty.

"Go get some sleep, baby girl." His lips press to my forehead, lingering only a second before he lets go of me completely, backing into the shadows.

Even after he disappears, I know I'm not alone. He'll watch me until I get inside safely, blanketing me in his warmth while he waits.

I feel it until I slide through my back door, shutting myself into my kitchen. It lingers so long that I convince myself it's here to stay…

But when I crawl into my cold bed, beside my best friend, I know it's only temporary.

He leaves, and his warmth disappears with him.

Chapter Twenty-Seven

Hayes

"Hey, Malec is here to see you," Lochlan announces as they both walk into the garage. I've been holed away for days, trying to keep my promise to give Liv space.

I want to see her again, and I really want to make sure she's okay. I think my record is 13 minutes for the span of time that I've not been hyper-focused on her well-being.

"What can I do for you, Sheriff?" I wipe my hands on my rag as he eyes my punching bag.

"Another gift arrived for Liv today. I've been keeping an eye on her cottage while she's been at Thea and Jesse's house, and this was in her driveway this morning." He holds his phone out, showing me the image he took.

'YOU ARE MINE' Is written in spray paint, surrounded by rose petals and scraps of white.

"What the fuck?" I grab his phone, looking at it closer. "Is that paper?"

"Her wedding program, torn into pieces."

"Her son of a bitch ex is behind this?"

"That's what I thought, too. He seemed angry enough when

she called off the wedding." He sighs. "But I checked his alibi already. He arrived for their hotel reservation in Toulouse six days ago… With the wedding planner."

I stare at Malec in disbelief. "I'm going to kill that fucker. Does Liv know?"

Malec holds his hand up as if to ward off my idle threats from hitting his ears. "I'm going to see her next. I just wanted to fill you in since you've taken a personal interest in her safety."

"No, does she know he's with the wedding planner?"

"She knows. He made sure to tell her after she dumped him. Figured she would have told you."

"She isn't ready to see me. All I do is hash up bad memories for her."

"You didn't drop by the other night?" Lochlan calls me out, and I glare at him.

"I went for a walk."

"Right," he scoffs. "How do we know the Porters aren't responsible for this? They could be harassing her since she's prosecuting their case, trying to scare her off."

"Jeremiah has been held in jail since his arrest. Randall is on house arrest, and his lawyer has made sure he's unreachable.

"Whoever did this had to have been there at the wedding to get a hold of these programs, but she called it off before photographers started snapping pictures of guests. The hotel didn't have any cameras pointed toward the venue space."

"Any other thoughts, Jensen?" Lochlan enunciates my first name to grab my attention because I've started to zone out. This fucker was at her wedding… What was he going to do? Would he have hurt her?

"I hardly know anything about her personal life now. She's

kept me at arm's length. Aside from Thea and you all," I wave towards Malec. "I don't know who she's been around."

"She has a lot of former clients, and a lot of cases on the docket in Rollins County. I've been going through all of them, but even the more difficult people she's represented have had nothing but nice things to say about her."

"She's always been the golden girl, even if she couldn't see it."

"Is there anyone from her past that might still be holding onto lingering feelings? Besides you." Malec asks, and my head snaps up. "Don't bother. Everyone with a pulse can tell you're in love with her."

My gaze tips up to the rafters, ignoring the latter statement. "She was adopted. As far as I know, she's never met her birth parents. Her adoptive mother has to be in her late 70s by now."

"I know all of that. I need the less formal information. The stuff she doesn't want to disclose."

"Dammit, Malec. You're asking too much of me. I just got her back in my life. If I betray her trust, she'll never speak to me again."

"She'll never speak to you again if she's dead, either."

My body lunges before my brain catches up, but Lochlan anticipated it, trapping me in an arm bar before I attack the Sheriff. I know he doesn't mean it as a threat, but it doesn't stop the visceral reaction.

"I'm not trying to rile you up, Hayes. I'm trying to get to the bottom of this. I'll ask Liv again, but think about it. If there is someone I need to know about, I expect a name as soon as possible."

Lochlan lets me go, and I shove away from him, nodding. "I

know you're trying to help, but this whole situation is pissing me off."

"Give me the names by Monday, or I'll start digging myself even if Liv pushes back. She can be mad at me, not you."

I nod in thanks, and he turns to leave, glancing at the punching bag again.

"You can hit it if you want."

Malec stares at it briefly, contemplating it. "No, I gotta go." He waves it off and stalks out of the garage, reminding me that he's just a normal guy who ended up on a different side of the law than I did.

He's not a bad dude. He cares about Liv.

He's not my enemy.

"He can probably punch it harder than you can."

My head turns eerily slow towards Lochlan. "Do you want me to beat your ass right now?"

"Would it make you feel better?"

I think about it longer than probably necessary. "No, it wouldn't."

"Well, I tried. Stop pouting and get some work done." He leaves out the same door Malec did, taking the distraction with him.

If she'd just let me see her, I'd stop worrying so much.

20 seconds. I didn't even make it 20 seconds without thinking about her.

I still haven't told Lochlan about the ridiculous way I've been distracting myself since I saw her last. A major life decision that has already been causing me back-breaking grief.

But after a million initials and a handful of signatures, the spontaneity of my decision felt so idiotic that I haven't had the courage to say anything.

My phone rings on the workbench, and I almost let it go to voicemail while I'm lost in thought, but I catch it on the last ring.

"Hello?"

"Taking the girls to Casa Amigos tonight to dance. I did not call you." Jesse hangs up without any more context.

Well, fuck. There goes being distracted.

* * *

"Does she know that you called me?" I approach Jesse from behind, and he doesn't even flinch. He probably clocked me the second I entered the bar.

"No, and I will deny it if she asks. Thea's worried about her," he sighs, turning to lean across the high top table we're next to.

"Why?" I glance at the sea of women on the dance floor, spotting the one I want immediately. Her rich brown hair bounces, catching every gleam of light as she jumps and sings nearly dead center in the crowd.

Her charisma radiates around her. You'd never be able to tell she's struggling with anything.

"She's been acting pretty nonchalant about everything but almost reckless at the same time." My eyes narrow, and he catches it. "I mean, it's Liv. She isn't going out and robbing banks, but she's talking about going to a cryo-clinic to freeze her eggs one minute and then talking about selling her cottage and joining her mom at Burning Man."

Another guy I recognize as Jesse's friend walks over with a bucket of beer. He sets it on the table and positions himself firmly against the wall before scanning the crowd and finding his invested interest.

He spots his redhead and then finally turns to address me. "Hayes, right?"

"Yeah." We shake hands, and he leaves it at that, grabbing a beer out of the bucket and offering me one. "Thanks."

"Nathan is Thea's brother," Jesse finishes the introduction. "We've served in the military together, going on... A lot of years." He shrugs like he's lost count, and Nathan doesn't offer any more insight, keeping his eyes on his wife.

"So why am I here?" I ask Jesse. Not that I care to have an excuse to see Liv, but I also don't want to piss her off when she sees me.

"Liv thought it was a great idea to come out tonight to lure her stalker out."

The beer nearly spits from my mouth. "What?"

"That's why I dragged Nathan along, too."

"You didn't drag me anywhere. Callie insisted on coming with her friends," he corrects, forming his longest sentence yet. Jesse only rolls his eyes.

"Malec doesn't have jurisdiction here, but he spoke to the local precinct just in case, and he should be here soon. Incognito," he adds sarcastically.

"Yeah, you can spot him as being a cop from a mile away."

"That's what I told him."

"I mean, you guys kind of give off a cop vibe, too."

Jesse laughs, and Nathan looks at me like I just kicked his shin. "And, you look like you prefer concrete walls and slop."

I bark a laugh, and it's the first genuine amusement I've felt in weeks. Jesse shakes his head but visibly relaxes when he realizes neither of us are about to kill each other.

"What makes Liv think her stalker will come out of the shadows now?"

"She claims that baiting him will get all of this over with quicker, and I didn't want her to attempt to do it alone." He sighs and glances at me. "When I married Thea, I went from having no family to being surrounded by people that I cared about. Liv included. I forget sometimes that she's not actually a sister-in-law.

"I'm used to watching over her, but to be honest, she doesn't usually need it. Men hit on her, and she laughs in their faces. God forbid they get snippy. I've seen her smile like Medusa in a grown man's face and then laugh when they run away.

"But the added variable of someone being out to get her makes me nervous. She acts tough, but I can tell she's scared. She doesn't like the threats. And she definitely doesn't want to admit that she feels safer when you're around."

"She doesn't want to put your family at risk. I'm expendable," I laugh to conceal the cold pit in my stomach.

I'm a shield, and I'll gladly be that for her, but that's all I am.

He shakes his head. "Not what I mean, Hayes." He looks at me pointedly. "That girl won't stop looking at the door, but I think she's only waiting for one of her stalkers to walk through it."

"Funny." I smile sarcastically, and he laughs. "Any thoughts from you?" I ask Nathan mockingly.

"No," he states bluntly.

"Great." I down my beer and toss it back into the bucket. "I need something stronger."

Chapter Twenty-Eight

Liv

The base thrums in my chest, pushing me to dance more, sing louder. Anything to drown out the battle between my heart and my head.

I shouldn't be concerned with matters of the heart this soon after ending an engagement, but the truth is that my feelings for Elliot waned a long time ago. I liked that it wasn't hard to be away from him.

I never wanted to risk another catastrophic heartbreak. Which is why Hayes being back in my life has turned everything upside down.

My brain tells me that I can't trust him. He broke me once. He'll do it again. My heart can't stop beating for him.

Even now, I imagine I see him in a mass of people. I squeeze my eyes shut, tipping my face towards the ceiling and submerse myself in the music. I don't need Hayes.

I don't need men.

I'll be okay.

An arm slips around my waist, jerking me out of the forced musical retreat in my head, making me gasp.

"It's just me," Natalie says. She must've just gotten here.

"I'm going to the bar. Want anything?"

"Anything with tequila."

"Sweet or strong?" She asks, backing towards the bar. It draws my attention over her head, and I blink a few times to clear my vision… *Is that?*

"Both," I breathe, spinning away from her.

Thea registers my face immediately, closing the gap between us. "What's wrong?"

"He's here."

"Who?" She asks, startled.

"Hayes."

"Oh," she sighs in relief. "I thought you meant your stalker."

"I don't know who my stalker is."

"I know, I thought it was just some lawyer hunch or something."

"Do you think he's seen me?"

She peeks around my shoulder towards the bar. "Mmm, probably not."

I whip my head around to check where he is, and he's looking directly at me. Our eyes connect, and my breath escapes me.

"Yeah, sorry, he definitely sees you." She rubs my arm. "Go talk to him."

"I can't."

"Why not?"

"I don't know what to say."

"It's Hayes. Your Hayes. You don't have to know, it'll come to you."

"And you think this is a good idea?" I ask skeptically. This is usually the type of thing my best friend should warn me away from.

"If he were anyone else, I'd say no." She nudges my butt forward, giving it a soft tap-tap when we get to the edge of the dance floor. "We're all here, you're safe. Let loose and have fun. Don't worry about anything else."

"This is starting to feel like a setup."

"I don't know what you're talking about," she sing-songs as she skips back to the table where Jesse is. He won't even look me in the eyes… This was definitely rigged.

"I believe this is your drink." A short glass with a sugar rim appears in front of my face. I don't have to look to know whose hand is holding it. The scars on his knuckles are a pretty dead giveaway, too.

"How do I know it isn't drugged?" I ask as I grab the glass.

"My existence depends on you speaking to me, so rendering you unconscious would not benefit me in the slightest."

I take a sip before I'm brave enough to face him. When I do, I wish I had downed the entire glass.

His subtle smirk and those crinkled blue eyes nearly melt me on the spot. How am I supposed to protect myself from someone who throws me so off kilter just by looking at me?

I take another sip from my glass because forming a sentence feels too complex right now.

He leans forward, and the liquor stills in my mouth, burning my tongue. "That is a very small tank top," he whispers huskily, letting his breath skate over my shoulder.

"You don't like my outfit?"

"I *love* your outfit."

My mouth parts, and I force it closed. "Are you flirting with me?"

His grin widens, and if it were the sun, I'd shield myself from the overwhelming intensity. I love his smile.

"Does it offend you?"

It coils up my insides into a million knots, twisting all that I know about myself, but… "No, it doesn't offend me."

It feels good.

Too good.

"I think I need to dance," I blurt out. I'm not ready to talk, I don't know if I have the right words to say, even if I was. But I know dancing makes me feel better.

His mouth upticks in another smile just before he downs his glass of amber liquor and sets it down with a clink on the table behind him. "Is this another hobby you picked up in college?"

"Dancing? I guess, since no one ever asked me to prom," I say pointedly, staring at him over the rim of my drink as I take another sip.

"And I'll regret that the rest of my life, dove," he says earnestly, taking my glass from me.

He threads his fingers through mine, pulling me back to the center of the dance floor. Everyone around us shifts naturally as if the spot was reserved for us.

Or maybe an ex-con and a 5'8 woman in heels just have that effect on people.

"You're going to dance with me?"

"Do you want me to dance with you?"

Somewhere in my brain, I've frozen him in time, and he's still the boy I knew in high school. It doesn't make sense that he would even know today's music well enough to dance to it.

I can't fathom that he's had his own life since then, and he's probably danced with countless women in bars.

He's probably taken them home.

He's probably taken a lot of them to bed.

My stomach twists, souring my buzz. "I don't know," I admit.

He doesn't react. He is too in control now as a grown man, but I've always been able to see under the facade. He's reaching for me, and I'm running away.

I don't want to run, but I'm afraid to stay.

The music picks up, and the lights start flashing as bodies around us react to the quickening tempo of the song.

He leans in close so I can hear him. "Dance, Liv. I'll hold your drink," his lips brush my ear, and a chill zips down my spine.

I'm dazed, watching him walk away and wishing he wouldn't, but not being brave enough to tell him that.

Bodies collide with me, but it's only the girls joining me on the dance floor. Thea smiles as she grabs my hands, forcing me to move my body while Natalie and Callie bounce around us, screaming to the song.

It's all I need to let myself go. I don't know how long I'm dancing or how many songs pass, but I know I've had one set of eyes on me the entire time.

My gaze washes over the crowd mid-twirl, and they always find his. Leaning his elbow against the high top table with that subtle, delicious smirk that tells me he's thoroughly entertained by what he sees.

He never holds a grudge when I push him away. He's always just watching and waiting.

This time, when my eyes lock with his, I can't will them away, and my body gravitates towards him. His attention doesn't stray as I work my way through the people dancing, and finally find myself standing in front of him at the edge of the dance floor.

"Thirsty?" He holds out my margarita, and I nod.

I step closer, drinking straight from the straw without taking the glass from his hand. I blink up at him after I've gotten my fill, feeling my buzz surge inside of me as he stares at me through hooded eyes.

His lips part, but I interrupt before he can speak. "I'm ready for you to dance with me, now."

His mouth closes and opens, but he doesn't form a word before I slip my hands up his sides, pulling him towards the dance floor. He's still holding my drink as my body resumes its chaotic free styling of the beat.

Everyone is dancing, jiving, grinding, but he's watching me, fueling me as my body twirls. Heat kisses my waist, and I gasp in surprise, but the contact disappears quickly, leaving my skin tingling in its wake.

My hands dance in the air as I bounce to the music, and his palm covers my belly, spreading more tendrils of the warmth that I crave, and turning me liquid in his embrace.

Except the warmth evaporates when I whip around to face him, as if he was never touching me at all.

My lungs heave, transfixed by the lights and the noise, tuning out anything else that isn't in this bubble of just the two of us.

I lean in, and his adam's apple bobs, swallowing thickly as I steal another sip from my drink. His gaze shifts from my eyes to where my lips are wrapped around my straw, and he doesn't blink as I suck the stray liquid from my bottom lip.

His jaw ticks as his teeth grind together, but I turn my back to continue dancing, pretending I'm impervious to the inferno behind me.

It's only seconds before fingers brush my hip, and then I'm seared by a lingering palm on my back. Always brief, always respectful.

Never enough.

Another chorus and every woman in the room throws their hands up to shout the lyrics, and when mine go up, his calloused hand engulfs my side from my bottom rib to my hip, sending sparks across my belly.

I need more. I need both of his hands on me everywhere.

His fingers begin to slip off me, and the subtle inklings of fire are replaced with panic as he rips my pleasure away.

We're not dancing. This is a game of cat and mouse.

Each brief contact is edging me towards a pinnacle that I have no hope of reaching, and I might combust in a bad way.

I snatch my glass from him, sucking down the last drink with no cutesy teasing this time, and tap the closest random man on the shoulder.

"Hey, go put this somewhere for me!" I shout at him, shoving the glass in his hand. The poor guy looks dumbfounded but complies like a good boy.

I don't bother confirming because my fingers are already threading around either side of Jensen's neck, pulling him closer so my lips brush his ear.

"Dance. With. Me."

Chapter Twenty-Nine

Hayes

"Dance. With. Me." Her demand raises goose bumps on my arms, but it's her fingers tightening around my throat that does me in.

This woman could tell me to do anything, and I'd do it.

Set her ex's house on fire? Done.

Buy a round of drinks for the entire bar? Here's my wallet.

Step off a ship into the middle of the vast, dark ocean? Liv proves that sirens lured men into the seas.

I'd follow her anywhere.

She doesn't wait for my response. She doesn't need to. She knows men obey her.

Especially me.

Her figure grazes my body, and I'm already a live wire. My hands find her hips as she sways to the music, hypnotizing me with every move.

Her body begged to be touched, but I was afraid to go too far. Now, she's pulling me in closer, holding my hands steady as she shimmies to the beat.

My palms skim the skin above her jeans, and my immediate reaction is to pull back.

Don't scare her off. Don't scare her off.

But her fingers thread mine, shackling my palms around her waist. She's thin and toned, and I can feel her abdominal muscles flex as she sways. Her tiny little tank top flutters along her rib cage, barely grazing my forearms.

She's the sexiest woman I've ever seen, and if she keeps backing towards me, she'll know exactly how much I think so.

Don't scare her off.

Don't–

Her ass grinds against my front, and my whole body stills as hers does.

Electricity shoots down my spine, overpowering any rational thought to move away… But then she moves.

Into me.

Her hips rock, planting her ass firmly against my hard length. Other than that slight movement, we're both statues on the dance floor as the entire bar buzzes around us.

Her fingers twitch in mine, and the mass behind my zipper responds without my permission, flexing against her tight backside.

"Olive," I breathe her name, starting to apologize, but she glances over her shoulder, silencing me with a single look.

She starts dancing again, grinding her body against mine, torturing me with her curves.

Fuck it. If I'm going to hell for this, I want the deluxe deal.

My right hand flattens on her stomach, forcing her against me until there's no space between us anywhere, while my left hand caresses every inch it can reach.

I feel the muscles in her leg working as she dances against me, and I drag my fingertips up the front of her thigh, carving a path towards her hip.

She pushes against me as I anchor her waist, pulling her in impossibly closer. Her fingernails climb the back of my neck, digging into my hair and scraping at my scalp.

Pure carnal frustration escapes my throat, and she gasps as I silence myself on the soft spot between her shoulder and neck.

No one has ever been able to elicit such impulses from me, but it's Olive, and I'm hard enough that I'm hallucinating taking her right here in the middle of the dance floor.

She tugs my palm higher on her stomach and up her ribs until my thumb brushes the underside of her breast. Not over her tank top, but under the flowy fabric, my rough skin caresses her soft flesh.

I hold her sternum steady, plastering her shoulders to my chest. "Don't fucking start something you don't intend to finish, dove," I murmur in her ear.

Her whole body shudders when I bite her earlobe, and she twists in my arms, always beating me at my own game. Because it's her and she *owns* me.

"You don't like how I dance?" Her lips flutter against my cheek, and it takes everything in me not to turn my head to claim them with my own.

My hands dance up her back instead, capturing every inch of her exposed skin between the two fucking strings holding her top together. "I *love* the way you dance," I growl, feeling every inch of her body melded to mine.

She wraps her arms around my neck, and I breathe in her scent, losing sight of everything around me. This can't be real life. I've dreamed of this for too long. I must've fallen and cracked my head open.

Or maybe I got in a car accident on the way here.

No, I rode my bike. I probably got taken out by a trucker.

The volume of the music dips as the strobe lights cut off, yanking me from my stupor.

"It's closing time, open all the doors and let you out into the world."

The song rips the idiocy from my brain as I blink at the woman in my arms.

"Closing time, turn all of the lights on over every boy and every girl."

I'm holding Liv, and I'm acting like a fucking animal.

It's Olive. *My* Olive. And, I'm not taking this moment seriously enough. She deserves better than this.

"Jensen," she whispers, holding my cheeks in her soft hands, forcing my attention to her mouth. It's still loud enough in here that I need to read her lips as she speaks.

But her lips. I want to feel her lips.

"My friends are going to make me leave now."

"What?" I blink. Take her?

"That's girl code. Come together, leave together." That means I need to let her go. "Unless..." She starts, and I don't wait for her to finish, anchoring my arm around her waist and lifting. She squeals, but her legs wrap around my hips instinctively.

I'm moving across the room and through the crowd before someone comes for her. She's mine, dammit.

"Jensen," she breathes my name again as we crest the outside air and the cold bites her skin.

I set her on my bike, whipping my long-sleeve shirt off, and draping it over her head. She giggles as I help guide her arms through the sleeves.

My white sleeveless shirt exposes more of the tattoos she hasn't seen, but none of the incriminating ones. It also exposes me to the elements enough to realize I can't take her on my bike.

She'll freeze, and I can't put her through that.

Instead, I lean in, dragging my nose along her neck, memorizing her scent. If I wake up tomorrow, I need to know this was real.

Her arms wrap around my shoulders as she tips her head back, exposing her throat, and I take it... Letting my lips caress her skin.

"Jensen," she breathes. My name on her fucking lips is a God damn miracle.

Her eyes are hooded, skating across my arms and across my chest, where her hands trail up towards my neck.

"Olive," I warn her when her lust-filled gaze lands on my lips.

A sudden shrill whistle from behind me berates my eardrum. "Hey, buddy. Off our girl," Natalie yells at me.

My head tilts to look over my shoulder, and Jackson just shrugs. "Sorry, Hayes."

I feel Liv's body shake as she giggles in front of me, and another wave of self-hatred hits me. She's fucking drunk.

I'm acting like a fool, and I almost kissed her in the parking lot of some random bar. God dammit, I'm fucking all of this up.

"Are you warm enough?" I ask her, sighing. She shakes her head and giggles, again, opening her arms for a hug. Fucking, Olive.

A smile tilts my lips as I wrap my arms around her, lifting her off my bike. "Where to?"

"I came with Thea and Callie."

"Hey, she's ours!" Callie and Thea burst through the double doors of the bar, giggling the same tune as Liv.

I help her into Thea's car, only after I confirm that Jesse is driving and not one of the tipsy women piling into the backseat.

"Nope, you're coming with me," Nathan states, dragging Callie back out of the car. A chorus of protests erupts, but she only laughs as he leads her to his truck.

I want that. I want Liv to be mine. I want there to be no question of who she is coming home with.

"Do you want your shirt back?" Liv leans out the window just as Jesse starts to pull away.

"No, dove. I don't."

"Good, I wasn't going to give it back anyway. See you Monday," she winks, and my whole fucking face grins. *This woman.*

They pull out of the lot, and I feel Malec's skyscraper shadow next to me. "Yeah, I'll be seeing you Monday, too. Hopefully, you two had a chance to discuss some things while you were fused to each other's bodies."

"Fuck off, Malec."

He pats my shoulder. "Monday."

How do I broach the subject with Liv that Malec wants me to spill all her dirty secrets? Especially now that I practically took advantage of her drunkenness and pretended that everything between us was fine and easy.

Nothing between Liv and me is easy. Not anymore. The comfort we used to share was shattered the day I nearly killed a man in front of her.

Now I'm supposed to ask her if she's had contact with a

man that I'd still want to kill if I saw him today.

And any other gritty details from her life that I've missed over the past decade… She'll go back to slamming doors in my face.

Chapter Thirty

Liv

For the better part of the last two weeks, I dreaded returning to normal life. Facing the people who knew I was leaving to get married but showing up to work this morning, single and scorned.

Except, I can't really convince myself that I care now. Feeling Jensen's body against mine and being showered with uninhibited adoration healed something deep inside of me.

I've wanted that part of him for so long that nothing else seems to matter. All I want is more of it.

I slip on my heels before fluffing my hair in the mirror when I hear the wrap tap tap on my front door. It's a little early, but he's probably just as eager to see me as I am him.

Swinging the door open, my smile is ready on my face, preparing to see him, but instead, I come face to face with a man I've never seen before.

He's young, but he's big. He's at least a head taller than me and almost fills the width of the doorway.

My smile drops.

He doesn't say anything, staring at me with wide eyes as I stare at him, waiting for him to murder me.

He shoves a bouquet forward, uttering. “Delivery.”

Over the bloom of roses and daisies, I see his brown collared shirt and name tag, and his white delivery van in the driveway.

I don’t touch the flowers, forcing him to hold them out awkwardly. “Who are they from?”

“Oh. Um, I don’t know. I just deliver them, I don’t read the notes.”

“Read it for me.” I clear my throat. “Please.”

He tucks the vase under his arm, pulling the card from the clip in the middle of the bundle, and I watch his face attempt to rival the color of the flowers. “I can’t read this.”

“Read it,” I demand, making him gulp.

“His hands touched you when it should have been me. I dream of slicing the skin away and keeping it for myself,” he stutters through the last of it, shoving the card back into the depths of the flowers.

His gaze stays averted as I stare at him, processing what I just heard.

“So, do you want the flow–” His voice cuts out suddenly, and my vision tunnels as everything around me goes black.

* * *

“Who the fuck are you?”

Hayes.

“Liv!” He touches my face, and I try to focus on feeling his warm fingers on my skin.

“Who. The. Fuck. Are. You?”

He’s angry. Why is he yelling?

"I didn't do it." Oh. The delivery boy.

I hope he doesn't hurt him.

"If you did, I'll fucking kill you," he threatens, and I hear a crash. "Call 911, ask for Malec. And, don't fucking leave my sight."

As hard as I try, I can't open my eyes.

"Wake up, Olive," he murmurs, stroking my cheeks again. "It's me, open your eyes."

I hear crinkling.

Cinnamon.

My nose tingles.

"That's it, baby girl. Wake up." He thumbs my bottom lip, tipping my mouth open slightly, letting the cinnamon bite my tongue.

I bite down instinctively, chewing to get the burning sensation off my tongue, and blink up at the face in front of me. "You didn't have to shove the whole piece of gum in my mouth."

He laughs breathily. "I thought your fainting spells were getting better," he murmurs, holding my cheeks in his hands.

"Me too." I lean into his palm, looking up at him. "I guess I can't blame the stress on a wedding."

He helps me sit up until my back is resting against the chair in my living room, and brushes my hair back gently.

"We'll find out who is doing this. I promise."

As much as it scares me, I'm worried about what will happen when my stalker's identity is discovered. Jensen won't rest until I'm safe, and we've already paid the price for that once.

I kick at one of my shoes that came loose when I fell, and my foot struggles to right it until his fingers circle my ankle, steadying it. He slides my heel back onto my foot easily, and

I don't breathe until his hand falls away.

I wish he would have left it there.

"Did I scare the flower boy away?" I ask with too much hoarseness in my throat, trying to stand. This time, when he reaches for me, helping me up, he doesn't let go as I peek over his shoulder.

There's a broken porch rail lying a few feet from me, and flowers scattered everywhere.

"No, but I scared him thoroughly." He nods to where the kid is cowering next to his van in the driveway. "He didn't hurt you, right?" He asks me under his breath, wrapping his arms around my waist to support my weight.

"No, he's just a delivery guy."

He nods against my head, and I lean into him, sighing deeply. "You can probably let me go now."

"You're still pretty unsteady. I probably shouldn't."

A laugh bubbles up out of me, and I feel his smile against my hair. "I don't think I've been taking all of this seriously enough."

He pulls back to look me in the face, suddenly. "Why?"

"I accepted that I had a stalker, but it's hard to remember to be scared when you're around."

He looks at me earnestly. "Are you flirting with me?"

I knock his shoulder with my palm. "Shut up, I just fainted." I smile bashfully towards the floor.

He tips my chin up, forcing me to look up at him. "I don't want you to be scared, but I am worried. I'd like to be around even more… If that's okay with you?"

He's asking to be with me more so he can protect me. Nothing else, Olive.

But as his thumb rubs little circles under my chin, my recent fainting spell becomes a distant memory. The words on my flower card don't ring so clear... When we're together, I'm always sucked into *him.*

He's waiting for a response, but I can't stop staring at his mouth, inches from mine. I know kissing him wouldn't solve any of my problems, and it might actually make things worse... But I bet it'd be fun.

"Whatever is happening in your head right now, I want to revisit later." His deeply spoken words draw my gaze upward. "Malec's here."

My first instinct is to pull away from him, but I meet the resistance of his muscles wrapped around me, reminding me that I'm a single woman now.

I don't have to hide this from anyone. I don't have to justify who I'm receiving comfort from.

Especially when that person is Jensen Hayes with our years of history.

Malec talks to the flower delivery guy and quickly sends him on his way before meeting us on the porch. "He's only been on the job three weeks. He doesn't know anything, and I think you made him piss himself," Malec sighs, looking at Hayes disapprovingly. I hide my amusement on his shoulder.

"I rolled up, and she was on the ground with some kid hovering over her. What would you fucking think?" He challenges.

"I didn't say you were wrong, but flying off the handle without cause could really make this blooming friendship a little awkward," Malec says sarcastically, motioning between him and Hayes, and I don't bother hiding my laugh.

"That was sweet. You should put it on a Hallmark card," Hayes responds, dripping with just as much sarcasm. *Men.*

"Speaking of cards. Where's the one that came with the flowers?" Malec asks, bringing us back to reality.

A fresh wave of anxiety washes over me as I glance at my feet and all the scattered roses, but I don't see the card. "It was stuffed in the bouquet. It must be here somewhere."

"It's right here," Hayes announces, finding it behind one of the planters. I don't have a chance to warn him not to read it before his eyes go dark as night...

His hands touched you when it should have been me. I dream of slicing the skin away and keeping it for myself.

I remember the words crystal clear, now.

Malec plucks it from Hayes's stony grasp and reads it himself before releasing a slow breath. "Yeah... Not good."

"Do you think he followed me to the bar? Was he there Saturday night?" That's the only place that he could have seen Hayes's hands on me. Besides... "You hugged me on my back patio that night, right after my wedding. Was he watching then?" I look at Hayes, but he's still standing eerily still, staring at the floor.

"So, Lochlan was right, you did sneak over here to see her," Malec accuses Hayes, but he doesn't react.

I'm wondering how often they talk about me when I'm not around... But I can't stop looking at his steely posture.

"Jensen," I say softly. "I'm okay. It was only words."

He forces air through his nostrils and tips his head back like he's attempting to regain some composure.

"Now is the time that I need to know everything, Liv," Malec states, opening up a notepad. "Every person you might have a hunch about. Every person from your past. It was only words this time, next time it might not be."

"Fuck," Hayes swears under his breath, stalking across the

porch to grasp his hands on the railing.

"I told you everything already. All my boyfriends from college. Elliot. I gave you all my case filings from the past few years."

Malec shuts his notepad and shoves it back into his vest pocket, but he doesn't take his eyes off me. "Jensen. Have any one to add?"

His head shakes in frustration, but not as if he's saying no. "Tell him, Liv. Or I will."

"Tell him what?"

He turns to face us, but doesn't leave the porch railing as he stares at me in silent contention. "Landon Arkett."

My mouth pops open. "You're kidding? I was 17, I haven't heard from him since the day you..." My words trail off, and I glance at Malec because I don't know how much he knows about Hayes's history. "Nearly killed him."

"He seemed pretty obsessed at the time," Hayes spews. He *hates* the man.

"The victim of your assault?" Malec asks, looking at Hayes to confirm.

"He's not a fucking victim. He was a pervert."

Malec tips his head in understanding and doesn't argue.

This type of fury in Jensen is the exact thing that makes me nervous to find my stalker. "The last I heard, he spent months in the hospital recovering from his injuries. I never spoke to him again. He never reached out. It's not Mr. Arkett."

Jensen only shakes his head in disgust when I say the name again.

"I'll look into it, but you're probably right, Liv. A grown man who preys on teenagers would likely lose interest the older his target gets. Even if he wasn't caught in the act and punished for it, he would have probably moved on to another young victim once he got what he wanted from you," Malec says, and I realize that he knows a lot more than I thought.

"I didn't have any other boyfriends. Hayes was practically my only friend until he wasn't. Are we finished? I need to get to work." I glance coldly at Hayes across the porch. I feel like I'm being blamed for everything all over again.

As if I asked to have a stalker.

As if I asked to have a teacher prey on me when I was 17.

Or have the boy I was in love with go to prison for protecting me.

"I'll get with you after I look into your old teacher, and I'll look at the security tapes from the bar on Saturday in case someone stands out. Keep close to Hayes, though, for the time being."

I smile stiffly at Malec because I know he's only doing his job, but I really don't want to be around either of these men right now.

"Hayes, don't have a stroke," he bids his farewell to him over his shoulder before walking back to his cruiser, and Hayes gives him the middle finger. "I saw that!" He yells.

Chapter Thirty-One

Hayes

The door clicks shut behind my back as Liv drops her briefcase on her desk. "Are you going to be in your office for a while?"

"Oh, he speaks. I thought you forgot I was here."

I was stewing in quiet rage the entire drive here, but she should know better. She always stays at the forefront of my thoughts.

"Do you have any appointments? Or will you be in here for a while?" I repeat my question, ignoring her remark as tension rolls across my shoulder blades.

Reading that note has me keyed up, and I haven't been able to squash it.

"I'm catching up on emails and paperwork all morning," she sighs, rolling her chair under her desk.

My fingers work the button of my shirt, loosening my collar so I can crack my neck properly. I lose the jacket next, throwing it on the fake leather couch that sits off to the side, acting as decoration more than anything.

The cushion barely gives when I sit on it. Bracing my elbows on my knees, I rub my hands roughly over my face before undoing the buttons at my wrists and rolling my sleeves up my forearms.

Liv peers at me over her laptop, her eyebrows quirked in question. I never sit.

I've never removed my jacket or acted anything less than professional in this setting. I've always respected her workspace, but I feel like I'm going to implode.

"I'll fix myself before you have to leave the office," I assure her, staring at my clasped hands in front of me.

"I'm not worried about that."

I glance at her, and she tips her laptop screen down to see me clearly. "I just need a minute to collect my thoughts. I'm fine."

"You need to punch someone," she scoffs sarcastically.

"Yeah, you have someone in mind?" I look at her seriously, and her eyes narrow.

"I don't know who is stalking me, Hayes. I don't know what you want from me!"

"I know!" I launch up from my seat and stalk to the window, bracing my hands on the windowsill. "I'm sorry. I'm losing my mind here, Liv. How am I supposed to keep you safe if I don't even know who I'm protecting you from?"

"You stay close," she says softly, grabbing my arm. Her hand on my bicep is an anchor, keeping me sane and bringing me back to earth.

Her ringless finger stares at me like a beacon of hope. She's still Olive Greenwood, so for now, she's still mine. Whether she believes that or not.

"Is that what you want? I don't want you to feel like you're trapped. I know how that feels… "

"Prison?" She sighs sadly.

"Yeah. Wouldn't recommend."

"I'm sorry," she utters, leaning her forehead against my shoulder blade. "If it weren't for me, you wouldn't have gone through that."

"Please, don't apologize. It wasn't your fault."

"Yes, it was."

I twist to face her, pulling her closer when she doesn't back away. "I never blamed you. I made my choices, and I stand by them. He never should have touched you. I'd do it all again, because I did what I thought was right."

"Don't. I can't go through that again." Her eyes are moist with tears, and I can see all those broken pieces lying dormant inside of her.

"Come here." I wrap her in my arms, hugging her with all that I have. Trying to heal what I shattered, comforting her after what happened this morning, and selfishly enjoying having her like this again.

My Olive.

"Even if you decide my life is too dramatic and you'd prefer the old Olive, I'd rather watch you walk away on your own volition than to see you go to prison again." She huffs a sad laugh, but I only hold her tighter.

"I'm not going anywhere," I promise. She looks at me thoughtfully with her head tilted and eyes filled with hopeful wonder.

"Besides, I thought you were beautiful when we were kids, but..." I blow a dramatic breath out. "I think I'd die if I went even a day without seeing you now."

"Whatever," she laughs, rolling her eyes.

I tip her chin back to look up at me. "I'm serious. The woman you are today has blown me away. Not only because you're brilliant and successful. You're–"

Her eyes fall to my lips, and my stomach clenches. I've never wanted anything more in my entire life than to kiss her.

"Gorgeous," I whisper, rubbing my thumb across her cheekbone.

I've dreamed of this. Having her look at me this tenderly, and wanting me. When we were kids, there was a world of reasons for me to say no. Her age, our friendship, my bad influence...

Now I can't think of a damn reason not to give her what she wants. What I want desperately.

My head dips until my nose traces hers, and her breath catches in her throat. Her fingers curl into my shirt just above my chest, and my heart thrums beneath them.

One touch of her lips is going to crack my chest wide open.

"Miss Greenwood." Liv jumps as her office door flies open, and her wide-eyed intern stares at us in shock. "I'm sorry, I didn't– I'm sorry."

"What can I do for you, Miley?" Liv asks in exasperation, straightening her jacket before walking towards the girl in the doorway.

I take my time, rolling my sleeves back into place and correcting all of my buttons as casually as I can. We weren't doing anything relatively scandalous in here, but I'd never want it to look that way either, for Liv's sake.

"Can I get you tea, Miss Greenwood?" I ask her after I slip my suit jacket back on. Miley's still thumbing through a stack of papers, asking her questions.

Liv's lips quirk up in a soft smile as she avoids looking at me, as if she knows looking at me directly will dissolve her tough lawyer facade in front of her employee. "That'd be great."

"Be right back." I let my hand caress her lower back as I walk by, out of the intern's view.

"Thank you," she whispers, daring to look at me briefly as I exit.

I wink, and her eyes snap back to the paperwork in front of her, biting her lip to keep herself from smiling.

My Olive.

* * *

"Thank you for meeting with us today, Curtis. Your testimony is important to the county's case, and we appreciate your willingness to help us after what you've been through."

I stand behind Liv's chair in Curtis's room at the rehabilitation center, looking at the bandages covering my friend in the seat across from her.

Curtis sustained a spinal fracture, a traumatic brain injury, and second-degree burns on 40% of his body after Jeremiah's attack. Before that, before he ever came to Second Chance Sanctuary, his arms were covered in skin grafts from a bombing incident.

The poor kid has been through it in his 25 years of life.

"Tell me what you need. I'll do what I can to help." His voice is low and scratchy, his shoulders are undeniably slumped. His whole being is defeated.

"I would like to go over your story and prepare you for the questions I'll be asking on the stand. If you're up to it, I'll coach you on how to respond to some of the defense's tactics when they cross-examine."

"Yes, ma'am," he responds plainly, and it takes everything in me not to turn away. It's difficult to see him like this. The young guy, so full of life, is nothing but a shell of himself.

"Can you tell me in your own words what happened the night of the incident?"

He clears his throat before adjusting in his seat stiffly. "We were celebrating Jo's graduation when the smallest barn on the property caught fire. During the commotion, my boss's niece, Emory, went missing. I, along with some of the others, split off into different directions to look for her. After some time, I stumbled upon a man that I assumed was a volunteer firefighter–"

"And, why did you assume that?" She asks, properly, as if we are in the courtroom.

"He was wearing a fireman's jacket and helmet. I couldn't see his face at first."

"What happened next?" Her voice is soft as she leads him through his testimony.

"Jo called out for me. She was trapped inside the bear enclosure and tied up." He moves around in his seat again, showing signs of discomfort, but I don't know if it's physical pain or if he is having a hard time reliving the story.

"Before I knew what was happening, I was taken to the ground, and we started fighting. Even when I got a few swings in, my hands were too weak to do any real damage because of my scars. He blindsided me, and I got knocked out." His face twists in pain as he spits the words out. "That's all I remember."

"That was great. Thank you."

The door to his room opens suddenly, and a woman in scrubs stops halfway through. “Oh, I’m sorry. I didn’t know you had visitors. I’ll come back tomorrow.”

“No, wait!” He calls to her, perking up more than he has in the past thirty minutes. The nurse peeks back through the door. “You can stay.”

She nods shyly before walking across the room towards us.

“This is Sienna. She was one of my nurses at the main hospital.”

“Hayes,” I introduce myself, stepping forward to shake her hand. “I worked with Curtis at the sanctuary. This is Liv Greenwood, Prosecutor of Rollins County.”

She smiles at Liv as she sits at the end of his hospital bed. “I recognize you from the courthouse. I’m friends with Natalie. Her little brother and my son, Charlie, are best friends. Dec was there the night the fire at the sanctuary happened. He was pretty shaken up when Emory went missing.”

“Luckily, with Curtis’s account of the events, Dec and Emory won’t have to testify,” Liv tells her kindly.

“Dec and Charlie send me gifts,” Curtis admits, pointing to the wall beside his bed. “Makes the room suck a little less.”

I wander over to look at the pictures taped to the wall and the small LEGO figurines on his bedside table. “Huh, that’s pretty cool.” I pick up the LEGO bear.

“Jackson helps the boys build those,” Sienna says over her shoulder.

“Jackson plays with LEGOS?”

She laughs and nods, but I’m watching Curtis over her shoulder, locked in on her every move. When she turns back toward him, though, he forces his attention out the window.

“I’m totally busting Malec’s balls the next time I see him,” I mumble. Liv clears her throat, obviously trying to reel me back in. "Sorry."

"Curtis, at any point during the incident, did you know who was attacking you?"

"Yes. I was the rookie at the sanctuary, and I had to go to the junk yard quite a bit to look for parts. Jerry is the owner, so I knew it was him as soon as his helmet came off."

"How many times would you say you had been to the junk yard if you had to quantify it?"

He glances at Sienna quickly but away again, delaying his response.

"How many times did you go to the junk yard if you had to put a number on it?" Sienna clarifies the question softly as if she knew exactly why Curtis was hesitating.

"I don't know. Once or twice a week for close to a year."

Liv nods in approval because that's exactly what she needed to hear. You don't see someone that many times and not recognize them. That's a solid identification.

"The next thing I'll do is explain your injuries to the court. I will give them all the gritty details and pull at their heartstrings because I want them to know how badly Jeremiah hurt you. I want them to feel how he changed your life. This might be difficult to hear, so I would understand if you tried to tune it out in the moment. Focus on a dot on the wall or something to distract you. Whatever helps you get through it."

He nods, swallowing thickly.

"It would also be helpful to have people there to support you. Friends and family. Anyone you can lean on."

He glances back out the window and sets his jaw.

"I'll be there. Lochlan and the guys, too," I tell him. A fresh wave of sadness hits me. If I could take his pain away, I would. "And when you're up for it, you always have a place at the sanctuary."

"I'll come, too," Sienna says. "If you want me there."

Curtis turns to look at her, nodding subtly, choked with emotion. He's been through a lot, and this won't be an easy feat for him.

Chapter Thirty-Two

Liv

"You're being quiet again," I say after we're nearly back to my house. He hasn't spoken since we left the rehab center.

He scrubs a hand over his chin and sighs. "I wish it had been me. Hearing all the pain he is in... I don't know. Just feeling a lot of regret right now."

"You can't protect everyone, Hayes. You can't be everywhere at all times."

"Still, if I could take his place, I would."

My head jostles lightly against the headrest as I watch him stare stonily out the windshield as he drives. His left hand rests atop the wheel, but his right elbow leans against the center console as he fidgets with his fingers.

He looks cool on the outside, but his warring emotions are on the edge of bursting out of him. He's always had such a big heart, even though he refused to let people see it.

"The man you are today blows me away, too, Jensen," I admit softly.

His fingers still, turning to look at me as if he imagined the words he heard. My palm covers his hand, and I squeeze.

He merely blinks before turning his attention back to the road in front of him, but his thumb dances in circles on the inside of my wrist, sending tingles up my arm.

Things are different between us now. We always had friendship as the foundation of our relationship, but after years of living different lives, we're relearning each other… And the depth of what's building doesn't feel like friendship at all.

It's raw and simmering to the surface every time he looks at me. Especially when he touches me, giving me a glimpse of what's underneath.

As a girl, I desperately needed a friend, and Jensen filled that role. But as a woman, I have enough friends. What I want from him is beyond that.

I want to know how it feels to be at his mercy.

I want to feel everything he has to give.

My thighs rub together as I uncross my legs and recross them, and my pencil skirt rides higher, but when I move to fix it, his gaze falls to my legs…

I shouldn't play games with him, not when I don't know where things between us will lead… Or if it's even a good idea.

But when he looks at me like that, desire burns inside of me, and I can't think of anything else.

I shift in my seat again, settling his hand inches above my knee, and watch raptly as his calloused fingers grip my exposed thigh. They tighten and relax as he drags his palm back and forth, massaging every inch of bare skin from my knee to the edge of my skirt.

I'm a spectator to his teasing, melting into my seat as he touches me until my insides are burning.

A crazy woman would hike her skirt up and beg him to keep going, daring him to push it farther.

But I remember begging him to kiss me when we were kids. If he rejects me again, I don't think I'll be able to handle it, because what I want from him now is much bigger than a kiss.

I want him to make me forget everything.

"How many questions would you have if I didn't take you home right now?"

"What?" *All I want* is for him to take me home right now. I've been so focused on him that I hadn't realized he pulled into my driveway and stopped short.

But there is also another car in my driveway.

"Oh my God," I mumble. *Elliot.*

"I'll tell him to leave."

"No, I should talk to him and get it over with."

He sighs, gripping my thigh as he pulls the rest of the way down the driveway, and I'm not sure if he plans to let go.

"Thanks for bringing me home," I utter quietly, staring out the window at my front door. Elliot still has a key. He's probably waiting in the kitchen with a glass of scotch, waiting to lecture me.

"I'm not letting you go in there alone," Hayes says gruffly.

"It's just Elliot."

"As a lawyer, you should know this isn't an argument you're going to win."

I fling my door open, ripping my leg from his grasp, pretending that I don't immediately miss the warmth.

"Don't-" I point at him before we get to the porch, "start a fight."

"Yes, boss."

I roll my eyes and take a deep breath before entering my home. The space that keeps being violated over and over again by unwanted men.

"What the hell are you doing?" I screech as my point is proven once again.

Every drawer is opened, every cabinet. My bedroom door is wide open, and clothes are dumped on the bed.

"Where's the ring?" He yells, storming into the living room and coming to a halt when he sees Hayes behind me. "What the hell is he doing here?"

"The ring is none of your business. It was a gift, and I don't have any obligation to return it." I ignore his latter question, feeling the fumes rolling off of Hayes already because of the mess.

All Elliot has to do is light a match to ignite the explosion that's about to happen.

"That ring is worth more than this damn shack."

"Then it will do wonders for a charity of *my* choosing," I respond calmly. If I don't act bothered, maybe Hayes will behave.

"You bitch." As soon as I hear that word, my eyes slam shut. That's all it will take.

I expect the atomic bomb, but what I get is the soft click of the deadbolt on the door being locked.

I spin to face him, but he's not looking at me. He's looking at Elliot, and his eyes are wild with rage.

"Jensen, don't. He'll press charges and sue you if you leave a mark on him. Please, don't," I plead, grabbing his shirt.

He puts his hand over mine, squeezing briefly. "You're right."

I'm... right?

I was expecting more theatric–

My hair catches the wind as a high-performance machine darts past me, locking Elliot in a headlock.

"No!" I yell, but it doesn't matter. Hayes has him on his knees in an instant.

"Apologize."

Elliot grunts, unable to use his throat.

"Come on, you were so loud before. Apologize to her," he demands, and his bicep grows as he deepens his hold.

"Hayes, stop."

He looks at me, but his eyes are cold, now. Detached. "He called you a bitch, Olive." His voice is so low and menacing. I hardly recognize it.

"You promised." I look at him with pleading eyes. He can't go to jail again.

A seconds-long standoff takes place as he stares into my distress-filled eyes, begging him not to do this.

Finally, his arm loosens, and Elliot falls to a pile at his feet. Relief fills me when I don't have even the slightest urge to check on the man who ended up being the biggest slime-ball on the planet.

"That shouldn't leave a mark," Hayes says easily, standing over his body as if he didn't do anything out of the ordinary. But his chest heaves with his need to cause pain, and the veins in his forearms are prominent and angry, straining as he clenches his fists.

As a non-advocate for violence... He's a man who makes it look too damn appealing.

"Now what?" My palms slap my sides. Elliot is passed out on my floor, and there's no protocol in law school for how to handle this.

"Do you want to tie him up and go feed him to the bears?" I ask, and Hayes shrugs. "No." I look at him pointedly and rub my hand across my face in exasperation.

When I open my eyes, Elliot's body is gone, and Hayes is dragging him halfway out the back door. "What are you doing?" I squeal, running after him.

Is he going to toss him into the woods?

Bury him in my backyard?

I skid to a stop on my patio as he picks up Elliot's limp body and dumps him into the ice bath. He goes under for only a second before he pops back up, gasping for air.

Hayes is there, yanking his head back by the roots. "Apologize," he grits through his teeth, inches from his face.

"III- I'm sss-ssorry, Livvy." Hayes dunks his head under the ice water again.

"Don't fucking call her that. Don't say her name ever again. Don't come back. Ever. Again," he threatens.

Elliot nods, and Hayes yanks him out of the tub, letting him drop onto the concrete stones. "Get the fuck out of here, prick."

"Can I at least have a towel?" He begs pathetically.

"You could have given me an STD… But you want a towel?" I ask him with narrowed eyes. "Go ask the wedding planner for a towel."

He climbs to his feet, shivering like a fool. "You're going to regret this," he mumbles, and Hayes steps towards him until I hold up my hand.

"I guarantee that I won't. I want my key back." I hold out my hand, waiting for him to comply, and he does, grumbling as he fishes it out of his soaked suit pocket.

He throws it on the ground next to Hayes. "I'm sure your

dog will need it."

Hayes smiles menacingly, and Elliot starts backpedaling off the patio in a flurry.

When he steps to go after him, I stop him with a hand to his chest. "Down, boy."

He looks at me in surprised amusement. "Funny."

Suddenly, my feet are swept out from under me as I'm tossed over his shoulder.

I have to blow my hair out of my face as it dangles around my head, and I see Elliot staring at us in open-mouthed shock.

"Say bye to your ex, you'll never see him again," Hayes states seriously with a hearty slap to my ass, making me squeak. He doesn't give me an actual chance to respond before he's gliding effortlessly back into the cottage.

The entire backyard disappears from view, along with my ex-fiance, as I'm taken into the kitchen.

Chapter Thirty-Three

Hayes

As soon as I set her on her feet, she's pacing the length of the small kitchen, getting more heated with every pass. I don't know if she's going to wring my neck for manhandling her ex or manhandling her.

"What the fuck was that?"

"You didn't want me to beat him to death. I had to make it hurt somehow." I rub the palm that just slapped her ass, wishing I could have enjoyed that feeling a little longer, but I know I was out of line.

"You do realize that your actions have consequences, right?" She doesn't give me a chance to respond. "You keep promising that you're going to stick around, but the second someone scorns me, you're begging to be thrown back in jail."

"I can't stand by and let someone disrespect you."

She digs her fingers into her hair. "But I don't care. Don't you understand? Elliot can be as nasty as he wants, but it doesn't matter. He doesn't matter to me anymore."

"He had his ring on your finger, Olive."

"So?" She stares at me with furrowed brows. "Oh, I see. This isn't about him being mean to me today. You're mad that he had me and you didn't."

I squeeze my eyes shut, fighting the anger building up. "Of course, I'm mad. He got everything! He got your heart... Your trust. He got to touch you... And, I hate him for it."

"Well, clearly I shouldn't have given him my trust," she scoffs.

"What the hell did you see in him, Liv?"

"Really? You want to blame me?"

"No. I want to know why the woman who could have any man she wants chose some douche bag with a trust fund."

She shakes her head and starts pacing again.

"Tell me!"

"Because he was nothing like you!"

I stare at her in shock.

"Do you think I could look at anyone with blonde hair and blue eyes and see anything but the boy I loved and then lost?

"I tried finding someone else. Someone better. I dated my way through my college campus and law school. Do you know how many men asked me out?"

Okay, this is not what I want to hear.

"I couldn't look at anyone with a nice smile without wishing it was yours. God forbid a man looked like he knew how to throw a punch. So if you want to beat up every man I dated, and everyone I fucked, trying to erase you from my heart, then go ahead. They'd probably give you just as much fight as Elliot could."

"Liv," I start, but she cuts me off.

"No, Hayes. No. You don't get to judge me. I never wanted anyone else. *You* forced me to move on." She turns away, bracing her hands on the counter.

"Have you moved on?" I force the question from my

throat because I'm terrified to hear her response. She doesn't respond, hanging her head between her shoulders. "Does any part of you still want me, Olive?"

"I want you more than I've ever wanted anything in my life," she whispers, and all the air in my lungs escapes my chest. "But you destroyed me once, and I won't let you do it again."

She stiffens slightly as my front brushes against her back, reaching around her to cover her hands with mine.

"I'll do whatever you need me to, for as long as it takes. Just don't close the door on us. Not yet," I breathe, nuzzling into the side of her neck.

She gasps, reaching back to grab my nape, pulling me in closer. My lips trace her skin, and I feel her tremble against me. Her body already knows she's mine, but her mind won't accept it.

"Did it work?"

"What?" She shivers as my hand skims up her arm.

"Fucking guys who were nothing like me."

"No."

My palm traces down her rib cage until I reach her waist. "Did you think about me?"

"Yes."

I flatten my hand over her stomach, sandwiching our bodies together. My cock is stiff against her ass, and she whimpers when I shift my hips into her. "You know I'll fuck you better than anyone else."

She whimpers but doesn't respond as I snake my other hand up her neck, capturing her jaw. "Tell me, Olive." She shakes her head in defiance, and a smile quirks my lips.

"You fucked other women," she spews as if that's an argument.

"A few." She jerks in my arms, trying to get away from me, but that's not happening. "Turns out there are only so many leggy brunettes to choose from, and they don't like being called the wrong name."

She twists again, trying to escape my words. "Too many to keep their names straight?" She hisses.

"No, there's only one name that leaves my mouth when I cum, dove," I whisper, biting her ear.

This time, when she struggles, I let her spin in my arms, keeping her trapped between my body and the counter.

"You don't mean that." Her eyes narrow as she looks at me, but her pupils are blown wide, breathing shallowly as if she can fight how turned on she is.

"Ask me about my tattoo, again."

Her gaze dips to the numbers on the hand she asked about before.

50.1.5

"How well do you know Roman numerals?"

Her eyebrows scrunch, and she twists her head to look at the numbers more clearly. Then she shakes her head. "No," she gasps as she reads each number differently now.

L.I.V.

"Yes."

"You put my name on your hand?"

Each step is painful as I back away from her, taking off my white dress shirt. She watches me slip each button out of its hole until I pull it off and drop it to the floor.

I lift my arm to show her the inside of my bicep. "A marigold."

Her mouth pops open, recognizing her birth flower, and she doesn't fix it.

"You've seen these." I pull at the collar of my undershirt to reveal the olive branches.

When I pull at my t-shirt to remove it, her eyes pop open wide.

"Stop!" She rasps, desperately. "I don't want to see any more."

"All I've done is think about you, Olive. There's never been anyone else for me."

"I can't do this, Jensen. This is too much. I just broke things off with Elliot a few weeks ago."

"But you were never truly his, were you?"

She jerks her head to the side as if my words slapped her. "I need some space. The Porter trial starts tomorrow, and I need to focus."

I shake my head in frustration. "I'm not leaving you alone."

Her palms meet her temples, and she squeezes her head between her hands. "I can't be near you all the time. I need time to think, and I suffocate around you."

"Olive…"

"Please." Her voice cracks, and I know I can't be the cause of her suffering.

I'll do whatever she asks.

"Right… Get some rest. I'll see you in the morning."

"Only to and from work. I need you to leave after you drop me off."

"Liv…"

"You cut me off without any explanation, and I had to live with it for years. At least I'm taking it easy on you," she whispers.

"I guess I deserve that."

"I'll call if I need you," she states softly, but coldly, bottling herself up again.

I know it's my fault, but it doesn't make it hurt any less. I'm slowly dying, being tortured by decisions of the past, and all I can do is take the pain and bear it.

Hoping that it makes her pain even a millimeter less.

* * *

She gathers the paperwork she needs, double-checking each page as she files it away in her briefcase, ignoring me as if I'm not even in the room.

It's a painful reminder that she holds our fate in her hands. With each breath, I'm waiting for her to tell me to go and not to come back.

I don't know how I'll survive if she chooses life without me. I was barely living already before she came back to me.

Miley brings her a hot tea, and without a word, we're making our way to the courtroom. The way she catwalks in her heels is terrifying, because a woman that confident will eat your heart out, and every person in this building knows it.

Me, especially.

She takes one last sip of her drink, handing it off to the intern again, who scurries away to dispose of it, and takes her place behind the prosecutor's table. She's comfortable here, and without a hair out of place, she looks like she owns the room.

"Hi," Jo whispers, sliding in next to me in the first row. Lochlan beside her.

"What are you guys doing here?"

"Liv didn't think she'd need Lochlan to take the stand today, but she said it would look good for us to be here. To show a stand against Randall Porter and what he did."

This trial shouldn't be as intense as Jeremiah's next week because Randall didn't actually get his hands dirty. But we all know he's the evil mastermind.

The judge enters and goes through his normal motions, and nerves creep down my spine. This is the first real trial I've witnessed Liv partake in, and as confident in her abilities as I am, I don't know how she handles the pressure.

"Mr. Porter has fired his legal counsel and chooses to represent himself today. All testimony will be done under oath. Do you have any objections, Miss Greenwood?" Judge Fulton asks.

"No, your honor," she replies coolly, but there is humor in her voice. Porter is an idiot.

"Very well, proceed."

"Thank you, your honor. Ladies and gentlemen of the jury," she starts. "We have an obligation as a society to adhere to the laws that keep us safe. Protected. We're here today because Mr. Porter did not believe in following the law. He tried to take shortcuts, and people got hurt because of it.

"I realize that many of you might recognize the man in the courtroom today. He's from a local astute family. He was even the mayor of the neighboring town of Langston. Don't be fooled by his outward appearance. He has only let you see what he wants you to see.

"If you'll look this way." She points to a projector that the intern is manning. "These are the documents that he does not want you to see. Intimidation. Falsifying penal codes.

Blackmail. Extortion."

Some of the jurors scribble in their notepads as the different images flash on the screen. Images of papers that I've seen on Lochlan's kitchen table. All the attempts by Porter to steal his property.

"Mr. Porter wanted Mr. Dane's property. He didn't like that it wasn't for sale, and he really didn't like that he couldn't bribe his way to it. Mr. Porter is a bully–"

"Objection!" Porter screeches, but the judge puts his hand up to calm him down.

"Miss Greenwood," Judge Fulton urges.

"It's relevant, your honor."

"Proceed."

"Mr. Porter is a bully, but he could not bully Lochlan Dane. Does that man look like someone who can be threatened?" She gestures to Lochlan, and it takes everything in me not to smirk.

Lochlan hates this level of attention.

The jury looks aghast at Lochlan's intimidating presence, agreeing with Liv easily.

"So instead of taking his loss, Mr. Porter stooped low. He decided to harass Mr. Dane's property. His animals. His employees. Not only is this against the law, but it's simply unacceptable. We cannot take things that don't belong to us."

She takes a stroll from her table towards the jurors.

"Mr. Porter wants you to believe that his brother, Jeremiah, is at fault for all the damage he caused, but that is not the truth. He back-stabbed his brother in this very room, splitting from his defense to save himself. My guess? He split from his lawyer this morning for the same reason. Mr. Porter does not like to lose, but unfortunately for him, I'm here to ensure that happens today." She walks back to her table, but I'm not looking at her.

My eyes are glued to Porter behind his table. He's looking at Liv as if he's holding a knife to her throat, and I don't fucking like it.

His anger rattles his voice as he starts his own defense, but it's sloppy and not nearly as articulate as Liv's. I hardly hear his argument because each time his steps take him within feet of her, my body tenses.

I don't like this guy, and I don't like how she is forced to be close to him. He hates her guts.

"I did not have a hand in any violence, and the prosecutor cannot prove this. That is why she chooses to assassinate my character," he spews, pacing the floor.

"As many of you probably relate, I am not forced to be friends with my family members. I am not close to my brother. I am not his keeper. I had no say in his criminal actions. I think the lack of evidence from Miss Greenwood proves this." He sits in his seat and adopts a smug look on his face, preparing for Liv's counterargument.

She stands, rounding her desk before leaning against the table top with a casual air. She points her remote at the projector and clicks one time.

A screen filled with texts appears. "Mr. Porter's text history to his brother. You might have destroyed your phone, Mr. Porter, but your brother was not that smart."

She steps towards the jury as she speaks, and his evil eyes don't stray from her.

"Not only can we see just how often the two brothers communicated, but his exact words when requesting his brother to burglarize Second Chance Sanctuary. Damage

Second Chance Sanctuary, and worst of all… Assault and kidnap an employee at Second Chance Sanctuary. And, his panicked text messages to you when his actions went too far."

"Bullshit! These should be inadmissible."

"If you hadn't fired your lawyer, Mr. Porter, he would have taken care of that for you," Judge Fulton explains dully. "Can you explain why you think they should be removed as evidence?"

Porter's silence lingers.

"Didn't think so. Proceed, Miss Greenwood."

"Mr. Porter did not physically put his hands on another person, but his actions directly resulted in one Second Chance Sanctuary employee being kidnapped and held against her will, and another nearly losing his life."

"I didn't tell him to beat the man to death!" He cries.

"So, you admit that you did speak to your brother?"

"Wait, no!"

"Mr. Porter," Judge Fulton thunders. "Sit down. Stop speaking out of turn. You're under oath, and she hasn't finished yet."

"Mr. Porter, do you admit to unlawful harassment of Mr. Dane?" Liv hammers him while he's still shaken up from the judge's hand-smack.

"No."

"Did you create unlawful documents in an attempt to obtain Mr. Dane's land?"

"No."

"Mr. Porter, do you admit to conspiring with your brother to commit crimes against Second Chance Sanctuary?"

"No!" He pounds his fists on his table in frustration.

"Last question, and remember you are under oath, Mr.

Porter," she continues calmly despite my need to jump across this bar and put a wall between her and Randall Porter.

"Did you conspire to kidnap JoAnna Montgomery?"

He hangs his head. "No," he utters, losing his fight.

"Then why do your text messages say otherwise?" She adds at the end, speaking directly to the jury instead of giving him a chance to respond. "That's all, your honor."

"Mr. Porter, your closing statement." He doesn't look at the judge. "Mr. Porter," Judge Fulton encourages again. When Porter doesn't move or speak, he hits his gavel. "We'll go to recess while the jury deliberates."

Liv packs her briefcase slowly as Porter is led to another room, but as soon as the courtroom begins to empty, she spins around to face us. "I totally got him!" She beams, and I'm struck by it, grateful to be on the receiving end of it.

"You did great," I tell her, breathing for the first time in nearly two hours.

"Sorry to call you out. I knew you wouldn't show if I warned you about it," she says to my side.

"No, it was great, really captivated the jury," Jo agrees, but Lochlan only grunts.

"Now, what?"

"We have to wait until the jury comes to a decision. Could be ten minutes, could be hours. You guys don't have to stay for this part. I appreciate you coming." Liv and Jo hug, giggling about how pretty they both are or something, as I move over to talk to Lochlan.

"She's the most important person in the world to me, Loch. You can at least humor her with a few words when she speaks to you."

He looks at me like he might snap back, but he sighs,

reconsidering. "I'll work on it," he grumbles. "Jo really likes her, too. It won't be long until they suggest a double date."

"I'd love to buddy. All you had to do was ask." I slap him on the shoulder, and he tells me to fuck off under his breath.

Now if I could just get her to go out on a date with me first...

Chapter Thirty-Four

Liv

It feels good to make a grown man nearly cry in front of a room full of his peers. Really gets my blood pumping.

"Miley, go grab a quick lunch. You did well in there!" I yell to her as I stroll into my office, Hayes right behind me.

"Wow, complimenting the intern. You're on a high right now," he teases, shutting my office door. Despite the boundary I put up between us, he's remained his same charming self, and I'm thankful.

It's hypocritical of me, but I don't think I could handle it if he were cold towards me.

"Feels good to win." My smile stretches over my cheeks, and he shakes his head in amusement.

"The jury hasn't decided yet."

"Doesn't matter. I know I won." I shrug, sitting back in my desk chair.

"I'd be terrified to face you in court, Liv."

"Aw, that's sweet of you to say."

He chuckles. "Do you want me to get you some lunch?"

I shake my head.

"More tea?"

Another shake of my head.

"Do you want me to tell you how hot you looked handing Randall Porter's ass on a plate?"

"Mmm, maybe. Hold onto that idea." I stand up, waltzing towards him. His hands flex, but he doesn't move, watching me as I get closer. "Thank you for sitting in there, even if it wasn't fun being in a courtroom again."

"Not a problem, boss." The corner of his mouth kicks up in a grin as he looks down at me.

"You don't need to call me that. You've never cashed a single check I've offered for your services." I plant my hands on his chest softly, feeling his breath catch.

"I don't want your money." He looks at me seriously, searching my eyes, probably trying to figure out my wishy-washy behavior.

I practically tell him to fuck off one minute and then can't keep my hands off of him another. I'm a mess.

"I know. Thanks for being here, anyway," I whisper, meaning it wholeheartedly.

"Always." He covers my hands with his, and I fight the urge to lean in more… To take more.

He would do anything I want, but I'm too conflicted to let him.

He sighs, rubbing his thumb over the back of my hand. "I didn't like seeing how heated Porter got. It's a reminder of how much danger you can be in. Between your stalker and the nature of your job…"

"I love my job. Making people mad doesn't scare me." I've had enough people tell me that I have no business in law just because I'm a woman, and I don't need to hear it from him.

I start to tug my hands away, but he holds them tight.

"I know you love it. I'll be here to make sure you never have anything to be scared of. That's all I'm saying."

"Oh." I wasn't expecting that. "Next week will be worse. Jeremiah is the violent one."

"Are you worried?" He asks, smiling softly.

"No," I breathe as he tucks my hair behind my ear.

He leans in, and I stop breathing altogether. "That's because you know I'll take care of you."

I don't think we're talking about the courtroom anymore, and I can't stop staring at his mouth.

"Miss Greenwood, I brought you a sandwich–" He jumps away, smoothing his hand over his chest as my hands fall. "Oh. I'm sorry. I'll come back." Miley runs back out the door.

"She really needs to learn to knock," I grumble.

"I'm sorry, I shouldn't have…" he motions between us like he's flustered, and I'm not sure what he's apologizing for. "You're at work."

"Don't…" I start, and he glances at me. "Don't be sorry," I tell him softly, not quite meeting his gaze.

I'm so conflicted by my feelings, but it's not because I don't want him… It's because I want him so badly it hurts, and I know how dangerous that is.

Giving him my heart again is a lot scarier than my job will ever be.

I pop out of my office to clear the fog from my head and to get whatever Miley was going to give me, but she's talking to someone by the stairwell.

I can't see his face. He has dark hair and appears to be older than her, quite a bit taller, too.

"Who was that?" I ask when she scampers back.

"Oh, that's my boyfriend. We're both sort of new to this

area. I was just asking him if he thought I should ask you and Mr. Hayes out for drinks sometime. Since it seems like you two are… Something."

We're something alright… *Just not sure what that something is.*

"That's really sweet of you, but I don't think it would be appropriate since I am your boss. Maybe once your internship ends," I tell her kindly, though with empty intent.

"Of course. Here you go!" She hands me a bagged lunch, and I turn to see Hayes watching our interaction with amusement on his face.

"Shut up," I whisper as I walk past him.

"That's the second double date I've been offered today."

"What? Who–" I don't have a chance to finish before my phone rings.

The verdict is in.

* * *

"On count one: Conspiring to unlawfully inhabit land. We, the jury, find the defendant guilty.

"Count two: Conspiring to burglarize. We, the jury, find the defendant guilty." I don't react as the head juror reads the verdicts. I'm a professional at maintaining my composure while Porter is growing more agitated in his seat.

"Count Three: Conspiring to kidnap. We, the jury, find the defendant guilty."

Porter's hands hit the table, and Judge Fulton gives him a warning glare.

"Count Four: Conspiring to assault. We, the jury, find the defendant not guilty." I take the blow coolly, letting the disappointment wash over me quietly.

That one was a long shot since Randall didn't know about Jeremiah's beating of Curtis until afterward. But it was worth it to try to stick it to him.

"In light of these decisions, I have the duty to uphold the law, Mr. Porter. You are sentenced to four years in a state penitentiary. Time served. Eligible for parole in two years." He hits his gavel, and I exhale in relief.

This was the easy one. Next week, it's my job to put Jeremiah away for a lot longer.

"I can't go to prison," Randall yells, swiping his table of all his paperwork.

"My ruling is final, Mr. Porter. This court is adjourned. I suggest you leave quietly with the deputy." The old man walks towards him, preparing to cuff him, but Randall jumps away.

Before I can react, a wall falls in front of me. Not a wall… Hayes.

He stands between us as Porter throws a temper tantrum. The older deputy attempts to grab him, but fails again. Within seconds, Sheriff Malec is striding to the front of the room.

"Randall Porter, you are being detained per Judge Fulton's ruling. If you resist, you will be charged with resisting and causing a disturbance." He grabs his arm and easily yanks it behind his back to put him in cuffs.

"Fuck you," he spits at the Sheriff. "And fuck you, too!" He yells towards me.

Hayes stiffens, but he doesn't react rashly, and I know it's solely for my benefit. He doesn't want to embarrass me at work.

"Make sure he gets in the transport van with no issues," Malec tells the other deputies as they take Randall off his hands. "I had a feeling there wouldn't be a smooth ending to this. If Jeremiah's trial goes without trouble, I'll be shocked," he says as I start packing up my table.

Hayes is too still beside me.

"It'll be fine." I squeeze his arm, and he finally nods his head, shaking off his rigidness.

"I wanted to wait until today's proceedings were over, but I'd like to discuss some things with you regarding your stalker," Malec says under his breath.

There are still plenty of people in the room that I'd rather not know about my personal situation.

"Sure, let's go to my office."

Hayes grabs my briefcase before I can and holds the swinging gate open to lead me out of the courtroom. I'm afraid that I'm getting too comfortable with this special treatment.

"What is that smell?" My face pinches as I step into my office. "It smells like pee." If someone pissed in my office, I'm going to freak out.

Jensen is the first one to investigate, sniffing around to find the source while Malec calls for someone to bring him his forensic kit.

"It's your lunch." He leans into the brown bag that Miley brought me. I left it untouched before the verdict.

"It didn't smell like that before."

"The food was fresh. It might have hidden the smell, but now it's been sitting for an hour."

"Someone peed on my lunch?"

He shakes his head. "I think it's ammonia. They used it all the time in the prison."

"Don't touch it," Malec tells him, pulling on rubber gloves. He gently opens the bag, pulling out the sandwich inside, and puts it into a crime scene bag.

This is unreal.

"Your assistant brought you this?" Malec asks after he seals all the bags.

"My intern. But she's just a kid. She wouldn't have done this."

"You didn't ask for lunch, Liv. She brought you this willingly," Hayes says, his face hard with anger.

"We get this from the restaurant across the street almost every day. I always order the same thing, she was just being nice. What if someone came in here after we went down to the courtroom?"

"Maybe." Malec looks at me like he's trying to choose his words wisely. "I'll have to question her."

"No, absolutely not. Not without a lawyer."

"You can't represent her, Liv," he tells me sympathetically. "You can trust me."

I look at Hayes for support, but when he turns to look at me, I can tell that is not what I'm going to get. "I don't like cops, but I trust Malec. I think you should, too."

"Traitor," I mumble. "Fine. But give her the opportunity to obtain her own lawyer, and I'll be watching. I swear to God, Malec, if you trap her into some bogus confession, I'll ruin your life."

He puts his hands up. "I wouldn't dare." His lack of defensiveness makes me believe him.

I nod, and he leaves, taking the evidence with him.

"If you had eaten that, it would have destroyed your insides," Hayes grits through his teeth, finally letting his rage show. "If I find out it was the fucking intern all this time..."

"It's not," I say, mostly confident.

But that means we're nowhere closer to finding out who my stalker really is.

Chapter Thirty-Five

Hayes

"Are you sure you don't want a lawyer present?" Malec asks Miley on the other side of the glass partition.

Liv and I are standing silently behind the window, she's watching them, but I'm watching her. Having someone so close to her be a suspect is bothering her more than she'll admit.

She hasn't been the biggest fan of her intern, but they spend hours a day together. That's a type of betrayal she isn't ready to accept.

"I didn't do anything wrong. I don't need a lawyer."

"Idiot," Liv mumbles.

"Why did you decide to bring Miss Greenwood lunch earlier today?"

"I was already getting my own lunch across the street. It wasn't any more trouble to bring hers."

"Do you do that regularly?"

"Well, yes, kind of. I bring her lunch all the time, but normally she tells me ahead of time when she wants something. I usually order it and then walk over to get it."

"But today was different?"

"Yes. I didn't know she wanted anything until I was already there."

"What do you mean?"

"The guy at the counter handed me her usual order when he handed me mine."

"Did you pay for both?"

"No, it was already paid for."

"By who?"

"I don't know, I didn't ask. I assumed Miss Greenwood's bodyguard called it in after I left the office."

Liv glances at me. Miley has no idea how complicated our relationship is.

"You picked up the lunches and walked straight back to the office?"

"Um, yes."

"Did you come straight back to the office after picking up the lunches?" Malec asks again.

She hesitates.

"What did you do after you picked up the lunches?"

"I stopped to see my boyfriend. He was outside the courthouse, waiting to say hi to me."

"Who is your boyfriend?"

She bites her lip, avoiding the question.

"Miley, you're not in trouble. I'm trying to get the big picture here. Miss Greenwood has had issues with unwanted attention, and I need to rule out everyone that I can."

"My boyfriend's name is Landon... I met him a few months ago."

Liv's shoulders stiffen, and my fists clench.

Mr. Arkett.

Malec doesn't make any obvious reaction, continuing his

questioning without skipping a beat.

"Where did you meet him?"

"He is a professor at my college. But I'm 19, it's not illegal."

"I know, Miley. You're not in trouble." She nods, and he keeps going. "Did Landon hold the lunches for you at any time?"

"No. I mean, I left them sitting on the park bench between us for a few minutes while we talked, but he never touched them."

"Are you sure?"

"Yes. We only had a few minutes. We mostly kissed." Her cheeks flush. "And then he asked me about work, and then I came back inside."

"What did he ask you about work?"

"He asked if my day was going okay? If my boss was being nice to me…" She looks down in embarrassment.

"What did you tell him?"

"I told him that she's been happier since her bodyguard has been around. She isn't so short with me."

She glances at me again, but this time I reach for her, threading my fingers through hers. She turns her attention back to the interview, but her hand squeezes mine.

"What did Landon say?"

"He asked to walk me to my desk, but I told him no."

"Was he okay with that?"

"Yes. I came back to the office alone, but I left my scarf outside on the bench, so he had to bring it back to me anyway."

"How nice of him," Malec compliments dully. "Do you have a photo of Landon?"

"Um, no. He didn't want to have any photos in case someone from the college found out about us and gave him a hard time, but he's very sweet. He gives me flowers all the time."

"Can you tell me where he orders them from?"

"Why?"

"Honestly, it's my wife's birthday tomorrow. I need to send her something before she bites my head off," he lies.

I know he would never be so careless about getting Natalie a gift... And they already celebrated her birthday a month or two ago.

I hate that I know that, and I think that means Malec is my friend.

"Oh, he orders from the Blue Ridge Florist Company online. He says that they're more efficient than the local flower shops."

And anonymous. That's the same florist Liv's stalker used.

"Thank you, I'll have to check it out. Can you write down Landon's phone number for me?"

"Why?"

"I'd like to talk to him, too. Rule out his involvement in today's incident."

"I don't know..."

"Someone tried to hurt Miss Greenwood. The faster we can rule out innocent parties, the faster we'll catch the person who wants to hurt her."

"Okay... I guess." He hands her a notepad, and she pulls out her phone to find the number she needs.

"What's Landon's last name? So, I know when I call him?"

"It's Smith."

"Ah, right. Thank you. You're free to go."

She scurries out the far door, and Malec turns in his seat to look at us through the window.

Someone is lying.

Chapter Thirty-Six

Liv

My laptop jostles in my lap as Hayes drives me home. He hasn't spoken since we left Malec's office, and I haven't been able to shut my brain off.

I can't fathom that Mr. Arkett is the one stalking me. It's been so long, and I've never had any reason to believe he's held onto any idea of me.

I don't use Facebook, I haven't logged on in years, but I open it reluctantly, searching 'Landon Arkett'.

A few profiles come up in the results, but I think I've forced my brain to forget what he looks like. I have to click on each one before I recognize anyone. Even the profile that I think belongs to him doesn't convince me.

It's private, but there are profile photos visible when you click through them. It isn't until I see the one from years ago with visible facial scarring that I realize that I definitely have the right guy.

Still, there isn't any reason for me to believe that he's up to no good. All his profile pictures over the last ten years are boring. One in sunglasses. One with a woman I don't recognize. A sports team he must like. And, a selfie that looks like he did when he was my teacher.

"What are you looking so serious at?" Hayes asks as he pulls into my driveway. I shut my laptop quickly.

"I forgot to send an important email."

I shouldn't lie to him, but I'm terrified of what will happen with Arkett back in the picture. If we find out that he's my stalker, chaos will follow.

Hayes will lose his temper, and I can't deal with the repercussions. Not again.

"Are you sure you don't want me to stay?" He asks after walking me to my door.

"I'll be okay. I'll keep my doors locked."

He doesn't look nearly satisfied, but he only grits his teeth.

"I need to prep for Jeremiah's trial next week." I don't know why I tell him that, but I can't come up with anything else to say.

He nods, tipping his head to look at me as if he's debating something before he tugs on my blazer to pull me in for a hug.

I savor the way it feels because I'm too weak to miss out on a chance to be held. Especially when I'm already warring with myself about wanting him to stay.

But despite how desperately I want to forgive him for all the heartbreak he put me through, I can't forget how it felt. And that is the only way I can get myself to pull back.

His lips brush my forehead as he turns to leave, though, and I feel more of the bad memories fade away…

Replaced by something new.

* * *

They tell you not to bring your work home with you, but it's the only way that I'm making it through the days without having an existential crisis.

Every day, Hayes drops me off at home, and I lie about wanting him to stay. I immediately distract myself with my case, ignoring my heart and the way it aches for him.

I pretend all day to be fine, and suffer all evening because I'm trying to resist his irrefutable pull.

And yet, when there is a knock on my door, his face is who I hope for first.

"Surprise!" Thea says when I open the door. "We came to check on you."

I let her and baby Kate in, her little blonde curls bouncing as Thea carries her inside. She reaches for me, and my heart melts.

There is nothing that a sweet baby can't fix. "How's my girl, today?"

"Oh, I'm fine, thanks," Thea giggles at herself. "Kate's cutting some teeth. She's been a little grumpy."

"I don't believe her, Kate. You're an angel." I swing her around in circles, dancing through my living room before hitting the snack cabinet.

"So why are you really here?" I ask after setting Kate up with her favorite puffs.

"Just checking in." Thea smiles.

"We text all day long and have three separate conversations happening at any given moment. Why the sudden visit?"

"Hayes has called Jesse three times this week, wanting to

know if you were okay."

The pit in my stomach I've been trying to ignore grows heavier. "I'm fine."

"Obviously, you are not fine because despite our hundreds of texts back and forth all week long, you failed to mention a rift happening between you and him or that your old teacher might be your stalker."

"Mr. Arkett is not involved. It has to be a mistake. And, there isn't a rift happening. The rift was already in place. Nothing has changed."

"Oh, Liv." She looks at me sympathetically.

"What?"

"You're so cute when you try to lie to me."

"I am not lying."

"Wow, this is worse than I thought. You're really fighting this."

"I'm not fighting anything. Being around Hayes is just so… Intense. He acts like just yesterday we were still best friends, and the last 11 years never happened. Like he's waited for me all this time…" I shake my head in disbelief.

"What if he has?"

"I can't believe that."

"Why not? You said yourself that you would have waited for him."

"That was a long time ago."

"Was it?"

Kate squeals, and I look at her, avoiding Thea's knowing gaze. "It doesn't matter. He stole my choice from me all those years ago. He changed my life, and I had no say in it. How am I supposed to get over that?"

"Is your life so horrible?"

"Of course it isn't."

"Then how do you know he wasn't right? Do you think it was easy for him to accept that you were better off without him?"

"Why are you taking his side?"

"I'm not. I'm on your side, and I think your stubbornness is only punishing both of you."

"That's not fair."

"I see the way you light up with him. I've never seen you like that with a man, not even Elliot."

"Yeah, Elliot was a sick joke."

"No, Elliot was a safe bet. Or, so you thought." She sighs. "You didn't have to unthaw your entire heart for him because you weren't in love with him."

"I loved him."

"But you weren't madly in love."

"No, I wasn't."

"You're in love with Hayes."

I hang my head in my hands. "It's not that easy."

"It can be. He's made it pretty clear where he stands, but he's waiting for you, and he doesn't get to make the choice this time."

He doesn't get to make the choice this time.

Hours after Thea and Kate leave, I pull his dress shirt from under my pillow, the one he left behind last week, and I bury my face in it like I have every night.

I slide my arms through the sleeves, draping it over my satin pajama set, and stare at my reflection in the mirror. The fabric of his shirt touches my skin, and tears well in my eyes because I'm craving his touch so desperately.

Memories of this same feeling haunt me. I drop to my

knees, digging out my suitcase from under my bed. There's only one thing inside when I open it.

A faded gray hoodie. More illegible than the day I received it because of the nights I cried myself to sleep in it.

The months that it went unwashed.

The panic attacks it endured.

I caress the rough fabric, remembering all the bad that it's seen.

I had this sweatshirt, and he had a photograph.

That wasn't a photograph that he kept tucked away in a drawer. He must've held it as many times as I've held this sweatshirt. The edges were worn, and the image was discolored.

Except when our reminders started to fade, I tried desperately to move on... I focused on my career, stuck to my life's plan, and ignored how hollow I was inside.

He tattooed permanent reminders of me on his skin so he wouldn't forget.

I wanted to erase him, and he refused to lose those pieces of me. I didn't even let him show me all of them.

He doesn't get to make the choice this time.

I have to see him.

I snatch my keys off the kitchen counter, and I don't slow down when I realize how hard it's raining outside. I jump in my car, pedaling down on the accelerator.

My windshield wipers work overtime as I struggle to see through the dark downpour, but I don't stop.

Second Chance Sanctuary is ghostly dark when I pull through the gates. The house is barely lit, and the lone floodlight by the barn is casting light on the streams of water coming down.

I still don't hesitate, jumping out of my car to bust into the garage. I stand there catching my breath, inhaling the thick scent of oil and gasoline, but he's not here.

The garage is empty.

I look down at my dingy slippers for the first time and my soaked clothes. His dress shirt is molded over my body, sticking to my skin. I can't go into the bunkhouse like this.

"Liv?"

I spin around, startled by a voice that doesn't belong to Jensen. Lochlan is standing in the doorway with soaked hair dangling over his concerned forehead.

"Do you know where Hayes is?"

"Is he expecting you?"

"No."

He scrubs his hand over his chin. "If he's not here, he'd only be in one other place, but you'll have to follow me."

Chapter Thirty-Seven

Hayes

I never planned when I'd become a homeowner. It was always a goal I had in the back of my mind, but my place was at the sanctuary. I had no reason to leave.

But when a future I wanted desperately was dangled in front of my eyes, I knew my time in the bunkhouse needed to come to an end.

The property next door to the sanctuary had been abandoned and then taken by the bank after years of illegal comings and goings. Lochlan spent hours crunching numbers, trying to figure out a way he could purchase the property himself to expand the sanctuary, but more so to eliminate the potential of getting new bad neighbors. Seedy shit happening next door to his bears is too risky.

Three-quarters of this property borders his, and now I'm his new neighbor.

Unfortunately, the house is in major disrepair. It's not just a fixer-upper; it was nearly condemned and demolished.

I had no business taking on such a project, but it felt like the right thing. I'd finally have a place of my own, and I could ease some of Lochlan's burdens after years of him easing mine.

That alone made it worth it, but I've still been cursing like a sailor every time a floorboard gives under my foot or something new starts to leak.

I've had a lot of time this week to submerge myself in the mess.

I've taken my frustration out with my hammer and worked myself like a dog instead of thinking about Liv.

She's still all I think about, but the projects have kept me from camping out in her driveway. Malec assured me he put extra patrols out in her area. Thea and Jesse were kind enough to give me enough details to know that she was in one piece when I couldn't have eyes on her.

I feel like I'm barely holding all of my pieces together. She's finally close, but it doesn't matter. She'll never forgive me for the past.

Now, I have to live with it.

I rock back and forth in my first housewarming gift from Lochlan and Jo, staring out at the sheets of rain coming down. There are at least five buckets inside catching drips already, and I suspect I'll find more holes in the roof by morning. I'm almost positive there are bullet holes in the siding, too.

A slow sigh escapes me right before headlights sweep across my driveway, and two vehicles pull up the overgrown grassy lane. The landscape is entirely in disarray, but I wasn't expecting visitors. No one even knows I'm here besides Lochlan.

His bronco pulls toward the porch, blinding me momentarily with his headlights as I stand to greet him, but he only flashes and makes a U-turn. Once he flips around, I can see the other car clearly, and my feet start moving on their own.

Liv's Jaguar comes to a stop, and I'm at her door before she cuts the engine. "What's wrong? What happened?" I ask in a panic, flinging her door open, barely giving her room to get out.

"Nothing, I'm fine." She swipes her already soaked hair away from her face. It's dripping down her shoulders onto her– *my shirt*. It's molded to her body, and her legs are completely bare. Her shoes are... Mud-caked slippers.

"You're okay?" She doesn't look like a woman who is okay.

She doesn't respond, but a shiver rolls over her, and I usher her to the porch anyway.

"What's going on?" I finish swiping the hair out of her face that's stuck to her skin, but she's still just looking at me.

"You're freaking me out." I hold her face between my hands, searching her enigmatic eyes. "Did something happen, baby?" I coax her softly, and her damp lashes flutter.

"I want to see the rest," she admits, trembling slightly.

"The rest of what?"

"Your tattoos."

"You came here at night in a rain storm because–"

"Yes," she cuts me off, gripping my hands where they rest on either side of her head. "I need to see all of them."

She's serious. In fact, I don't think she's ever been more serious about anything, and whatever her reasoning is, it is obviously extremely paramount.

"Let me get you inside to get dry and warm." She lets me take her in, but that's as far as we get.

"How many times did you look at the photograph of us? The one I saw at the bunkhouse."

"Liv..."

"How many times?"

"I don't know. A million. Maybe more."

Her breath catches. "Every day?"

"Every hour if I could."

She's so closed off, I still can't tell if my response is good or bad. I don't know if it's what she wanted to hear or not.

"And the tattoos… Why did you get the tattoos?"

"Prison is dark and ugly… I was struggling to find reasons to live. You were already a part of me on the inside, but I needed to be able to see it on the outside, to keep moving forward."

"I didn't know you were allowed to get tattoos in prison."

"You're not." A small smirk tilts my lips. "I did most of them myself in my cell. The more difficult ones, I let someone else do once I got out."

Her eyes blink in shock. "You got more even after you were free?"

"I was free from prison, but I wasn't free from you, Olive."

She steps forward, wrapping her fingers in my wet t-shirt, looking up at me with those big, beautiful eyes. "Let me see them," she demands breathlessly.

I oblige, pulling my shirt over my head, letting her hands fall to my naked skin. Right above the one that means the most to me.

She gasps softly, tracing the letters under my sternum.

No secret meanings, nothing to decipher. Just the name of the woman who owns me.

"It's always been you, Olive."

She blinks up at me again, but this time there's heat behind her eyes. She's looking at me like she did in her office, the way I haven't been able to stop thinking about. When her gaze falls to my lips, my breath stills in my chest.

"Don't," I plead reluctantly, and her eyes snap to mine.

"Don't kiss me until you mean it. With your entire soul."

She blinks at me, but doesn't respond.

"I've waited for this, for you, for well over a decade. And, I'll wait longer if you're not ready, but when you are… It's the end. All the bullshit, all the lines drawn in the sand. I'm yours, I always have been. I'm only waiting for you to choose me so I know I fulfilled my promise not to derail your life."

"What about your life? You'd wait forever if I never gave in to this?" She whispers huskily, still trembling in her wet clothes.

"My life doesn't exist without you."

"Don't say that. I almost married someone else."

I thread my fingers into her hair. "I'd still be here, even if it meant watching you get married to someone else. Watching you have children. Sending them off to college after giving them the childhood we always dreamed about. I'd watch from afar as your hair grays and your body weakens. I'd wait until your last breath and then take my own so I could be with you every possible second."

"Jensen," she breathes, wrapping her hands around the back of my neck and drawing my head closer to hers.

"I'd wait for you forever, Olive. But I won't live a day on this earth without you."

The final inch between us disappears as she forces her lips to mine, taking exactly what she wants, and kissing me mercilessly.

My Olive.

I palm the back of her neck, pulling her closer until her damp body molds to mine because I'm convinced I'm dreaming. I've waited for this for so long. A soft whimper escapes her throat, and I respond fervently, needing all of it. All of her.

My tongue swipes at her lips, and they open on a gasp as I delve inside. She's as sweet as I imagined.

Her nails dig at my neck and my chest, demanding more.

God, I want to give her everything.

Electricity shoots down my spine when she bites at my bottom lip, and a groan rumbles my chest, making her still. Her hooded gaze is filled with excited wonder as she leans in again, nibbling along my jawline.

"Fuck," I moan, completely at her mercy as her lips graze the spot below my ear and continue downward.

Her teeth scrape along my neck, and when she sinks them into my collarbone, I'm nearly a goner.

"Olive," I beg breathlessly, lifting her by her ass and forcing her legs around my waist. My fingers dig into her soft flesh as her center settles over my stomach, and I almost forget how to use words. "Are you sure you want this? Me?"

She tips her head back, looking at me tenderly before capturing my mouth in a gentle kiss. "It's all I ever wanted."

Joy and relief hit me all at once, and I sink to my knees with her in my arms. "I've waited so long," I breathe, resting my head against her chest as she wraps her arms around me, holding me close.

"It feels like a lifetime," she whispers into my hair.

I tip my head back to look at her. "I've loved you since the moment I set eyes on you. I'll love you for the rest of my life, dove."

Her breath catches. "Are you sure?"

I nod, and she can't squeeze her eyes shut tight enough to stop the tears that escape. "Meeting you changed my life. I knew it even back then," she says, wiping at her tears. "Your karate sweatshirt is so faded now," she laughs, smiling at me sweetly.

"I can find a new sweatshirt to give you."

"No, I like the one I have." Her smile widens, and I can't help but mirror it. This time, when I kiss her, it isn't urgent.

I capture her lips gently, savoring her like I dreamed about so many nights. Even if it takes another lifetime, I'll make up for the moments we lost.

She giggles as I kiss her cheeks and nose, battling with me to bring my lips to hers so she can kiss me back.

"I love you, Jensen. I'm trusting you not to break my heart," she utters against my lips, and I still.

"I won't lose you twice. I'll chase you to the ends of the earth before I let that happen, again." I hold her face, forcing her to see the truth in my eyes, but I don't expect to see hers flare.

"Is that what you want? To be chased?"

"I always wanted you to come for me," she admits, resting her forehead on mine. "I hoped you'd steal me away and take what was yours."

My cock flexes against my zipper, and I can feel her heat through her barely there silky shorts. "You've always been mine," I growl, thrusting against her.

"Always yours," she whispers, shifting her hips atop me until it turns to a languid grind. Like she can't help herself.

"You're so sexy," I utter as she rides me, snaking my hands up her spine under her tiny satin tank top. "Is this what you wear to bed every night?"

She nods, smiling. She knows exactly what she does to me.

"But not this." I peel my dress shirt off her body, stealing it only to see more of her.

"I've slept in it every night this week."

"I'll give it back once it's dry."

Chapter Thirty-Eight

Liv

"This is wet, too." I let my finger drag down the satin on the center of my chest, watching his eyes follow it.

"I've been a very patient man, Olive." His finger hooks the thin strap above my shoulder. "But I won't be gentle."

The strap falls down my arm, and so does the satin, exposing my right breast. He stares at the perky flesh in a trance until his thumb brushes the dainty barbell donning my nipple, and I gasp.

"Did it hurt?" He leans closer until his lips nearly brush the sensitive peak.

"Yes." I tremble in his arms, not even close to being cold.

"You liked the pain, didn't you?" The warmth of his tongue covers my nipple, and I throw my head back as he sucks, tugging my piercing into his mouth.

"I did," I admit, writhing in his lap as he feasts on my breast.

My answer pleases him because in the next moment, my left breast is ripped free from my pajama top, and the fabric pools around my waist as he attacks.

My arms anchor his shoulders and neck, clinging to him

as he licks, bites, and sucks at my breasts. My skin quickly paints the picture of his attention, marred with pink love bites and marks of affection.

He's not going easy on me, but I know he could do worse. "Does this place have a bed?" I beg as he licks a path between my breasts.

He smiles against my chest, kissing my skin. "More like a mattress in the middle of the floor."

"Perfect."

He laughs, lifting me effortlessly as he stands, but then he sets me lightly on my feet. "I'd carry you chivalrously up the stairs, but I'm afraid a board will give out."

"That's okay." I back away from him towards the staircase, letting my top fall down my legs. His gaze is heavy on my naked chest until my fingers play at the waistband of my shorts.

"Let me," he pleads, dropping to his knees in front of me to replace my hands with his own. My shorts slide down my thighs, and he moans as he admires my nakedness for the first time.

"Everything you imagined?" I breathe as his face hovers inches from my soaked center.

"Better." His tongue swipes up my slit, and my knees nearly give out. "So much better."

He buries his head between my thighs, and I have to grip the banister to keep myself from collapsing. But he's devouring me, and the pleasure building in my core is stealing strength from the rest of my body.

His big hands lower me to the steps, continuing his assault on my clit as he squeezes my ass. When his tongue penetrates me, my vision blurs.

It doesn't matter that I'm butt naked on a dusty staircase; all I care about is Jensen Hayes between my thighs.

My hips jerk, and I know I'm close when he sucks my clit between his lips and tugs. "Oh my God, yes," I cry, thrusting against his face for more.

His fingers grip my thighs roughly, spreading my legs wider as he tastes every inch of me, licking every fold and crease, fucking my pussy with his tongue, and teasing the entry of my ass.

He's taking every part of me for himself, and I'm completely at his mercy. He can have anything he wants from me, but I'm a burning ball of need, and I want to cum so desperately I could cry.

"Please, I'm dying, please," I beg, tugging at his hair, but he doesn't relent, swirling his tongue into my pussy again as if he can't get enough. His fingers open my lips wide as he dips his tongue into my hole over and over, fucking me with it, and trying to go deeper with every thrust.

Then he pushes a finger inside, and my eyes roll back. "Jensen," I plead, letting my head fall back onto the steps.

He goes slow, adding another finger, reveling in exploring me for the first time. His mouth dances over my clit, making love to it with his tongue, and my eyes flutter as each wave of pleasure builds higher, bringing me closer to the brink.

He's torturing me, and it's only fueling my addiction to him. My need to have all of him is consuming me.

Just when I think he's going to push me to the edge and give me what I want… He pulls back, sliding his finger through my folds and disrupting the momentum he had.

"You did that on purpose," I accuse, whining at him.

"I've waited a long time for this, Olive." He squeezes the

globe of my ass roughly as he bites my inner thigh. "Let me play."

"You have the rest of our lives to play." He groans in pleasure at my words, and it vibrates against my sensitive flesh. "I want to cum on your face."

"Never thought I'd get to hear those words." He sucks my clit into his mouth, and my eyes roll back in my head as I moan in relief.

But when I blink them open, trying to watch his head between my thighs, I have to blink multiple times before I realize my eyes are open, but the lights are gone.

There weren't a ton of lights on in the house, but now it's nearly pitch black.

"I hope you're not afraid of the dark," he murmurs against my thigh when he notices the storm has taken the electricity out.

"Not when you're with me."

"Maybe it's me you should be afraid of." He bites me, and I giggle. "I have a couple of candles in the bedroom."

"Sounds romantic." I scoot away from him slowly, as his hands drag the length of my legs.

"Are you trying to get away from me, dove?" His hand grips my ankle before I've made it even three steps higher.

"That'd be silly." I tug my leg away from him, and he lets me back further up the stairs.

"You can try to run, but once I catch you, and I will catch you… I'm not letting you out of my bed until morning."

"Is that supposed to be a threat?"

"Only a promise, baby girl." I can't see him well enough, but I know he's smiling. "5… 4…"

I turn, scampering up the final few steps before stumbling

down the dark hallway.

"3... 2..."

I don't wait to hear the last number... I take the first door I feel, and duck inside. It's completely absent of light, but my hands grasp the porcelain sink, and I know it's the bathroom. It has one of those sliding glass doors, and I slip inside the small stall shower, tiptoeing on the cool tile.

I try not to breathe, but every breath is amplified in the confined space. The floorboards in the hallway creak, and I know he's close.

The excitement of being caught makes my body tremble, and as soon as the door eases open, my stomach clenches in anticipation.

The dim moonlight streaming in from the hallway is the only glimpse of him I get before the door shuts again, and he's trapped us both inside.

My heart thunders as the glass door rattles, sliding open, and I don't know if he can see me, but my back hits the shower wall on instinct.

He steps back, and I think he's leaving, until I hear the clink of his belt coming undone and the rustle of his jeans falling.

His body fills the shower suddenly, and I gasp as his hand wraps around my throat.

"Gotcha," he whispers as his thumb caresses my hammering pulse. "Now, how should I punish you for running from me?"

"What?" I squeak. I anticipated the chase but not what comes after.

His other hand grips my hip bone, flipping me with ease and pressing my chest against the cold wall. My nipples pebble as he sandwiches me in, and his stiff cock digs into me. He's still wearing underwear, but I can feel the distinct outline of every inch of him along the crease of my ass.

His hand around my throat, and his body behind mine, cages me in everywhere, giving me no room to escape. "Spread your legs," he demands, kicking my feet apart.

His fingers find my clit, circling the swollen nub until I'm squirming in his arms. I was already so worked up, I'm nearly at an orgasm when he pulls his hand away and slaps me. One quick swat to my clit, making me jerk in his arms.

Was that my punishment?

That wasn't so bad, that–

He works my clit again, distracting me with pleasure until he rips it away.

"No, fuck," I utter against the shower wall as my legs shake.

His fingers hook inside my pussy from the front, fucking me ruthlessly with them, and rocking my clit with the heel of his hand. My hole clenches in desperation as he abuses it, forcing my ass against his cock.

I grind into him, submitting to the intensity, and just trying to survive until he finally lets me cum.

Tears stream down my cheeks, and I'm so close, but his fingers disappear, making me cry out in disappointment.

He flips me around like a rag doll, again, dragging his lips up my neck and to my jaw. My nipples brush against his chest, and I arch against him, needing more contact.

My whole body is shaking. Being brought so close to a climax so many times without release has my adrenaline soaring.

His thumbs wipe away my tears as he captures my mouth, kissing me tenderly. It's loving and sensual, but all-consuming. It's what I've waited my whole life for.

"Are you ready for me to take you to bed now, baby girl?" I

nod, too hazy to form words, and I feel his smile against my lips. "Good. I wasn't giving you a choice anyway."

His hands are under my thighs in an instant, hoisting me up around his waist before carrying me down the hallway to his room.

He wasn't lying about the mattress on the floor. It's the only thing in here besides a useless standing lamp in the corner and curtains that frame balcony doors. The doors are cracked open as the rain continues to pour outside, making the curtains billow.

We always dreamed about having big lives when we were teenagers. We'd sit at our rusty park and talk about the houses we'd want to live in and the cars we'd drive. We'd name foods that we didn't know how to pronounce properly, that we wanted to try, and talk about all the money we'd have.

Yet, somehow, being in this nearly abandoned house, in an almost empty room, with cobwebs in the corners and no power, is absolutely perfect.

Because all I need is him. Having each other is all we ever needed.

He lays me on the mattress gently and steps back to admire my stringy hair and tear-streaked face, and all I can do is smile at him.

His chest heaves as he stands above me, looking at me with eyes full of pride and pleasant disbelief.

"What are you waiting for?"

He takes a shuddering breath, flexing his hands. "I'm terrified you're going to disappear, and I'll find out this was all just a dream."

"How can I convince you it isn't a dream?"

He slides his underwear down his legs, and a soft gasp

escapes me. His cock bobs as he kneels in front of me on the bed, pushing between my thighs to cover my body with his. "Just stay," he pleads, kissing me softly. "Don't leave."

He's not asking me to stay the night. He's not asking me to stay in this house. He's asking me to *stay.*

And, I have every intention of doing just that.

"You're in my soul, Jensen. There's no running from that."

"I love you, dove." He kisses me again, tenderly. All the games are over, the silly prolonging... This is it.

Making love to Jensen Hayes was always just a fantasy, but now it's real, and the air is heavy as we breathe each other's oxygen, anticipating what we're about to do.

I can sense his nerves, and I kiss his cheeks, his nose, urging him to continue.

"You're my girl, Olive," he whispers gently, guiding his cock to my entrance. In one slow, but confident thrust, he pushes inside me like he's always belonged there, and I gasp as he settles to the hilt. "So beautiful."

All of my overwhelming feelings stream from the corners of my eyes, but he holds me close, wiping my tears as he begins moving inside of me.

"My Olive," he murmurs, kissing me softly.

Our bodies glide together as he moves on top of me, and it's all too much. I was already prickling with my need to climax, and every time his hips thrust against mine, it takes my breath away.

I claw at the back of his neck and shoulders, clinging to him as he makes love to me. More tears well in my eyes as I realize that I've never experienced anything like this.

No one has ever loved me like this, so effortlessly, and authentically. I don't know how I survived without it.

I sink my teeth into his bottom lip, eliciting a moan from his throat as I suck it into my mouth. I want him closer, I want him inside my skin.

His strokes inside of me become more demanding, stealing my grasp on my control. Each time he hits me deep inside, an unintelligible noise escapes my throat, and I can hardly keep my eyes open as my back arches, accepting the climbing pleasure.

"Cum on my cock, gorgeous."

"I'm… I–" Nothing coherent comes out.

"I've waited a long time for you, baby girl. Give me what I want," he demands, rocking into me deeply until the pressure is too intense. My spine locks and muscles tense as I'm swept away in an orgasm so incredible, I see stars.

He captures the scream from my throat, kissing me passionately until my vision returns and my breathing steadies.

He stopped moving, and when I blink up at him, he's only gazing at me in wonder, smiling softly. "You're the sexiest thing I've ever seen."

A breathy laugh escapes me. "That's good because I forgot to try to be sexy."

"You don't have to try with me. I'm obsessed with you." He kisses where my smile has stretched my cheeks.

"Then you should know…" I push him until he rolls off of me. "I like being on top."

I straddle his hips, admiring the way his cock falls impressively against his stomach. His hands land on my thighs, gripping me fiercely when my fingers circle the base of his girth and squeeze.

It's heavy as I position it upward and shift my hips over him. "This is what I've dreamed about… Watching your face as I ride you."

A choppy exhale is all he has time for before I impale myself completely on his rock-hard shaft. We both gasp in pleasure from it.

I start slow, grinding in his lap until it feels like I'm adjusted to this angle. I feel fuller, intoxicatingly so, as every inch stretches the walls of my pussy.

My hands support my weight on his chest as I roll my hips, taking exactly what I want from him, but when my ass bounces, and I start truly fucking him, his death grip on my hips only intensifies.

"Fuck, Olive," he groans as I find my rhythm.

Chapter Thirty-Nine

Hayes

"Your cock feels so good," she whimpers, rising to the tip and dropping back down repeatedly until she's out of breath.

I've never wanted to prolong anything more than this, but I don't stand a chance. She's going to work me dry.

I hold her hips steady, thrusting into her from below to give her a chance to breathe, but to give me a break from the fucking magic spell she has me under.

Her tits bounce as I pound into her, and she rakes her hands through her hair, taking every thrust.

"Touch your clit, baby. I want you cum, again," I beg. She sticks two fingers in her mouth to her bottom knuckles, sucking them out slowly without tearing her eyes off mine. *Fuck me.*

My stomach clenches as my release builds, and she's so fucking hot, I'm not going to be able to stop it.

Her fingers work her clit, and she throws her head to the side as she chases her second orgasm. My fingers are probably bruising her hips as I bounce her, but I know she doesn't mind.

She likes the pain.

"Olive," I breathe her name in warning, nearing the edge of no return.

"So close," she utters, jerking as she nears hers, too.

I want to feel her everywhere, but even as our chests meet, I can't get close enough. Her hips gyrate against me, and she gasps at the same time. I feel her walls choke down on my cock, and that's all it takes for her orgasm to milk mine right out of me.

She moans as she accepts my cum, rocking lazily against me until I'm depleted. My cock twitches inside of her as our breaths return to normal.

"I was hoping to last a little longer." I have to clear the frog from my throat. "But I didn't know you were going to fuck me like that."

She throws her head back and laughs, making me smile as her core clenches around me again.

"You know that I like to be good at everything." She kisses me softly, and I take her with me as I fall back onto the mattress.

"You're perfect. So damn, perfect." I kiss her head as she settles against my chest.

"No, you and me, together. That's perfect," she whispers, tipping her head to look at me.

"I still think I'm dreaming."

Her teeth dig into my chest. "Nope. Very real." She smiles, kissing the spot.

"Careful, Olive. I might have to get another tattoo." Her eyes crinkle with a smile, and I make a note to make that idea come true.

"Can you tell me about your other tattoos?"

"Only if you come take a shower with me."

She nods, and I slap her ass as she climbs off of me. I'm nowhere near done with her tonight.

The power is still out, but I have a couple of candles that I light and bring into the bathroom, somehow making everything more perfect. It's like the outside world doesn't even exist.

"What about this one?" She points to the snake on my arm.

"Snakes are deadly, but they're protectors." She nods, not asking for any clarification.

"This one?" She drags her finger over the dagger on the lateral part of my bicep.

"An act of sacrifice." Her finger lingers there for a moment before she leans down to kiss my wet skin.

"The compass?"

"My moral compass."

She smiles and traces it with her fingers. "Very deep."

"I spent a lot of time wanting to kill myself. I needed something deep to believe in." Her fingers still, and I cover them with my own. "I only attempted once when I was in prison, but it was a long road to stop hating myself."

She doesn't speak as she guides her hand over the scar above my wrist. The one hidden by the claw marks.

"Lochlan got to me in time. He slowed the bleeding down until the medical staff could save me. Then he kept saving me. Gave me a home once I got out of prison, and purpose. He saved my life in a lot of ways, but keeping me alive and out of trouble so I could find my way back to you is the highest on my list."

"So I should thank him?" She looks at me sadly, filled with grief over the decisions I made.

"I mean, you can... But he'd probably just grunt in response."

She grins as I wipe her rogue tears with my thumb.

"I guess I see what Jo sees in him then."

That makes me laugh, and she leans into me as the shower streams down on us.

Her hand follows the path of water down my stomach, her fingers graze my thighs as she traces the tattoos there.

"First ones I did to myself," I tell her, as her nails dig into my muscles.

"Doves?"

I nod, and she brings her hands back to my chest, looking at me, thoughtfully, waiting for an explanation.

"I did them in my cell once I figured out how to get a hold of tattoo equipment. They don't look great. But each one is a little better than the last."

I have two on one thigh and the best one on my other thigh.

"What other tattoos am I missing?"

"My back is empty. Saving it for a big piece."

"Have any ideas?"

"Yes." Her eyes narrow at my short response. "Another Liv tattoo."

Her mouth pops open. "Like what? You already have so many."

"Lady justice, with a blindfold covering a beautiful face that I've had memorized since I was 18 years old." I trace her jaw with the backs of my fingers. "Clinging fabric draped down sexy long legs, and a spine of steel that I've had the pleasure of getting to know more recently."

"Hmm, doesn't ring any bells." She squints her face teasingly until I push her against the cold shower wall.

"I could leave her naked, but I would kill any fucker that had to look at these long enough to tattoo them on me." I suck her nipple into my mouth, swirling her silver bar with my tongue until she writhes in my arms.

"I bet the asshole who did these was hard as a rock." I pinch her other nipple, and she cries out.

"He was very professional," she says, and I squeeze her tits roughly in my hands. "But he did give me a discount."

I spin her around, slapping her ass sharply. "Did his discount involve touching you anywhere unprofessionally?"

"No," she moans when my fingers sweep over her pussy from behind.

"Good. Wouldn't want to add anyone else to my list."

"What list?" She gasps when my finger enters her.

"The list of men I can't be in the same room with because if I see them looking at the parts of you they've touched… I'll gouge their eyes out."

Her pussy squeezes my fingers, and I reach around her waist with my other hand to reward her by playing with her clit. "You like that, don't you? You want me to despise all the men who have had you before I could."

"Yes," she breathes against the tile.

"You like that I'm jealous."

"Yes," she cries, riding my fingers as I fuck her with them.

A growl escapes my chest, and I can't get my fingers out of her fast enough to replace them with my cock, shoving inside her heat brutally and without warning.

Her hips push back to meet mine, completely unperturbed and taking me greedily because her pussy is ready for me.

I fuck into her forcefully, slamming my hips against her ass as I pin her to the shower wall. "Should I let you cum? Or should I make you beg for it all night long?"

"No, don't make me beg. Not tonight. I want everything you can give me tonight," she pleads, meeting me thrust for thrust.

"If I give you everything tonight, we won't walk for a week," I whisper in her ear as my hand cups the front of her throat

"Good." I feel her throat work against my hand, and my balls tighten. I'm already close.

The fingers of my other hand slap her clit, making her cry out, and I do it again, circling the sensitive nub and then swatting it. Her nails scrape at the wall as she struggles for breath until her hips rocket back into mine as her orgasm demolishes her.

The rolling waves of her climax wrap around me so tightly that I cum before she's completely released from hers, both of us gasping and groaning in tandem.

"Oh my fuck," she breathes, leaning back into my chest.

"Yeah," I agree, letting the blood return to my brain.

* * *

"Thea was my roommate since freshman year. She was so kind to me when I started college as a blubbering fool. She'd crawl into bed with me and make sure I didn't feel alone anymore while I was crying myself to sleep. We'd go to parties and bars. We were both inexperienced in life, but we got to be dumb college kids together."

After our shower, Liv rummaged through my empty kitchen to find some snacks, and we've been listening to the rain in bed for an hour, talking about anything and everything.

"Then she came back the summer after undergrad, and something had happened to her... She was hurt by someone, really badly, and it was my turn to hold her. We shared a full-size bed more than we ever stayed in separate rooms. She was falling apart, and she almost dropped out, but I refused to let her. I picked up her pieces just like she picked up mine. I knew how it felt to lose one best friend. I couldn't do it again."

Hearing about Thea stirs anger in my gut, and I realize how much I've grown to care for Liv's friend. I understand why Jesse feels so protective of both of them. They're a packaged deal, and I'm grateful that they've had each other all these years.

"Is the person who hurt Thea..." I can't finish my sentence because I'm not sure what answer I'm hoping for.

"It's a long story. Jesse had a run-in with him once, but he's moved across the country now. I'm pretty sure he and Nathan keep tabs on him to make sure he never comes back to this area."

"Nathan seems like a protective brother."

"He is. It simmers beneath the surface. He always kind of reminded me of you in that way... I'm surprised you guys don't get along better."

I like the guy just fine, but she starts again before I have a chance to defend myself.

"Once Thea started getting better, I convinced our local college bar to host a ladies-only night once a month so we could still dance. I threatened to sue them if they didn't," she snorts in amusement. "I hadn't even taken the bar exam yet."

"I guess I assumed she had an aversion to me. I didn't realize she was afraid of men."

"She's getting better. Jesse helped her a lot. His presence alone makes her feel safe enough that she almost seems back to normal. She'd never go onto a packed dance floor with men lurking about, though if it weren't for him."

"Well, I'm grateful that she brought you to this area. Not sure where we would have crossed paths if you hadn't come here to watch Kate grow up." I kiss her temple, and she smiles.

"We all joke that Thea is like the sun. Everyone sort of revolves around her because she makes your life better, you know? I hated having a long-distance friendship, but our lives were just in two separate places... But then she had Kate, and I realized that Kate was the sun."

"She is pretty cute."

"If anything ever happened to Thea and Jesse, I'd take Kate. And, if you are choosing me, you choose her too. She's the only person on this planet that I would drop you in a split second for."

"Damn. I didn't even have a chance to agree." I rub my chest teasingly.

"Sorry, just had to put that out there." She laughs, swatting my hand from my chest. The power surges suddenly, but the lights stay out. "Why did you buy this house?"

"What? You can't see the appeal?"

"I see a lot of things peeling..." She giggles under her breath, and I squeeze her ass.

"After all the shit that went down here over the years, I knew Lochlan was worried about it."

"So you bought it?"

"I also knew that if I wanted you in my future, I needed

something to offer you. I haven't had time to fix this place up yet, but I see potential. It has five bedrooms, a study beside the living room... The kitchen is pretty small, but I thought I could bust out a few walls and add an island. I don't know, it has good bones."

She searches my eyes, seeing the truth in them. She still doesn't understand how committed I am to having her in my life, but I think she's starting to. "You didn't need the house. I only wanted you."

I squeeze her fingers. "And, all I ever wanted was to give you everything. A home. Stability."

"A swing set that doesn't have rust?" She whispers against my chest.

"No graffiti either." I kiss her head.

"I like my cottage."

"I know."

"But it only has one bedroom."

"Kate will need a place to sleep when she's old enough to have sleepovers with Aunt Liv."

"Yeah, she will." She smiles, and I tuck her closer, still in disbelief that I'm holding her at all.

"You can put your cold plunge tub on the back porch."

She shakes her head, wrapping her arms around my waist. "I'm done being cold."

Chapter Forty

Liv

"I haven't been brave enough these last few months to ask about your mom. How is she?"

I feel his smile against my hair. "She's great."

"She is?" I prop my chin on my hand to look at him.

"When I was in prison, I was able to work through a program they had, and any little bit of money I got, I saved. As soon as I got out, since I was able to move into the sanctuary for free with Lochlan, I sent all my money to my mom."

"And your dad?"

"No, I made her promise to leave him. That was my stipulation. I needed her to be willing to start over."

"She was okay with that?"

"She was more than okay with that. She only stayed so long because of me, and she didn't have any way to leave. My dad made sure she was trapped. It was still hard on her, but I got her into a little apartment. She got a job at a diner. She's happy."

"Is she around here somewhere?"

"About an hour north."

"Have you heard from your dad at all?"

"No, not a peep. I assume he's drinking himself to death in the same trailer." He sighs. "It's exactly what he deserves."

"Did you ever think it could have been different if he had gotten sober?"

"No, even without the alcohol, he's evil to his core."

"You're everything good despite what he put you through, Jensen. I'm proud of you."

He twirls a piece of my hair around his finger mindlessly. "If I was good, I wouldn't have stolen you back when I knew you'd be better off without me."

"It's not stealing if I came willingly."

He nods, holding back a depth of emotions that I can only begin to guess. I don't know if I'll ever be able to convince him that he's worth everything to me.

"What did you think about when you were in prison?" I sit up, straddling his stomach.

"What did I think about…" He trails off, distracted by my nakedness on him.

"How did you think about me, Jensen?" I scoot down, feeling his cock stiffen as I slide over it and to his thighs. "Like this?"

"Fuck, Liv. I thought about this in every direction. I was suicidal, but I was 19 and horny as hell."

"Mhm, tell me."

His gaze sears me, traveling the length of my body until it lands on my mouth.

"Your lips. I dreamed about our first kiss. No matter how fucking vile my fantasy got… It would always start with a kiss."

I lean down, sealing my lips to his, but only letting them linger a second. "More," I encourage, running my hands down his torso.

"Then your tits. I'd imagine how they looked. Felt. I'd picture them bouncing in my face. Running my tongue over them and sucking them into my mouth. Fucking them."

"Like this?" I cup his shaft between the curve of my breasts, stroking him gently. I don't have a large chest, nothing that would get the job done effectively, but he does not seem to give a fuck as he stares.

"Just like that," he exhales in relief.

"Did you cum on me this way?"

"Yes."

"On my titties or in my mouth?"

"Both."

"Good boy." His eyes flash to mine. "How many times did you cum all over my face?"

"Too many to count."

"How many times did you fill my pussy with your cum?"

"Every night."

My core tightens, making me tingle everywhere. Hearing how hot he was for me before he ever had me stokes the fire inside me.

"What else, baby? How did you fuck me?"

"Fuck," he moans as I work his cock with both of my hands, stroking him gently from base to tip. "I'd wake up every morning wishing you were sitting on my face or sucking my cock. Sometimes I had already finished in my shorts because my dreams were so desperate for you."

"Did it feel like this?" I don't wait for a response before deep-throating him as far as I can go.

His hands cling to my scalp as he groans in pleasure. "This is better," he breathes.

"Mmm, good answer. Tell me more, or I'll stop," I threaten, licking up and down the length of him.

"I thought about your pussy so often that I'd lie awake, wishing I was between your thighs just so I could stare at it. Taste it. I wanted to know how every finger felt sliding inside your wetness."

"More," I demand.

"I'd fuck you so often in my dreams that I ran out of positions. I'd imagine you sitting on my face and my cock, holding onto the top rails of my bunk, and riding me until the bed broke. I'd fuck you so hard from behind that you screamed my name for the whole fucking prison to hear."

"Yes, baby. I would have. I know there was more. Tell me how filthy you got."

His hips jerk as I tug and twist with my hands, and suck on his head at the same time, making his legs tremble under mine.

"I'd make you beg for my cock."

"More."

"I'd make you beg to have it in your ass. I'd fuck your tight little asshole and fill you with my cum until it dripped into your pussy. And then I'd fuck it into your pussy and cum in you again!" He thunders the words as his climax bursts out of him, filling my mouth. I flatten my tongue as he fucks his seed down my throat, taking every drop.

I fall onto the mattress beside him, catching my breath, and grinning like an idiot. "That was so hot."

"I didn't even touch you," he pants.

"You don't have to touch me, and I'm still soaked."

"Is that right?" He hums, hooking his arm under my leg suddenly, yanking me to a perpendicular angle. His head finds a comfy spot between my thighs like his own personal pillow.

When his lips brush my clit, I moan, expecting him to continue, but then he merely opens my legs wider, staring at his prize.

"So beautiful." He kisses me again, teasing me with his tongue. "I want to die right here."

He inhales my scent, spreading me with his fingers and sliding his tongue through my slit. The next time he does it, he goes a little farther, dipping into my pussy. Then he does it again, swirling my puckered hole, making me gasp.

"Is that okay?" He murmurs.

"Yes."

He does it again, teasing my ass again, and my entire body tightens. No one has ever dared… I've never given them the privilege.

"I'm going to fuck you here, Liv. Not tonight, but I'm going to own every one of your holes."

"Why not tonight?"

He chuckles. "I don't have any lube. I don't want it to hurt."

I groan in frustration, and he relieves me by stroking my clit. "How do you want to cum this time, baby girl?"

"On your face."

"Good answer." He sucks my clit between his lips, and my hips buck against him. "Fuck my face, Olive."

I sigh in sweet relief as I grind against his tongue, and he laps at my clit happily, gripping my thighs and pulling me closer.

When he nibbles on me, lightning zaps my muscles, and my whole body clenches as he starts working me left to right.

He flattens his tongue, applying more pressure as he

forcefully moves my hips with his hands, demanding me to fuck his face.

That's all it takes to draw my orgasm out. My thighs clench his head, and my hips leave the mattress as I crest to the peak of my climax, finishing with his tongue buried deep inside my pussy.

The second the tension in my muscles fades, his attention turns to my inner thighs, where he kisses me tenderly until I'm clawing to get my next fix.

Without having him inside of me, I'm horrifyingly vacant.

Only one thing will cure me. "I need your cock inside of me, please."

I'm so high on lust, his dick pushes inside of me before I even realize he's changed positions. My back molds to his front as he moves behind me on the mattress, spooning me as he fucks me.

His arm hooks under my thigh, widening my hips to take more of his brutal thrusts, and my moans turn to whimpers. My head rocks back and forth on the mattress in near delusion. I can't even keep my eyes open as he plays with my clit.

He's using me like a fuck doll, and I'm incoherent, overwhelmed by pleasure. "Yes, you fuck me so good… Your cock fits perfect inside of me… Yes, Jensen… Fuck me…"

He bites my shoulder as I praise him, and the words keep flowing nonsensically from my mouth as his powerful body rocks mine, taking me like the feral beast I know him to be.

"You own me, baby… Yes… Fuck me harder… You're such a good boy… Fuck, fuck, fuckkk–" Another orgasm tears through me, ripping a scream from my throat as he continues to fuck me harder, faster, applying bruising pressure to my clit.

Tears stream down my cheeks until his hips still, and I feel his cum flood my insides.

A sleepy smile stretches my lips.

I'm such a whore for Jensen Hayes.

* * *

My final swipe of mascara applies perfectly, fanning my lashes across my eyes exactly to my preference. The last thing I do is peel my lip tint off as I do every morning, leaving my lips a deep but subtle berry shade.

My attention shifts in the mirror, though, as Hayes walks into my bathroom, adjusting his tie. He never wears a tie. I must have really flipped his world upside down this weekend. That makes me smile to myself.

After we peeled ourselves out of bed on Sunday morning, he grabbed what he would need for a few days, and we came back to my cottage.

Every part of my hips and thighs aches, a delicious reminder of his affection, and I'm counting down the minutes until work is over today and I have him to myself again.

"You look handsome," I admit softly to him in the mirror. He glances up, catching my heated gaze, and smiles.

"And you…" He shifts towards me, sliding his hand across my waist to pull me into his chest. "Look absolutely beautiful." His lips brush my neck, and my whole body melts into him.

"How am I supposed to work when I could be getting more of this?" I sigh, letting him tease my exposed skin.

"Because you love what you do, and I'm not going anywhere. There will be plenty of time for me to reward your patience later."

"Wow, you sound like the responsible one."

"Only when it comes to you, baby." He kisses my neck again and slaps my butt as he leaves the bathroom, forcing me to follow.

"I'll just slaughter Jeremiah Porter's defense and be done by lunch. How about that?"

"I have no doubt." He twirls his keys on his finger and sticks them into his pocket, where he waits by the door. He's going to ensure we leave by 7:30, and I've never been so annoyed by it.

"Okay, one more kiss before we leave our safe zone." I slink towards him, and he watches me skeptically, but when my arms circle his neck, his hands find my waist without hesitation.

"You're wearing lipstick."

"It's a stain, it won't transfer."

"I'm not worried about me, dove. I don't want to ruin your makeup," he whispers against my lips. I capture his mouth, moaning when his hands roam downward to cup my ass.

I force my tongue against his, and he growls, gripping my cheeks in his hands roughly. When my palm sneaks down his chest, he doesn't react until I'm dragging it over the stiffness behind his zipper.

"Dove," he warns.

"I can't get enough."

"You're killing me, baby." He groans as I stroke my palm over the length of him repeatedly.

"Are you complaining?" I hum against his lips.

He smiles softly as he shakes his head. “I’m exactly where I want to be.”

Chapter Forty-One

Hayes

I've created a monster. I can't keep her hand off my cock the entire drive into the courthouse, and I'm about to cum in my pants by the time I park.

All she wants is to fuck, and I'm garnering all my self-control to keep her from being late to work. This is an important case, and I can't be the reason she's distracted.

If it were a different day, I would have bent her over her couch and slapped her ass raw as I fucked her.

My balls tighten against me at the thought... *Focus... Focus...*

She's pouting in the passenger seat, and luckily, she's so adorable that it helps distract me. "Time to be a lawyer, you sex fiend."

"I can be both."

"I know you can, but today is a big day. I'll make it up to you later."

"You better," she grumbles, grabbing her briefcase from the floorboard.

I smile as I meet her around the back of the car and take it from her hands. "I'll follow your lead. Everyone will still see me as personal protection, an employee. Nothing more.

But if you need me to spank your ass behind closed doors, I'll oblige happily."

"I'll decide if you deserve that or not," she snips, but smiles as she struts in front of me.

I follow behind her like the obedient dog I am, trying not to make it obvious to onlookers that I know how it feels to be buried inside of her. Better yet, that I know how big her heart is, and I've never been more infatuated with her.

As soon as she's through her office door, a switch flips, and her professionalism is at an all time high as she readies herself for trial.

Someone knocks on her door, and my spine stiffens because something about this trial today is putting me on edge. "Who is it?"

"Sheriff Malec."

Liv rolls her eyes as I go to unlock the door. "Jackson, you don't have to use your formal title with me," she says.

"Sorry, seems weird announcing my first name at your office."

"What can I do for you?"

"I was going to update you on some stalker stuff, but I can wait until after the trial."

"No, it's okay," she says too quickly, and Jackson looks at me questioningly.

"Tell us."

He hands Liv a paper. "Landon Arkett lives in Oregon. There is nothing that shows me that he's been out of that state in years. Unless he's traveling across the country by car and only using cash, I don't think he's been here."

"Really?" I ask skeptically.

"Yeah. I even called his current employer. I didn't let them know why I was calling, but they were happy to offer up that he hasn't missed a day of work."

"So he isn't my stalker?" Liv breathes in relief.

"No, I don't think it's possible."

"Mr. Arkett isn't my stalker," she mumbles in disbelief this time, plopping down in her seat. That still means that someone else is.

My eyes flash to Jackson. "Then who the fuck is it?"

"Unfortunately, it seems like someone who knows more about your life than you'd like, Liv. I looked into Miley's boyfriend, Landon Smith. It's a false name, and the number she gave is now disconnected. When I asked her about it, she started crying. Apparently, he broke up with her after he found out about my interview. I think this guy created a false identity to plant himself near you. "

I scrub a hand over my face, trying to rein in my frustration.

"I didn't want to tell you this before the trial, but I don't want you looking over your shoulder for Arkett when your stalker is still out there and unidentified."

"No, I understand. Thank you."

"We're all in your corner, Liv. Good luck today."

"Thanks, Jackson." She waves as he leaves her office, but her eyes find mine.

"Are you okay?" We both ask at the exact same time.

I huff a laugh and sit down on the stiff couch to keep myself from pacing. "Don't worry about me. I'm fine."

She tilts her head as she looks at me from her desk. Too far away.

"Come here." I watch her closely as she walks across the room, stepping between my legs. I pull her in close because I don't care who walks through that door next. I need her in my arms.

"Talk to me, don't keep it bottled up," she says softly, stroking her fingers through my hair.

"I'm fucking worried about you, Liv. Every damn minute, I worry about you."

"I know. I'm worried, too. I'm so tired of feeling ten steps behind this guy. I'm scared that…" She trails off, but her frown deepens. She opens her mouth but closes it again.

"Liv," I press, not wanting her to hide anything.

"I'm afraid that you won't handle bad news well," she whispers, and I let my head fall against the back of the sofa.

"Because I can't control my temper?"

"I don't know."

"I'm not a kid anymore. I might be a hot head sometimes, but I know there's a time and place for everything."

She nods, but it falls flat.

"You don't trust me?"

"No, I do." She says quickly, trying to convince herself as much as she's convincing me, and a heavy silence falls between us.

My phone vibrates in my pocket, and she shifts to let me look at it. "Curtis is here. I'm going to help him to the courtroom. Stay here until I come back for you." I stand stiffly, pulling her to her feet.

She might love me, but she still doesn't trust me, and that stings.

"Wait," she starts, but I shake my head as I cross the room.

She might want me in her life, but I won't be the reason things go south. I won't let my feelings screw with her head.

"Time to be a lawyer, Liv. Don't worry about me."

Chapter Forty-Two

Liv

Hayes locks me into my office without another glance, letting my nerves for today rise to the surface. I have a strong case, I know that, but I also have a lot of friends who are going to be personally affected by the verdict.

Including me.

I haven't told Hayes, but I was offered a new contract for the prosecutor position if this trial goes well. That means my life here will officially be permanent.

We're finally figuring things out, and so many life changes have happened within a matter of weeks that I'm fighting the feeling that I'm going to fuck it all up.

Breath escapes me roughly, and I rub my palms across my blazer to dry the dampness before shoving all my papers into my briefcase.

People are counting on me, and I have a job to do. My personal life does not belong here right now.

My job status and my stalker are not my priority.

It's getting justice for everyone impacted by Jeremiah Porter.

Curtis. Lochlan. Jo.

A light knock on my door, and Hayes appears. "Ready?"

My breathing comes easier just having him near me, but he doesn't return my familiarity when I smile at him. He keeps his eyes averted and stays three steps behind me as we exit my office.

He normally keeps a professional distance when we're in the building, but when everything feels so unsteady, I want him right beside me.

I stop short before walking into the courtroom, and he nearly runs into my back. People are milling about, and more than a few eyes are on us as I turn to look at him, but I only see him.

I thread my fingers through his, searching his eyes for what I need. His brows furrow in confusion, but then a sly smile quirks the corner of his mouth, and his fingers squeeze mine.

He leans down to whisper in my ear. "No time for a quickie, baby girl. You've got a job to do."

A laugh escapes me, needing that bit of unseriousness when it feels like the weight of the world is on my shoulders.

He told me he'd be whatever I needed him to be, but I just need him.

Exactly as he is.

This time, when I turn to walk through the doors, it happens with ease, and I'm feeling a little stronger. I can do this.

"Is everything prepared, Miley?" I ask her as I approach the prosecutor's table.

She's pacing back and forth, fidgeting with her fingers. "Yes, ma'am. The projector is cued up," her voice wobbles.

"What's wrong?"

"I'm so sorry about whatever trouble my boyfriend caused. I mean, ex-boyfriend now. I had no idea he was lying about who he was."

"It's okay, Miley, you couldn't have known."

"I just feel so stupid. I haven't been able to stop crying. I let him… I let him touch me," she whispers, on the verge of tears.

"You're young. Boys suck. Don't beat yourself up." I really don't have time for this pep talk. I need to focus on the trial, but Miley is falling apart, and I need her assistance to present all the evidence smoothly.

"I'm sorry, Miss Greenwood. I can't do this. I need a break." She turns and flees out of the room before I can try to stop her, leaving me dumbfounded.

"What was that?" Hayes asks from the other side of the bar.

"She took off."

"Is she coming back?"

"No, I don't think so," I admit in disbelief.

"What do you need?"

"I need someone to run the projector, hit my cues when I'm presenting evidence to the jury."

"Do you want me to see if someone else in the office is available?"

"No." I look at him closely. "No, I need you to do it."

"Excuse me?"

"You know this case inside and out. You know what's on these slides already. All you have to do is sit next to me and pay attention to my talking points."

"I'm not meant to be on that side of the bar, Liv."

"I need *you*."

His conflicted eyes search mine before he relents. "Okay."

"Thank you." I look at him tenderly as he settles in his seat, fixing his already perfect collar and suit jacket.

His hand squeezes my knee subtly under the table as Judge Fulton enters, and just like that, the trial begins.

Jeremiah's defense attorney does his job and comes out of the gate swinging, but it's nothing I can't handle.

Sometime after hour three, though, a blister starts forming on the back of my heel, and it's all I can think about.

After hour four, the grumbling in my stomach is so loud that I have to fake a cough to hide it. I was so distracted by everything this morning that I forgot to eat. It's a rookie mistake.

"I want to call Vanessa Porter to the stand, your honor. My last character witness," the defense attorney states.

I sigh internally. This is the fifth character witness, and I'm struggling not to show my annoyance.

Jeremiah's mother takes the stand, and they start droning on about how sweet Jeremiah was as a child and how easily he was influenced as a boy.

As if him being meek as a kid changes the fact that he nearly murdered Curtis. It doesn't.

A wave of dizziness hits me, and I have to blink through it. I really need to eat, but I'd never halt the trial for that.

A hand knocks against my thigh, and I glance down at a piece of gum resting there. I shouldn't take it. It's not professional to chew gum during legal proceedings. But neither is passing out.

The cinnamon gum burns my tongue as I slide it into my mouth without drawing attention to myself. He swoops the wrapper from me without prompting, and I focus on quietly letting the tingling flavor boost my focus.

"Miss Greenwood, do you have any questions for Ms. Porter?" Judge Fulton asks.

"Yes, your honor." I stand, subtly depositing the chewed gum into Jensen's hand as I round the table. He doesn't flinch as he hides it away under the table.

"Ms. Porter. You said that Jeremiah was a kind boy. He loved his big brother, but you worried about him hanging with the wrong crowd."

"Yes," she replies, stiffly, looking at me with utter disdain.

"Did you ever consider that he was the bad crowd?"

"No, not my boy."

"Right. And, I'm sure your other son, Randall, would never have committed fraud or conspired to a kidnapping... But he did."

"Now you listen–" She starts, but I cut her off.

"And you never would have believed your husband and brothers, all now deceased, would have been involved in human trafficking... But they were."

"That has nothing to do with my boys!" She yells, and Judge Fulton clears his throat in warning.

"Right. They were innocent..." I say sarcastically. "Your entire family simply got mixed up with a bad crowd. Your father thought he was above the law, too. Right? And he's now deceased. Correct?"

She locks her jaw but doesn't speak.

"That's okay. I have the police report here." Jensen clicks the remote, displaying what I need on the screen.

"Reverend Jefferson Porter confessed to his crimes of drug trafficking, human trafficking, and kidnapping before he pulled a weapon on Sheriff Malec. Suicide by cop."

"You're a rotten little bitch," she sneers, and I only smile smugly in response as Judge Fulton knocks his gavel, reprimanding her language.

"No further questions, your honor." By the time I make it to my seat, my knees are nearly gelatinous.

"We need a recess, but the prosecution hasn't had a chance to call any witnesses yet today. Do you want to proceed, Miss Greenwood?" Judge Fulton asks, and even though everything in me is begging for a break, I need to get the final word in before the jury breaks for a late lunch.

Then I'll hammer them right away when we get back, too.

"If you don't mind, Judge Fulton. I'd like to call my first witness, Sheriff Malec. It will be short and sweet."

"Proceed."

Malec comes to the front of the room and takes his oath, as I prepare my questions, breathing through my lightheadedness.

"Sheriff Malec, can you tell me about the night of the arson at Second Chance Sanctuary?"

"The barn on the far side of the property was torched after being doused with lighter fluid. That resulted in a large outpouring of response as everyone either searched for Mr. Dane's missing niece or worked to put out the fire."

"Was his niece found?"

"Yes, luckily, she was fine. It was a distraction technique to take attention away from the other side of the property where Jeremiah was able to kidnap JoAnna Montgomery and then attack Curtis."

"What else?"

"Jeremiah used the same means of arson to start a fire in the wooded area surrounding the bear enclosures."

"Lighter fluid and a lighter?"

"Correct."

"Not easy to track. Pretty easy to find at any store... What made you suspect this wasn't the first time Jeremiah was involved in arson?"

"Jeremiah was a trained volunteer firefighter, though his certifications had all expired. He also admitted to carrying out the dirty work for his family members. An apartment here in Lawson was set on fire two years ago. Fire Marshall Max Robbins suspected an accelerant such as lighter fluid was used."

"Why would Jeremiah be a suspect?"

"The victims of the fire were targeted by a man that Jeremiah's grandfather was working with."

"You believe that Jefferson Porter commissioned his grandson, Jeremiah Porter, to commit arson?"

"Yes."

"Objection. Speculation." The defense attorney pipes in.

I nod to Judge Fulton. "That's all I have, your honor."

Chapter Forty-Three

Hayes

"If I stand up again, I'm going down for sure," Liv utters as I pack away the papers on the table.

I could see her energy waning, but I didn't realize how bad she was feeling. "What can I do?"

"Sit here with me and pretend that everything is fine. Let the room clear." She grips my forearm as I sit next to her, shielding her from the remaining people in the gallery.

"You need to drink some water and eat."

"I know."

"Hey, what's wrong?"

Liv nearly jumps over me to see the person who asked that. Thea is leaning over the bar, looking concerned.

"I didn't know you were here."

"I snuck in the back. I wanted to be here to support."

Liv's face relaxes like having Thea in her proximity brings her great relief. "I feel like I'm going to faint."

"Do you need gum?"

"I already tried that," I tell her.

"Here." Thea pulls a fruit bar and an applesauce pouch from her gigantic purse. Clearly, snacks meant for Kate. "Get your blood sugar going."

"Thanks." Liv takes a bite of the bar but ultimately guzzles down the applesauce instead. Only finishing the bar once she's got something on her stomach.

"Any better? I also have pretzels, and…" Thea looks at Liv quickly. "Saltines."

Liv goes still, staring at her friend. "You're pregnant?"

"What?" *Did I miss something?* We just went from A to Z so fast.

"I'm sorry, I meant to tell you in a much cuter way. I just found out, so I'm only like four weeks… The saltines are just a precaution right now."

"No, don't apologize. I'm so happy for you!" She leaps up to hug her friend, and my hands go wide, preparing to catch her if she falls. "Another baby," she exclaims gently.

"I'm terrified," Thea laughs.

"It'll be great. You just made my whole day."

"Well, come on. I'm eating for two, and you need to fuel up for your afternoon. Hayes, take us to lunch," Thea instructs, and I nod, happy to oblige.

* * *

Trial resumes after lunch, and the gallery seems to fill up significantly. It's time for Liv's victim statements, and she has quite a few of them.

Curtis is outside with his nurse, Sienna. Jesse joined us at lunch and followed us back to the courthouse to help support Curtis. Jo and Lochlan are here because Jo has to take the stand this afternoon, so Callie came to support her new friend. Which means Nathan is here too, because where Callie goes, he goes.

Natalie and Jackson are here with half of the Rollins County police force because so many of them were affected by the Porter family's crimes. Jeremiah also has quite a few people here in his corner, though they look more like his mother's associates, and not his.

If Liv is feeling the pressure, she isn't showing it. She swears that lunch fixed her up, and she doesn't feel faint anymore, but I'm on high alert regardless.

Jeremiah is going to prison. It's just a matter of how much Liv can prove that will affect the severity of his consequences.

Curtis is the star witness. The gravity of his injuries will put Jeremiah behind bars for a long time if she can prove it was attempted murder.

"I'd like to call my first witness to the stand. JoAnna Dane, formerly JoAnna Montgomery," Liv tells the judge, and she waits calmly as Jo takes the oath.

"JoAnna, can you tell us about the night you were kidnapped?"

"Yes, of course." She begins recounting the night of her postgrad graduation party when Emory went missing, and then Jeremiah took her against her will.

She gets to the part about being chained inside the bear enclosures, but I'm hardly listening. My body is angled, keeping Lochlan in my peripheral vision.

His jaw is set tight, and I know he is imagining serving his own kind of justice. His eyes are on Jo, but his anger is penetrating Jeremiah's back.

"JoAnna, at any point, did you believe that Jeremiah meant

to harm you?"

"Yes."

"He claims that he was only going to chain you up and leave. Is that accurate?"

"Yes, but he told me that he wanted to let the bears handle me."

"As far as you know, the bears at Second Chance Sanctuary are not tame. Correct?"

"Correct."

"Jeremiah knew that leaving you at the mercy of adult black bears could result in your death," Liv responds to Jo, but is speaking towards the jury. "His actions were not merciful. Even if he did not wish to harm you with his own hands, he had ill intent."

"Objection!" Jeremiah's lawyer stands. "Speculation. She can't prove that my client knew anything about the bears' mental state."

"Move on, Miss Greenwood."

"Of course, your honor. JoAnna, did you witness Jeremiah's attack on Curtis?"

"Yes."

"Do you think that Jeremiah intended to kill, Curtis?"

"I don't know."

"At any point, did you believe that Curtis was going to die?"

Jo clears her throat. "Yes."

"Tell me about that point."

"Jeremiah picked up a thick branch and hit Curtis on the back of the head. It knocked him to the ground, and he stopped moving. I couldn't tell if he was breathing," her voice breaks. "I thought he was dead, and I was chained up. I couldn't help him," she cries, and I sense the room collectively feeling her sadness.

Except, Lochlan. My focus is still on him and the way his knuckles are turning white in his lap. *Don't cause a scene, buddy. Don't cause a scene.*

"I can only imagine how difficult that was for you. But I am happy that we have Curtis here today to tell his story. My next witness, your honor. Curtis Debaugh."

Thank God. I can finally breathe again once Jo is in her seat next to Lochlan, and he visibly relaxes. I did not want to fight that battle today.

Curtis's testimony can make or break the severity of Jeremiah's punishment today. Liv also has to prove that Jeremiah is not just a victim of his brother's bidding.

Curtis is summoned from the hallway because he asked not to be forced to watch the trial from the gallery. It was too much, hearing all the details all over again.

He walks down the main aisle between all the spectators, hobbling slightly and visibly in pain as he uses a cane to assist him. He's wearing a knit hat to cover the scars on his head, and Sienna walks closely behind him, ready to help him if needed.

She looks different outside of her nurse scrubs. Smaller and more fragile. Her hair is tied back in a ponytail, and her glasses make her look young, though I think she's a few years older than Curtis.

She sits in the pew closest to the swinging gate after holding it open, letting Curtis make the final steps to the stand by himself. Natalie is sitting behind her and leans forward to squeeze her shoulder.

"Curtis, thank you for being here," Liv tells him after he takes his oath to tell the truth.

He nods but doesn't respond. His hands twitch nervously.

"Can you tell us about the night you were injured?"

"Yeah, um... I was looking for a little girl. Lochlan, I mean, Mr. Dane's niece. I was looking for her, and it was late. When I saw..." He clears his throat. "When I saw him."

"Him, who?"

"Him." Curtis points to Jeremiah, but his other fingers are crooked slightly, splayed outwardly when they should be tucked against his palm.

"Let the record show that Mr. Debaugh is pointing to the defendant, Jeremiah Porter." She pauses, letting that settle. "What is the first thing you noticed?"

"He was a firefighter. Or, he looked like one. The barns were on fire. There were a lot of firefighters on the property."

"When did you realize that something was wrong?"

"I heard my name. Jo, err, JoAnna, screamed my name. She yelled that she was trapped and that Jer– He had trapped her." Curtis is struggling to speak, and he keeps refusing to say Jeremiah's name.

"What happened next, Curtis?"

Curtis rubs at his head, but he doesn't speak.

"Curtis?"

"I'm sorry," he mumbles, fidgeting in his seat.

"That's okay. I know this is difficult. Let's move on; we can circle back later. Okay?"

He nods in agreement, but continues shifting in his seat uncomfortably.

"Can you tell us about the injuries you sustained that night?"

"Um, spinal fracture. Burns... Uh, I'm sorry." He presses his palm to his forehead. "Sienna can tell you. My nurse. She can tell you, I'm sorry." He rocks back and forth in his seat, as everyone in the room watches on, visibly worried.

"Your honor, I'd like to stop and give Curtis a break. Can we hear from his nurse? She's in the gallery today."

"Go ahead, but medical diagnosis only."

"Yes, your honor. Sienna?" Liv strolls over to her, throwing her a look of apology as she puts the timid nurse on the spot in this packed courtroom. "Can you state your full name and title for the court?"

She stands stiffly, tucking non-existent stray hair behind her ears. "Uh. Yes. Sienna Teller, BSN, RN, CCRN."

"Can you tell us what those credentials mean for the record, please?"

"Bachelor of Science in Nursing. Registered Nurse. Critical Care Registered Nurse."

"Thank you, Nurse Teller. Can you tell us about Curtis's injuries?"

"Curtis came into the Emergency Department with Second-Degree burns on more than half his body. He was diagnosed with a spinal fracture to his C7 and T1 vertebrae. This resulted in nerve damage to his arms and legs. He was also diagnosed with a severe Traumatic Brain Injury."

"How did the TBI affect his health?" Liv asks.

"He lost consciousness at impact, and as a result, he was not responsive when he arrived at the ED. The medical team decided to induce a coma to help him heal from his injuries. Severe swelling and bleeding in his brain made his condition unstable for weeks. He was in the ICU for weeks. He has memory loss, confusion, dizziness, and ongoing headaches. His burns are healing, but he'll be left with significant scarring."

"Thank you, Sienna. Is there anything else the jury should

know about Curtis's medical condition?"

"I don't want to speak out of line, Miss Greenwood, but I think the court should know that Curtis should not be here today. The doctors in the emergency room did not think he would make it the night he came in, and they also weren't sure they could wake him from his coma. His injuries were severe enough that we spent weeks searching for a next of kin in case he died. Luckily, he did wake up, but that led him on a path of more surgeries. 12 before he could leave the ICU. He has been in the rehabilitation center for months. He's supposed to be in a wheelchair. The doctors couldn't believe his strength to not only survive, but to persevere."

"Thank you for sharing that, Sienna. Curtis is lucky to have a medical team that cares about him so much." She smiles gently and nods her thanks as she turns back to the judge.

"Your honor, I'd like to take a short recess. To give Curtis a break."

"I'll grant you a recess, but only to get your next witness in line. Mr. Debaugh is not fit to testify. I sympathize with his condition, I do, but I don't want to see the boy suffer in my courtroom. We'll pick things up first thing tomorrow morning." He hits his gavel, giving no room for argument.

Liv just lost her star witness.

Chapter Forty-Four

Liv

At this point, I don't know how this day could get any worse. I still have a stalker. My intern quit on me. I almost fainted in the courtroom. I lost my star witness before he could finish his entire impact statement. And, even though my best friend gave me the best news earlier, making me a godmother for the second time, it's left a hollow feeling in my gut.

I thought by the time she had another baby, I'd be closer to that phase of my life, too.

"What can I help with?" Hayes asks, watching me shove my papers into my briefcase.

"I don't know. I need a minute," I tell him coldly. I don't mean to, but I don't have any energy left after this crap day.

I don't look up, and I don't need to. I feel his body leave my atmosphere. He's been nothing but great to me, and I'm awful.

I'm a terrible person. I suck at my job.

Tears prickle at the back of my eyes, and I have to inhale deeply to fight them off.

Everyone is counting on me to put Jeremiah away for the

rest of his life… I'll be lucky to get him eight years now, and that is a hard pill to swallow.

When I turn to leave the courtroom, my friends are huddled around each other talking, and Hayes is in the corner talking to Nathan. All in their own worlds, and I can't bear to pretend that I'm optimistic about today's outcome.

I slink out the side door and immediately run into Curtis and Sienna.

"I'm sorry, Miss Greenwood. I thought I could do it."

"It's okay, Curtis. I asked too much of you. It's on me. It'll be fine," I assure him with a weak smile. "I'm sorry, I need to run. Thank you for coming, and thank you, Sienna."

She looks at me closely. "Are you okay? You look a little pale?"

"I'm fine. It's been a long day." I dismiss myself with a wave, rushing away and begging for the elevator doors to close so they don't see me fall apart. As the doors slide shut, I see Hayes exit the courtroom, and his eyes connect with mine just before I lose sight of him.

He's going to change his mind about me. I'm not the strong woman he thinks that I am. The one I swore I was.

I'm still the weak girl he met as a teenager.

Another deep inhale enters my lungs, and I blow it out slowly as the doors open on my office floor.

It's dark, everyone is busy with their own cases downstairs, or have left for the day. My office light is on, though, shining through my door.

I shove through my door, flinging my briefcase on my desk, and my spine stiffens. I sense immediately that I'm not alone.

The floorboard behind me creaks, and ice trickles down my spine. I don't move, I hardly breathe.

"Did you come up here to see me, Livvy?" His voice is low and gravelly. I don't recognize it, but something about it feels familiar.

Something presses against my lower back gently, and my body bows away from it. He scoffs at my reaction. "Bitch."

The pressure on my back turns forceful, shoving me face-first into my desk, but my palms smack the wood surface before my face does.

I gasp, breathing against my desk for several agonizing seconds before I shoot back up.

I'm alone.

He's gone.

I know I didn't imagine that.

He was here.

I'm standing frozen next to my desk when the elevator dings and I hear a triage of voices filter through.

"What happened?" Jensen asks first, looking at my face closely. "You're white as a sheet."

"My stalker was in here."

"Did he leave something?" He asks, looking around, but I still haven't blinked.

"He touched me," I whisper, finally looking at him.

He's gasoline, and I just flicked a match at him. The anger ignites behind his eyes, and it's exactly what I need to snap out of my stupor.

"What?" The heavy timber of his voice melts over me. It would scare anyone else, but not me.

"I'll call Malec." I glance over to see who spoke. And everyone is here. Thea and Nathan are standing in the doorway, but when Nathan turns to make his phone call, I see Callie and Jesse.

"Are you okay?" Thea asks.

When she moves towards me, Lochlan and Jo shift into focus. She's looking at me with concern, but Lochlan is focused on Hayes.

"He was in here, and he touched my back." All these people here, and no one saw him. "He got away," I mumble to myself.

"Is that all? Did he speak? Did you see his face?" Thea asks, assessing me for the same invisible injuries that Hayes did. Her hand brushes over my forehead, and I lean into her palm.

"He was behind me. He shoved me into my desk before he took off. I didn't have time to turn around or to look at him."

"Dammit. Dammit!" Hayes yells, throwing something from my desk across the room. It breaks as it hits the wall, and Lochlan steps into the room, but Hayes holds his hand up without looking, warning him off.

Jesse has already pulled Thea behind his back, planting her next to Callie and Jo outside my office door. He holds his hand out to me, urging me to move away from Hayes, but I don't take it.

I don't need to.

"I'm fine," Hayes barks at Lochlan as his friend steps closer still.

"Give us the room," I demand, watching everyone's eyes ping back and forth with worry. Lochlan doesn't move.

"Lochlan, I need a minute with Hayes, please," I tell him softly. If he makes me ask again, I'm siccing his wife on him.

He glances at me quickly, then longer at his friend before nodding.

"We'll be right outside," he grunts, closing the door behind him, shutting Hayes and me in alone.

I take one full deep breath before turning to Hayes, and

as soon as our eyes lock, my knees buckle. He catches me before I can fall, wrapping me in his arms to keep me from breaking apart.

"He touched me," I cry.

"I know. I'm so sorry, baby. I shouldn't have let you come up here alone. Fuck, I knew better."

"I was mad about the trial. I was pouting."

"I wanted to help. I brought your friends up here to help," he sighs, stroking my back. "But I let that fucker have access to you."

"He spoke to me."

"What did he say?" He growls.

"He asked if I came up here to see him… As if I knew he'd be here."

"Did you recognize his voice?"

I shake my head against his chest. "I have no idea."

"It's okay. I'm going to fix this. I'll keep you safe."

"Don't leave my side anymore. Okay? Even if I'm mean and you change your mind about me."

"What? Why would I change my mind?"

"I was awful today. I made you feel like crap this morning. I sucked at my job. I left the courtroom alone when I knew you wouldn't want me to."

"It's okay, Liv. You're human. You needed a minute."

"I froze. Again. I'm a grown-ass woman now, and I still froze when a man put his hands on me. I didn't even see his face. I could have ended this whole thing."

"This is not your fault. Some fucker came into your space and touched you without your consent. Your reaction kept you safe. If you fought or ran, he might have hurt you."

"I let my guard down because I was drowning in self-pity."

I sniff some of my tears away. "I'm pathetic. Now, getting Jeremiah on attempted murder is up in the air. The jury won't be able to decide on a verdict without reasonable doubt. I'm such a failure."

"You're not a failure, and I have a plan."

"What plan?" I ask in disbelief.

"It'll be easier to explain once we talk to Malec and everything here settles. Just trust me, okay?" He looks at me deeply.

I gaze into his eyes as he strokes my cheek, and I know without a doubt that I trust him. With every fiber of my being, I trust him.

"Okay."

* * *

"I got him on camera entering the building and exiting. He used Miley's employee I.D. She failed to mention that she lost it, but I don't think she's in on it… I think she's just kind of…" Jackson trails off.

"Spacey?" I finish his train of thought because he's too nice to say what he really wants to. He nods in agreement.

We all congregated back at Second Chance Sanctuary because it was decided it would be the safest and most guarded place now that my stalker has been bold enough to make physical contact.

I've had too bad a day to resist. I'll hold onto my arguments until tomorrow.

Someone picked up pizzas on the way up the mountain,

and now there are ten half-eaten pizza boxes scattered about, and what feels like twenty people piled into the main area of the bunkhouse, though the parolees are attempting to make themselves scarce per Lochlan's orders.

"I lifted fingerprints from the doors to compare to the ones from the past incidents, and we have a better picture of this guy's identity now from the cameras. He definitely had dark hair, but he might be dyeing it. If I had to guess, he's around 5'11. Slim build. Ring any bells?"

"No. That could be a million people, but no one comes to mind."

"How about you guys?" He asks Hayes and Thea. They are the two people who have known me the longest.

"I know you said he isn't a suspect, but Arkett had dark hair. He was shorter than me. It still sounds like him," Hayes says.

"I'll keep him on my radar, but he hasn't traveled to this part of the country in years."

Hayes nods unsatisfied.

"I swear I've been cataloging every new face I see in town or at the library. I'm always looking for someone who doesn't belong. I don't know who would do this… Everyone always loved Liv, but in a normal way. She was practically Miss Congeniality our senior year of college," Thea adds.

"Any bad attention in college?"

"No, not really. I had friends, and I dated. I flirted with everyone because it was easy and I–" I glance at Hayes. "I wasn't ready to get hurt again."

He hangs his head in guilt, but I keep going.

"Anyone want more than you wanted to give?"

"Not really. It was college. Everyone was flaky. They'd move on to the next hook-up within a couple of days."

"What about grad school?"

"I went into law school right after undergrad. Thea started her master's program. We kind of hunkered down the first year." I don't continue explaining, and he doesn't seek clarification. He knows about Thea's past.

"Did you ever go back home?"

"To the trailer park? Never. We got an off-campus apartment. I stayed there year-round. Worked for a catering company."

"Any high school reunions?"

"Definitely not. I didn't have friends in high school, especially not after… You know." I glance at Hayes again, and Jackson nods.

Hayes gets up and starts pacing the open room.

"Well, if anything comes to mind, let me know right away. From here on out, you're not to be alone. My deputies will take shifts sitting at your office and in the courtroom." He stands. "If you're not here at the sanctuary, one of these guys needs to be with you."

I look around the room and realize that they're all looking back at me. Nathan, Jesse, Lochlan, and Hayes. Thea, Callie, Natalie, and Jo. Tears sting my nose, and I have to glance away to keep them at bay.

"I don't want to disrupt anyone's life."

"It's not disrupting if we're all choosing to help," Callie says, sitting next to me. "It's a terrible feeling to be targeted. Unfortunately for your stalker, you happen to be surrounded by a lot of qualified men who can and will protect you. I will protect you. Thea and Jo will."

"I will literally fight anyone, Liv. Just give me a chance," Natalie adds, and it makes me laugh.

"Jesus Christ," Jackson mumbles, and it makes me laugh harder. "Come on, fireball, we need to go pick up Dec."

"I'm serious, Liv." She motions as if she's cutting someone's throat as she backs away, and it's exactly what I needed to feel better.

"She scares me. I love her," Jo says, sitting on the other side of me. "I know you'll want to stay in Hayes's room tonight, but come up to the house in the morning so you can get ready. I have anything and everything you'll need."

"Thank you, I will."

She squeezes my arm, and Lochlan takes her hand, pulling her up from the couch. "We'll see you guys tomorrow."

She starts to walk away, but Lochlan doesn't move yet, turning to look at me.

"You're safe here, Liv. We take care of our own," he says, gruffly. He nods at Hayes, standing behind me, and when I look back, his face is hard with an emotion I can't quite read.

Chapter Forty-Five

Hayes

I never needed Lochlan's approval when it came to Liv, but hearing him call her one of our own here at the sanctuary is probably the nicest thing he's ever done for me.

This place has been my home and my lifeline since I got out of prison. It made me the man I needed to be to get Liv back. I'll never be able to express how important it is.

"Do you want to tell her?" Thea asks, looking at me thoughtfully.

"Tell me what?" Liv twists to lean on the back of the couch to look at me. Her eyes are wide with uncertainty.

She can't handle any more bad news today, but luckily, that's not what I have.

"I won't try to pretend that I know what you need to slam dunk this case, but I think Nathan can help us."

"Nathan?" She asks.

He's been sitting off to the side, quiet as usual.

"He recognized Jeremiah when we came to watch the trial today," Callie informs her.

"I think you need to put him on the stand," I tell her. I'm not qualified, and she knows this, but as her wheels turn while she looks at me. She knows I'd never overstep unless it was important.

"Nathan wants to go on the stand?" Liv asks.

"No." He shuts her down immediately, but she doesn't even flinch at the rejection.

"Yes," Callie insists, crossing her arms.

"Nathan, if you know something that will add years to Jeremiah's sentence, then it's your civic duty," Thea tries to convince him.

He sighs. "I've done enough civic duty for a lifetime."

"He'll do it because I need him to," Callie insists, stepping towards her husband, applying the full weight of guilt onto him. "Seeing everyone from that family punished for their crimes will give me the closure that I need, too."

That did it. I can see it all over his face.

"Fine." He wraps his hand around the back of her knee when she steps between his legs and rests his head against her hip.

Whatever Callie went through fills him with anguish.

I recognize the signs. The lack of control makes it impossible for him to be apart from her. As if touching her will erase all the fear and grief.

"Perfect. Now tell me everything. Don't mince your words." Liv sets up her phone to record him, and we all fall silent as she forces him to talk through his and Callie's story.

Her Hail Mary.

* * *

"Are you going to be able to sleep?" I whisper, brushing my fingers through her hair, massaging her scalp. It's been a long-ass day, and we have to be up in three hours to get ready to be back in court.

She grilled Nathan for hours and then spent another couple of hours preparing her questions for his testimony.

She's a heap of exhaustion in my arms, and reluctantly sharing my bed in the bunkhouse. She'd rather be at home, and I would rather have her all to myself. But it's safer here when we're exhausted, and she's doing everything she can to focus on tomorrow's trial.

"I'm so tired, but my brain is wired. I'll blink, and the alarm will be going off." She sighs, snuggling into my chest. "I already feel like I've blinked and my entire life has passed by."

"What do you mean?"

"I was supposed to be settled by now. Starting a family. Thea and I were going to have babies at the same time, but I called off my wedding. Now she's having another baby without me."

"Did you tell Thea how you were feeling?"

"No, but I don't think I need to. I think that's why she waited to tell me," she admits solemnly.

"Waited? She's still pretty early along."

"Yeah, but with Kate, she sent me a picture of her pregnancy test while the pee was still wet," she giggles at the memory.

"So, how soon until you can send that type of picture back to her?"

"What do you mean?"

"If we start right now."

Her body stiffens, and then she whips her head back to look me in the face. "That's not funny."

"I'm not trying to be funny."

"You would want a baby right now?"

"Olive, I would do anything you wanted. If you had called me up after ten years and asked for my sperm to create your own laboratory baby, I would have done it. I'd probably counteroffer doing it the old-fashioned way so that I could feel your pussy wrapped around my cock just once... But I would have done it all the same."

"You're insane."

"Yeah, but you like me that way."

A slow smile stretches her cheeks. "Yeah, I guess you're right."

She hooks her leg over my hip, pulling her body on top of mine until the covers fall away. "So, if I sit on your cock right now and beg you to give me a baby?"

I tip the band of my boxers down, fisting my hard shaft and positioning it exactly where she needs it. "It'd be the easiest answer of my life."

A soft gasp escapes her as she shifts her hips to line up over my crown. She's naked under my t-shirt, and the warmth of her pussy cloaks my cock as she sinks down on me. Always the perfect fit.

"We've never used any protection, but I am on the pill."

"I know, baby. I saw them on your bathroom counter. But there's no harm in practicing."

She grinds back and forth on me languidly, rolling her neck as she takes her pleasure. "Maybe the odds will be in our favor, and you'll beat the birth control."

"Yeah, or I'll flush them down the fucking drain and fill your womb until you give me twins." Her walls clench around me, and I grunt. "You belong to me, Olive. Always have. If you were going to have anyone's baby, it was going to be mine. Always mine." I thrust into her from below, cupping my hand over her mouth as she whimpers.

We're not alone here. There are seven other men in the bunkhouse, some twenty yards away. My bed is the most secluded, but it isn't private by any means, and it squeaks.

"I only ever imagined my future babies would look like you," she admits softly, biting my palm.

Dammit, she's going to do me in already. I work her clit, demanding her orgasm before I lose it inside of her. She's so fucking perfect, and imagining her carrying my child is like kryptonite.

I can't beat it.

Her hips jerk back and forth in my lap as she nears her climax, and I only press harder, fuck her faster, drawing it out until her pussy is clenching my cock like a vise. "Yes, baby, take my cum," I groan as she forces my release from me.

She twitches and grinds against me, sucking every lost drop from me until I collapse back on the mattress with her sprawled on my chest.

"Do you think someone heard us?" She whispers.

"Probably."

She giggles against my chest, and I smile, despite deciding how I would kill anyone across the loft who might've gotten off hearing her moans.

"I bought a wedding dress because it made me think of you when I tried it on," she whispers her confession, making my hands still on her spine.

"When?"

"Last year."

A surprised breath escapes me. "Do you still have it?"

She settles back beside me on the bed, and I cover her up. "Yes. Does that freak you out?" She asks hesitantly.

"Not even a little bit. Will you show me?"

"Well, if you plan to marry me one day… Then it would be bad luck to see the dress."

"You tell me that you bought a dress with me in mind and you're going to make me wait to see it?" I utter in exasperation. "Can we get married tomorrow? We'll already be at the courthouse."

"No, absolutely not."

I grumble in frustration against her head. "This is going to kill me."

"I don't know, I think it feels nice to have something to look forward to. It finally feels like the good things are ahead of us, and not just in the past."

"I've never looked forward to anything more than having a future with you," I admit, pulling her in tighter. "And, I'm going to celebrate every fucking milestone with you, baby. I can't wait."

She smiles against my cheek and snuggles closer. "I love you, Jensen."

My lips capture hers, kissing her deeply.

My Olive.

Chapter Forty-Six

Liv

"In light of yesterday's proceedings, I'd like to call a new witness to the stand," I present calmly, as soon as day two of the trial begins.

No one in this room would ever know that I'm running on two hours of sleep, or how I refused to step foot in my office this morning.

The barrier that existed between my stalker and me was crossed yesterday when he touched me, and I did not need the reminder of that violation before today's proceedings.

"Objection. This is the first we're hearing of this," the defense lawyer states.

"My witness was unable to finish his testimony because of the injuries that your client subjected him to."

"Allegedly."

"I'll allow this new witness, Miss Greenwood. The defense will have their chance to cross-examine," Judge Fulton decides.

I nod. "I'd like to call Special Sergeant Nathan Wolfe to the stand."

The room audibly reacts as the stern-faced man approaches

from the gallery. Without saying a word, he elicits an imposing air of respect even without his uniform.

This isn't an Army matter, so he's only wearing a nice suit, but if I recall, it's the one he wore to Thea's wedding.

I've known Nathan for years, but I'll admit this is the most conversation I've ever had with him. He keeps to himself, and his hard exterior only melts around Callie; he gives everyone else a cold shoulder.

He's only "kind" to me because his sister treats me like family. If I were anyone else, he wouldn't be taking the stand today.

I wait until Judge Fulton does his part, swearing Nathan in, before greeting him. "Sergeant Wolfe, thank you for being here today."

He nods, stiffly.

"Before I get started. Can you tell the jurors a little bit about yourself?"

"I'm a resident of Whitewater. Moved here four years ago. I've served in the United States Army in some capacity for 15 years and currently serve in the Army Criminal Investigative Division."

"You moved to this area four years ago and have held residence on the outer edge of Rollins County. You live deeper in the mountains than most folks. Do you hunt?"

"Yes."

"Can you tell me about one of your most significant hunting trips?"

"It was early November, almost four years ago. I was sitting on top of a ridge waiting for game to appear when I saw a woman in distress." His gaze slips to Callie in the audience, but he recovers quickly.

"Did you help her?"

"Yes, I was able to deter the hostiles and secure the package." He shakes his head. "I deterred her attackers, and I got her to safety," he clarifies in civilian words.

"What happened next?"

"I brought her into my home to bandage her injuries and to prevent hypothermia. She was able to tell me what happened to her, and the next day we set out to find her vehicle and personal belongings."

"Why did you need to find her vehicle?"

"She was attacked on the side of the road after pulling over to fix a flat tire."

"Did you find her car?"

"Yes. It was still sitting on the side of the highway where she was taken."

"What do you mean by taken?"

"She was attacked by two men and kidnapped." One of the jurors gasps, but Nathan's face doesn't budge. Only I'm close enough to see the twinge of pain in his eyes. "They tied her up and put her in their vehicle and drove into the mountains."

"But she escaped?"

"She escaped."

I nod, bringing the conversation back around. "Were you able to fix her flat?"

"I put on her spare tire."

"Did she run over a nail?"

"No. Her tire was shredded by a handmade spike strip. The bits of scrap metal were still embedded in the rubber."

"What happened next?"

"A tow truck pulled up, and the driver was prepared to tow the vehicle."

"But you got the spare tire on?"

"Correct."

"So you didn't need a tow?"

"Correct."

"Why was the tow truck there, Sergeant Wolfe?"

"The driver informed me that someone else had called on behalf of the vehicle to have it towed away."

"Why would they do that?"

"I suspected to get rid of evidence."

This is when Jeremiah's lawyer should object... But he has no idea where my line of questioning is going. I'm trying not to let my cards show.

"Who was trying to get rid of evidence?"

"The former sheriff, Sheriff Chuck Donahue. He and his wife's brothers were working together to abduct innocent people from their vehicles."

"Why?"

"They were involved in human trafficking."

"Jeremiah's father and his uncles. Correct?"

"Yes."

"Objection, your honor, this has nothing to do with my client."

Judge Fulton dismisses his objection, and I turn to hide my smirk, raising my voice an octave to capture the attention of the room. "Sergeant Wolfe, can you tell me who was driving the tow truck that day?"

"Yes. Him." He points to Jeremiah.

The audience gasps. "Did you know that it was Jeremiah Porter at the time?"

"No, I did not. I only knew the face I saw that day."

"Nearly four years ago, Jeremiah Porter was driving the

tow truck that was used to dispose of evidence in his family's crimes," I speak directly to the jury. "Does this sound like a man who has just suddenly been tempted to commit a crime? No. Jeremiah comes from a crime family. He wasn't in the wrong place at the wrong time. He's not a victim. He has been involved in their illegal dealings for at least four years, and I would bet longer."

"Objection!" The defense shouts, though they don't have more to add. I know they're halting my speculation. I hold my hand up in understanding.

"Fact: Jeremiah Porter owns three different towing vehicles. Fact: Jeremiah Porter owns a failing junk yard. Fact: He has the resources to tow vehicles and dispose of the parts. Fact: Jeremiah Porter has been a single father for six years."

"Objection. Relevance?"

"Miss Greenwood." Judge Fulton encourages my next response.

"This is relevant to Jeremiah's motive and mental state, your honor."

"Proceed."

"Jeremiah has been a single father for six years, and there is no documentation of any received child support. He's kept his business all these years despite making less revenue than the expenses to keep it running.

"Fact: Jeremiah needed money to support his family. And, he was desperate enough to steal, lie, and hurt people to get that money. He was complicit in his family's human trafficking ring. He willingly abducted JoAnna Montgomery, and he attacked a man when he got caught. He was willing to *kill* for *money*," I enunciate passionately, making sure to look each juror in their eyes as I speak. "He left Curtis Debaugh for dead. Curtis is alive today because of his own strength. His own grit. Jeremiah should not get off easy because Curtis survived the terror inflicted upon him."

I stroll calmly across the floor, listening to my heels clack in the deathly somber room. "I'm finished with this witness, your honor."

"Defense, any questions for this witness?"

He stands up, stacking his papers together, pretending to have his life together. "Mr. Wolfe, this incident with a random tow truck took place four years ago. How can you be sure you are getting your identification correct?"

"I'm sure."

"Eyewitnesses are wrong all the time. Nearly 69% of wrongful identifications happen every year."

Nathan leans towards the microphone. "Those are civilian statistics. I'm not a civilian."

"So you are more qualified to identify faces?" The defense lawyer scoffs.

He leans in again. "Yes."

He responds so seriously that everyone in the room would be remiss to argue. Even the defense lawyer looks scared.

"No further questions, your honor."

And that's all I need.

* * *

"On the count of arson with malicious intent: We, the jury, find the defendant... Guilty.

"On the count of unlawful abduction: We, the jury, find the

defendant… Guilty.

“On the count of second-degree attempted murder: We, the jury, find the defendant… Guilty.”

Judge Fulton knocks his gavel, signifying the end of the trial, and I let the wave of success wash over me. I did it.

I nailed Jeremiah Porter on all counts. He’s going to prison for a long ass time.

“Congratulations,” Hayes whispers in my ear as I’m packing my briefcase. I don’t look at him as I finish my task, but the smile glows on my face regardless.

I want to wrap my arms around his neck and plant a big kiss on his lips, but I’m forced to maintain my composure until we exit the courtroom.

“So do we all go out to celebrate now or what?” Thea asks, pulling me into a hug.

“I definitely want to celebrate, but please, let’s rain check. I’m exhausted,” I laugh, and she squeezes my arms.

“Fine, I’ll get my mom to babysit tomorrow night. Don’t argue.” She points at me before backing away. “I’m telling everyone. I need a good night out before the pregnancy sickness hits me like a freight train.”

“Yes, mother,” I tease her.

“Hayes, make sure she looks sexy,” she whispers through her hands, winking before she joins Jesse and the others outside the courtroom.

“I can only imagine you two were menaces in college.”

“Yes. Yes, we were.” My hand creeps down to his butt after I notice we’re the last few remaining in the room, and the others aren’t paying attention to us. “Take me home, baby,” I utter raspily, and his eyes darken.

“Liv, your stalker is out there. We shouldn’t go back to the cottage yet. We shouldn't be going out tomorrow either."

"Fuck my stalker. I won't be alone. I'll be with everyone. I'll be with *you,*" I pout, batting my eyes.

"Yep, definitely a menace," he whispers, leaning down to steal a firm, molten kiss.

Chapter Forty-Seven

Liv

"Thea told you to look sexy, but this is fine work even for you." He whistles as he leans against the door frame of my bathroom.

I only smile in response as I put in my earrings. I'm wearing a matching bra and panty lingerie set, and I know that he knows this is not something I'd wear outside.

My nipples are almost entirely visible through the sheer lace cups of my bra, and my ass is completely bare.

"How late can we be before your friends worry?"

I watch in fascination in the mirror as he slinks towards me to kiss my shoulder.

"They're your friends, too."

He smirks against my skin but doesn't say anything about that as his lips trail up my neck. I've been asleep most of the day after my action-filled past few days. This is the first time that he's made a move on me since my trial ended.

He prioritizes my well-being even when I want him to use me like his own personal whore.

It's excruciating.

"Please, touch me," I breathe when he nibbles the soft flesh between my neck and shoulder.

"Mmm, my pleasure." His hands find my waist, but very quickly descend to my lace thong as his fingers play with the string around my hips.

He snaps the band, and it bites my skin, but the sound makes me jump more than anything. When my eyes find his in the mirror again, he's watching me with intense interest as his hands move towards my bra.

His large palms capture my breasts, squeezing my flesh without remorse, eliciting a moan from me as he manhandles me. He rips my lace cups down, and my breasts bounce as they're freed.

"Mmm, perfect," he mumbles, squeezing them again without the barrier. When his thumbs flick my piercings, my back arches, and I feel his hardness against my ass.

I try to reach back to run my hand over it, but he gently shoves my hand away and not so gently slaps my bare ass cheek. "Not yet. I'm not done playing with you."

I groan in frustration, but he silences me quickly as he unhooks my bra and slides my straps down torturously slow until it falls to my feet.

"I want your tits out whenever you're at home with me. You walk through that door, chuck that stiff blazer off, and I want these tits in my hands. In my mouth." He spins me around suddenly, forcing my feet off the floor as he sets me on the counter in front of him.

"Tits out," he insists, sucking my nipple into his mouth.

"Oh fuck," I moan as he tugs it to the point of pain, flicking my piercing with his tongue just before it becomes too much. He soothes me with a kiss before he does the same to the other side, making me squirm on the cool counter.

I'm on fire already, and he hasn't even touched me down there. I need relief, I need… "Fuck me, Hayes. Don't make me wait. I need your cock inside of me, now."

He pulls his t-shirt off, throwing it to the ground, and my mouth waters. His toned muscles flex as he tugs at his belt and pants, dropping them next to his shirt.

"Next time, when we have more time, I'm going to edge you until you cry and fuck you until you lose your voice."

"Oh my God," I utter in excitement. Hopefully, he means tomorrow because we officially have no other plans.

"Show me your pussy," he demands, starting to pull his boxers off.

I finger the lace between my thighs and tip it to the side, exposing myself to him. He grunts his approval as he strokes his cock. "Slide your finger in."

I push my finger through my folds, dipping into my tight hole as his eyes darken. When I start to finger fuck myself, his hand matches pace, jerking off as he steps closer. "Let me in."

As soon as I vacate, he notches his head at my entrance and shoves inside, stealing my breath. "Let me taste you," he begs, looking at my glistening finger.

The pad of my finger traces his lips, but as soon as he sneaks his tongue out to steal a taste, I shove it in my own mouth, sucking it clean with a moan.

His eyes widen in challenge. "That was mine," he growls, claiming my mouth in a brutal kiss. His tongue invades mine, forcing me to give him a taste of my essence.

"Open," I whisper against his mouth, and he obeys right away, letting his lips part.

I stroke my tongue along his, and then I do what I've wanted to for months...

I spit directly into his mouth.

He doesn't blink, looking deeply into my eyes as he licks his lips and swallows. "Better than candy," he murmurs against my lips.

I smile, wrapping my arms around his neck to kiss him deeper. His arms band my waist, holding me steady as he pulls out almost completely and drives his cock back in forcefully.

"Again."

He does it harder, and I feel the bruising force against my cervix.

"Again."

This time, he continues thrusting, pounding me mercilessly. If he wasn't holding me still, I would slam back against the mirror, but I'm safe in his arms as he takes me exactly how I want.

I'm not made of porcelain. I want fucked without remorse.

He does it so well.

"Dammit, Liv, you're clenching me so tight, I'm losing my mind." He pulls out without warning, and my walls squeeze nothing but air, making me whimper. He scoops me off the counter to turn me around, pinning me against it so he can slide my panties all the way off onto the floor.

I feel his cock line back up to continue where he left off, but... "Wait." My voice stops him, and he looks at my reflection in the mirror.

"Not there."

Realization hits him, and he glances down as he strokes his crown over my puckered hole. "You want me to take your ass, baby?"

"Yes. I want you everywhere."

"Do you have lube?"

I shake my head, and he glances down again before looking at me in the mirror and letting spit fall from his mouth. It hits the crack of my ass and rolls down to where his blunt head presses against my ass hole.

"Do it."

He watches my face in the mirror as he presses harder, barely entering my virgin hole. His eyebrows pinch in concentration, but he doesn't look away from my face. He pushes inside me deeper, but nowhere close to completion, and I feel my inner walls stretching in ways they've never been tested.

My jaw falls slack, experiencing the sensation for the first time, and his fingers tighten on my hips as he struggles to maintain his composure.

"Are you okay?" He breathes, and all I can do is nod. He spits again, lubing the latter half of his cock, and I brace myself to take all of him. "Your turn, baby girl. Take what you want, I won't force it."

He's so sweet. He reaches around to circle my clit with his fingers, and I know in that instant, I'm going to take every last inch of his fat cock.

"That feels so good," I utter breathlessly. "I'm going to cum with your cock in my ass, Jensen."

"Fuck yes, you are." He works my clit like an expert because he is; he already knows my body like the back of his hand.

My hips flex back and forth, slowly taking more of him until it feels like he's in my throat. It's a feeling I've never experienced, fullness that defies logic. But all I want is more.

The ripples of an orgasm are growing, and it makes it easier to sheath myself on him fully, lighting all my nerve endings on fire. His happy trail brushes against the curves of my butt as I settle fully to the hilt. Taking every inch.

I smile in sweet relief as he fills me whole, and I let him take the reins, drawing an orgasm from me as I grind dreamily against him. So full. So nice.

"You're so sexy, baby," he grunts, and I feel his cock flex inside of me.

When I blink at his reflection, a drop of sweat snakes down the side of his face as tendrils of control escape him.

My climax is so close with his demanding fingers on my clit, all it takes is a few circles of my hips for my eyes to roll back and every muscle in my body to clench like I've been hit by a bomb.

"Fuck, ahh," I scream as my ass clenches with exertion around his steel length. My palms smack the counter as I'm rocked by the explosion.

His heavy breathing and rough grunts of pleasure hardly hit my ears, but his cock flexes, extending my orgasm as his release fills me.

"Jesus Christ," he sputters as he tries to catch his breath, bracing his hands on the counter on either side of me. "You're going to kill me, baby. You're incredible."

I smile against the cold granite and feel the wetness under my cheek of my fallen tears.

Deliciously good tears.

* * *

"I'm really happy for you." Thea's arms wrap around my neck

from behind, where I sit on a bar stool. Hayes would only leave my side to go get drinks once I was surrounded by all our friends.

He and Jesse promised to get the first round while Nathan, Jackson, and even Lochlan stand around the table of girls like our own personal bodyguards. You would never know I'm the one with the stalker, the way they watch over all of us.

I've had groups of friends here and there, but nothing like this. People who care about you like a big family would.

"You're just glad that I won the case and you didn't waste your time coming to watch."

"Nooo," she laughs. "Well, that too, but I meant I'm happy for you and Hayes. I love seeing you guys eye fuck each other from across the room."

"Ha! We were not."

"Uh, you are constantly, but at least now you get to actually do *it*. Watching you two dance around your feelings for one another was torturous for everyone."

"Wow, thanks." I scoff in fake offense, and she giggles.

"Drink extra for me tonight since I'm sober for at least the next year." She sighs.

"We were supposed to do it together," I finally admit to her.

"I know," she says, knowing exactly what I mean. "My third one might be our golden ticket, though."

"Maybe."

She spins me around in my chair, and I have to grasp the table to keep from falling over. "Unless you're pregnant now?"

"What? No," I laugh, smacking her arm. "But maybe I won't wait." I shrug. "I've loved Hayes since I was 16 years old…"

"There's no right or wrong time if you feel ready. Jesse and I hardly waited, and my family is the best thing that's ever happened to me."

I bite my nail, looking at my friend and glancing over towards the bar where the love of my life is balancing four drinks in his hands.

"I could use a little more one-on-one time with him. Make up for lost time, ya know." I wink at Thea, and she laughs.

"Oh, I know."

Chapter Forty-Eight

Hayes

It's surreal being here and being a part of the group. I don't feel like an outsider anymore. Liv joked that Thea was the sun, that everyone revolved around her, but if she's the sun, Liv is the atmosphere.

She pulls you in like gravity to earth, keeping you close and making you belong.

I know I belong with her.

"This is my song! Let's go!" Callie grabs Jo's hand and pulls her onto the dance floor as Natalie and Liv suck down the last of their drinks before joining them.

"You coming, Thea?" Liv asks as she scoots closer to the dance floor.

"No, you go! I need to conserve my energy to last all night." She waves Liv away, but her face falls quickly.

"Are you okay?" Jesse asks her.

"I'm fine, the sickness is starting to come and go." She smiles weakly. "I'll be fine. I just get to hang out with you guys." She sits down on the stool between Jesse and me, leaning against the table.

"Yeah, we're thrilling," I tease. "Lochlan is having the time of his life."

Lochlan glances at me. "I hate this," he grumbles

"Jo is having a great time, so you love this."

He ignores me, drinking his beer, but I see the spark in his eyes watching her have fun.

"I'll get you a Sprite," Nathan states without waiting for an answer from Thea, and goes to the bar. He's a different level of protective when it comes to his baby sister. I don't know how she or Callie get anything done.

My eyes stay on the dance floor where Liv and Natalie grind all over each other, practically losing their balance because their legs are so entangled. I smile as Liv throws her head back and laughs.

"Do you ever get used to it?" I ask Jackson, and he turns his head to acknowledge me. "Loving a woman who might cut your dick off if you piss her off."

"No." He takes a drink of his water, but then he smirks. "It's quite a thrill, though. I wouldn't change it for anything."

For a moment, we're lost in the entertainment of watching the women in our lives lose themselves to the music, and peace settles over me. Maybe all the years of suffering were leading me here, and now the second half of my life begins. Uninhibited happiness with Liv.

A delicate hand grips my forearm with force, and I glance down at it.

Why is Thea touching me?

Thea has never touched me...

My gaze goes from her nails digging into my skin to her other hand on Jesse's thigh, and when I look up, Jesse is looking at me with just as much confusion.

We both look at her at the same time, but she's intensely

focused on something across the room.

"Him," she utters, hauntingly.

"What?" Jesse says, scanning the crowd, trying to find what she is seeing.

Her head snaps to the side, looking at me with wild eyes. "Get Liv!" She yells, and chaos erupts.

Every man at the table is on their feet, dispersing into the crowded bar. I'm barely dodging people and spilling drinks as I sprint to the dance floor.

I'm within feet of the squared-off section when Liv's eyes find mine. She stops dancing and grabs all the girls, seeing the trouble on my face.

My arms are around her and her friends within seconds as I whip my head around, still looking for the person that Thea saw. If only it were as easy as having a red beacon arrow over their head, but no one stands out.

Lochlan is at my side, clearing a path to get the girls back to the back corner as curious bar patrons stare at our odd behavior.

We get them to the table where Jesse is holding Thea behind his back and effectively put a wall around all of them.

"Where's Jackson?" Natalie asks, looking over my shoulder.

"He went to try to find the guy I saw," Thea says against Jesse's back.

"Who was it?" Liv asks Thea, looking at her as if she's trying to read her mind.

"I don't know. It was a boy I remember from college. He was looking right at you. And then he turned and looked at me. He was angry."

"What was his name?" Liv asks more urgently.

"I don't know," she cries. "Parts of undergrad are a blur now.

He used to show up at our dorm room asking for you, but you were depressed and bedridden. I ignored all the Freshmen hallway socializing those first few weeks to give you time to adjust. I always turned him away, and eventually he stopped showing up. I totally forgot he existed until I just saw his face."

"It's okay, we'll figure it out." She hugs her friend, and I fight the urge to throw her over my shoulder to get her out of this bar. But there is safety in numbers, and I have to let myself take advantage of that now that I have it.

"There's Nathan," Callie says, looking on worriedly.

He pulls her into his arms when he reaches the table, and we all watch as Jackson stalks back towards our group.

"The manager won't give me access to the cameras, and I don't have the jurisdiction to force him," Malec admits.

"What's his fucking problem?" I fire out before I can control myself.

"He claims that the other bar patrons' privacy is important to him, and technically, a crime hasn't been committed here."

"Liv's stalker is on those fucking tapes, and we're supposed to just sit here and let him get away?"

"I know, Hayes. I know," Malec argues. "If I obtain evidence unlawfully, then Liv is screwed when it comes time to prosecute this jack ass," he thunders. "If I don't do this right, he'll walk free."

"He's walking free now!"

"Stop, Hayes. He's right," Liv agrees, letting her head fall to my chest. I hold her tightly, letting my anger boil inside of me.

"I'll scour social media. I can try to find all of the alumni from our university. Someone has to be mutual friends with him," Thea suggests, but Liv only nods against my chest.

The conversation flows around me as they all discuss ways to solve our problem, but I can't focus on it. I'm struggling not to lose control of the temper that I've worked so hard to keep at bay.

The temper that will take me away from Liv when I've finally got her back.

In my peripheral vision, I watch Nathan kiss Callie's head and slink away from the group, unhurriedly making his way through the crowd of people that still linger in the bar.

When my curious gaze catches her attention, she shakes her head subtly, telling me not to draw attention to his absence.

I don't look at him directly, but I glimpse his back as it disappears down the back hallway…

Only a few moments later, he reemerges, continuing his casual pace as he threads through the people and back to our corner.

"He changed his mind," Nathan says, holding a flash drive.

Malec sighs, glancing up at the ceiling in exasperation. "Don't tell me what you did… Just tell me we don't need to call a medic."

"Nothing a janitor can't clean up." He smacks Jackson on the shoulder and glances at his wife, who is hiding her amusement behind her hand.

"I can't look at this, legally," Malec says, looking at Liv and me. "If we do this, there is no case."

"I know," Liv says, staring at the flash drive in Nathan's hand.

I look at him, but he's already watching me closely. He didn't get the drive for Jackson or Liv. He got it for me because he knows prosecution is the least of my priorities.

"Thank you," I tell him earnestly, grabbing it from him.

Liv whips her head to look at me, but I assume it's disapproval so I ignore it.

"I can't let this guy win, dove," I whisper, so only she hears.

"I want to see it, too," she responds, and I look at her in surprise. She wants to do it my way.

"Come back to our house. Dec's at Charlie's house. I'll make food, and you guys can look at the footage," Natalie suggests.

"We're all coming," Thea adds.

"Okay." Malec nods, already on board. He finds Natalie's hand. "Good thing we bought all those chairs," he mumbles to her, making her smile.

* * *

Somehow, Malec's kitchen is louder than the bar we were just in, as the girls hover around the kitchen island while Natalie makes a late-night snack. With all of us here, we're taking up every last chair in the kitchen and dining room.

Jackson is glaring at his laptop screen while Jesse looks over one shoulder, and Nathan stares intensely over his other shoulder.

I don't look. If I recognize anyone on the video, I'm liable to sneak out the back door and handle it without witnesses.

I can't lose Liv again.

Which is why Lochlan is watching me from across the table as if he's waiting for me to snap.

"I'm fine," I assure him, just to get his intense stare off of me.

"You don't look fine."

I lean back in my chair, crossing my arms. "Don't ask me to pretend, Loch. If Jo was being stalked, you'd be losing your mind, too."

He stiffens slightly but leans in to rest his forearms on the table. "That's exactly why I am here. We're going to keep her safe, but I am not going to let you do anything stupid."

"Easier said than done," I utter. When I glance to the side, feeling eyes on me, I'm surprised to find Nathan watching me.

There's an understanding in his eyes, and even though we're different people who come from different worlds, somehow I know we're more alike than we'd ever admit.

"Thanks for getting the footage," I tell him.

He nods. "If I didn't, you would have, but there would have been a lot more cops involved."

I huff a laugh. "Yeah, you're probably right."

"Technically, we are cops," Jesse says to him, while Malec just ignores all of us.

"Civilian shit doesn't really concern me," he shrugs.

Jesse rolls his eyes as his friend walks into the kitchen to get another beer. "Keeping him in line is like keeping a rabid dog in a cage," he sighs, squeezing the bridge of his nose.

"I think I found the time stamp I need," Malec says suddenly, walking over towards the TV to plug his laptop in.

Everyone gathers round, but I grab Jesse to hold him back. "Whatever happened to the old Sheriff and Jeremiah's uncles?"

I heard the story from Nathan on the stand, but I never got the ending.

"One day, after a lot of beer, I'm sure he'll tell you." He

raises his eyebrows as he takes a swig from his bottle and joins Thea on the couch.

"Okay, Thea, this is two minutes before Nathan gets up to get you a Sprite from the bar," Malec says, queuing the video on the big screen.

Chapter Forty-Nine

Hayes

"You're fucking kidding me? We pay a cover fee to get into this place, and that's the camera quality? I can't tell who that is, I can't even tell if that man is 20 or 60," Liv huffs.

Malec sighs. "Yeah, it's not the best, but that's probably for a reason. These places don't want the liability of knowing what's going on when alcohol is involved."

"Now what?" She says, glancing over at me, but I'm too busy staring at the screen as if I can jump through it and see who the stalker is.

"Now, I call in some favors. I'll see if I can get someone to enhance this video and see if any other businesses in the vicinity of Casa Amigos will cooperate with their security footage."

"That could take a while," I utter.

"Yeah, it could. And, if he's bold enough to walk into a room with all of us in it, and to be as angry as Thea said he looked... It's time to take this more seriously."

"We have been," Liv says, defensively.

"Not seriously enough," I state, and her head snaps in my

direction.

The silence in the room is thick as everyone looks at us.

Malec clears his throat to get our attention back. "I'm not trying to scare you, Liv, but nothing is going to get better before we get this guy. He's escalating. Stalkers only want one thing, and they'll kill for it."

Liv doesn't respond; she doesn't even blink, but when I pull her into my chest, she comes willingly. "I've got you," I whisper against her hair.

She takes a deep shuddering breath before righting herself. "So what do I do?"

* * *

"I've showered and packed, and you haven't said a word to me. Can you stop pouting now?" Liv asks, leaning over the couch beside me.

We haven't slept, and it's nearly dawn, but the plan is for the cavalry to be here first thing in the morning to move Liv out of her cottage as quickly and quietly as possible. That only gives us about another hour to package her life into a neat little bow.

"We still don't know who this guy is, Liv. I'm pissed."

"I'm pissed, too. But I'm the one being terrorized by this creep. I'm the one being forced out of my home. So, get it together!" She stalks to the kitchen, and her flimsy robe flutters behind her.

Someone wants to take her from me. Someone wants to hurt her. I'm losing my damn mind, and she's walking around without clothes on.

Doesn't she realize what she does to me?

Her stalker's obsession wouldn't hold a flame to mine.

Her hand is shaking as she attempts to pour herself a drink, but I'm on her before she sees me coming, pushing her into the counter from behind and gripping her robe around her waist.

"Is this for me? Or are you hoping *your stalker* is peeking through your windows?" I whisper in her ear, dragging my teeth along her neck.

"You're sick," she huffs, but gasps when I bite her earlobe.

"Would you fuck me while he's watching?"

"I would fuck you if anyone was watching."

"Naughty girl." I rip the robe down her arms, raking my teeth along her shoulder blade. "No one gets to see how pretty you look falling apart in my arms."

She gasps, arching her back as my lips trail down her spine.

"Do you need my cock just like I need you to fucking breathe?" I grumble, digging my fingers into the soft flesh of her ass.

"Yes," she breathes, moaning when I bury my face between her cheeks.

"Bend over and spread your legs, dove."

She complies eagerly, laying her chest on the counter in front of her until her ass is propped perfectly in front of my face.

I give her one solid swipe of tongue before a resounding smack fills the air. Her body jumps, reacting to the slap. A red handprint glows on her ass cheek, and I admire it as I soothe the spot.

"What was that for?"

"Because I can. This ass belongs to me, and your whole fucking body is mine. No one is taking this from me." I grab her other cheek roughly. "Do you hear me?"

"Yes."

Smack. "I didn't hear you, baby girl."

"Yes, I'm yours."

"Good." I pop my belt buckle quickly, stroking my cock as I notch it at her tight opening. "Now fuck what's yours," I demand.

She drives her hips back, swallowing my cock in her pussy until her red ass flattens against my lower stomach. She grinds against me as she adjusts to the intrusion, but once she's comfortable, it's on.

Her ass bounces back and forth as she fucks me, throwing it back against me so hard that I can barely keep myself still. She grips my crown with her tight opening before sheathing back to the hilt, and I'm fucking mesmerized, watching her juices coat my shaft.

"God, you're sexy." She whimpers at my words, fucking me brutally until her legs start to shake. I grab her hips, slowing her momentum. "You don't get to make me cum until I've made sure you get yours."

"But–"

Smack. "Hear me?"

"Yes."

"Roll your hips over me… Fuck, I love it when you do that." My fingers find her clit, and she moans as I circle it.

We stay like that, languidly fucking in the middle of her kitchen as I pepper her spine with soft kisses. She loves it rough, but she needs this, too. I need it just as badly.

"I'm so close," she gasps, jerking as she nears her climax.

I wet my middle finger, pushing it into her tight ass without warning, and her entire body tightens. Her pussy chokes down on my cock as I fill both her holes, sliding my finger in and out of her ass as she twitches in my arms.

"Fuck me with both your holes, baby girl."

She drives against me harder, taking it in both entrances until it's too much. She falls apart in my arms as her orgasm rocks her.

I hold her taut, letting her feel how full she is as her body clenches me, and it isn't until she takes a deep gasping breath that I start thrusting again.

My control was teetering on the edge already, and plowing into her a few times is all it takes before my cum rockets inside of her, and she's gasping, again.

"Fuck," I say breathlessly against her back, still buried inside of her.

We needed this distraction, a moment of connection to get lost in, but I feel the moment reality returns. She leans back against me, letting me take her weight as I hold her against my chest.

The longer we stand here in silence, the heavier she feels in my arms, deflating in front of my eyes.

"Are you ready to go?"

"No." I can't see her face, but I hear the frown in her voice. "I don't want to leave my cottage."

"I know, but it's temporary, and it's safer behind the gates." My arms tighten around her, and she leans further into me as I kiss her head. "You put oxygen into my lungs, Olive. I have you back, and I will do whatever it takes to keep you safe."

She nods, and I reluctantly let her go as she pulls away from me.

I hate that her life is being flipped upside down.

"I need to find my phone," she says as she straightens her robe back over her shoulders. "I think I lost it while I was packing."

"I'll call it."

"It's on silent."

"Did you leave it in the car?"

"Maybe. This night has been a mess." She presses the heels of her hands into her temples.

"Are you okay?"

"No dizziness. Just a little bit of a headache."

My lips press to her forehead, lingering longer than necessary as if I can take away the pain. "I'll take your bags to the car and look for your phone."

She nods as she glances around the kitchen, looking nothing but lost. Her thoughts are a million miles away from what's in front of her face, and I don't blame her.

It only takes me a few seconds to slide her bags into the back of my SUV, and one glance in the front seat makes me scoff. We both left our phones in the car, stacked on top of each other in the center console tray.

Both of the screens are filled with notifications. Missed calls, missed texts...

"Shit." I sprint back into the cottage, trying to thumb through the texts from Malec, Thea, and Jesse.

"Liv! Thea's been trying to get a hold of us. She found him! It's–" My steps skid to a stop at the entrance to the kitchen, and both the phones fall from my hands, clattering to the floor.

Chapter Fifty

Liv

I worked so fucking hard my entire life for everything to go to plan, just to end up at the mercy of some lunatic. I can't believe this is happening.

I finally feel at home, at peace, and it's being ripped away. Outgrowing the cottage is inevitable, but it's my sanctuary, not the one with big black iron gates.

If Hayes's house was in better condition, I'd insist he take me there instead of the bunkhouse, but I understand the risks. He wants to keep me safe, and I'd rather make that easier for everyone.

Putting myself in harm's way only increases the chances that Hayes will do something rash and end up in hot water again.

I can't let that happen.

The floor creaks behind me, and I sigh again. I haven't moved past the kitchen in the search for my phone. I'm getting nowhere. "Was it in the car?" I ask him as I turn around.

"Hi, Livvy."

I blink.

It's the only part of my body that functions.

A man... A version of someone I knew a million years ago.

"That's what he called you. And, you liked it. Remember?" *His voice is deeper than I remember.*

His hair is darker. Unnaturally so.

His eyes used to be so kind, but now they look desperate and dull.

"I've missed you, Livvy." His clothes hang on him like they're a size too big for his slender frame. He was never much larger than me, but he looks sick or malnourished now.

"I don't understand."

"Come with me."

"No."

His eyes narrow. "Yes."

"Why are you doing this?" *He was always so kind to me.*

The front door swings open, and he lunges at me before Jensen's footsteps reach us.

"Liv! Thea's been trying to get a hold of us. She found him! It's–" Our phones fall from his hands like bricks, but I can't see them hit the linoleum because a sharp blade is tucked under my chin, keeping my neck taut.

"Noah..." His name falls from Hayes's lips as a warning.

I feel my old classmate's muscles tense against me. I don't know if they ever interacted in school, but Noah saw Hayes beat Mr. Arkett that night. He held me back while I screamed...

"She's coming with me," he forces through gritted teeth right beside my ear.

"No, she's not," Hayes says, holding his hands out in front of him.

"I've been waiting for her for years. If you hadn't shown up again, she would have finally been mine!" He spits out, and I flinch at his outburst.

"What are you talking about? I haven't seen you since high school," I cry, trying to pull a fraction of an inch away, and reaping the consequences immediately as the sharp stinging rips across my throat.

"Don't move, Liv!" Hayes thunders, his wild eyes locked on the blade under my chin.

Noah's other hand drags the length of my spine over the thin fabric of my robe, and it takes all of my will not to retreat from it. "I wanted you to see *me.* But it was always *him,"* he spits at Hayes. "And, then Mr. Arkett swept you off your feet, and I was nothing, again!"

"I didn't even know you liked me," I utter, gasping as the first drip of blood rolls down the column of my neck.

"Liked you? I was in love with you!" He yells, gripping my hair suddenly, making me cry out in pain.

"All those study sessions. Computer lab dates. The first night you got in Mr. Arkett's car instead of getting in mine was a slap in the face, but I forgave you. But watching him touch your body after prom when it should have been me, killed me!"

I feel Hayes take a step forward like I can always sense him, but Noah is focused on my face.

"I even applied to the same college so we could be together."

My eyes blink rapidly, still trying to recall him from undergrad.

"You were upset. You needed me! But your stupid little friend wouldn't let me near you," he sneers. "She didn't know what we had together."

I only remember the nights I cried into my pillow, wishing for Hayes… I never thought twice about Noah once I graduated high school.

"Why didn't you say anything years ago?"

He lets his fingers dance across my cheek. "I liked watching you. So, I waited for you."

"Why?"

"Because you weren't ready for me."

"What?" I can't make sense of any of this, but if I keep him talking, it'll distract him from Hayes.

"I followed you to law school," he murmurs in my ear.

I can't believe it, and he sees the confusion on my face.

"You're such a conceited whore. Never seeing what was right in front of you. Then you moved into the top floor of that fucking condo, and I lost my mind. I couldn't watch you. I never knew if you needed me. I knew you would need me, Livvy."

"I don't understand," the words tumble out of my mouth, and his blade only tightens on my throat, making me whimper.

"You were so independent, but you were consistent. You grabbed the same tea from the grocery store. You ate the same lunch every day. I watched you. Waited. And when you didn't *see* me because you were always self-absorbed by your own life, I forced you to slow down."

"What did you do?"

He brushes his fingers down my hair. "Turns out, you can tell any doctor some sob story, and they'll give you enough medication to tranquilize a horse. Or in my case, micro-dose you until you would swoon at my feet, and I could save the day."

"You drugged me?" I gasp, jerking in his arms, feeling the

knife slice into my skin.

"Calm down, it was prescription drugs, not meth," he spews, struggling to control me. Hayes uses that moment to lunge for him, grabbing his wrist in a vice grip.

The surprise only lasts a moment before Noah attempts to recoil, but Jensen is stronger. He yanks him and the knife away from me, but the force of it knocks Noah off his feet. His body crashes into Hayes, and both of them fall to the floor in a heap of limbs

"No!" I scream, watching Noah flail until he rolls off of him and to his feet. Jensen is holding his stomach, and his face is pinched in pain. "No!!"

"Fucking animal!" Noah yells, wiping Jensen's blood off his hand and into his pants as he turns to me. "He took you from me! He always saved you, but not anymore! You're mine!"

"I was never yours, you psycho!" I scream, gripping the counter behind me as he points the bloodied blade at me.

"Don't say that!"

"Just leave, Noah. Go and let me help him. I won't tell anyone, please," I cry, needing to check Jensen's injury. He hasn't moved from the floor, and the blood has already drenched the front of his shirt.

"I can't leave." He shakes his head. "It's too late."

"It's not. You can go," I beg.

"Come with me. Let's run away." He holds his bloodied hand out for me, and I fight the urge to vomit.

"No."

"Livvy…"

"Don't call me that."

"Fine. You've given me no choice." As he steps towards me, he pulls handcuffs from his back pocket and dangles them in front of me. "Turn around, or I'll gut you like I gutted the felon. Then I'll go find your little bitch friend and gut her and her baby."

"You bastard," I sob.

"This is your fault, Livvy. He's dead because of you. Now, turn around."

With shaky limbs, I do as he says, turning until my hip bones hit the edge of the counter.

"Hands," he demands, and it takes all my strength to move my arms behind me.

"Please, don't," I whisper, feeling the warmth of my tears stream down my face, the saltiness burns the wound on my neck as I weep.

"I thought if I looked like Mr. Arkett, you'd notice me. I guess I should have scribbled shit on my arms and copied the felon instead," he grits out. "The lawyer and the ex-con. How cliché?"

"You don't know me at all, Noah. You're deranged," I utter the words.

The first wrist is cuffed with a finite clink, and my entire body shakes.

"You're right, Livvy. I don't know you at all..." His fingers touch the back of my bare thigh, and a strangled noise leaves my throat, "But I can't wait to know every inch of you." He inhales deeply against my hair at the nape of my neck, and a sob heaves out of me.

His hand trembles as his palm slinks up my hip, and it lifts the hem of my robe above my butt, making me flinch aggressively. The movement forces his hand to snap back to my wrists to keep me secure, and my bones cry out in agony as he attempts to finish shackling me.

I almost whimper in defeat right before the second cuff clicks, but instead, I yelp as the metal ring breaks away suddenly, and his hands are ripped from mine.

Jensen's arms are locked around him in a bear hug from behind, tearing his body from mine and dragging him across the kitchen with a burst of guttural exertion.

"Go!" He grates out, and Noah makes desperate swipes at his forearms with the knife. His arms don't loosen, giving me a chance to run, but I can't move.

Jensen's face is washed out, and sweat is pouring off his skin as he struggles. This is all my fault. He is going to die because of me.

I don't want to leave without him. I can't.

The knife strikes bone, and he grumbles in agony, squeezing his eyes shut. "No!" I scream, lunging for them as he falls back, being sandwiched between Noah and the wall.

I don't think. I don't hesitate, grabbing Noah's wrist with both of my hands and shoving upward as hard as I can.

I don't know how...

But the blade lodges in his trachea.

His eyes go wide, but mine are wider, watching the blood pour from his throat.

Bursts of wet rasps escape him until his grip loosens, and his hand falls, but the knife remains buried deep in his windpipe.

When the frothy sputtering stops, his body goes limp in Jensen's arms, and both men collapse to the floor.

"Jensen," I breathe, swaying as I fall to my knees. The kitchen is spinning as I search his face, his body.

"Please, Jensen. Please," I beg, crawling over him. His shirt is saturated, but my hands search for his wound, covering it with my palms when he cries out in pain.

"I'm sorry, dove," he murmurs, not even opening his eyes.

"No, no, no," I mutter. I need help, I need someone.

There's no one here to save him.

I lift my hand, staring at the blood that belongs to the man I love more than anything, and bring it to my cheek, dragging the warmth of it across my face until it feels real.

I need to do something.

There is no one here to save him but me.

My trembling, bloodied fingers dig into my jaw until the gripping pain surges me into action. I stumble, attempting to stand, but on the second try, I make it to the sink and rip open the drawer there, pulling out all my dish towels and throwing them to the floor where Jensen lays bleeding to death.

My knees skid to the floor beside him again, and my hands twitch above him. I don't know what to do; I'm not a doctor. I've never been able to stand the sight of… *Blood.*

I need to stop the bleeding.

His shirt is slick in my hands as I shove it up and away from his stomach, exposing the puncture a few inches below my name on his sternum and the blood welling from it.

How much blood can a person lose?

I shove a dish towel on it, putting all my weight against his abdomen.

"Jensen, please, wake up. Please, I need you, baby. Please, wake up."

His eyelids hardly flutter, and my tears pour from my eyes, mixing with the blood coating his skin.

"I love you, Jensen. I need you. Do you hear me? I need you! Don't fucking die on me. You promised not to leave me!"

Sound sputters from his mouth, but so does a drop of blood,

smearing red across his lips. *No, no, no, no.*

I lunge for my phone a few feet away, using my body to keep the towel pressed to his stomach, and I scramble to unlock it with blood-soaked fingers, barely managing to do what I need.

The phone doesn't ring a full ring before Malec answers. "Liv, I've been–"

"Help! Please, help us! Jensen's been stabbed, please," I cry hysterically, letting the phone fall from my hand.

His words are inaudible as he relays to dispatch that we need an ambulance, but I leave him on speaker on the floor. I need both my hands on Jensen. I refuse to take my hands off him.

"I am only a few minutes away, Liv. I knew something was wrong when we couldn't get a hold of you guys," Malec says. "I'm so sorry. Dammit!" He yells, and I hear his engine revving louder. "Where's the perp? Are you safe?"

"I– I'm safe," I mutter, leaning down to rest my cheek against Jensen's.

His chest is still rising and falling, but his face has paled completely. He's fading right in front of my eyes.

"Jensen, please. Fight for me, one last time. I'll never ask you to fight again. You died once and came back from it; you can do it again. Please, for me," I beg. "If you don't survive this, I can't live without you. I will end my fucking life if you die. Do you hear me?"

I don't know if he can hear me. And, I don't know if he has enough fight in him left to care… But I will fight for him. I'll beg God. I'll do anything.

I will do *anything*.

I stabbed a man to death.

And, I only wish I had done it sooner. So I could save Jensen.

I would kill for him.

I would go to prison for him.

I would give my life for him.

But I need him to live.

Chapter Fifty-One

Hayes

I never dreamed of heaven. I only dreamt of Olive.

I only ever wanted Olive.

I needed her to breathe.

I need her…

"Jensen, please."

She's crying.

I need to comfort her.

"I love you, please stay with me."

My Olive.

She needs me.

"How long has he been bleeding?"

Someone's here… She's not alone anymore. I don't want her to be alone.

"I don't know... Five minutes. Ten. I don't know," she cries.

She needs me.

"Medics are pulling in. Hang on, buddy."

"Ma'am, we've got him now. We need space."

"No, no, I can't leave him. No!"

"Let them help him." She's not alone; someone's with her. *"We'll follow them to the hospital."*

She'll be okay…

She lost me once…

She'll be okay…

My Olive–

* * *

It's so bright.

I can hardly peel my eyelids apart as if someone glued them together.

Everything was black, and now I can see.

Is this the afterlife?

A face appears in front of me, too blurry to make out.

"There he is." A woman's voice… So soft. So familiar.

"Mom?"

"It's me, honey." Her soft hand strokes my cheek, and I startle.

"Am I… Alive?"

A sad laugh escapes her, and her eyes finally come into focus in front of me. Pain-filled eyes, gazing down at me.

"You're alive. Thank God. Your stab wound was an inch from being fatal."

Stab wound...

"Olive! Where's Olive?" I shift to move, and every part of me cries out in pain.

"Shh, shhh, she's right here. She's finally sleeping. Let her rest."

I glance to where my mom is looking and see the curled-up form on the hospital couch. There's a blanket covering her from her chin to her toes, curled under her tightly. Her back is to me, but I can see her chestnut hair, pulled into a ponytail, falling over the edge of the cushion.

She never wears her hair up anymore. It reminds me of when we were younger.

"They said she's been awake nearly two days, since you've been unconscious, but I convinced her to rest when I got here. I think she needed to know someone was watching over you. Though I don't know why… There is a lobby full of people down the hall, and the nurse said they haven't left since you got here either."

My eyebrows furrow, and even that hurts as I let my head fall to my pillow. I've never felt so heavy and immobile. Lifting my arms is nearly impossible, but I do it just enough to see the bandages wrapped around my forearms.

"They said those are mostly superficial. They'll heal quicker than your stomach."

"I hardly remember…"

"There's a sheriff outside, too…" Her face is cast in worry. "I think he wants to speak to you."

"It's okay." I grab her hand where it rests beside mine. "He's one of the good ones," I assure her.

She nods and smiles softly. Her hair is more gray than the last time I saw her, but it's still long. She likes to keep it braided down her back, and some of the front wisps have surpassed gray and turned white. But her face is as youthful as it's always been. The lines forged from stress can't dictate her beauty.

"You finally got the girl, huh?" She smiles softly at me, squeezing my fingers delicately.

"Yeah. I guess I did. Now, I just have to keep her."

"I don't think that will be a problem. Well, maybe if you stop dying," she scolds, tipping her head to look at me sternly. It only makes me smile.

"I'm sorry, I haven't visited in a while. I've been..."

"It's okay. You've made a good life for yourself. I'm glad you're happy."

"I'm happier now," I tell her softly, tipping my head to look at Olive again.

"You always were so smitten with her. Does she know about your dad?"

My eyes snap back to her. "No. She doesn't."

She nods, sensing my reluctance. "Okay, let me go get your nurse. I want them to make sure you're alright." She pats the top of my hand before she lets go.

"I'm so proud of you, Jensen. I always have been."

The door shuts behind her, and I take the deepest breath that I can manage, which still feels overwhelmingly shallow.

Chapter Fifty-Two

Liv

"I know you're awake, dove."

A soft whimper escapes me, and my shoulders heave as I let out the cry I've been trying to keep hidden. Hearing his voice for the first time sent waves of relief over me, and I'm too raw to hold it back.

"Come here, baby. I can't move," he groans as if he were attempting to anyway.

I roll to the edge of the couch and sit up, letting the blanket fall. He looks so broken and fragile… But he's alive.

Another burst of sadness escapes me, and I can't contain the tears streaming down my cheeks as I jump up and bury my face in his neck. "I was so scared," I cry, hiccuping against the valley of his collarbone.

"I'm sorry, baby. I'm so sorry," he murmurs against my head. His lips brush my forehead, and I lean into his kiss, needing to feel him.

His bandaged arms come around me, and he holds me gently, but the weight of it is heavy after almost losing him.

"Are you okay?" He asks, and for the first time in days, I smile.

"You're the one in a hospital bed. I should be asking you that."

"Olive. Are you okay? Did he hurt you?" He asks again, ignoring my remark as his eyes search my neck.

"He didn't hurt me. Seeing what he did to you nearly killed me... But he didn't hurt me." A regular large bandage is all the evidence I have of what happened. On the outside at least.

Jensen's entire body relaxes as he takes a breath, wincing slightly as he does.

"Is he?"

"He's dead," I answer definitively.

"Good."

A quick knock at the door is our only warning before Malec walks in, dressed in his uniform and with an exhausted expression on his face.

"Glad to see you're awake," he says, walking over to the bed and glancing at Jensen's bandages. "Did Liv fill you in on the investigation?"

"Not yet," I answer. "He just woke up."

"What investigation?" Jensen says, trying to track our conversation. I can tell he's still not up for all of this.

"I have to do a death investigation for Noah. It's required–"

"I did it," he says suddenly. "I killed him."

"Jensen..." I start, but he keeps going.

"I stabbed him to get him off of Olive."

I rest my hand over his heart to get his attention as Malec smirks. "Jackson already knows what happened, Jensen. We're not in trouble. *I'm* not in trouble. I don't need you to take the fall for me."

"It was self-defense. I know that. I was only telling you that an investigation is required, not because I'm assigning guilt."

"Oh," he sighs, letting his head fall back to his pillow again.

"I need your side of things for my report, but it can wait. I just wanted to come in and check on you. I'll let everyone else know you're awake and just as thick in the skull as before."

I conceal my laugh, but not well enough. Leave it to Jensen to take the fall for a crime just to protect me… Even when it's totally unnecessary.

"Malec," Jensen says suddenly as Jackson goes to leave. "Thanks for getting there, and being there with her when… When I could have…" He clears his throat. "Thank you for not letting her be alone."

"That's what family does, Hayes. I only wish I had gotten there sooner." He tips his head and leaves us, letting silence fill the room.

I don't have a chance to say anything, though, before a nurse and a doctor walk in to check on him. I stand back, watching them poke and prod at him, and I flinch every time he winces.

"The pain killers will need to be alternated every six hours, but you should be able to go home tomorrow," the doctor says, and the room empties once more.

I can't move. Jensen's looking at me tenderly from across the room, but I can't get my limbs to cooperate. I almost lost him…

"Come lay with me, dove."

I shake my head. "You're hurt."

"I don't give a fuck. Come here."

His insistence has my feet moving, but I stop at the side of my bed, not going any further.

"I need to have you right here." He pats the sliver of mattress beside him. "Nothing you can do will hurt me more than what already happened."

My face tugs down in a frown, and he taps the bed again. This time, I take my time, gingerly crawling in beside him. If I hurt him, he doesn't say. He doesn't make a noise or flinch at all as I ease down on my side next to him.

"Head right here." He uses his chin to point to his chest by the inside of his shoulder. "That's perfect," he says with more grit in his tone than I would like, but if he wants me beside him, then I'll stay right here.

"Malec found Noah's car. And his apartment. He wasn't bluffing… He had photos of me all the way back from undergrad and beyond. He had photos of you. Mr. Arkett. Elliot. And some of my random dates in college."

"I don't even remember him from high school," Hayes utters.

"He had journals filled with rants about Mr. Arkett preying on me. He wrote that he wished he had intervened when you had, so he could have been the hero… He was delusional, but I guess I blacked him out completely."

"Did the doctors check you out? I remember him saying something about drugs…"

"They ran an extensive blood panel, and they think it was adderall and clozapine that he was slipping in my tea. A stimulant and an antipsychotic drug that was likely making me tachycardic. The doctor said I'll be fine once it's completely out of my system. I won't have any more dizziness or fainting."

"Thank God, you're safe." He kisses my forehead.

"If you hadn't grabbed him, he would have taken me, I don't know where…" I whisper into his chest. "He nearly had me."

"If that was my last dying action, I'd do it a thousand times over. I wish I killed him… So you didn't have to."

"After I saw what he did to you, I was glad I was the one to do it," I admit sincerely. "I would do it a thousand times over if it means saving you."

"I don't deserve you, Olive. Never have, never will."

"Malec was right. Just as thick-skulled as ever." I glance up at him, careful not to jostle us. "What did your mom mean about your dad?"

"Ah. So you were awake for that part?"

"I was ripped from sleep as soon as I heard your voice," I whisper. I thought it was a dream at first.

"My dad was awful. Can we just leave it at that?"

"No."

He sighs, but there is humor behind it until he starts to speak. "My dad liked to use the law to his advantage. Before I met you, he blackmailed my karate teacher into financial ruin. He smeared his name until he couldn't face his family, and he killed himself because he couldn't escape my dad's evilness."

"Why didn't you ever tell me?"

"I couldn't stand the thought of filling your mind with such dark thoughts. You were so full of light," he says, tracing his thumb over my forehead. "You were good when nothing in my life was."

"Jensen…" I start, but he cuts me off.

"Meeting you was the only thing that kept me alive back then. And, your friendship was the only reason I kept living. So, when my dad threatened to ruin your life, I kept my mouth shut."

"What?"

"He knew I hurt Arkett because I was protecting you… He didn't care. He wanted everyone to see me as a monster, and that didn't bother me. I was way past caring about my father's opinion. But then he brought you into it.

"He said if I told the judge I was defending you, he was going to claim that you were an accomplice. He was going to make your life a living hell while I was behind bars. I would have been helpless to stop it," he admits softly, staring at the ceiling.

"You didn't fight for lesser charges because you wanted to protect me? After you had already protected me so many times?"

He shrugs like it was a no-brainer for him.

"If I hadn't stood up and said something to the judge, you would have gone to prison for 20 years!"

He nods against my head.

"You stupid, selfless man. I wouldn't have wanted you to do that."

"I know. But you were my whole world, and I couldn't leave you at the mercy of my father."

The choices he made changed the course of both of our lives... But I finally understand that it was never a choice at all.

He did all that he could to keep me safe, so I could keep living.

I lost him because he loved me. He sacrificed himself for me.

"I love you, Jensen. I'm going to prove to you how much for the rest of our lives."

"I'll never have enough time to prove how much I love you, Olive. But I'll show you every damn day how grateful I am to have you."

Epilogue

Liv

T*wo years later...*

It's been raining for days, and even now, with a small break from the moisture, the clouds are dark and angry, casting out any chance of sunlight. The woods beyond the yard are filled with the smoke so aptly representing these mountains that we call home.

The porch swing I mentioned wanting to Jensen once in passing sways gently under me as I admire the landscape from under the covered porch. And the occasional distant grunt of a black bear over at the sanctuary.

I never did move back into the cottage. We focused on renovating the big house, as I like to call it, and moved in right away. Leaks and all.

The first six months were full of challenges and home-improvement projects. So many hang-ups and snags in our plans, but nothing felt more right.

Every challenge with Jensen didn't feel like a challenge at all. None of it mattered, not when we had each other.

I cleaned the cottage out and started renting it out. I didn't want to sell it, but it deserves to be loved by someone.

The front screen door squeaks as Jensen comes out to join me, carrying one of his thick flannel jackets draped over his forearm and two steaming mugs. His coffee, and mine tea.

I know without even checking, it'll be the perfect temperature to drink. I don't need a bodyguard at the courthouse anymore, but he always sends me to work with a to-go cup prepared exactly how I like it.

And he welcomes me home, whether he's done with his workday at the sanctuary or not. Sometimes that means just a kiss, sometimes I use him until he puts off whatever else he needed to get done until the next day.

He hasn't complained at all.

"I ordered the supplies for the play set," he says proudly, sitting down on the swing beside me and gently handing me my mug. He gazes out across the yard to where he plans to put it, in the spot where we said our vows last year.

He looks at that spot a lot, like he never wants the moment to leave his head.

I rest my head on his shoulder, smiling to myself. We both wept like babies through the entire ceremony. His mom was here. My mom came. All of our friends. The sun beamed down on us as we said 'I do'. It was perfect.

"Don't you think that is a little premature? We still have so much that needs to be done inside."

"I know, but Kate will like it when she visits. Besides..." He reaches over with his free hand to rub my round belly. "It won't be long until this one wants to play."

A smile stretches my lips as I gaze at him. My Jensen Hayes... The man that he is. He has proven himself, as he said. Every day, he loves me louder than the day before.

I never imagined I'd get a life better than the one I dreamed of.

I never knew how much it depended on simply having him in it.

Everything else is extra.

He takes the flannel jacket off the swing and drapes it around my shoulders. I wasn't cold, not with him so close, but I take the extra layer graciously.

"Thank you for keeping me warm," I whisper, leaning in for a kiss. From the very first day we met, until now, he has been the only warmth I needed.

"Always," he promises, kissing me tenderly.

Chance Encounters Series

If you've been here since the beginning, I can't begin to thank you for reading these stories and supporting me. You've read my start as an author, and I hope you've seen the growth I've experienced as a writer. I'm grateful for these characters and their stories, but I'm not finished...

I couldn't close this series until I gave Curtis his happy ending. In addition to these five full-length novels, I've decided to write a short novella for Curtis. No new trauma, no heartbreaking suspense, just a happily ever after for a character that so many people are rooting for.

Stay tuned!

About the Author

Amber Cassidy is an independently published author and full-time SAHM to two beautiful little girls. Writing has been a passion of mine since childhood and has enabled me to maintain my sense of self while in the thick of motherhood.

I am passionate about romance in any genre, but my current focus is small-town romantic suspense.

You can connect with me on:

- https://www.instagram.com/@ambercassidy_author
- https://www.tiktok.com/@ambercassidy_author